NO PLACE LIKE HOME

"*No Place Like Home* is witty and bright, sparkling with friends and family who love each other. . . . The novel is heartbreaking as only the best love stories can be, yet it fills the reader with hope and promise. I will have these characters with me for a long time."

—Luanne Rice

"A lyrical novel of family, loss, and redemption, beautifully written, beautifully told."

—Jennifer Crusie

THIS PLACE OF WONDER

"*This Place of Wonder* is a wonderfully moving tale about four women whose journeys are all connected by one shared love: some are romantic, some are familial, but all are deeply complicated. Dealing with loss, love, hidden secrets, and second chances, this stirring tale is utterly engaging and ultimately hopeful. Set along the rugged California coastline, *This Place of Wonder* will sweep you away with the intoxicating scents, bold flavors, and sweeping views of the region and transport you to a world you won't be in any hurry to leave."

—Colleen Hoover, #1 *New York Times* bestselling author

"Kristin Hannah readers will thoroughly enjoy the family dynamic, especially the mother-daughter relationships."

—*Booklist* (starred review)

"Barbara O'Neal's latest novel is simply delicious. Engrossing, empathetic, and profoundly moving, I savored every sentence of this story of several very different women who find solace and second chances in each other after tragedy (though not before facing some hard truths and, yes, a few rock bottoms). *This Place of Wonder* is one of the best books I've read in a long time."

—Camille Pagán, bestselling author of *Everything Must Go*

"I have never much moved in the elevated circles of California farm-to-table cuisine, but O'Neal makes me feel like I'm there. Rather than simply skewering the pretensions, *This Place of Wonder* pinpoints the passions. Some of these characters have been elevated to celebrity, some are newcomers to the scene, but all are drawn together by the sensuality, the excitement, and ultimately the care that food brings them. Elegiac but also forward-looking, this is a book about eating, but more than that, it's a book about hurt and healing and women finding their way together. I loved every moment of it."

—Julie Powell, author of *Julie & Julia* and *Cleaving*

WRITE MY NAME ACROSS THE SKY

"Barbara O'Neal weaves an irresistible tale of creativity, forgery, family, and the FBI in *Write My Name Across the Sky*. Willow and Sam are fascinating, and their aunt Gloria is my dream of an incorrigible, glamorous older woman."

—Nancy Thayer, bestselling author of *Family Reunion*

"*Write My Name Across the Sky* is an exquisitely crafted novel of three remarkable women from two generations grappling with decisions of the past and the consequences of where those young, impetuous choices have led. A heartfelt story of passion, devotion, and family told as only Barbara O'Neal can."

—Suzanne Redfearn, #1 Amazon bestselling author of *In an Instant*

"With its themes of creativity and art, *Write My Name Across the Sky* is itself like a masterfully executed painting. Using refined brushstrokes, O'Neal builds her vivid, complex characters: three independent women in one family who can't quite come to terms with their fierce feelings of love for one another. O'Neal deftly switches between three points of view, adding layers of family history into this intimate and satisfying study of how women make tough choices between love and creativity and family and freedom."

—Glendy Vanderah, *Washington Post* bestselling author of
Where the Forest Meets the Stars

THE LOST GIRLS OF DEVON

One of *Travel* + *Leisure*'s most anticipated books of summer 2020

"A woman's strange disappearance brings together four strong women who struggle with their relationships, despite their need for one another. Fans of Sarah Addison Allen will appreciate the emphasis on nature and these women's unique gifts in this latest by the author of *When We Believed in Mermaids*."

—*Library Journal* (starred review)

"*The Lost Girls of Devon* draws us into the lives of four generations of women as they come to terms with their relationships and a mysterious tragedy that brings them together. Written in exquisite prose with the added bonus of the small Devon village as a setting, Barbara O'Neal's book will ensnare the reader from the first page, taking us on an emotional journey of love, loss, and betrayal."

—Rhys Bowen, *New York Times* and #1 Kindle bestselling author of
The Tuscan Child, *In Farleigh Field*, and the Royal Spyness series

"*The Lost Girls of Devon* is one of those novels that grabs you at the beginning with its imagery and rich language and won't let you go. Four generations of women deal with the pain and betrayal of the past, and Barbara O'Neal skillfully leads us to understand all of their deepest needs and fears. To read a Barbara O'Neal novel is to fall into a different world—a world of beauty and suspense, of tragedy and redemption. This one, like her others, is spellbinding."

—Maddie Dawson, bestselling author of *A Happy Catastrophe*

WHEN WE BELIEVED IN MERMAIDS

"An emotional story about the relationship between two sisters and the difficulty of facing the truth head-on."

—*Today*

"There's a reason Barbara O'Neal is one of the most decorated authors in fiction. With her trademark lyrical style, she's written a page-turner of the first order. From the very first page, I was drawn into the drama and irresistibly teased along as layers of a family's complicated past were artfully peeled away. Don't miss this masterfully told story of sisters and secrets, damage and redemption, hope and healing."

—Susan Wiggs, #1 *New York Times* bestselling author

"More than a mystery, Barbara O'Neal's *When We Believed in Mermaids* is a story of childhood—and innocence—lost, and the long-hidden secrets, lies, and betrayals two sisters must face in order to make themselves whole as adults. Plunge in and enjoy the intriguing depths of this passionate, lustrous novel, and you just might find yourself believing in mermaids."

—Juliet Blackwell, *New York Times* bestselling author of *The Lost Carousel of Provence*, *Letters from Paris*, and *The Paris Key*

"In *When We Believed in Mermaids*, Barbara O'Neal draws us into the story with her crisp prose, well-drawn settings, and compelling characters, in whom we invest our hearts as we experience the full range of human emotion and, ultimately, celebrate their triumph over the past."

—Grace Greene, author of *The Memory of Butterflies* and the Wildflower House series

"*When We Believed in Mermaids* is a deftly woven tale of two sisters, separated by tragedy and reunited by fate, discovering that the past isn't always what it seems. By turns shattering and life affirming, as luminous and mesmerizing as the sea by which it unfolds, this is a book club essential—definitely one for the shelf!"

—Kerry Anne King, bestselling author of *Whisper Me This*

THE ART OF INHERITING SECRETS

"Great writing, terrific characters, food elements, romance, a touch of intrigue, and more than a few surprises to keep readers guessing."

—*Kirkus Reviews*

"Settle in with tea and biscuits for a charming adventure about inheriting an English manor and the means to restore it. Vivid descriptions and characters that read like best friends will stay with you long after this delightful story has ended."

—Cynthia Ellingsen, bestselling author of *The Lighthouse Keeper*

"*The Art of Inheriting Secrets* is the story of one woman's journey to uncovering her family's hidden past. Set against the backdrop of a sprawling English manor, this book is ripe with mystery. It will have you guessing until the end!"

—Nicole Meier, author of *The House of Bradbury* and *The Girl Made of Clay*

"O'Neal's clever title begins an intriguing journey for readers that unfolds layer by surprising layer. Her respected masterful storytelling blends mystery, art, romance, and mayhem in a quaint English village and breathtaking countryside. Brilliant!"

—Patricia Sands, bestselling author of the Love in Provence series

No Place Like Home

ALSO BY BARBARA O'NEAL

No Place Like Home

a novel

BARBARA O'NEAL

LAKE UNION
PUBLISHING

Published by Lake Union Publishing, Seattle

www.apub.com

Amazon, the Amazon logo, and Lake Union Publishing are trademarks of Amazon.com, Inc., or its affiliates.

ISBN-13: 9781662521294 (paperback)
ISBN-13: 9781662521287 (digital)

Cover design by Shasti O'Leary Soudant
Cover images: © Teri Virbickis / Shutterstock; © Jetrel / Shutterstock; © ChrisGorgio / Getty

Printed in the United States of America

This one is for my son Miles, who loves the net of Sunday breakfasts and watermelon cut into chunks in the fridge all summer long and two degrees of separation and friends you've had since you were four and playing pool on Saturday afternoons, and who will, when he grows up, cook biscuits for his children and sing along to the music and cut watermelon into chunks and make a home that's worth living in.

FROM THE AMTRAK DINING CAR LUNCH MENU:

Santa María Cheese Enchiladas—$6.50—Monterey Jack and cheddar cheeses rolled up with scallions, then topped with tomatillo sauce and served with black beans and Spanish rice.

Chapter One

The April I was thirteen, I went to sleep a good Catholic schoolgirl, and woke up the next morning burning. The transition was like the flip of a coin, and made me as dizzy as an airborne dime.

I was sick for days with it—drunk on the new green of globe willow leaves against the slate of a heavy spring sky; feeling the itch down my spine and the sides of my legs from the seams of my clothes; eating gluttonously of every lasagna, every olive, every bowl of cream I could put my hands on. A cat crawled into my lap, and I petted him for hours, a cat I had known all my life, and I ached with the incredible softness of his long fur, the astonishing sound of a purr.

My mother said it was puberty. It would pass.

More than twenty-five years later, the great cosmic hand flipped the coin again. I went to bed a woman of the world, and awakened the next morning desperately homesick for the world of the girl I'd left behind. I turned over in my bed—a futon shoved against the wall of the living room of my Greenwich Village apartment—and remembered, suddenly, what it was like to awaken to complete morning silence. Not a plane or a taxi or a clatter in the street, only the voices of birds or the purr of a cat. I stared at the square of obstructed sky I could see above the curtains and remembered a bowl of sky stretched hard from the yellow, elm-pierced east to the dark jagged blue of mountains to the west. It seemed I could smell sage and rain, dust and onions, lasagna and perfume, all at once, mingling like a siren song.

That day, a registered letter came from Passanante, Corsi, & Cerniglia, Attorneys-at-Law, and I opened it to discover that my aunt Sylvia, ninety years old, had passed away and left me her house and all the lands that went with it. It was so wildly unexpected, I knew my grandmother must have been very, very busy lighting candles to every saint on her list for a special intervention. Saint Jude—oh, he of hopeless causes. And certainly Magdalene, who would understand fallen women so very well.

It would not have surprised me if it had been Sylvia herself who'd brought all that homesickness to me, sitting on my bed in mischievous, ghostly humor, taking care of one last thing before she went on to meet her husband, Antonio.

Truth was, though, I had probably known that going home was the only answer. My best friend, Michael, had collapsed on the stairs the week before, unable to manage the steep narrow flights of our building any longer, and I'd accepted—even if he hadn't—that he'd be living with us soon. Which, considering I'd blown the engine in my delivery van and didn't have anywhere close to enough money saved to think about a new place, was more than a small hurdle.

And as if that weren't enough, the building was sold out from under us to a developer who wanted to put in condos. We had two months to find a new place.

I moved my index finger over the embossed name on the letterhead. No choice.

When Shane, my seventeen-year-old son, came out of his room, rubbing his chest in an unconscious gesture, I said, "Babe, we're going home."

"Home?"

I took a breath, waved the letter. "Pueblo."

For one long moment, he blinked at me, maybe waiting for me to say, *Just kidding*. When I didn't, he scowled, his dramatic dark eyebrows beetling above the brilliance of his blue eyes. "I'm not going there."

"Yeah, kid, you are." I tossed the letter down and poured some coffee into a ceramic mug I'd picked up from a street stall. "It doesn't have to be forever—but we have to take care of Michael."

He slumped on a stool, leaning his elbows on the counter and putting his big, dark head in his hands. Although he was a fairly typical mix of the arrogance and uncertainty that represents seventeen, he was both more and less—thanks to his music and the lessons of the past couple of years. It hadn't been easy, for either of us, and now we were facing the hardest hurdle of all. "Mom—"

"I know." I took a breath, let it go, focused on the irregular rooftops I could see from our fifth-floor window, grimy with soot even though I tried to keep it clean. "A year, Shane, tops. You finish school, we take care of Michael, you can meet your family . . ." I shrugged. "Then you're free. The music isn't going anywhere."

His broad shoulders hunched against me, or maybe against the knowledge that he couldn't really refuse this request. After a minute, he nodded.

I touched his shoulder on my way by. "Thank you."

~

I'm sure the thought of going home and taking Michael with me must have been in the back of my mind for months, triggered by little things—the cadence of Italian-accented English in the voices of people walking below my window, the wrong taste of salsa made by recipes that were nothing like the ones at home, an illusory scent of sage and rain on the wind. After more than twenty years away, there were suddenly reminders of my hometown on every street corner in New York City.

But until we were actually on the train, settling in the generous seats of the Three Rivers Amtrak, I didn't really believe I was going to do it. And even then, as the wheels started to clack across the rails, making that particular and hypnotic sound, I was absolutely sure something else would come up and save me from having to face it. Michael looked at me. "You okay, kid?"

I smiled brightly. "Fine. I really think you'll like it."

"I'm, uh, really sure I won't," Shane said from across the aisle. He used Marlon Brando's *Godfather* voice, slumping deeper in his seat, his electric bass guitar slung over his knees, a badge and a shield. He'd been hustling every avenue, every lead, every possible way to keep us in the city—which was, after all, pretty much all he remembered—until it was plain we really did have no other option.

His idea of Pueblo was my fault. I'd spent most of his life making wry little asides about the place—had perfected an entire spiel on Pueblo, a one-horse little steel town that barely managed not to die when the industry collapsed in the eighties. I delivered the monologue in that peculiar accent I'd worked so hard to lose—a blend of Spanish and Italian and Irish cadences, mixed with a good helping of country Colorado—making insider jokes about the mill and neighborhoods and ethnic groups that nobody outside the city could understand.

Home sweet home. In my memory, it lived under a white-hot summer sun, one of those dog days of August when all the colors in the fields had been bleached out, when the mercury shot up to 101 and the world thumped with the sound of swamp coolers and overhead fans.

My father, too, walked through my memories of home. Romeo, who made me dolls of hollyhocks and spent rainy afternoons with his daughters, cooking zeppole in the shapes of letters and animals and stars.

My father, with whom I had not exchanged a single word in twenty-three years.

It took two days. We spent most of the time sitting in the observation car or in the lounges, staring out the windows at those pastoral landscapes. The hours were very melancholy, at least for me. I don't know if it was for Michael—it's hard to ever know what Michael is really thinking. He's made an art form of inscrutability. For the trip, he turned himself totally anonymous in a pair of jeans that bagged around his skinny rear and a pair of mirrored sunglasses.

Not many people recognized him, of course, not like they did in New York when his restaurant was in full swing and in the papers, so he didn't have to deal with those expressions of hastily hidden dismay he'd often run into in the city, but some people still remembered him from the days when he and my nonhusband Billy were still making records. Michael, being Michael, made it easy for them by cracking jokes about being a missionary in Africa, where rations, you know, are slim. They loved him for it, as they loved him for everything he did. To a lot of people, Michael Shaunnessey was a god.

He was never a god to me, though I sometimes think of him as my angel. Hard to imagine where I'd be without Michael.

Shane, who looks exactly like his father and was, like Billy, also born with some talent to go along with the face, was bearable on the train only because he managed to charm a trio of three young females. They were college girls making their way to LA for some dream or another, and in spite of his age, they were smitten. There's not a female on the planet who can resist that exact combination of smoldering intensity mixed with genuine openness and admiration. Fatal charm.

Or at least it had been fatal for Billy. I hoped it wouldn't prove fatal to Shane.

"Damn, that boy looks like his daddy," Michael said, his voice as gorgeously southern and raspy as ever. We were passing silos at the time. I saw a barn lettered with the name of a feed store pass behind his head.

"I should never have named him Shane," I said. "If I had called him Horace or Porfino, I'm sure he'd be wearing thick glasses by now." Shane had seemed such a dangerous, romantic name to my twenty-two-year-old self. And it is.

"Nah," Michael said. "His friends would have nicknamed him Killer or Charm or something. Count on it."

He was right, of course. Men are even more awed by a lady-killer than women are. That's part of the trouble.

I gave myself up to the rocking of the train, the endless, soothing sound of the wheels clunking over the tracks. I was tired. Scared. Michael and Shane had made peace with the need and the reality of this upheaval in our lives, but I had a lot more baggage than they did.

Roots. It wasn't just that I'd lived in the same house while growing up, though I had. Same house, same neighborhood, same families that had known one another since forever. The whole group of them had emigrated from Sicily ninety years before. Two hundred families left a village in the southern reaches of that island and transported themselves—lock, stock, and secret wine recipes—to America, plopping themselves down in a section of blocks in South Pueblo.

So it wasn't just a generation or two, it was hundreds of years of roots. Stories about things that happened before Napoleon was born, traditions that started in the sixteenth century, family feuds left over from 1742.

It only *sounds* romantic, trust me.

And yet, here is how it happened, my coming home: the train came into La Junta at nine o'clock on a cloudy, late spring morning. We found the TNM&O station and got on a bus filled with migrant workers to ride the last little stretch into Pueblo, sixty miles or so away. I took the window, my limbs heavy with remembrance as the potholed two-lane highway rushed under the bus. I spotted Pikes Peak, way off to the north, and the Sangre de Cristos to the south, blue and distant. They came closer as we trundled west, and a part of a Paul Simon song wound through my head, about a man and a woman winding through the Blood of Christ Mountains.

I'd forgotten how beautiful the yellow fields were in comparison to that soft blue of the mountains, how unbelievably huge the sky appeared. In my years away, I'd had a chance to visit Sicily and had immediately understood why my ancestors had settled in Pueblo. There were a lot of things that had the same feel, even now.

We passed through Rocky Ford, where the best cantaloupes in the world are grown, and I thought about eating piles of them when my mother bought them, five for a dollar, at roadside stands in August. We made ourselves sick on cantaloupe. I thought about telling Shane, but he was slumped deep in his seat, his hair hiding most of his face, and I didn't.

But when we got to the Lanes, I sat up and poked him. "The house is right over that rise." He roused himself, mouth slack, and nodded blearily.

Michael peered out the window, his hands folded easily across his lap, and showed not a flicker of emotion. He read a road sign. "Ah, Thirty-Second Lane. I get it, the Lanes, capital L."

"Not all the names are that simple, so don't get cocky on me."

He put a long slim hand on mine. "You okay, kid?"

"No. But there's nothing you can do about it." I just had to live through it somehow, these first few days. Twenty years was a long time to be a runaway. It would have been a lot easier if I'd shown up every year or two in the meantime.

It wasn't like I'd been incommunicado. It wasn't that dramatic. When my sisters Jordan and Jasmine, one year and two years younger than me, respectively, got out of the house, we set up friendly lines. They kept me up to date on Jane, our baby sister, who was sixteen years my junior. My mother got over wanting to kill me for dropping out of school within a couple of months, and told me to call her every Tuesday night from then on. Tuesday is my dad's bowling night.

My father, on the other hand, has not spoken to me one time in twenty-three years, but I can't say I didn't know it would be that way. I did.

The city arrived outside the windows, so much bigger than it had been that I was blinking. "Shane," I said, "time to wake up. We're almost there."

My sister was going to meet us and drive us out to the house. My sister Jordan, that is, the only one I'd told I was coming—the only one, in all honesty, that I was absolutely sure would come to get us. As we pulled into the station, I sat up tall, straining for a glimpse of her. Entering the driveway, the bus rocked side to side like a lumbering elephant.

We came around the corner, and there they were. I don't know how many. Twenty or thirty at least—my sisters and their families, some of my cousins and aunties, and my mother standing anxiously at the front. Someone had made a big sign that said WELCOME HOME, JEWEL AND SHANE with five exclamation points.

Shane said, "Are they for us?"

"Yeah." That was the thing I'd forgotten to tell them about roots, the upside. Even when you totally screw up, your sister will organize a giant surprise welcome for you. She'll be wearing a medieval velvet hat she bought at the Renaissance festival, and she'll have put on a dress for the first time in five years, even though she lives in clay-stained jeans or surgical blues.

I saw her standing there and waited until I caught her eye, then put my hand on the window, palm out. She raised her hand. Both of us had tears running down our faces.

Then I was up and running down the aisle. They spotted me, and everybody started cheering. All of them, I swear, surged forward, arms out to enfold me and touch my head, to exclaim and kiss my cheek. They blurred together in their clean shirts and good haircuts and the solid shoes of the old women, and the rosary in my nana Lucy's hand. She felt like sticks when I hugged her, and all at once I was dizzy with the recognition that she was still alive. How could I have dared let so much time go by?

My father wasn't there. I hadn't realized until then that I'd been harboring some hope that he might be ready to throw in the punishment towel.

At last, everybody kind of cleared away, or maybe they surged around Shane. Either way, I was just standing there, looking at my mother, who also had big fat tears rolling down her pretty face. "Finally," she said, and hugged me.

~

Jordan had convinced everybody that maybe we wouldn't want a big party after being on a train for two days, and the family, mollified by the promise of a real celebration on Saturday afternoon, got in their Buicks and SUVs and drove home. Jordan took us to the farm in her slightly battered old Volvo.

The farm, like everything else, has a bit of a story attached.

Most of those Sicilians who came here went to work in the steel mill. A few did other things—grocery stores and the like. My mother's line has a restaurant that's justly famous, called simply Falconi's, which is where I learned to cook.

But in 1919, my grandfather Sal and his brother Antonio Falconi had a fight about a woman, Sylvia Rosario. She was a lush beauty who, by all accounts, bewitched—and I do not use the word lightly here; there are still people who say she knew more than she should about herbs—half the men in Bessemer when she came to Mass for the first time on an August Sunday morning. She was fresh from Lucca Sicula, the younger sister of a man who had finally saved enough money from his job as a smelter to send for his siblings.

Sylvia, so the story goes (and I heard it often enough from Sylvia herself to know), took one look at Antonio Falconi and made up her mind in that instant that he and no other would be her husband. Unfortunately, my grandpa Sal had made up his mind that Sylvia would be his wife, and he was the older brother. This might not be a problem where you live, but it was a really big problem for Antonio and Sylvia.

Obviously Grandpa got over it, because he was married to my nana Lucy for forty-nine years. But at the time, it meant war. The restaurant would go to him, of course, so Antonio had to find something else. He bought a farm out on the mesa, where he grew apples and peaches for cider, and although he never got as famous as Merlino's, he actually became rather wealthy once he started growing the chilies and beans that thrive in those hot, irrigated fields. The apples liked the irrigation, too; it just infuriated my uncle to have to outguess the last freeze every year.

What they never grew, Antonio and Sylvia, was children. So eventually they healed the rift with the family, and it became a tradition to have holidays at the farm. The house was a rambling Victorian with a porch that wrapped around three sides. Nearly all the downstairs windows opened on to it. My aunt used to put out dozens and dozens of red geraniums in clay pots every summer, and over the years, some got so big she had to put them on wheels. I used to help her move them, every spring.

It had been a long time since I'd seen the farm. The trees had grown a lot bigger since the last time I'd been there, and a bank of lilac bushes, just about to explode into blossom, had taken over the western property line. There weren't any geraniums, only a forgotten basket that had withered on a hook over the winter.

Other than that, it looked exactly the same. Outside.

And, sadly, inside, too.

Shane surveyed the living room with its overstuffed furniture and dusty carpets, its plaster walls made grimy by years of cooking and my uncle's cigarettes. Probably the result of failing eyesight on my aunt's part, too. If she could have seen the grime, she would have scrubbed it away. Shane couldn't know that. Couldn't know that my imagination filled the room with Christmas trees and the four of us girls and innumerable cousins all racing around the grown-ups' legs until somebody shouted at us to get outside.

He said, "We aren't really going to live here?"

"As a matter of fact, we are."

"What's with all the little statues?" He pointed to an altar in the corner and one visible in the dining room.

Jordan and I exchanged a smile. "Saints," I said. "Sylvia was big on saints."

Jordan shuddered. "I think you're brave to take it on, Jewel."

"Bravery has nothing to do with it." I moved inside, beckoned for Michael to join us. He was hanging back, his hands in his pockets, looking over the fields. I wondered what he was thinking.

I wondered what *I* was thinking. Jordan put the keys in my hands ceremoniously. "There's some bread and a lasagna Mama sent over from the restaurant; just bake it for an hour. I got some groceries stocked for you, and cat food's in the cupboard below the sink—you know about the cats, right?"

They came with the house, three of them. I nodded.

"Sylvia only gave them Science Diet, so you have to feed them that or you'll be sorry. Mama and I aired things out and cleaned things up a little, but she's been fretting over Dad so much—" A touchy subject and she skittered away from it.

"Thanks, Jordan." I kissed her head, surprised still at the height difference between us. I hadn't quit growing until I was pregnant with Shane, and I felt my height almost everywhere. Jordan had halted just shy of five feet, and I could easily kiss her crown. "You'll never know how much it means to me."

"Well, watch out. Not everybody is thrilled that you inherited this place."

"Who wanted it?"

Jordan lifted a shoulder. "A few people. Land values have gone up like you wouldn't believe, and even without the house, a hundred acres of land is worth something."

A hundred acres. I'd forgotten that. I wondered about taxes on that much land and when they'd need to be paid. "Was it making any money before she died?"

"Some, maybe. I don't know how much. Her estate paid off any encumbrances, though, so you should be okay until you get your sea legs." She grinned and clasped my arm. The bells on her bracelet rang. "Buck up. She really wanted you to have it."

Jordan went out and stopped on the porch to put a hand on Michael's skinny waist, looking up at him in concern and no awe whatsoever. She's a nurse, and a good one, though she is at heart an artist. I'd asked her a million questions about things when we'd first found out he was sick. I loved her for the gentleness of that hand.

FROM THE *PUEBLO CHIEFTAN* CLASSIFIEDS:

Thank you to Saint Jude for answering my special prayer. This is my publication.

Say this prayer for nine days, nine times each day.

"May the sacred heart of Jesus be adored, glorified, loved, and preserved throughout the world now and forever. Sacred heart of Jesus, pray for us. Saint Jude, worker of miracles, pray for us." On the ninth day your prayers will be answered. It has never failed. Publication must be promised.

—Rose Falconi Sabatino

Chapter Two

Two months after we got there, the phone rang at 3:00 a.m., starting what would turn out to be one of the longest days of my entire life.

I picked up the receiver from a sound sleep, then dropped it and had to fumble around in the covers to find it. Pushing my hair out of my eyes, I said, "Talk to me."

"Mom, hi. This is Shane."

"I know."

"First, before you get mad, I have a good reason for being late."

He was always late, and he always had a good reason. "Mmm."

"Mom. Are you listening? Are you awake?"

I settled deeper into my pillows, waiting for him to come to the point.

"Mom? Mom! This is important. I'm in jail, and I need you to come get me."

"Jail." As well as I could remember at three o'clock in the morning, it was Shane's first brush with the law, but I was familiar with the procedure. Way too familiar. "I hope you don't need bail money, because I don't have it."

"Um. Yeah. Well, actually, I do."

A boy named Horace wouldn't end up in jail at the tender age of seventeen. Wouldn't happen. No how, no way.

"Mom?" Nervousness was creeping in now. "Are you there?"

"I'm here." Sitting up, as a matter of fact. "How much?"

"Uh, I don't know." He said something to someone else, and I imagined some bored cop in a starched uniform, his pockets pressed neatly against his chest. "Hundred bucks."

I closed my eyes. "I don't have it."

A long pause at the end of the line. "You aren't going to leave me here, are you? I swear, Mom, it wasn't my fault."

"It never is, Shane." And I did something it had never occurred to me to do before: I hung up the phone. Since I knew for a fact he'd get only one call, I didn't have to worry about him calling back to wheedle and cajole and try to wear me down. It would be good for him to stew there.

While I figured out where to get his bail. A hundred dollars. So he'd done something very stupid this time—and got caught. It crossed my mind that maybe I ought to just let him stay there all night, teach him a lesson. I'd done it with his father.

I fell back on the bed, feeling a dull kind of pain across my shoulders, and thought about the pies I'd have to start baking in two hours, then deliver to various spots all over town. If I didn't bail him out right now, he'd be stuck there until at least noon.

Leave him, said the annoyed mother in a voice that sounded a lot like Madonna's—the singer, not the saint.

But what about all the creeps in the holding cell? This one was June Cleaver's.

Be good for him, Madonna said.

But what if they hurt him? June argued.

I squeezed my eyes shut and ripped out a good, solid roar of frustration. Shane, brilliant and bad, arrogant and sweet, lost and proud and troubled, was driving me out of my mind. June's voice said quietly, *He needs a father, you know.*

Yeah. Madonna snorted. *To beat him.*

In the end, I decided to bail him out for purely practical reasons. If I left it till noon, I'd be exhausted and wouldn't be able to mete out punishment well enough. If I did it now, especially without coffee, he'd get a furious earful.

But that meant I had to get the bucks. The only two people who wouldn't either make me eat crow for the next six months or throw a fit were Jordan and Michael. Michael had no money, either. Jordan might scrape it together, but it would be a sacrifice, and I couldn't stand to ask.

My father wouldn't talk to me about the weather. Little chance he'd bail out my bad-seed child. My mother might have done it on the sly, but it was kind of tough to hide a middle-of-the-night phone call.

Which left only one person. Jasmine, my other sister. She'd have the money, and she'd get up in the middle of the night to give it to me. I would also have to live with the polite tsking and ladylike sighs for ages and ages.

It amazed me faintly, lying there, that I had so many resources after so many years of having only myself to rely on. Another good side of roots, I guessed, but it was hard for me to settle back into it, to remember that I did have options.

With fierce, quick stabs, I dialed the number. The phone rang four times before Jasmine picked it up and answered in her perfectly accentless voice, which was fluty and sweet even in the middle of the night. I wondered if she did drills.

"Jasmine," I said before I could chicken out, "I'm sorry to wake you up, but I need a huge favor, and you're the only one I can ask."

"Jewel! Tell me, honey. What is it?"

Honey. Like *I* was the younger sister. "I need your help, and I wouldn't ask, but you're the only solvent person I know. I need a hundred dollars right now to bail Shane out of jail."

"Jail?" There was as much glee as dismay in the word. "How awful! What did he do?"

"I don't know yet. Can you help me?"

"Of course!"

"Cash, Jasmine."

"Even I know that, Jewel. I've got it in my cookie jar. Just run by on your way and pick it up."

"Thank you. I owe you big. I'll take the kids for a whole weekend so you and Brian can get away."

"Don't worry about that right now. Just get that boy out of that awful place."

I thought, suddenly, that maybe it wasn't June Cleaver mouthing those worried words in my head. It was Jasmine, the sport-utility-driving, aerobics-going, Lands' End–wearing version of June. God love her. And in spite of everything, I was glad of the blessing of family. "Jasmine," I said. "Please don't tell Dad."

"Oh, Jewel! I won't."

She would, of course. I don't know why I cared. It would be just what he expected, and things were so bad between us anyway it wouldn't make any difference, but for once I wanted to keep a thread of dignity.

I think I'd hoped that my father would drop the war after I'd been home for a little while. After two months, I fit right back in with my sisters and my mother, the relatives I was beginning to reacquaint myself with. They moved, my family, as easily as water, to incorporate me and Shane and Michael, embracing us in that mercurial fluid of *la familia*. It was as if I'd never left.

Except for my father, who considered me banished and invisible. I didn't go to my mother's house or even call there. The family water flowed around the banishment, making a pocket for my father to occupy without me, and I was trying to live with it.

Turning on the lamp by the bed, I made myself put my feet on the floor and straighten up, forget about my father. There was enough to worry about without tossing him into the mix. My jeans were flung over the back of a chair, and I put them on, then shucked my nightgown and turned around, yawning, to look for my bra. My hair swished over one shoulder, brushed across my breast, and for some reason it brought awareness to my skin. My body. Maybe it was being awakened in the

16

middle of the night. Maybe it was just that there was no father in this boy's life that made me feel so alone.

Whatever the reason, I stood there in the lamplight in the middle of the night, thinking about how long it had been since I'd touched anybody. A man. So very, very long. So long that I'd forgotten to notice that the soft air of an almost summer predawn could arouse me.

Touch. Once, my greatest comfort had come from lying, naked flesh to naked flesh, with Billy. Not having sex, necessarily. Just touching him like that, shoulder to foot, arms entangled. It somehow healed wounded places in me, eased the tension of a day.

Standing there in the coolness, I honestly couldn't remember the last time I'd been touched in any but the most cursory of ways. Michael held my hands, and I touched him a lot when he needed help or when he was hurting. Since I'd been back home, I'd fallen back into the hugging and kissing my family does, and it was great, really, so much better than I remembered.

None of that was the same as touching a man. But then, what had touching men ever gotten me? Trouble. Nothing but trouble.

At my knee, a dog collar rattled, and Berlin made a soft woofing noise. Oh, yes. I do have animal touches. There was Berlin, ostensibly Michael's dog, who had named me Favorite Human years ago. And on the bed were the three cats, who'd likewise nominated me FH, inherited from Sylvia. Two were sort of neurotic and needy and wanted attention all the time. The other one was an aloof and gorgeous tuxedo male named Giovanni. It was naturally him that I liked the best, and I reached over to give him a little scrub.

It was only then I realized I was still half-naked, and it made me feel very silly. Moony. I put on the rest of my clothes and pulled my hair out of my eyes with a scrunchie, then went to get my rotten child out of jail.

∼

Women often tell me, with a piercing kind of longing in their voices, that they always wanted sisters. I somehow end up being friends with women who don't have them—Michael said once that I must be such a sister that they gravitate to me instantly.

My mother had four sisters and is so entwined with them that I think the force of her pleasure is what caused her to have only daughters. She has four and would have kept going, but my father insisted they couldn't afford any more children. She once confessed to me that she wanted twelve kids. I don't know why. The four of us gave her fits enough as it was.

I don't hate my sisters, but having a crew of them is not exactly what these sisterless friends of mine always seem to think it is. I have the scars on my arms from Jasmine's fingernails—which was her usual response to my borrowing one of her shirts, even if all of mine were in the laundry and she didn't like the shirt I borrowed—to prove otherwise. She and Jordan used to gang up on me and call me conceited and vain, which I admit I was. They tattled when they got mad at me.

And when I left them behind, I missed them more than I could ever tell you.

The thing is, there is no more complicated relationship on the planet than that between sisters. I completely adore them. They get on my last nerve. I can't imagine my life without them and have often said I hope I'm the first one to die, because I don't want to have to bury them. I think it would kill me. I've watched my aunts and grandmothers bury sisters. They just fall all to pieces, and I know I would, too.

Maybe that's what all my sisterless friends are looking for when they wish for a sister of their own. That connection. I mean, we might have called one another names and said awful things, even *done* awful things, but when it comes down to the wire, sisters are there for you in a way you can't always count on from your friends. Or maybe you'll just ask your sisters for the support you need when you know they'll be pissed but will help you anyway.

Like Jasmine now. I drove to her house, a luxurious Mediterranean-style adobe built in a community that would have been gated anywhere else in the country, and made all sorts of pretensions to being gated here, though there was no earthly reason for it. True to her word, she'd turned on the porch light. I left the car running in the street—I'd never dare drive that old car into that pristine driveway and risk dripping oil onto the concrete—and dashed up the sloping, curved walk to the porch. Jasmine must have been waiting. She opened the heavy carved door just as I landed on the top step and said, "Come on in." Her voice suited the moment—subdued and quiet. "I've got it right here."

I followed her inside. Even in the middle of the night, she looked like a Hollywood version of a southern belle. Her robe was apricot satin, showing a glimpse of the negligee beneath it, the fabric swooping dramatically over a chest that was her pride and joy, and neatly flat in the back. Billy had made a joke about that lack of rear end, once upon a time. Remembering that made me miss him suddenly.

From the table beside the door, she took two crisp fifty-dollar bills. Her manicured nails matched her robe, and I wondered if she coordinated the polish color and her clothes for a week or changed the nails every day or if it was a coincidence. "Here you go," she said.

I took the money, feeling a sting that I'd had to ask at all, but another surge of gratitude that Jasmine had it to loan me. "I'll pay you back in a couple of weeks."

"Whenever, Jewel," she said in a hushed voice. "I know it's hard for you right now."

Without her usual armor of makeup, Jasmine's skin glowed pearlescently, and her eyes were as purply blue as the gloxinias she grew as a hobby. I shook my head, knowing my own skin was greasy with summer and sleep. "It's unbelievable that you look this good in the middle of the night."

Her eyes went soft. "Thank you. That's the nicest thing you've said to me since you got home."

I bent down to hug her—she wasn't quite as short as Jordan, but it was close. Jane, who would be twenty-four this summer, was the only one who'd come close to my height. "I know. I'm sorry. I'm evil and you are a goddess. Thank you."

Jasmine allowed it for three seconds, but it wasn't her nature to be comfortable with the loving attention of women. "Go on, now," she said. "Get that boy out of jail and tell him to come see me in a day or two so I can kick his little bottom for him."

"I will."

~

I got Shane, who was shamefaced and contrite but also a little giddy on the actual fact of being arrested, home and into bed in time for me to start making the pies. I'd built up a fair amount of business in two months, trading mostly on nepotism at first, then, as word spread, capitalizing on the fact that I was a master of that particular food form.

I'm a great cook—when you're raised in a restaurant, it comes naturally—but I studied cooking seriously in New York, and my passion is for pie. The family kept asking me when I was planning to get a real job, but this was my real job. I hoped, eventually, to build it into a catering business, something I'd run from Michael and Andre's restaurant for nearly seven years, but at the moment, Michael needed my attention a lot more than my business did. We had a roof over our heads and utilities were cheap. As long as I could bring in groceries and start building a savings account again, we'd be okay for now.

Since flats of blueberries were on special, I'd decided to bake blueberry pies this morning. The fruit mixture and pie shells had been prepared the night before, but I liked baking them in the morning so they'd be aromatic and maybe still a little warm when I delivered them. It went quickly. By ten thirty, they were loaded into the station wagon and I was on the road into town. By one, I was back home, considerably richer and definitely on my last emotional nerve.

In the middle, at exactly eleven, I had walked into Falconi's, which technically belongs to my mother and her sisters, so my father couldn't keep me out, even though I was fairly sure he wanted to. I was a little nervous each time I dropped pies by there, but my father had taken pains to avoid me, managing to run an errand or be out talking to somebody when I showed up.

Torture, right? Why would I bother? Because I needed to. Because Shane needed him. Because he could pretend all he wanted, but I knew he still loved me.

I was always his favorite. Except for my height, which comes from my mother's side, I look like him more than the others. I have his winged eyebrows and golden eyes and curly hair. My mother says the internal angle is even more similar: our birth dates are three days apart, under the sign of Leo—which is probably at the heart of our falling-out. Lion pride.

As if to prick that pride, the car started screaming as I drove up. I had no idea why it did it, just started screaming at the top of its lungs at odd moments. Three mechanics had looked it over to see if they could find the source, and all three shook their heads in bafflement. I told everyone it was just haunted, but Shane said if that was true, I'd have a ghost following me from car to car, making special noises in each one. We'd had a brand-new Buick off the lot once that had a weird, deep squeak in the front left tire. A delivery van that turned the radio on and off at will.

Anyway, I wasn't expecting much out of an '83 Chrysler station wagon I bought for seven hundred bucks. It ran very well, so I put up with the occasional scream. Except that I hated it totally when it did it that morning, commencing when I turned the corner from Northern and made my way through the blocks to the small, unassuming corner building that had housed Falconi's for seven decades. It screamed until I turned off the engine, drawing Lorenzo, the daytime bartender, outside the kitchen door to wave at me, a grin showing off his big white teeth.

I rolled my eyes and stuck my head out the window. "Don't say it or I'll keep driving, and you won't get any blueberry pie with your lunch today."

"Ah, cruelty, thy name is woman!" He put his hand over his chest and came to open the back gate fitted with racks for the pies. I got out and went to help him. Four pies, twice a week. I suspected sometimes that my grandmother, who no longer worked but reigned from her back table for a few hours every day, made everyone in town eat those slices of pie so she could get me back in there as often as possible. No one else on my list used anywhere close to eight pies a week.

Lorenzo carried two and I carried two. "You gonna marry me yet?" he asked. He was already married, to a tiny neat lawyer who'd bought them a very nice house in University Park, and he was crazy about her. But he was also insane for my pies.

"Well, you'd be handy enough around the house"—something I desperately needed in the old farmhouse—"but you'd be back to being poor."

He inhaled the scent from the still-warm pie. "It would be worth it."

It's a cliché to say that Italian men have a flirting disease. It's also, to some degree, true. I'd probably be disappointed if he didn't find some way to appreciate me every day.

He pushed open the door and let me go ahead, laughing when I had to squeeze close. I pretended to be scandalized. "You should be ashamed of yourself, young man."

"I am, I tell you. Every single time."

So I was laughing and playing word games with the married bartender when I came in and saw my dad sitting there at the table with my grandmother, listening to everything we said.

He's a good-looking man, my father, even now, just past sixty. His hair had silvered a little, and he combed it straight back from his forehead, which showed off his hawkish, gorgeous nose. As usual, he was wearing a clean, starched shirt with a collar, this one in blues and tiny threads of yellow, tucked into a crisp pair of gabardine trousers. His shoes had a shine. His nails were neatly trimmed. He's natty, is Romeo. Probably where Jasmine gets it.

When he saw me, he didn't give me any long, meaningful look or anything. Just stood up, picked up the papers he'd been going over with Nana Lucy, and walked off. Like I was invisible.

So maybe I was wrong. He would never acknowledge me again. He really meant it when he said I was dead to him for the rest of my life.

Beside me, Lorenzo said, "Don't take it like that, babe."

Right. Easier said than done. I wondered suddenly if Jasmine had already told my father about Shane ending up in jail, but realized it didn't matter. It wasn't as if it would make any difference, one way or the other.

Stung, I rushed through my business, stopped for a minute to kiss my nana's white head and agreed to bring Shane and Michael to dinner on Sunday, and got out of there as fast as I could. The whole time, my cheeks felt hot, and I could feel the sympathy of the waitresses and even some of the early customers. I hate it when they feel sorry for me, and it made me want to do something dramatic, like scream an epithet at my father's stiff back, which is something I would have done in my youth.

Twenty years had given me the wisdom to know it wouldn't change anything. He'd still ignore me. I'd look like more of a floozy than ever, and not one pair of sympathetic eyes would be fooled into thinking I didn't care.

~

Back at the farm, I rousted Shane out of bed and put him to the most miserable tasks I could come up with: scrubbing both bathrooms, the kitchen floor, and even—I have to admit I assigned it with a certain glee—the baseboards. It was a task Sylvia had tackled every third Saturday of the month, and it had not been done once since we arrived. They were the old style of baseboards, six inches of carved wood, and required a tremendous amount of elbow grease. It would take him hours to take a rag and Liquid Gold to every single one in the house.

Michael was up, a good sign, and sitting on the screened porch. "Hey, good looking," I said, kissing his head and covertly checking for fever with my hand. He didn't like being fussed over, and it killed him to have to be so dependent, so he wouldn't always say when he was feeling bad. "Did you eat?"

"Yeah, Shane made me breakfast."

"Well, I brought you a treat for later, then." I settled in a chair opposite and held out my prize, a filled éclair from a bakery he liked. "Ta-da!"

He grinned at me, those deep eyes flashing mischief the way they'd always done. "A woman after my own heart." He took it out and started nibbling it. Savoring it. "So what happened with Da Kid? I take it you had to bail him out of jail in the wee hours of the morning?"

"Oh, it's good this time." I ticked off the violations on my fingers. "They were tagging a billboard over on Fourth Street when a cop spied them."

Michael raised his eyebrows.

"Wait," I said. "It gets better. Being a fairly bright pair of idiots, they had an escape plan in place. They scrambled down from the sign— drunk, of course—"

"Naturally."

"—and got in Justin's car to outrun the cop." It made me nauseated to imagine what might have happened.

"Obviously they were not successful in their flight." A tiny smile quirked the corner of Michael's mouth.

"No. Getting caught with spray paint cans in hand, drunk, after curfew wasn't enough. They had to add eluding the police." Watching him make his way through the éclair, I regretted that I'd resisted buying a cruller for myself. "What is *wrong* with him?"

"Ah, it's not that bad. He's seventeen, that's all. In the long run, you know he'll be all right."

A pang went through my chest. "I'm really not that sure right now. He's got no strength of character. He's too charming, he's too good looking, and he's too much his father's child."

Michael thought about that as he licked some custard off his thumb. "All true but the last bit. He's not really like Billy. He's more like you."

It wasn't all that comforting, to tell you the truth. It's not like I have a record of outstanding successes. "I wish my father would pay attention to him. I don't care anymore if he forgives me, but he could do a lot for Shane."

Michael looked at me. No words. He didn't approve of my father, but only because he didn't understand him. Michael loved me and hated that I cared so much that my father has not spoken to me in twenty years, a reality that had grown more excruciating with every passing day. "You can't judge everybody by the way your father was, Michael."

"Is that what I'm doing?"

I shrugged. Relented. "No."

"Truth is, darlin', I can't really think of anything your father and my daddy would have had in common. 'Cept rotten children." He winked, a shadow of his former self.

We sat in the quiet of the gathering heat, not talking. I propped my feet on the rail and listened to Shane's music on the CD player inside—something new and alternative in a minor key. It expressed remorse, and I had to smile. The kid has great taste in music, actually, loves everything from Celtic to jazz, Bach to metal in addition to his beloved, blasting rock 'n' roll.

Music. Would it save him or kill him? Did so many musicians self-destruct because the music failed them or did self-destructive people end up in music? A familiar knot of panic tied itself in my gut.

"Have you heard from your father lately?" I asked, taking my mind from the immediate worry.

"Not for six or eight months. He was working in Indiana. Asking for money in a roundabout way." He gave me a bitter smile. "Didn't have the heart to tell him I didn't have any left."

"Sorry."

A lift of one bone-thin shoulder. "Not your fault."

"I think you need to call him, Michael. You need to see him."

Slowly he examined the last of the éclair, then ate it. "We been through this, darlin'. No point in breaking his heart just yet."

I sighed. There was no way to *make* Michael do anything he didn't want to do, and he'd somehow made up his mind to spare his father the pain of his eldest son's lingering illness.

Michael's parents had been ordinary, blue-collar southern people, salt of the earth as they say, until they got together. And they turned from normal to completely abnormal, alternately obsessed with lust for each other or caught in a spiral of jealousy and revenge that had ultimately ended with Michael's father in prison.

Where my life had been as stable and ordinary as, well . . . pie, Michael's had been as turbulent as a hurricane. In spite of that, I'd never heard him actually speak ill of his parents—in fact, he was a hell of a lot more forgiving of their foibles than I would have been—but their double-edged passion for each other had been a disaster for their children, Michael and his brother, Malachi, who was a few years younger. Michael had been their meal ticket during low times—they'd parade him out to sing and play guitar in any little honky-tonk or hole-in-the-wall lounge they could find to pay them. Michael laughed about it and said it was those times that had made him a musician in the end, but I hated to think of him, skinny and gawky at nine or twelve, singing in some dive in Texarkana.

He did it because he could, because he had to, because the family needed him to do it. And because he was fiercely, deeply, rabidly protective of his little brother.

Malachi. I'd never met him, and considering I'd known Michael for two decades, that was saying something. They got together sometimes, but Michael always met him someplace private, and they'd go off and have a few days of good-old-boy fishing or some such thing. His brother led adventure tours all over the world, and it almost seemed that Michael had to chase and capture his brother each time he wanted to see him, that Malachi was so restless he couldn't bear to light in one place for more than three minutes at a time.

Case in point: for six months, I'd been trying to find the mysterious Malachi. I'd written letters to a post office box number in—of all places—Biloxi, Mississippi, where he stopped for rest when he wasn't wandering the world in search of Hemingwayesque adventures.

Not that Michael knew I'd written. He didn't want his brother here, either. I'd had to rifle through Michael's things in search of Malachi's address when it became clear that he wasn't going to tell either his paroled father or his footloose brother that he was dying and they ought to come visit. I couldn't find an address for the father, but I'd written to Malachi. Repeatedly. No answer.

A fact I'd finally decided was for the best. What kind of man is named Malachi, anyway? I'd seen some photos, but there was always something wrong with them—a streak of light that obscured his face, or a weird blob of color that rendered him all but invisible. He was as big as Michael had been, and dark where Michael was fair, but that was really all I'd ever been able to make out. And that he was one of those rough-and-ready guys. I imagined him posing with a dead fish the size of a small boat or running with the bulls in Spain—something I knew for a fact that he'd actually done and struck me as completely insane—or putting his foot on the side of some precious animal he'd slain. He probably carried a knife in his boot and swilled liquor made of alligator blood.

A magpie flitted over the fields just beyond my feet, screaming a warning, and it startled me so much I realized I'd nearly drifted off. Blinking, I straightened and looked over at Michael to discover he had fallen asleep. It pierced me. In the bright afternoon light, the blue veins running beneath the thin white skin of his temple were clearly visible. His big nose, once so aggressively sexy, seemed to be only bone, and his beautiful hands were whittled down to knuckles.

But here, on my aunt Sylvia's porch, he could doze in the quiet. He could look at the blue, blue sky and listen to birds twittering in the trees. He could sleep at night without hearing sirens or worrying about how we'd get the rent or any of those things. He had Shane. He had me. He had my sister Jordan, who knew how to make him feel better in ways that were beyond me and how to check his medicine and nag doctors when things didn't feel right.

I wished he also had Malachi. I went inside to write another letter.

SHANE'S GREEN EGGS AND HAM

This was my favorite story when I was a kid, and my dad read it to me like thirty-seven billion times. Even though it's been a really long time, I can still remember him making all the voices, and he's the one who cooked green eggs and ham for me all the time, since he was home in the mornings when my mom was working.

Mix 8 large eggs, 1 cup chopped ham, ½ cup chives, chopped to mush, grated cheese if you want, or even a little bit of blue cheese. Mix 'em up, and be sure and get the chive juice into the eggs. In a big iron frying pan, melt a big chunk of butter until it's sizzling and popping. Pour in the eggs and scramble till they're soft. Serve with sliced tomatoes and milk and orange juice.

Chapter Three

Shane finished the baseboards in less than two hours, and although I went through and examined them, I had to admit they were pretty decent. I'd expected it to take most of the afternoon and could tell by the glitter in his smoky blue eyes that he knew it, too.

"Good job," I said, reluctantly.

He laughed. "Now what, master? And just for the record, am I working in the house to pay back my bail or is this just punishment work? If it's work to earn money, could you let me in on how much I'm earning, so I'll know when I'm done?"

"Two cents an hour," I said, trying not to look at him. It was partly my fault that he was so bad—I mean aside from the name business. He charmed me. It was also very difficult to punish him, because he turned everything into a big game. In some ways, I guessed it was a blessing. I was also afraid it would get him killed.

"Cool," he said, and leaned around the corner to check the clock. "Only five thousand hours to go." He gave me a bland look and rolled up his sleeves. "What next?"

"Lunch. For everybody. I'm going to take a shower."

"I don't know if Michael will want anything. He ate a lot this morning. I made him some scrambled eggs and he ate every bite. Drank a big glass of orange juice, too."

"Really? He ate an éclair, too." It was a truly astonishing amount of food for him these days, and my heart lightened.

Shane bent—even though I'm five ten, he's taller—and gave me one of his spontaneous hugs. "Maybe he's gonna have a good summer. Maybe your witchy aunt is casting a spell over him."

I hugged him back, laughing softly. "Maybe." I wondered if she had any spells hidden away for troubled teens. "Just fix lunch for us, then. I really want a shower." Probably a nap, too.

The bathroom was badly in need of updating. It was a tiny room, barely big enough to hold a claw-footed tub, toilet, and tiny sink set on top of a truly ugly pressed-wood vanity that at least provided some storage. It did have one long frame window that let in plenty of light, and Aunt Sylvia had done her best to make it appealing with cloth shower curtains hung around the pitiful, added-on shower. A fern, overgrown in the moist heat, crouched in one corner. A small ceramic statue of a saint—I had no idea which one—perched on a little shelf above it, hints of mildew edging the folds of his skirt.

Pinning up my hair, I thought about Shane and what Michael had said. The kid really was a lot like me in many ways—the fact that he cooked to Michael's appetite was a good example, and he did it without being asked. It was his own little quest, to discover and cook all the things Michael most liked and prepare them perfectly. He'd learned a lot about cooking when Michael had the restaurant, so his offerings were a cut above the usual teen fare.

Damn. Drinking and driving—that wasn't the life I wanted for my child. How could I convince him that was an idiot move?

I turned on the water in the shower and let it warm up. Outside, a motorcycle cut through the quiet, roaring by the front of the house in obnoxious noise. It sounded like it stopped, and I worried that it might be one of Shane's new buddies—the troublemakers—but the only one who could drive was Justin, who had been arrested with him last night. I suspected he would not be driving again for a very long time.

Whoever it was, they could wait. I stepped into the shower and washed away the grime of cooking and the sweat of running all over town. In the shower, where no one could see or hear, I let myself have a good cry over everything—the struggle of single parenthood, the pressure of trying to make ends meet, Michael's illness, my father's rejection, all of it. It doesn't always help to cry it out, but I've found it doesn't hurt.

~

I didn't hear the voices on the porch until I got to the bottom of the stairs. Three of them, very animated. One belonged to Shane. One to Michael. One to our mysterious visitor, a voice I didn't recognize, and although it was indistinct, it was one of those baritones that carry in the best possible way—much too deep for any of my family members.

So I was grateful I'd taken a shower and didn't look like something the cat dragged in. I smelled coffee brewing, and as I made my way through the room Sylvia had called the parlor and we used as a dining room, Shane popped back in through the screen door and gave me the funniest look. Pleased. Abashed, even. An expression I didn't see much anymore and that had once been reserved for his father, the odd celebrity, or a dazzlingly beautiful girl.

"Who is it?" I whispered, trying to see out the window to the porch. The lace curtain blocked everything but the shape of a man's shoulders. Fairly burly shoulders topped by a dark head.

Shane said, "I gotta get to the lunch," and grinned at me, ducking away before I had a chance to corner him.

So there wasn't really anything to do but be glad I was clean, even if I didn't have any makeup on and had tossed on some comfortable, ancient jean shorts and a tank top in preparation for a good nap after lunch. I stepped out onto the porch.

Michael was facing the visitor, who had his back to me, and whoever it was, I smiled, because Michael was laughing. Laughing the way he used to, the way that infected everyone around him and made them laugh, too. That was the big thing that drew people, not just the size and beauty of him, but that infectious zest. He loved everything, and it made you want to love things, too.

"Jewel!" Michael said. "Look who's here."

And instantly I knew who it was, a man so large that I had a sense of him unfolding as he stood up and turned around. There was something familiar about his movements, the shape of his shoulders, the set of his head.

Malachi.

Other than body type, the brothers could not have looked more different. He was as dark as Michael was fair—hair the darkest shade of cinnamon brown, eyes the color of bitter chocolate, skin tanned as dark as the earth. He'd been leading an adventure tour down the Amazon.

He wore a white shirt with the sleeves rolled up and a pair of jeans and heavy boots for riding that motorcycle I'd heard. Covered with road dust, hair sweaty from the helmet that sat on the ground near his chair, and obviously exhausted, he still kindled a flash of instant lust.

And to my dismay, I could see it was hitting him, too. His eyes touched my arms and body, my knees and hair. Especially my hair.

The lust didn't appear to make him any happier than it made me.

I had at least five years on him, maybe more. And guys like this, they want girls—emphasis on *girl*—with pierced belly buttons and skinny thighs, neither of which I own. Forget about it, I told myself.

"Malachi," I said.

"And you're the famous Jewel."

I wanted to slide my eyes down his body but didn't, kept them firmly fastened to his face. "Or infamous, depending on which tabloids you read."

That made him grin. "Right."

Shane came out, bringing mugs of coffee. "Milk and lots of sugar," he said, like a waiter, putting one down on the little table for Malachi. "Black," for me. "White," for Michael.

"Thanks, babe." I picked up my cup, glad of something to do.

Michael said, "Malachi's been in Brazil. Just got back three days ago and blazed out here. He seems to think I'm in dire straits."

"Oh, surely not!" I met Malachi's eyes, hoping he'd give me a chance to talk to him before he went further. He blinked, slow as a cat, and I took that as agreement. "I'm glad you got my letter, though. If you'd gone looking for Michael in New York, you might have been pretty worried."

He gave a nod. "Yeah." And he wiped his face in a telling gesture.

"Can you stay for a while?" I asked. "We have plenty of room."

"I'd like that. Got some time." His voice was devastating, even more so than Michael's. Not only that carrying baritone, but laced with a drawl as slow as a southern river. "Thank you."

"Good," I said. "Shane, why don't you get the bed made in the blue room? And put out some clean towels."

"Got it." He hopped up with a kind of enthusiasm that made me frown. What about Malachi caused this excitement?

"You looked wiped out, bro," Michael said. "Why don't you go grab a shower and some sleep? I'll make a big supper and you can tell me about your adventures."

Malachi pushed his fingers through that thick, damp hair. "All right." He stood up and then bent down again, all long legs and arms, and gave Michael a hug. I liked him for that—a lot of men these days won't hug even their brothers.

"We'll eat in a few minutes," I said. "Sure you don't want to wait and have some sandwiches first?"

"I'm pretty beat. Had some doughnuts at a Kwik Way a little while ago." His smile was rueful.

"Come on, then, and I'll show you where you can put your stuff."

I waited in the living room for him to get some things from the bike—an impressive thing, by the way, with saddlebags and all the extras. A bike for long trips, and one that had made many by the wear on it. He took a heavy, well-worn canvas bag off the back.

I watched him from the shadows, where he wouldn't be able to see me. He was a very watchable man. A sex god. My type exactly, even though you'd think I'd have learned my lesson by now.

Don't mistake me—I'm not talking about pretty. Or just good looking. Most really good-looking men are so self-centered they aren't worth bothering with. I'm talking about an entirely different quality.

Billy had it. So does Shane, even though I try not to think about it. Michael, for all his beauty, doesn't, because he's gay. I guess maybe gay guys see the same thing in him because he never lacked for love, but I'm talking strictly the man-woman thing.

Malachi moved easily in his skin, rare in anybody, but really rare in a man who must have to duck under doorways constantly and buy his clothes from special shops. He was that big. Lean, but very powerful through the shoulders and chest, probably from that hale life he led. At least six six, and neither skinny nor ripped up like some silly wrestler, but perfectly in proportion so that you wouldn't really notice he was so big until he filled a doorway.

And his size doesn't say it, either. My dad is five six, and he has that quality and a name to go with it: Romeo. Women have been falling all over my father since he was a baby. I'm sure they'd been doing the same for Malachi.

It's a look, a way of moving, an awareness quotient. A man who is present now, in this minute, his attention on whatever is right in front of him. I knew he'd be able to tell somebody that my eyes were brown, that my hair reached my waist, that I had more flesh on me than was strictly allowed these days, but that it was arranged in a way that people could call voluptuous instead of fat. I suspected he might be able to tell the color of my bra, too, because I'd almost caught him taking a long look down my shirt when I stood up. He lifted one eyebrow, like *couldn't help myself*, which is really the most natural response. A man who pretends he's not looking or a man who makes a big deal of it are both annoying. One's prissy, one's a lout.

Anyway.

Sex. That's how I was thinking from the first minute I saw him, and it wasn't all that easy to lead him up the stairs, because I'm sensitive about those not-skinny thighs. I chattered to make myself feel calmer, and wished

I'd put on jeans instead of shorts. "It's kinda hot up here as the summer moves in, but we've got a million fans, and you should be all right."

"I've been in Brazil, darlin'."

I smiled over my shoulder. "Good point."

The room was tucked under the eaves on the north end of the house. He dropped his stuff on the bed Shane had made, and I showed him to the bathroom, still pretty humid from my shower, and illustrated the wonky controls. "That's really it."

As I said, the bathroom is tiny, tiny. Malachi just stood there in the doorway, filling it up entirely. "Tell me about Michael," he said. "How long has it been AIDS?"

I took a breath. "Two and a half years."

"After Andre died," he said. Not a question.

"Yeah." I blinked, looked down at my toes. "It took a lot out of him, losing Andre, then the restaurant."

"And he's dying," Malachi said.

"Yes."

"What about drugs? All the antivirals and whatever?"

There were times that the reality was almost more than I could stand, and a wave of that hit me just then. "He was HIV positive for a very long time, Malachi, since the late eighties. He took the drugs then, and they worked, but he developed resistance to some of them and allergies to some others, and he can't tolerate anything anymore." I raised my eyes. "He's pretty much down to some antibiotics and some pain meds, but that's it."

"He looks tired and very thin, but not like he's gonna die."

"I know." It was one of the more difficult aspects of the whole thing. "Sometimes he's back to his normal self, he feels that good. And sometimes he's really tired and won't get out of bed for days. You've caught him on a good day. I swear I'm not lying—although he will."

A small frown pulled down his heavy brows. "No." He took an envelope out of his back pocket. Three envelopes folded together, actually. "I didn't doubt you were serious."

Seeing those three letters, each one more desperate than the last, sparked the anger that had been lurking since I'd seen his gorgeous bod on the porch. I glared up at him. "What took you so friggin' long to get here?"

"I was in Brazil."

"For six months?"

A lift of those arched brows. "That's right."

"Doesn't anyone get your mail and tell you when something urgent is going on?"

He looked down at the letters, smoothed them between the index and long finger of both hands, framing my handwriting on his name: *Malachi Shaunnessey.* His mouth tightened a little; then he looked up at me, very directly. "It's not like there's some big network of people in my life. My mother is dead. My father's an asshole and I don't care what happens to him." A little jerk in his throat or maybe the jaw, just enough to show that if he weren't such a big, alligator-blood-drinking tough guy, he'd probably have tears in his eyes. "I never expected . . . Michael's always landed on his feet."

Damn. I'd had nearly two years to come to terms with all of this—a stage at a time. And although he was my best friend, he wasn't my brother. I put my hand on his arm. "I'm sorry."

He gave that guy-nod, eyes downcast, throat working a little.

"I'll let you take your shower, get some rest. We can talk later."

"Thanks." The sound was a little rough, but he attempted a faint smile. Didn't step back, just lifted his head and gave me a rueful half smile, acknowledging his almost breakdown.

And, just like that, I was very aware of the fact that he dwarfed me—which is a good feeling when you're tall and hippy—and that his eyes were soft when they were sad. He smelled like the outdoors on a summer afternoon, like clothes just taken off the line, and I wondered in a distant way why he didn't smell like sweat and exhaustion.

It went on a little too long, and that initial zing I'd felt upon seeing him expanded into a roar. Lust. Deep and somehow clean, perfectly obvious for what it was. I wanted to see his chest. He tilted his head, quirked his mouth a little, and his gaze flickered downward, and I suspected the same thought—a bared chest—was crossing his imagination.

I dropped my hand from his arm. He was in the way and didn't seem to notice for a minute, and then he grinned. "Sorry," he said, and stepped back. I pushed by him, my shoulder bumping his biceps.

In the hall, I backed away. "The faucet sometimes makes a loud noise when you turn on the hot water. Just turn it on a little more and it'll stop."

"Hmm." He held up a finger for me to wait, ducked into the bathroom, and turned on the water until he got the noise—a shuddering that seemed to shake the entire room. He came out. "Got a wrench? I can fix that in about three seconds."

"You don't have to do that."

His wink was pure sex god. "I'm sure you can figure out a way to pay me back."

I rolled my eyes and went to find a wrench.

SYLVIA'S LOVE POWDER

On Saint Anthony's Day, cut long branches of rue, collect the freshest flowers, and mix with the petals of the reddest rose in the garden. Dry in a secret place where they will be safe from the breath of others. When they are dry, grind them with a mortar and pestle to a fine powder, then pour it into a bag. Take the powder to the river on the Feast of Our Lady, think of your heart's desire, and toss the herbs into the water and ask the Lady's blessing on your love. If he is meant for you, he will come by the turn of the season. If he is not, your true love will appear.

Chapter Four

Not even the arrival of the delectable Malachi could keep me from my nap. It's a lifelong habit, one my mother says kept me out of afternoon kindergarten. "She needs her sleep," she'd tell my aunts, brushing hair off my forehead as I dozed on her lap in one of their living rooms. "Hasn't missed her nap since the day she was born."

And I still try not to. The animals trailed me upstairs, taking their stations around the bed, Berlin at the foot, Giovanni the aloof tuxedo on the windowsill above the bed, the other two cats on each side of my body. I fell on my stomach, grabbed a pillow to throw an arm across, and closed my eyes. A breeze came through the open windows, sweeping over my face with the smell of summer water, making me think of Malachi's white shirt flapping on a clothesline. I took the image with me into the dark, cool well of sleep.

When I woke up, one cat had moved to slump over the small of my back, paws on either side of my body, and another was curled right at my nose. She squeaked at me when I stirred. By the thickness in my head and the sweat collected on the back of my neck, it had been a long nap. Deep gold light, colored by dust in the air, slanted through the windows to fall on the dresser and floor and wall. Pueblo has the same artistic light that has made Florence and Taos and southern France so famous, but its steel mill image somehow stunted any artist colony that might have developed. Lying there, waiting for my mind to come back from the wild world of dreams, I admired the quality of those rectangular bars of light, thinking maybe I wanted to try some butterscotch pie sometime soon. Maybe my auntie Gen had a recipe, or maybe Carol.

The smell in the air brought me around fully. Michael was cooking. I turned over on my back, breathing it in with a smile, identifying the food by the notes in the air. Barbecued chicken wings, messy and sweet and tangy. He'd make a spinach-and-orange salad to go with them. Blinking heavily, I stumbled down the hall, passing the closed door to the silent blue room where Malachi still slept, and washed my face, thinking about the extra-strong coffee that was the secret ingredient in Michael's sauce.

But before I went down, I went back to my room, took off the old T-shirt I'd slept in, and shuffled through my drawers for something else. It all looked boring—the short-sleeved Henleys and simple little scoop-necked summer shirts. Mom stuff. I glared at them, digging deeper, wondering when I'd let this part of myself go. When had I turned into this person?

Finally, near the bottom of the stack, I found a green silk tank. Not great, but a hell of a lot better than the rest of the junk. I shook it out, and the cool heavy weight of it suddenly made me remember wearing it in previous summers, good times, sometimes with Michael, sometimes with another man or some of my girlfriends. Finding a club where the music was good, the tables crowded into some dark, small space. The rush of excitement of getting ready, going out, having a few drinks and laughing, dancing, letting down our hair.

Outside my window, there was no sound of traffic, no horns or rumbling trucks, and a part of me was suddenly, deeply homesick for those noises, for the rush and excitement of the city. Why had I come back here?

A step sounded in the hallway, and I heard the bathroom door shut. Malachi, almost certainly.

Maybe it was thinking of my old self, or maybe it was that lingering hint of man hunger that had been crawling on my spine all day, but

I suddenly reached around and unhooked the ordinary white bra that had taken me through the responsible roles in my life—the business-woman and the mother and the caregiver—and dug into the bottom of the drawer for a dangerous black one, made of soft lace. Just in case he needed to take another look down my shirt—the silk shirt that made a man want to run his hands over a woman. I could have told myself I was doing it for me or to celebrate Michael feeling good enough to cook or even to celebrate Malachi's arrival here, but I learned a long time ago not to play those kinds of games with myself. He stirred me up, and I wanted to stir back.

But in that instant I happened to catch sight of my body in the mirror over the dresser and got a crashing dose of reality. Why does that happen, over and over? In my head, especially in a good mood, I'm thinking I'm still a hot mama, a little more of me than there was, maybe, but still pretty sound female stuff.

The mirror is so brutal. Especially since I was standing in that bright-gold sunlight streaming in the second-floor windows. It showed the fish whiteness of my belly, which would never stand the scrutiny of a bikini again and hadn't for five years. Soft grayish stretch marks there along the sides. And the breasts that had once stood so high and proud were lower, not anywhere close to perky. It wasn't an awful body—how can you really hate the body that gives you babies and pleasure and walks you around in the world?—but it was just so obviously skin and hips and breasts that had been around for forty years. For one tiny moment, I wanted a belly button that could tolerate a tattoo.

Never gonna happen. But I put them on anyway, the black lace bra and the silk tank, because I was liking the sense of pleasure it gave me to make the best of whatever those years had left behind. Michael would love it—he hated for me to be anything less than 100 percent siren—and I was pretty sure Malachi wouldn't *mind*. I let my hair down, too—what the heck. Maybe I'd just be a wild woman and ask him for a ride on that big old bike, and use it as an excuse to lean into his body, smell him again.

"You are such a slut, girl," I said to the mirror. The slut looked back and lifted one rueful eyebrow. She didn't look nearly apologetic enough for a woman who'd been estranged from her father for twenty years over the whole thing.

~

I beat Malachi downstairs, which gave me a minute to wander into that hot, spicy-smelling kitchen and see Michael happily tossing greens in a big wooden bowl. Baby spinach and mandarin oranges, as I'd suspected. He wore a black shirt and black jeans, a silver bolo at his neck, and his pointy black cowboy boots. The blond hair gleamed in a thick mane down his neck, completely unaffected by his illness.

It pierced me to see him looking so normal. He gave me a big grin over his shoulder and held out a cup of the rich, almost thick coffee he made for barbecue sauce. "I heard you moving around."

I took the cup and drank a grateful sip. "I smelled it. And the wings. How long till dinner is ready?"

"About a half hour, I guess." Whistling, he turned around to toss the salad some more, and he suddenly seemed so dear, so perfect, so himself, that I set aside the coffee cup and put my arms around his waist, my head against his back. His ribs and shoulder blades were sharply defined, belying the happy good humor of the moment, and the recognition of the fact that I would lose him drove itself home once again, deep and hard and unbearable. I gritted my teeth against revealing it to Michael, but he felt it, and he put his hands over mine, gently lifting one to his mouth.

"Thanks for getting Malachi here," he said.

"Sure." I just leaned into him, smelling his particular scent—a hint of grass and spices—for a long time. Against my cheek and my hands, wherever we touched, there was a tingling sensation, not at all sexual. Maybe it was just healing, just love—a strength transfer. He put my hand on his faintly stubbled cheek and pressed it there for a minute, and I let him go.

In the big window by the breakfast bar was a shelf for Saint Anthony. I gave his head a pat as I sat down, remembering when Sylvia would turn his face toward the wall when she was mad at him.

I sipped my coffee. "You never told me your brother was a sex god." Michael grinned. "Runs in the family."

"What does?" Malachi himself appeared in the doorway, much cleaner than last time I'd seen him, dressed in jeans and a turquoise T-shirt printed with a parrot and some Spanish slogan. No shoes. I didn't look at his feet, naked and white against the worn linoleum of my aunt's floor, but this time, I couldn't help but notice his waist. Impossibly narrow beneath those shoulders. And the kind of radiating presence that slams you if you're within twenty yards. Maybe twenty miles.

Trust Michael to get that mischief in his bright-blue eyes. "Being a sex god," he said.

Malachi looked at me, slightly sleepy, his hair just a little untidy. "Yeah?"

Sex sex sex sex sex. It came off him in waves, reminding me how long it had been since I'd let myself indulge. Such promise in that little quirk of a smile, the edges of his eyes crinkling in a solid fan of sun lines. "Trouble with sex gods," I said, "is that they're so damned predictable."

He laughed. "Too true." He came into the kitchen, Berlin—traitorous creature—trailing behind, and took the other stool at the breakfast bar.

His eyes said that he didn't care if my body was a decrepit forty and he was used to twenty-four. They slid with that cheerful familiarity over my neck, my hair, my arms, liking what they saw. He even—shameless creature—touched his lower lip with his tongue, showing it to me like the manifestation of original sin. He saved himself—just—by winking.

I laughed. Overt I could handle. "I should have known he'd have a brother like you."

Michael laughed, too.

"Where is Shane?" I asked, having finally gathered enough brain cells to notice his absence.

"Your sister Jasmine came by and wanted him to babysit, so she and Jane could go do something for the wedding," Michael said. "They should be back any minute."

Jane, my youngest sister, who was fourteen years younger than Jasmine, which meant sixteen years younger than me, was getting married in August. Word was that she had somehow remained a virgin and actually had earned the right to wear her $2,000 white wedding dress. "What are they doing?"

Michael made that helpless face. "Fittings or something?"

"Ah." I understood and neither of them had to. I also understood that Jasmine had picked Shane to babysit in order to give him a caring lecture about going to jail, and also to illustrate that even when a kid went to jail, he still had value. Something else I owed her for.

And because Malachi was sitting there sipping coffee, and I kept noticing the thick, raised veins in his forearms, I was also grateful when the group of them showed up. Jasmine and Jane, both as clean scrubbed as a Noxzema ad; and Shane, carrying Karen, Jasmine's youngest; *and* my mother and grandmother; and Jasmine's other child, a monster boy of eight named Daniel, who was born to do manly things like mow down other boys on a football field and swoon over army tanks at the state fair. "Yo, Danny-boy," I said. "Give me five."

"Hey, Auntie," he said, being cool. He noted the guys in the kitchen and swaggered over, hands in his pockets, to pop my palm smartly.

He had stitches across his nose. "What'd you do this time?" I asked. He already had scars from a dog bite, a fall from a trampoline, a long skid across a sidewalk from riding a skateboard face-first, and a particularly impressive thick snake of a scar running up his thigh that he received jumping over a fence. Caught a nail that ripped through his jeans, his flesh, and six muscles. He never dropped a tear until they gave him drugs for the pain. The Sabatinos and Falconis bragged about Daniel, I can tell you.

"Oh, I fell off my bike."

Jasmine elaborated. "He smashed into a truck and broke the windshield with his nose."

Malachi gave a quick, bright hoot of laughter. "Whoa," he said, sticking out his hand for a high five, too, and Danny, who'd been deeply hoping for such validation, tossed his buzz-cut head and slapped him five.

The women all swiveled their heads around at the robust sound of that man laugh in the kitchen. Jasmine straightened prettily, just slightly thrusting out her impressive chest. My mother's black eyes narrowed, while Nana Lucy impaled him, the Stranger Who Would Bring No Good, with her gaze. It was nothing personal—strangers were always trouble, in her opinion.

Only Jane acted like a normal person. Tall and leanly muscled, Jane is as healthy as anyone I've ever met. Her dark-blonde hair bounced in its ponytail as she stuck out her hand. "Hi," she said to Malachi. "I'm Jane. You must be Michael's brother, Malachi. Shane told us you got in this morning."

He was already standing, exhibiting the good southern manners I'd always found so charming in Michael, and guided Nana Lucy to his seat. It earned him a solid half point with her. Only ninety-nine and a half to go. "That's right," he said, and took Jane's hand. "Nice to meet you."

Jasmine gave him her best, toothiest smile, tossing back her mane of shiny hair. "Jasmine," she said in her perfect voice, her hand fluttering at her neck.

He smiled and nodded. "This child can't be your boy," he said with the right note of awe.

Her eyes widened. "Oh, he's mine. If I live through it."

Mama hung back, looking from him to me with her arms crossed over her chest. "Malachi," I said, "this is my mother, Rose, and my grandmother Lucy."

Nana Lucy had been picking over the black grapes in a bowl on the table until she found one that met her standards. Holding it between her long, gnarled fingers, she scowled. "Malachi?" She said it with a particularly nasal whine, *MAH-la-ki*. "What kind of name is that?"

I saw Michael and Malachi exchange an amused glance, and it struck me that they were *brothers*, with that long, unspoken knowledge of each other. "We always wondered what my mother was thinking," Michael said.

"Why didn't she just call you John?" Nana asked. She ate half the grape, slowly.

Malachi's big white teeth flashed. "It would have made my life a lot easier, I can tell you that."

He seemed enormous in the middle of them, towering over all the women, even Jane, who only came up to his shoulder. Lost in the forest of legs and knees, Danny adamantly slapped Malachi's big thigh. "Hey! You want to come outside with me?"

"Okay with me." He raised his eyebrows for permission from Jasmine. "But you gotta promise no blood, all right? I get kinda woozy."

Michael met my eyes across the room, that little secret smile on his mouth, like he wanted me to notice his big sex god brother taking a little kid outside to play. "Predictable," I said.

Malachi got the joke, chuckling low as he took Danny's hand and headed for the door. He winked. "Works, though."

Nana, who also got the joke, pushed my hair off my face. "You're too old to wear your hair down like that."

I didn't look at Malachi, who left the room with Danny, leaving only the chaos of my family behind. Manageable. "I like it this way," I said, and pulled the hair down that she had pushed back.

Jane touched it. "I *love* it," she said, her fingers lazing through the curls. "Very Renaissance."

"Thank you," I said, and plucked a few grapes out of the bowl myself.

My mother still hadn't said a word, and I looked up to see her staring out the kitchen window at the man and boy playing in the yard, her mouth in a straight, measuring line. "Hey," I said, "let's take this out of Michael's kitchen. He's creating." I grabbed the bowl of grapes. "Come on, Nana."

She waved me away, and I knew she wanted to sit alone with her guy. For whatever reason, she'd adopted Michael Shaunnessey, and loved coming here to fuss over him. He loved it, too. He gave me a nod. "About a half hour," he said.

We settled around the giant dining room table, little pockets of chatter rising and falling. Shane deposited Karen in a chair. "I'll be upstairs," he said. The long, long day was starting to tell in his face. He'd be asleep in five minutes.

"Don't you want something to eat?"

"Not right now." He went up the stairs, his combat boots heavy, even clumps instead of the usual two-at-a-time race. I smiled to myself. A hangover is a good teacher.

Jane caught the smile. "Not feeling top of his form, is he?"

"Nope," I said. "But tell me what you guys were doing. How's the wedding going?"

"Oh, it was just a fitting," Jane said. "They still have to take up the waist a little more, but the dress looks good. The big thing is," she said with glowing eyes, "we found a house!"

"A house?"

"It's real pretty," Mama said, relaxing enough now that That Man was out of the room to take a handful of grapes into her palm and start eating them, one at a time, gesturing with them as she talked. "Even has roses growing up the porch. We can get over to Eagles and fix it up in no time." She pursed her lips. "What's that paper Carol got for her stairway?"

"Oh, the paisley! Yeah," Jane said. She took my hand. "It's so beautiful, Jewel. You'll love it—the light is so pretty. Two bedrooms and even a family room. Over by City Park, so we can take walks in the evening, and when we have babies, it will be so easy to go to the zoo."

I listened to her descriptions with a sense of missed possibilities. She was so responsible, this baby sister of mine, and it hadn't appreciably ruined her life. She had been going steady with her boyfriend, Steve Candelario, since they were both juniors in high school. They'd done everything by the book, these two—homecoming dances with corsages, and the prom in tuxes and evening gowns and limousines. They both went to college right here in town, achieved their degrees in four years flat, and graduated together, and now that they'd been out in the workforce for two years, had decided they'd saved enough to get married. It was almost scary how sensible they were.

The wedding itself promised to be an undertaking of Herculean proportions and would require the careful diplomatic planning of a peace treaty. Steve's family was at least as enormous as ours, with roots that went back in the area a hundred years, with another three hundred before that in New Mexico. And while both families were Catholic, his family was Hispanic, with their own long traditions.

"I'm so proud of you," I said, touching Jane's hand. "It's going to be so wonderful."

Nana Lucy came to the doorway. "I'm ready to go home now."

Everyone stood up. Jasmine said, "I'll just dash out and get Danny, and meet you around front."

Jane rolled her eyes at me, and I kept my face straight. Mama swatted Jane's arm, which only made her grin. She leaned close to me. "Can I talk to you for a minute?" She glanced over her shoulder. "Alone?"

"Yeah. Let's go on out."

Dusk was gathering along the edges of the sky, and between the two mesas to the west, where the Arkansas River flowed through, the sun glowed like a magic ball. I looked over my shoulder to the cotton-wood at the edge of the yard, and the very top of it caught those long, burnished fingers of light the way it always did, a reliable and beautiful thing that never failed to capture me.

"What's up?" I asked Jane, putting my butt on the porch railing so I could see in the door. Mama and Nana Lucy were fussing over Michael.

Jane took a breath. "Well, um . . ." She tossed a lock of hair off her forehead, glanced down at the tip of her blazingly white tennis shoe. "This is hard."

"Hey, it's me, remember?"

"Yeah." She raised her head, a charming little flush on her cheeks. "Okay, I'll just say it. Can you teach me how to be sexy? Nobody else can do it. They don't get it—they're giving me white-lace nightgowns, Jewel, and I don't know if that's good or bad, and nobody wants to tell me anything, and I just thought—" Her cheeks went completely crimson. "Oh, that's bad, I mean, uh . . ."

"You really are a virgin," I said in some wonder. "That's so cool!"

"I guess," she said in some misery. "But so is Steve, and neither one of us knows anything, and what if it's a big disaster after all these years of waiting?" She was very close to tears.

Impulsively I took her hand. "First of all, you are so beautiful that he's going to just die when you take off your clothes. Trust me."

"Really?"

"Yeah, really." I squeezed her fingers, and thought about the rest. How did a person learn, except by fumbling along in the back seats of cars or trading idiot stories with friends or making mistakes—unless someone told them? "I'll help you pick out something decadent for your wedding night, if you like. And if you have specific questions, I'll be happy to answer whatever I can. But most of the mechanical stuff you can find at the library. The rest, you'll teach each other."

She wiggled a little, bending at the knees, then up again, a move-ment that made me remember her so clearly as a toddler. So much time.

I'd lost so much time with her. "I just wish I could look like you," she said.

I felt ancient. The wise woman, the crone. "No, you don't. You look like you, and that's good."

"I know that part." She sighed and pulled her hand out of mine, frustrated. "You aren't listening. I mean look at you tonight—Nana was clucking her tongue before we even got in the house, and Mom got all worried, and I couldn't see you, so I didn't know what the big deal was, but then I did see you, just sitting against the wall, so comfortable in your body and so sexy I just wanted to be you for five minutes."

"Keep talking, Jane," I said. "You are *so* good for my ego."

"Jewel! I'm serious."

"I know. I'm sorry—and I know what you want." She wanted sueded silk and black bras. Very easy stuff, that. "We'll go shopping, just us."

"Thank you."

Malachi and Jasmine came around the side of the house, Danny complaining all the way. Jasmine had that grim, exhausted look she got when she had to match wills with him, and I whistled sharply to distract him. "Yo, Danny-boy. Wanna go see the street rods with me this weekend?"

"Can Malachi come?"

"Mr. Shaunnessey," Jasmine corrected.

"Whatever. Can he?"

"If he wants," I said. Across the purpling dusk of the world, our eyes met, mine and Malachi's, and it was that strange, rippling thing again. Feeling him, the force of him, across a big space of grass. Purely physical, and somehow very pleasant. He was so very climbable.

My mother tsked. "Guess you don't want to help with Jane's new house, then, huh?"

Immediately I felt defensive. I could fool a lot of people, but my mother saw through me like cheap glass. "I just thought maybe—" I stopped. "I was just trying to help."

She met my eyes, that clear, no-bullshit look that had made me so angry so often when I was a teen. "I know what you were doing," she said quietly. "I thought you'd wised up a little after all you've been through."

I crossed my arms, stung, but took the offensive. "If Jane's working on her house, my dad will be there, won't he?"

"Probably."

"Then I guess that solves that, now doesn't it?"

She took Nana Lucy's arm to help her down the steps. Nana pushed my hair back. "Think about what I said. It's time to cut your hair. You're not young anymore."

Ouch. I nodded in deference to her elder status and stood on the porch until they left, struggling to keep a smile pasted on my face. I felt cheap and silly in my tank top and my too-long, little-girl hair.

Michael's hands landed on my shoulders, and his body was warm against my back. "Don't," he said against my ear. "You look fabulous."

I let go of a pained little laugh and surreptitiously wiped a tear from the corner of my eyes. "What do you know?"

He laughed, his old laugh, full and deep and so infectious. "I'm the king of the fairies. It is in my power to know these things."

Even though I'd known it was coming, I laughed with him. Long ago, when we first met, Michael's ethereal beauty had enchanted me. Naive and young—and made brave by the copious amounts of wine we'd all drunk—I'd blurted out one night that he looked like the king of fairies. Needless to say, he'd roared with laughter along with everyone else, but I think the description has always pleased him. He fancies himself to be a magical being in ways, Pan or maybe Apollo.

"What's this?" Malachi asked, coming up the steps.

"An old, old joke," I said.

His mouth stretched up on one side. "The king of fairies?"

Michael straightened, pushing a little between my shoulder blades. "Malachi, this woman needs some wind in her hair. Y'all go get some tequila. We need margaritas."

"But dinner must be almost ready!" I protested.

"I can hold it for ten minutes. Go on," Michael said. "Can't eat chicken wings without margaritas."

"We can go in my car," I said.

Malachi snorted, looking at the station wagon. "Nah."

Malachi pulled out his keys. "Come on, sugar," he drawled. "Let's go for a ride."

MICHAEL'S MAGNIFICENT CHICKEN WINGS

6–8 lb. of chicken drumettes, washed
For sauce:
1½ cups coffee
2–3 cups water
½ cup Worcestershire sauce
1 orange
1½ cups ketchup
¼ cup cider vinegar
2 tbsp vinegar
3 tbsp chili powder
pepper
2 tsp salt
2 cups onion, chopped fine
nutmeg
¼ cup minced hot chilies
jalapeño or serranos
6 cloves garlic
honey

Put chicken in a large ceramic bowl. With a fork, poke holes in the skin all over the wings—don't get fancy about it, it's just to let in a little more flavor.

In a large measuring cup or bowl, mix 2 to 3 cups of water (enough to cover wings), the juice of an orange (plus the fruit, shredded up into little pieces, if you want), a couple hard shakes of Worcestershire sauce, a couple tablespoons of vinegar, plus a dash each of pepper, salt, and nutmeg. Pour over the chicken; cover chicken with plastic wrap or foil. Have a beer or two and come back later for part two.

Put on some music. Probably best to have some southern rock, blues, or even some good bluegrass kind of gospel for this particular under-taking, though I have used K.T. Oslin to good effect some days. Also, it's

good to open another beer.
In a big pot, mix all sauce ingredients except the honey.
Simmer for a half hour. Thicken with honey, and pour over chicken wings. Bake at 350 degrees for an hour and a half, turning halfway through, basting as necessary. Really good with margaritas.

Chapter Five

So I got my wish. Malachi got on the bike and pulled it upright, turning the ignition to bring the engine to rumbling, low-throated life. His thighs tensed, big and strong beneath the black jeans, and he handed me a helmet. "Spoiling your image now," I said, taking it. "Don't you want the wind in your hair, freedom man?"

"Not if it means a cracked skull." He pulled his own helmet on and shifted forward, leaving room for me.

There's a reason bad boys ride motorcycles. They're very dangerous machines. I put my hand out and braced myself on his shoulder, feeling giving flesh and hard muscle beneath the turquoise T-shirt, and slid behind him, settling as far back as I could to avoid pressing against him.

"Hang on," he said, and when I put my hands on the seat, he added, "Hang on to *me*."

So I did. Put my hands around his waist and leaned into him. No way around it.

And this is what my mother knows about me: I could pretend all day and night to be holding myself rigid, but he smelled good, even better than he had this afternoon. Soap and clean breezes and healthy man. Against my arms, his sides were hard as iron, his back warm against my breasts and belly. I relaxed into him, enjoying it, enjoying him and the rumbling engine between our legs and the soft summer night air blowing over my skin. The moments sizzled along my nerves, worked their way into my chest, and untied some tight knot that lived there. Our bodies moved, into turns, out of them, and he called over his shoulder, "Not your first ride, I take it."

"No," I called back, and heard myself laughing.

At the liquor store, I realized I should have done something with my hair, which had flown all around in the wind. But somehow it didn't matter nearly as much here. I yanked off the helmet and carried it in my hand, feeling like a tough girl, like a wild woman. I loved walking in there with Malachi, too, and picking out tequila and fresh limes. He picked up a box of salt, and I took it out of his hand and put it back. "Kosher salt for margaritas. He'd kill you if you brought back regular." I picked it out and tried to remember if there was any triple sec around the house. Margaritas were my favorite, and I was picky about the way they were made, thanks to a long stint as a bartender in a Mexican restaurant in LA, back when Billy and Michael still thought they'd make the big time.

"Is it okay for Michael to drink?" he asked me suddenly.

I started to say, "What difference does it make?" but that would be too bold. Instead I looked up and smiled. "He's feeling great today, because of you. Let him enjoy it."

He turned his mouth down at the corners, an expression of acceptance. "I can do that." His boot heels made a solid, reliable noise against the tiles of the floor. "Your grandma's mean."

I smiled. "She's not so bad, once you get on her good side."

"How'd you come from that family?" he asked, and frowned over the bottles of sweet and sour.

"What d'you mean?" I pointed to the right brand.

He gave me an "oh, get real" look, which I ignored. "Do we need anything else?" he asked.

"I think that's it." We carried it all up to the cash register. The cashier called from the back, and I shifted, examining the tiny, pretty bottles of amaretto and Frangelico behind the counter, mainly trying to keep from eyeing Malachi's hands as he pulled bills from his front pocket. Hands are kind of a weakness. By now you're thinking that pretty much everything about a man is a weakness for me, and you'd be halfway to right, but there are certain things that cool my attraction pretty fast, and ugly hands is one. A lot of big men have spatulate hands, with blunt fingers and those weird-looking fan-shaped nails. Michael, for all that I love him, doesn't have great hands.

Malachi's hands were strong. I watched him flip the side of his thumb impatiently over the edge of the bills, and the tendon below moved beneath dark skin. His nails were oval at the end of straight, long fingers.

"All those women in your kitchen tonight are good girls," he said, tossing a twenty and a five on the counter. He braced himself on his palms and looked down at me, one knee cocked to sling out a hip. "You aren't."

Stung again, I made a noise and narrowed my eyes at his pose. "Do you practice every single gesture?"

"Nope. Do you?"

"What does that mean?"

A lift of one shoulder. "What did you mean?"

"This is a stupid conversation." I looked over my shoulder to see what was keeping the guy, and he was finally lumbering toward us. White grizzles of whiskers clung to his jowls, and he didn't make conversation as he rang everything.

Malachi picked up the bags. "After you," he said with a courtly gesture, and grinned. "That one, I've practiced."

I managed to smile only a little bit. Outside, I pulled on the helmet. "You didn't answer my question," he said. A streetlamp shone directly on his head, putting arcs of white light across his crown and the straight, aggressive bridge of his nose.

"Which one?" I twisted my hair into a long rope and tucked it down my shirt, feeling at a slight disadvantage because the helmet muffled my hearing.

"Do you practice?"

"I don't have to practice," I said, and put my hand out for the liquor.

He grinned. "Exactly." He put on his helmet and swung easily onto the seat. I slid on behind him, glad to have something to put space between us on the way back.

At the house, he caught my arm as we were going up the walk. "I didn't mean to hurt your feelings back there." He paused. "With the good-girl thing."

"Oh, that." I waved my hand. "You didn't."

"Yes, I did, and I apologize. I meant it as a compliment."

His big dark eyes were earnest, and I suddenly realized that he was a good deal younger than me. Maybe even more than five years. He was probably flirting with me not because of my black bra or anything else, but because he was being nice to his brother's best friend. The lonely older woman.

"I know," I said, and carried the bags into the house. "No big deal."

Shane was setting the table on the porch when we came in. He gave me a lift of his chin, but his smile was for Malachi. The same smile, I realized suddenly, that Danny had given him—slightly abashed and admiring, wanting approval. "Hi," he said. "Michael says we're eating outside."

I went to the kitchen to help Michael. Behind me, I heard Malachi join Shane outside, their voices braiding into the sound of crickets starting up their night song.

Michael had not heard me come in, and although he straightened quickly, I'd already seen him leaning hard on the counter. When he raised his head, I saw the strain that had settled beneath his eyes and around his mouth. Covering the pang it gave me, I cocked my head to the porch. "Go," I said. "I'll take it from here." I grabbed a long apron from the hooks by the door and tied it on.

He moved slowly, pushing up and away from the counter he'd been leaning on, and I turned toward the stove, giving him a little space for dignity. His big bony hand fell on my shoulder for a second, and I touched it with my fingers, then let him go and opened a drawer to find the tongs for the wings. For a long minute, I stared into the tangle of utensils, hearing distantly the sound of the male voices, rich and full against the silence in the kitchen. Berlin's nails clicked against the kitchen floor as she crossed the room to sit beside me, her sherry-colored eyes in a red face so very empathetic.

Shane appeared and carried everything out while I mixed a pitcher of margaritas. Malachi came in, too, and took the bucket of ice, the glasses, and the saucer of salt. Shane came back for a forgotten pile of cloth napkins and saw the pitcher. "Cool."

I made a noise. "Like you'll get one."

"Come on! I'm seventeen. It's a party. Just one? It's not like I never had anything to drink in my life."

"You're lucky I'm going to let you eat, boy." I picked up the pitcher and pushed him out of my way. "Go put some music on."

Michael, or maybe Shane, had gone all out. They'd gathered up dozens of my candles, all shapes and sizes and colors, and put them on the outside of the windowsills, on the table, along the railing of the porch. The round table was covered with a dark cloth—I smiled to think of Michael choosing the dark one in case people got barbecue sauce on it—and set as elegantly as a Martha Stewart picture. They were good at mood, these two. "It's beautiful," I said, putting down the pitcher. I pointed to Malachi's big blue goblet, and he handed it to me to be filled. "See how much better kosher salt looks than regular?"

"Yes, ma'am," he said, lifting the glass in a toast.

From within came the mellow guitar and whiskey voice of Bonnie Raitt. "Good choice," Michael said with a smile, handing me his glass. "If he flunks out at the music game, he can always be a DJ."

Shane clicked off the dining room light as he came through, so we were plunged together into the intimacy of the candlelit dark. I remembered to pull the apron off over my head before I took the seat next to Michael. Shane sat between Malachi and me.

I raised my glass. "To good friends and good food."

"And good God let's eat," Shane said. "I'm about to starve to death."

"When you went upstairs," I said, helping myself to a pile of wings, sticky and juicy, "I thought you'd be out for the night."

"I just had to get away from all the lectures." Shane scowled. "This is one part of living here I hate the most—getting a lecture from ten different people on the same thing. Most I ever got before was two."

"You might think," Michael said, choosing a chicken wing at leisure, "that a body'd want to avoid trouble after that."

Shane looked down, chastened. He'd been flying all day on the slight notoriety, and the strangeness of Malachi's arrival, and then the edge of teen righteousness at the repetitive lectures. Michael's slow, reasonable, southern voice let the air out of him in one sentence. "Yeah," he said. But he scowled at his plate, his knee wiggling in his discomfort. "I didn't mean to, really. Just . . . one thing led to another."

"Happens to the best of us," Michael said, licking his thumb with careful disinterest. Then his blue eyes pinned my boy right where he sat. "Happens a lot more when you're a fool about your liquor."

Malachi looked up at that, his eyes narrowing. "Damn," he said quietly. "You sound just like the old man."

Michael grinned. "Yeah, I do. Been hearing it for years." He looked at Shane. "What're the rules about drinking, man?"

"One an hour. No shots. No shotgunning beers. No driving."

Malachi made a noise I couldn't quite place. Derision, maybe. But Michael was focused on Shane. "And how many of those rules did you break last night?"

"I dunno." Shane raised a shoulder. Then his mouth quirked. "Uh, all of them. Not the beers."

Michael's mouth lifted on one side. "And you see where you landed."

Shane nodded.

I raised an eyebrow. "You've been giving him instructions on drinking?"

Michael took my hand across the table. In the candlelight, he looked almost like himself, his blond hair gleaming on his shoulders, the dual hoops in his ears glittering. "Did you think he'd never get around to trying it?"

"Maybe." Just like he'd never have sex or a broken heart, or be penniless and have to eat refried beans from a can rolled into a tortilla for six days straight. Michael's fingers moved on mine, and I didn't have to look at him to know he was smiling fondly.

"You mad?"

I shook my head, but there was a hollowness in my chest as I looked at Shane, bent over his food with the rare and passionate appetite of a boy. His hair, thick and long, shone with the brilliance of youth and good living. Candlelight exaggerated the shadows below his high, slanted cheekbones and the strong line of his jaw. He was beautiful, my Shane, and so much like his father it was eerie.

It was only a year until he'd leave me. Probably not to college, not if he didn't get his grades and life together, but somewhere. He wasn't the kind of kid who'd hang around a minute longer than he had to. Then he'd be off to the world. The music world, most likely.

And how could I stand not having him at the dinner table every night? I scowled at my margarita and picked it up with determination. "To growing up," I said.

He looked up at me, my beautiful son, with his father's brilliant and soulful eyes, and grinned. "If we're toasting that, I think I deserve a margarita, too."

"You're grounded until you're ninety, so it doesn't matter if you grow up or not."

~

I was the first one up the next morning. It wasn't a cooking morning—those were Mondays, Wednesdays, and Fridays—but in spite of the margaritas and the upsets, or maybe because of them, I awakened just after six. A farmer's sun, bright and clear to shine on all the crops, streamed in my windows, and I lay there and let it cover me, wash against my eyelids and my mouth and my neck. A breeze, cool from the night, blew the curtains up and touched the crown of my head.

The house was silent all around me, and I thought of the males in their various bedrooms, Shane sprawled in a tangle of sheets, his unbelievably hairy legs sticking out of the covers. Michael, neat even in sleep, a single sheet tucked under his chin in the dark room that faced west, a room I'd given him deliberately so he could sleep as late as he needed to.

And Malachi. The unknown quotient. I stirred my legs a little, dislodging cats, and imagined how he would sleep. On his stomach, naked or in a pair of white briefs. That brought up a picture of his beautiful behind clothed only in that thinnest of cotton. Mmm.

The luxury of having the silence of the house and no pies to bake was too great to waste lying in bed. I got up, pulled on a pair of shorts and a T-shirt, and went downstairs. I ground coffee beans and started the machine, then wandered outside to my aunt Sylvia's herb garden. There was still rain on the leaves from a fierce, quick storm the night before, and the dampness intensified the smell. I plucked a frond of lavender and held it up to my nose, thinking of the wands she'd made of these plants, wands she sold and gave away, wands we all stuck in our drawers, wrapped in their braids of red and yellow and green string. Nearby, Berlin sniffed along the rows, scenting a squirrel, maybe, or a field mouse. Her fur glinted deep red in the early sunlight.

But while I was doing all of that, there were ingredients tickling the back of my brain. A quiver of roasted garlic. A piquant bite of chili. Onion, of course. Milk? No, chicken broth. Even better, a good veggie broth, something hearty and nutritious for Michael, who would be exhausted today after so much excitement and movement yesterday.

I picked a huge handful of thyme and another of basil, and carried the damp leaves inside to wash in the deep porcelain sink. It was a great sink, and I've known a lot of bad ones. Shallow ones with no room to wash anything. Chipped ones that bred bacteria in their rusted wounds. Stainless steel—ordinarily such a great material for anything in the kitchen—abused by harsh cleansers and too much scouring.

But Sylvia's sinks were elbow deep, two of them, side by side. The porcelain had been carefully tended over the years, so the finish was as white now as it had been sixty years before. Showering the newly harvested herbs with the sprayer, I thought of my uncle Tony carefully cutting the hole for the rubber hose into the old porcelain, and hummed under my breath. The song came to me, a K.T. Oslin tune that made me happy.

I hated cooking without music and in spite of the budget crunch had splurged on a small, portable CD player. For Christmas a couple of years ago, Michael had given me a pair of cordless headphones, and I plugged in the little gizmo they required. From the stack of plastic cases on top of the fridge, I found the Oslin, and "Come Next Monday" danced its way into my head. I took out pots and bowls, singing along cheerfully.

The windows were full of early-morning sunlight. This morning, the Swedish ivy inherited from Sylvia gleamed on the wide sill by the breakfast bar, covering Saint Anthony's feet, and blue bottles stood sentry on either side, the light not so much breaking as expanding within the cobalt curves. Through the window over the sink, I had a good view of the orchards—trees that actually seemed to be putting out a little fruit this year—and from the mudroom, great bucketfuls of soft buttery light poured over the floor.

I chopped and sautéed, singing along, drinking coffee. In the corner on top of a cupboard was a small color television, and I turned it on to CNN with the sound on mute so that I could catch up on world events as I slowly browned a head of garlic and a huge onion in olive oil.

Almost nothing makes me as happy as food, cooking, kitchens. Family kitchens, filled with a multigenerational mix of women always talking, gossiping, moving around one another in a little dance. That was where I heard the best secrets, the best advice, the most profound observations of life. The aroma of garlic roasting makes me think of my uncle Joe, who caused a terrible scandal by having an affair with the waitress at Corsi's Bowl and crept back to his wife, broke and sorrowful, only when the waitress dumped him for an upper-management type at the steel mill, a man who wore polo shirts tucked into his slacks, not Joe's serviceable blue cotton uniforms. Basil leaves make me think of Sylvia's hands, gnarled and golden and rivered with blue veins even in my youngest memories. And as long as I live, I'll never smell barbecue sauce without thinking of Michael, I know it.

As great as family kitchens are, restaurant kitchens are even better. The big, gleaming stainless-steel stoves and ovens and wide, unbroken countertops. The wealth of knives—gleaming steel attached to heavy black handles: wide, angled butcher's knives, paring knives, corrugated bread knives, and sleek, small steak knives for customers. As a girl, I'd also loved the big graters with their multitude of sides, loved being given the task of grating piles of hard white Parmesan or soft, gloppy provolone, one of the secrets of the Falconi lasagna. I loved the big slabs of white cutting boards and the deft, graceful movements of an expert chopping vegetables, fingers curved to avoid the knife, the whip-whip-whip sound ringing out authoritatively into the air.

I can't think of a single thing that ever happened to me that doesn't have some food or cooking memory attached. When I met Billy and Michael, the night air was full of funnel cakes and Polish sausage and beer, the smell of the fair. When I went into labor with Shane, I cooked all night, piles and piles and piles of comfort foods: lasagna and beef stew. I'd even started on tamales when the guys got freaked and insisted two minutes apart meant I needed to go to the hospital.

It's another thing Michael and I share, this love of cooking and food and restaurants. He'd learned early that restaurant work was easy to get and not too hard to do—and between singing in honky-tonks, he worked as a busboy and a waiter and a bartender.

He'd inherited his love from his father, who cooked all kinds of things to make up for the desultory labors of his mother. Abe was famous for many things, but his Sunday morning breakfasts, country-fried everything, were the top of the list in Michael's memory, as was his apple pie. I made a mental note to dig out that recipe and make it for dinner tonight. In fact, it would be a good offering for the business, too. In a notebook I kept for the purpose, I made a list of the things I knew I would need, singing absently along with K.T.

Something—not a noise since the earphones muffled everything—made me look up. And there in the doorway to the mudroom, haloed by that gold morning sun, was Malachi. He had on a fishing vest, with lures and mysterious pins all over it. The khaki pockets were lumpy with stuff I wasn't sure I wanted to know about, though I imagined small, screw-topped bottles of slimy red eggs and an efficient Swiss Army knife. He wore a fishing hat—and not even Malachi could make a fishing hat look good. His was dark blue with a formerly cream-colored band laced with more shiny and feathered lures. At least he didn't pull it down too low on his forehead.

I yanked the earphones from my head, letting them circle my neck. "I thought you were still asleep."

He plunked his catch down on the breakfast bar, a shiny bass and a big catfish. I wrinkled my nose. "Been getting up early too long to sleep in," he said, pulling off his hat. "If you've got a good knife, I'll get these cleaned. Don't know as the catfish'll be any good, but we can stick the bass in the freezer and wait to get some more."

I plucked a good knife from the bar over the stove and gave it to him. "Thank God. I hate cleaning fish. It was always the girls' job when I was a kid."

He arranged the fish on the table. "And I bet you were wishing you got to be the one to catch them."

"Not really. I can't stand to see them alive and then eat them. I never mind somebody else killing them, you understand"—I strained olive oil from the pot—"but it grosses me out to have to do the killing myself."

His grin was easy.

"You hungry?" I asked. "I'm making soup, but I could cook some eggs or something if you want."

"Maybe in a little bit. I ate when I got up. Wasn't sure what the coffee customs were around here, so I didn't make any." With those strong hands, he sliced the body of the catfish open, and as if the odor held a magic lariat, suddenly all three cats appeared, crying out for scraps. "Now I'll know. You like it hefty."

"Strong enough to walk, your brother says."

He tossed tidbits of fish belly to the cats, who wove around one another in a frenzy. "Come on, you guys," I said. "You act like you never eat." Giovanni, the tuxedo male who allowed himself to be stroked only when he specifically required it, gave me a quelling look with his bright-yellow eyes.

Malachi laughed. "D'you get the message clear enough?" He bent, coming down from his great height with three generous chunks of meat for each cat, spreading them apart on the floor so they'd each get their own. Berlin, tail wagging, stayed where she was, but a soft little whine came out of her throat, and Malachi cut her a piece of meat, too, which she took with her black tongue very politely. "Man, you got a lot of animals."

"None of them are technically mine. The cats came with the house, and Berlin belongs to Michael."

"I can see that," he said, going to the sink to wash his hands. "Seeing how she sticks to his side every waking minute."

"Well, she stayed with me a lot in New York."

He settled and started efficiently gutting and then slicing the fish, his big hands capable and deft. I took some heavy freezer bags from the cabinet and brought them to Malachi.

"Did Michael live with you there?" he asked. "In New York?"

"No." Picking over a bucket of red potatoes, I said, "I was trying to convince him, but it took getting the building sold out from under us to move him at all."

His eyelids came down, hiding whatever emotion that had called up for him. "Glad you were there for him." The unspoken part was *when I wasn't*.

"He was there for me often enough." I carried the potatoes to the sink and started scrubbing them, wishing I didn't have to turn my body so my too-big rear end was exposed. I put one foot on top of the other. "When Billy died, I don't know what I would have done without your brother."

"Ah, Billy." He sighed. "Bad way to go—crack cocaine."

"Yeah." The memory could still slice me open after three years, the sight of the cops on the doorstep at eight o'clock in the morning, asking me to come identify his body. "We saw it coming for a year, but it was still a shock—a heart attack at forty-one."

"I always figured he'd get himself shot."

"I forgot you knew him." But of course he had. They'd all known one another. I carried the potatoes to the counter and dried my hands, grabbed a sheet of newspaper from the stool, and spread it out.

"He always did have a bad end written all over him."

"Think so?" I thought of him, my not-husband, with whom I'd lived for almost a dozen years. "He was driven, kind of given to a temper, but I didn't see that end waiting for him."

Malachi carefully layered translucent pink flesh in the bags. "You'd have had to have known him younger than you met him. He did some crazy shit." He raised his eyes. "Michael probably gave him a solid decade."

It was so strange to hear another side of an old story that I stopped in the middle of peeling the potato and looked at him. "Really," I said. Not a question. An invitation for more. I smiled, trying to imagine all of them at Shane's age. "You had to be quite a bit younger than they were."

"Seven years." Then a grin. "But big for my age. I didn't really have anybody but Michael, you know, so he was good about letting me tag along."

Seven years. So I was right—he was at least five years my junior. It made me relax, somehow, and stop thinking of my body. Men always want a woman younger than they are. Just read the personal ads sometime. The fifty-seven-year-olds want forty or younger, the thirty-five-year-olds want eighteen to twenty-four. Only eighteen-year-olds want somebody older.

For obvious reasons.

Malachi said, "The night we met Billy, Michael had a gig in this dark, old, tumbledown club in Alabama, singing for a country-*western* band, if you know what I mean—"

I grinned.

"—that tinny, awful stuff, and he made it sound good." He shook his head, knife still in his hands as he remembered. "I thought he was the best singer God ever made, you know, and I was sitting in the back with a Shirley Temple that Michael made sure didn't get any liquor in it."

He paused for effect, and although I knew at least most of what was coming, I stopped peeling to listen to his version. "And this guy walks in. Bad attitude written all over him. It's a country bar, with a bunch of farmers and rednecks, and Billy comes in with his hair down to his waist and black leather and tattoos and a bandanna tied around his head, and I thought, 'Oh, shit. Gonna be a fight.'

"But he just walks along the back of the room, jingling from all the metal all over him—"

I snorted.

Malachi grinned, pleased. "And just sits down next to me. 'How ya doin', man,' he says. And I just about fell out in a dead swoon. He was so cool, and I was fifteen years old and thinking, 'Oh, my God, I bet he gets laid every ten minutes.'"

I was still smiling from the memory of the metal and laughed out loud at this. Caught, I put the potato peeler down and folded my arms, leaning one hip on the counter.

Now that he had my full attention, Malachi launched into a full-blown retelling of That Fateful Night. "He hears Michael sing and whistles low under his breath, and me, I'm dying to get his attention—you know, like maybe he'd know how I could get under Jean Anne's blouse—and I tell him it's my brother doing that singing."

His eyes fixed on some place far in the past, a place he saw just over my shoulder. "And at the break, Michael comes over and shakes his hand, and I can tell they've talked a little, and I could see that kind of way Michael got, you know. He was attracted to this cool guy, and not like I was." He came back from that night, looked at me, a sad smile on his face. "And I was so damned humiliated I just wanted to kill him."

There was a raw edge to the words, and I smiled, shaking my head. "You were a kid. It's natural."

He bent his head, gave a twitch of a shoulder. "Billy saw it, too, but he was a hell of a lot more sophisticated than I was, and it didn't give him any heebie-jeebies."

"Did he tell you any tricks about getting under Jean Anne's shirt?" I asked lightly. "As I recall, he was very adept."

He laughed. "Well, not right away."

I went back to my potatoes, thinking about the age thing, trying to fit Michael's and Billy's stories with the new information about Malachi, whom I'd always believed to be only a couple of years younger than Michael. "How old were you when your father . . . uh . . . went to jail?"

"Ten." Gruff. Subject not up for discussion.

But I couldn't let it just go. "Oh, my God," I said, and remembered another piece of the story. "And you were the one home that night."

"Yeah." He gathered offal and walked to the trash. "Ancient history, babe, and I hate that sympathetic look, all right?"

"All you big tough guys do." I grinned at him.

"You just call 'em like you see 'em, don't you?"

The phone rang, startling in the quiet, and I wiped my hands. "I lived with Billy, remember?" I picked up the phone and said hello.

"Jewel, did I wake you?" It was Jordan. There was an edge of something to her voice, and I frowned.

"No, what's up?"

"I hate to ask, but my damned car won't start, and I need to get to work. Can you give me a ride?"

"Don't scare me like that, girl! I thought somebody was hurt or something."

"No. I'm just bummed. I hate begging favors."

"No big deal. I'll be right there."

I hung up and turned to Malachi. "My sister needs a ride to work, and I'm closest."

"Which sister is this?" He'd tucked the fish into the freezer and was wiping up the counter. A man who cleaned up after himself—wonder of wonders.

I turned the broth off, covered the potatoes with a sheet of plastic wrap. "The one you didn't meet: Jordan. She doesn't live far away."

"Mind if I ride along?"

It startled me. "Uh, no."

A glimmer in his eyes said he knew it unsettled me. "Sure?"

"Have to ride in the station wagon."

"That's all right."

I got my keys. "Come on then, big boy."

ROMEO'S ZEPPOLES

This is something you can do with the little ones—bring them all into the kitchen with you, maybe on one of those cold rainy afternoons when there's no place for them to play. You can make the dough into little animals or letters or numbers, and let them put the powdered sugar on when they're finished. Little ones, they like cooking.

7 cups of flour
3 eggs
1 package of yeast
1 orange peel
2 tsp salt
3–4 cups of warm water

Grate orange peel. Beat the 3 eggs. Add yeast to 1 cup of warm water and mix in the 3 beaten eggs, orange peel, and 2 teaspoons of salt. Take this and add it to the 7 cups of flour and mix with your hands. As you are mixing, continue to add the remaining cups of warm water. The dough should be soft and sticky. Once you have finished, take the dough and wrap it in a clean dish towel and place it in a big pan to rise. Once the dough has risen, take a fork and let the air out. Re-cover and let it rise again. Take the dough and shape as you like. During this time fill a pan with oil and heat it. It's hot enough when the dough drops to the bottom and comes right back to the surface. Once the dough has browned, take it out and place it on a brown paper bag.

Chapter Six

Jordan lived in "the county," as locals called it. Not quite the Lanes, as we did, though technically she did live on one of them, but farther east a little more, in an ancient adobe that we figured had been built around 1875, at the latest. It was crooked and required zillions of hours of upkeep, but it was also charming and very Jordan. The Arkansas River flowed not forty yards away, but the house stood on a little bluff, surrounded by huge, thick-branched cottonwoods, so it was safe from flooding. She lived there with her husband, a vague, friendly potter named Henry whom she'd met at the Renaissance fair years ago. They kept chickens and sold the eggs, grew an enormous organic vegetable garden every summer and dried it, and harvested rose hips to sell to a tea company in Boulder.

Together they'd developed a unique and interesting line of pots and bowls and dishes with whimsical forest creatures—the fey folk, not animals—peeking over brims and shaping handles. Henry sketched the designs and did the glazing; Jordan happily formed the actual pieces, painstakingly and by hand. Every weekend through June and July, they donned their Renaissance garb, loaded their goods, and went north to Larkspur for the festival, and made nearly enough money to live on most of the year.

Hippies, people would call them, I guess. But that's not the right word in Colorado. For one thing, neither of them is anywhere close to old enough to really be a hippie. For another, hippie implies drugs, a weird sort of zealousness for vegetarianism or organic sandals or uncut hair. They aren't like that.

They're just not exactly on the same time continuum as the rest of society. They move in tune with an inner directive, or maybe just a natural one. It's a kind of person you see a lot around here, especially the closer you get to the mountains—amiable and relaxed and content with what is.

Malachi didn't say anything as we pulled into the yard behind Jordan's old Volvo, just looked at the chickens pecking in a patch of sunny dirt behind a fence. Jordan came rushing out, dressed in her blue scrubs, her hair flying out behind her. I was pleased at how pretty she looked—the prettiest one of all of us, though she's never known it for one single minute. Or cared, for that matter. Golden brown hair springing in wild curls around a makeupless and perfect face, a big Sophia Loren kind of mouth that's always red because she's so healthy, a strong but very lush figure that looks truly awesome in a Renaissance gown. She halted halfway to us, held up a finger, and rushed back into the house for something.

Malachi said, "Wow."

I laughed as she came running back out, an empty cloth bag printed with flowers flying behind her. "Gorgeous, isn't she?"

"That's not what I meant—I mean, yeah, are you guys twins?"

"Keep it up, sailor," I said with a grin. "Flattery will get you anywhere."

He raised one eyebrow, looking at me across the small space, and he just seemed huge and tempting, all of a sudden—twelve feet of thighs to straddle, a jaw that my hands wouldn't cover, the chocolate-syrup look of those eyes. "Yeah? What'll it get me?"

"She's younger than me," I said. "But still older than you."

He opened the door and got out, gesturing for Jordan to get in the front seat, but she waved him back. "You've gotta be the brother," she said, patting his arm as she went by and yanked open the back door.

"I already heard all about you." She inclined her head. "You don't look anything like Michael."

They both got in, and Jordan pulled her hair into a scrunchie. The faint patchouli smell of incense clung to her, exotic and pleasing, and she leaned back. "Boy, you shoulda heard 'em last night. Jasmine cooed, I swear to God."

Tossing a glance toward Malachi as I turned around to back out, I laughed. "I noticed."

"Nana Lucy was not cooing." She raised her voice into the crone tones of the old woman, "'MAL-a-KI! MAL-a-ki! What kind of name is that for a man?'"

He laughed. "She'll come around."

"Ha! You don't know her. You know those old witches in fairy tales, the ones who bake little kids or feed them till they're plump so she can eat them? That's my nana."

"*Jordan!* That is not true."

"You were always her favorite, that's why." She scooted over to sit behind me as I got on Highway 50 back to town, so she could look at me in the rearview mirror and bring our passenger into the conversation. "Malachi, what do you think of this? When we were seven and six, Jewel and I both got Barbie dolls for Christmas. Jewel broke the knees of hers, and my nana took mine away and gave it to her!"

"Oh!" I looked at her in the mirror, laughing. "That is such a lie, girl! You broke my doll's knees."

He laughed and threw up his hands. "I'm not getting in the middle of this for love nor money."

Jordan laughed, and I asked about her car, which she said was dying. Henry would pick her up on his way home—he did construction work most days—and they'd set out for the festival tomorrow. "You like Ren fairs, Malachi? You should come with us some weekend. You're staying awhile, right? You'd look good as a knight. Nobody is ever really big enough to pull it off. You ever swing a sword?"

He looked at me, and I smiled, but carefully didn't look back. That's the thing about Jordan. Like a lot of artists, she's a little manic-depressive. In an up mood, she can outtalk anyone on the planet. When she's down, she tends to hibernate. It's not like she needs drugs or anything, it's just a natural cycle for her. My mother gave her her own room—even though I was the oldest, I might add—because of it. She needed her space more than the rest of us.

She talked all the way to town. Or at least until the car intervened. Just past the university, just as we got into serious traffic, in other words, it started screaming. Loudly.

"Jewel! What is that?"

I raised my chin. "I have no idea. Three mechanics have looked at it, and they can't find it." A guy in a three-quarter-ton pickup glared at me. I glared back. Did he think I wanted it to make this noise? "Shane says it's haunted."

"They check the fan belt?" Malachi asked, his head cocked, listening.

"Yep. All the belts." The light turned, and I headed down Elizabeth toward the hospital, going under a tunnel of thick trees that seemed to exaggerate the banshee scream. It sounded exactly like those shuddering electronic toys you can get for Halloween. "Checked the tires, the undercarriage, everything."

He was frowning intently, like he knew something, and I found myself with a teeny flare of hope. If he could fix that noise, I'd cook him pies for a year. "Do you know engines?"

"A little," he said. "I'll take a look."

We dropped Jordan off at the hospital, and as she got out of the car, I reached out of the window to catch her sleeve. "Hey! Do you know the address of Jane's new house?"

She smiled and gave it to me.

When I put it back in gear, the car stopped screaming as abruptly as it had started. "Do you mind if I run by the house and look in the windows?" I asked Malachi. "It's not far."

"Course not. Maybe while you're looking in the windows, I'll look under the hood." He shifted. Even this old station wagon wasn't really big enough for the length of his legs, the breadth of his shoulders.

"What do you drive when you aren't on a motorcycle?" I asked.

He grinned at me. "A truck, sugar. What else?"

"Of course. A big one, too, I bet. A Ford."

"Naturally."

Easy to imagine him hanging his elbow out the window of some giant pickup. What else, indeed. Pulling into traffic toward the center of town, I pointed out a graceful, exquisitely maintained Victorian house. "A museum," I said, even though he didn't strike me as a museum kind of guy.

"Looks haunted."

"Definitely. We used to have to go there a lot—with Girl Scouts or the church group or school—and after the first time, I had nightmares the night before I went back. Every time. My mama finally wrote me excuses."

"She didn't strike me as the type to let a girl off the hook like that."

I stopped at a light, tapping my fingers on the wheel. "Don't judge her by last night. She just worries about certain things. On the rest, she's all right."

A horn tooted next to us, and I looked over to see my cousin George in a low-slung sports car, looking clean and sweet smelling in his polo shirt and sunglasses. I rolled the window down and he rolled down his. "Hey! How's business, Rich Guy?"

"Not bad." He lifted his perfectly cut chin toward Malachi. "How you doin'?"

Malachi nodded.

The light changed, but George didn't move right away. "Call me, will you? Maybe there's a catering job for you—Dante Alighieri Society."

"Fantastic!" I blew him a kiss and waved, pulling out before the people behind us could honk, though usually people would give you a second unless they were out-of-towners. "Ah," I said, thinking aloud. "If I could do a great job for Dante Alighieri, I'd be in like Flynn."

Malachi chuckled. "Mixing the cultural metaphors there a bit, aren't you?"

I grinned. Brighter than he looked. "Yeah, well, hang around awhile. It's appropriate." I took a big deep breath. "I've been working so hard to get new accounts. Now, if none of my dad's old cronies are in Alighieri, I'll be okay."

"Good luck."

The possibility of the job warmed me all the way across town. I deliberately went through town to show Malachi the nicer areas of the city, Union Avenue and the emerging River Walk, then through the old, wide streets behind Mesa Junction to the quiet block where Jane's house was located. I pulled up beneath an ancient catalpa tree in front, the enormous heart-shaped leaves casting deep shade. Some people around town clipped them into lollipop trees, but the several around the Craftsman-style bungalow had all been allowed to attain their massive height. In the grass beneath them were snowy piles of popcorn-shaped flowers, and I kicked at them happily as I walked up to the front porch.

It surprised me that Jane had settled on an older home. I would have expected her to want a clean, neat ranch style, maybe freshly built in Pueblo West or in one of the small, new neighborhoods popping up all over the place.

But I approved the choice heartily. The gardens were neat and filled with the kind of perennials that let me know a passionate and long-term gardener had lived there—irises flanking the wall to choke out weeds, thick neat stands of exuberant coreopsis, clumps of pinks and daisies. The sidewalks were neatly tended, the paint obviously well cared for. I peered in the front window and saw the trim was preserved in its original state.

A beauty. I could see my little sister adorning the archways with gorgeous, tasteful bouquets of dried flowers, could imagine the chintz and soft fabrics she'd choose for the furniture. It was a *home*, awaiting the touch of the mistress.

That sudden, odd pinch of lost chances touched me again, and I frowned a little, seeing my reflection in the window when I straightened. Behind me stood my father.

I turned around, unable to stop the sharp catch of hope in my chest. He was as surprised to see me as I was him and not able to get his stony face on fast enough to hide his expression. For one long second, we stared at each other across the thick grass of the good daughter's house, while Malachi in all his sexy badness leaned against my car, summing up in one long body all the reasons my father still wouldn't talk to me.

But in that split second, I saw that his eyebrows were getting a few gray hairs, and long lines marked his lean face from nose to mouth. He was wearing blue mechanic's coveralls to protect his clothes and had a cleaning rag in his right hand, a bucket in the other. "Hi, Dad," I said, taking a chance. "It's a great house."

He looked over his shoulder at Malachi. Then his mouth twitched, and he marched around the house, following the path he'd evidently been on before my sudden appearance stopped him. He kept walking across the lawn to the side of the house, disappearing behind an overgrown lilac bush. I stared at the spot where he'd gone, willing myself to just walk away. To pull up my chin and throw back my shoulders and stalk over to the car with a saucy flip of my hair. The girl I'd once been urged me to do it, to show him it didn't matter.

But there were hollyhocks blooming around the lilac bush, tall stalks with red flowers, and I remembered the dolls he used to make for me out of them. I remembered riding on his shoulders, my hands tight in his thick hair, being so proud to walk into church with him, my dad, the handsome one, Romeo, the one the women all wanted to talk to for even a minute if they could.

At my elbow, Malachi said, "Come on, sugar. Let's go get something to eat, huh?"

I hadn't heard him approach, and his deep rich voice seemed suddenly very sexual, seemed as if it would carry a long way. Darkly, I hoped it would, and went down the steps.

~

We weren't far from my old stomping grounds, and on some strange impulse I didn't bother to dissect, I drove by my old high school, looking imposing on its hill. "That's where I went to school," I said, pointing. "And when Billy showed up to whisk me out of Pueblo, it was right on that front lawn."

"That's when you fell out with your dad?"

"Yep."

He looked around me at the tall steps, real interest in his face. His long arm stretched out along the back of the seat, a very ordinary thing for such a big man to do, but the suggestion of thumb so close to my neck made me a little more aware than I wished to be. "Tell me about it."

A kid in a primered Impala was bearing down on me from behind, so I pulled over. Where to begin?

"Have you ever gone to the state fair anywhere?"

"Sure."

"Well, it's a big deal in Pueblo—the biggest event every summer, especially for kids. We used to live really close to the fairgrounds, and we'd go as often as we could scrape up the money, just to hang out and listen to the bands and see all our friends." I stopped, rolling my hands on the steering wheel, the taste, the excitement of those summer nights coming back on waves of neon and laughter.

"The summer I was seventeen, Billy and Michael's band landed one of the free tent shows. A good way to get some exposure, all that, you know?"

"I remember. They did a lot of that for the first year or so."

"Everybody was talking about them, especially about Billy. He was just about the most gorgeous thing my friends had ever seen." I closed my eyes with a happy smile, remembering the astonishing pleasure of that music. "And you know how good they were. I didn't even notice Billy right away, you know? He was cute, but it was Michael's voice that got me—it was like that Roberta Flack song. I stood there in the audience and just cried."

"Does Michael know this?"

"Oh, sure. We've talked about it a lot." I took a breath. "Anyway, they went into a set of heavy rock and roll, to get the crowd all hot, and I started dancing. When the set was finished, Billy came looking for me."

We were quiet, looking at the wide green lawns, the imposing columns, the very high schoolish look of it. "I partied with them, Billy and Michael, that night, and I went back every night after that until they left six days later."

Oh, the pain of those long weeks afterward, spending hours and hours on the phone long distance with Billy in some other city, my heart eaten up with jealousy and longing! He swore undying love for me, but even then I was smart enough to know he was tempted every single day.

Which probably lent a good deal of triumph to what happened next.

"About two months later, when I came out of school, Billy was waiting." I could see the day so clearly, still. "I came down those steps, and it was a sunny day with a big wind blowing all these leaves into circles, you know? I didn't see him right away, because I was totally miserable being in school after that big adventure in the summer. All the kids seemed so stupid and shallow." I shook my head.

"I remember that feeling." He touched my shoulder, once and away.

I pursed my lips, remembering. "There was a big knot of girls at the bottom of the stairs, and they were doing that giggle-and-point thing, you know, a sure sign there was some boy who thought he was the baddest thing around." I glanced at him. "Are you getting how cool and together I was?"

He chuckled.

"So I look up, and there he is. Leaning against his motorcycle with his hair blowing all around him, his arms crossed. He even had on a leather jacket." My heart rushed a little, like it had then. "I thought I could see his eyes, burning me across the whole lawn, and it finally hit me that the kids were all whispering his name, telling each other, 'That's Billy Jake, from the Lost Boys Band.' And then they were looking back at me, waiting to see what I'd do."

"God, that was a stupid name," Malachi said. "I tried to talk him out of it, but his agent just thought it was so damned clever, he wouldn't listen to me."

I grinned. "Not as bad as Johnny Cougar."

"Huh. Mellencamp got it together eventually, though, figured out he was being used. Billy was never that smart." He realized whom he was talking to and winced. "Sorry."

"You're right. I knew it even then." I shrugged and looked back at the grass, at a day more than twenty years in the past. "I hated Pueblo— it seemed so provincial and backward and blue collar . . . and Billy knew how I felt. He sat there on that bike, and I knew he'd come for me, that all I had to do to walk away was just get on that bike and ride away with him."

I looked at Malachi and smiled. "I remember exactly what he said, too." I dropped my voice, let the southern drawl—did I mention I've always been a sucker for a man with a drawl?—slow my syllables, and said, "'Come on with me, Jewel. I don't know where we'll end up, but you know where this road leads.'" So many years later, my breath felt short over the enormity of the decision I'd made so easily in that instant. "And he was right, so I put down my backpack, zipped up my coat, and I went with him."

"And I bet they swooned, those kids watching."

"Maybe," I said, putting the car back in gear. "But I bet a lot more of them thought I was a fool."

"What do you think?"

I looked over my shoulder and waited for a car to pass so I could pull out, thinking of my father's snub. "That's the sixty-four-thousand-dollar question."

"So what's the deal with your dad, then? He's not talking to you twenty years later because you ran off with a musician when you were still a kid?"

"Not exactly." I took a breath as we passed an old Catholic church, and struggled for a way to put four hundred years of Sicilian tradition and women into a single sentence. "I shamed him in front of his friends and his relatives and his customers. The only way he could save face was to wash his hands of me."

And I remembered, too, with an ache that hadn't gone away in all these years, how it had happened. In a voice that was emotionless, I said, "I was afraid to go home, right then. I mean, I guess I knew it was crazy, but it was also what I needed to do, and I was afraid they'd talk me out of it."

"So I just went with him to Denver. And my father followed me. Tried to get me to come home." Oh, the memory could still bring tears to my eyes, my father standing there in the rain outside the little motel we were staying in, his eyes burning with fury, Billy behind me in the musky darkness of the room where we'd been making love. "He told me if I didn't come home with him right then that I'd be dead to him forever."

"That was a long damned time ago, Jewel. Why don't you just say fuck it and move on? Why are you still trying?"

I just shook my head, thinking of hollyhock dolls. Zeppoles in the shape of letters. Riding his shoulders to church.

We stopped at Burger King for lunch. The drive-in line was a million cars long—well, okay, three, but I don't like drive-ins in this car, never know when the screaming will start and then I'm trapped—so we went inside. The lunch rush was over, and the employees were laughing in a little knot behind the counter. Some young kids in the back, hair in nets, a middle-aged woman scrubbing down the counter, a boss type in a clean shirt on the phone, making notes on a clipboard, his back to us.

The woman put down her washcloth and looked at us. "Can I help youse?"

We both ordered, me a burger and shake, Malachi two giant burgers, a giant order of fries, and a monster-size Coke. He paid, gallantly, for all of it. I widened my eyes at his order. "Your arteries are hardening as we speak."

He flashed that grin, wiggling his eyebrows. "I work it off."

The boss type hung up the phone and gave us a distracted grin. "How you folks doing today?"

I smiled. "Good, thanks."

He took another look at me. "You related to Jordan Sabatino?"

"You think?" I grinned. "My little sister."

A subtle war happened on his smooth brown face. Admiration—he'd been one of Jordan's many suitors, that was obvious—but also a little avaricious curiosity over the "little" sister part. "Ah," he said, his eyes glittering. "You're the dangerous one, then."

"Yep," I said lightly, happy to have a straw to unwrap. "That's me. Ms. Dangerous."

He leaned closer. "I thought you lived somewhere else, New York or something, with that"—he glanced at Malachi, trying to decide whether he could be the rock star of Jewel's legendary flight—"band."

The band. Right. I poked the straw through the starred hole on the top of my shake, unable to stop the flicker of heat over my ears at the stories that had circulated about me. This was a new variation, and I could just imagine how it had gone. Jewel the Slut who ran off with the whole band. "I married Billy Jake," I lied with a level gaze designed to take that greed out of his eyes and sit him down in the back pew of the church where he'd atone for his gossip. "We were married fourteen years before he died."

"Yeah. Yeah, I think I heard that." He straightened, lifted his chin in the traditional parting gesture. "Hey, tell your sister Matt Sedillo said hi, eh?"

"I will."

Malachi had been quiet, but when we carried the red plastic trays over to the table, he said, "How many people live in this city? I thought it seemed like maybe one hundred thousand, maybe one hundred fifty thousand?"

"That's about right." I unwrapped my sandwich. "Why?"

He gave me a puzzled little frown. "You keep meeting people everywhere. It's like a small town."

"Ah. That's the two degrees of separation."

"What does that mean?"

"There was a play called *Six Degrees of Separation*. It was also a movie, one of Will Smith's early roles. You ever see it?"

He was busy with his giant burger and only shook his head.

"Well, it was about the connections between people. The idea that if you sit down with someone else, you can find a connection between you within six degrees—like your uncle was married to his first-grade teacher's mother." I frowned and counted, trying to find six degrees, then waved my hand. "Anyway, in Pueblo, that narrows down to two." I took a bite of my burger. "Sometimes two in seven directions."

He raised his eyebrows. "Like that guy."

I shrugged. "Yeah."

"Weird. Kind of claustrophobic, isn't it?"

"Maybe," I said, looking at the woman behind the counter. Truth was, I liked it. Nine times out of ten, I could find a connection with a stranger in five minutes or less. Not that I'd bother most of the time, but it's kind of comforting to know you can. It was one of the things I'd missed like hell while I was gone—that web, knotty and sometimes limiting, but also somehow secure. You can't fall too far with that web below you.

"You like it," Malachi said. "Even if a guy like that slobbers all over the counter?"

"I don't like that part," I admitted. "But it kind of means that people don't get too far off the track if they plan to hang around."

"Which you didn't."

"Right." I folded the paper from my sandwich, knowing outsiders didn't like the web, never had. It was hard to be woven into it, for one thing. Hard to like something you can't participate in. I cast around for a way to put it in terms he might understand. "It keeps the really dramatic, awful things to a minimum. If there's trouble, there are a lot of people to split the load and handle it."

"I'll buy that."

I nibbled the lettuce around the edges of my sandwich, a thousand examples of the way that worked running through my head. Then I smiled, looking up at him. "Divorce sucks, right? I mean, there are times that it's the only option, when two people are just totally wrong for each other, but in maybe ninety out of a hundred cases, the marriage'll work out if both people are committed, don't you think?"

He lifted a shoulder. "I guess."

"Well, even if you don't have the experience, you can see that maybe it's bad for kids, that it's a lot easier on everybody if the marriage works out in most cases."

"Yeah, okay. I can see that."

"Until I went to high school, I never knew anybody who was divorced except one family down the block, and that guy was such a loser that everybody really wanted to see her get rid of him."

"I see where this is going. I don't buy it, Jewel." He shook his big head stubbornly. "What that gets you is a bunch of really miserable families where one person or the other is just dying to get out."

"No, it doesn't. If the expectation is that you get married for life, the other option presents so many problems that people tend to put a little more elbow grease into making the marriage work however they can, sticking it out through the tough times."

A faint bitterness crossed his mouth. "Well, it sounds nice, but I still don't buy it." He met my eyes. "You had to get rid of Billy eventually. I remember when Michael talked about it. There was no saving him."

"Well, first of all, I wasn't actually married—and you know, I sometimes wonder if that might have made a difference." I shook my head. "But second, sometimes it just doesn't work out. He had a lot of problems before I made him leave, and even when he got addicted to crack, I didn't stop loving him. But I didn't want Shane to see his father that way."

He crumpled his empty sandwich wrappers carefully. "I gotta tell you, sweetheart, that I think the opposite is the real truth. People are happier without all those external ties, making choices day to day over whether to stay or go, change and grow. I think people get stuck in places like this, stuck in the expectations everyone has for them. You thought so, too, or you'd never have ridden off on that bike with Billy."

"I did think so, once," I admitted. "And this isn't right for everybody, I know that. All I'm saying is that there's a lot to be said for that web—I think people are very tribal, and we have to find ways to create those tribes if we don't have one."

"I don't have a tribe. Never wanted one."

"You had Michael."

A flicker of quick sorrow across those dark irises. "He was enough."

To lighten the mood, I tossed my balled-up paper at him. "Come on, tough guy. I've got some pies to bake."

FROM THE FALCONI'S MENU:

Lasagna—A Pueblo tradition since 1927! You've never tasted lasagna until you've had our special slow-baked pie made from a secret recipe passed down from father to son since 1902. You won't be hungry when you walk away from this meal!

Chapter Seven

I didn't end up baking that particular apple pie that day, or even for a week after that. In truth, the budget was screaming, and there were other pies that were cheaper to put together—and I hated being so limited by the cash situation.

It's never easy to get a business going. I knew that. With the onset of warm weather, some of the business was also bound to drop off as people opted to skip dessert or maybe eat some ice cream instead of pie. I didn't really have the delivery or storage capabilities for cold pies, either, though I could get away with a few now and then. The only answer was to build accounts, and I took advantage of the fact that Malachi was available to stay with Michael to get that in motion. Monday, after delivering the pies, I went to OfficeMax to get some materials printed, then spent most of Tuesday and Wednesday putting together a sales package. In attractive, professional folders, I assembled an informational piece about the business and another about myself and my professional credentials and a menu list. It felt incomplete, though I'd used the package to great effect in New York, and I finally sat down and wrote a friendly introductory letter emphasizing my connection to the community, to Falconi's. Roots. Connections. Two degrees of separation. I ran the risk of some people remembering which daughter I was, and therefore losing some business, but I thought the gamble was worthwhile.

Thursday, I dressed carefully in a straight blue skirt, modest heels with a slingback, and a tailored cotton shirt. My hair went up into a french twist, and I put on the gold-and-diamond necklace Billy had given me when Shane was born. Standing back to examine myself critically, I thought it worked okay. The women would be glad I dressed modestly, and they'd like that I didn't bother with stockings in hot weather. The men would like the glint of diamond just barely visible above the neckline. Putting my hair up made me look reliable.

I clacked downstairs with my briefcase and stood in front of Michael and Malachi, who were reading in the shade of the front porch. "How do I look?"

"Like a secretary," Malachi said.

I tsked. "Thanks. That helps."

"It's just right," Michael said. There were dark bruises under his eyes, and I wanted to just forget it all and sit with him. Impossible if we were going to be eating in another couple of months. "Need lipstick."

"Ah! I almost forgot!" I dug in my bag and came up with a nice brownish berry, smeared some on, blotted it with a scrap of tissue. "Better?"

"Perfect," Michael said.

"Take a letter, Maria," Malachi sang. Then he grinned. "Just kidding. You look great. I'd buy all your pie."

"Stop it." I inhaled, tucked the tube back in my purse, and bent over to kiss Michael. "Be good," I said, wiping a smudge of berry off his cheek.

"What about me?" Malachi said.

I clacked over to him, bent over, and kissed his cheek, too. "I'm not even going to bother to tell you to be good."

His wicked hand touched the back of my knee. "Go get 'em, babe."

~

It went pretty well—I covered the central and northside establishments during the low hours of late morning, timing things so I could meet my cousin George and a representative of the Dante Alighieri Society for lunch at Rosario's. It was pleasantly upscale, filled with professionals availing themselves of the buffet. This was New Pueblo, catering to the money coming in to the west and, by virtue of expansion, making many of the wealthy citizens—a great many of them Italian, by the way—even wealthier. The great American dream in action. I saw some of them, tanned from their cruises, in golf shirts and tennis bracelets, the women with acrylic nails, the men with very clean wrists. The menu offered goat cheese salads and veggie sandwiches along with lasagna and pizza.

I wondered how my catering plan would adapt to this new reality of the city changes and decided I'd play it by ear. In the meantime, the meeting with my cousin went well. Ellen Michelletti, the rep, was a smart, clearheaded woman who knew exactly what she wanted. I'd received the audience based on George's connections and my name, but I also knew what I was doing, and I could see that Ellen was quite happy with my answers. She promised to be in touch shortly.

I lingered in the courtyard, admiring the fountain tinkling in the midst of the shaded gardens, so that neither George nor Ellen Michelletti would see me get into that awful car. Or hear it scream. When the coast was clear, I pulled out my list and headed for the south side.

Old Pueblo. Or maybe traditional Pueblo. The difference was palpable as I stopped in one small establishment after another, asking to speak to the owner or manager. I introduced myself, pulled out the sales package, and saw the polite disinterest on the face of the listener—until I mentioned my connection to Falconi's. Then they'd shake my hand, open the folder, and either flip through and consider the offerings or say they'd give me a call.

It was exhausting. My face hurt from smiling. My scalp was starting to prickle with the heat, and I was starting to fantasize with great detail about ice-cold margaritas. Sitting in my car, looking over the list, I saw that it was nearly four, and I could probably call it a day. I'd signed one new client, with two more very serious contenders, and there would likely be more in a few days when I called to follow up.

One more. I drove to the last spot on the list, a family-run restaurant that had been in its spot by the steel mill for decades. A pair of girls were playing with Barbie dolls in a shady area behind a white picket fence, and some towels fluttered on a single clothesline strung between two elm trees.

I had to pause inside to let my eyes adjust. A young woman in a polo shirt and black pants approached me with a menu in her hand. "One?"

"No, thanks. I was hoping to be able to speak to the manager or owner."

"This is about . . . ?"

I handed her one of the sales pieces. "I'm establishing a pie service to the area and was hoping to interest your restaurant in a trial. I have samples, testimonials, pricing details."

Her lips turned down. "Okay, let me go tell him you're here. Have a seat. Would you like some water?"

"Yes, please." I settled at a nearby table. There was a bar, but this was a traditional establishment, and I wouldn't risk offending the owner if he was as traditional as his restaurant. There were three or four tables of early dinner customers, mostly old folks, and one young family with small children. Classical guitar music played over the speakers, and I could see the mountains through the big windows along the front. Excellent location, I thought idly.

The door to the back burst open, and a stooped, aging man came out, my sales piece in his hand. Seeing the disapproval on his face, I stood, pasting a regretful, polite smile over my dismay. "No, thank you," he said, and his accent was heavy. "We don't got use for this here."

"No problem," I said with false cheerfulness, and reached for my folder.

He yanked it out of reach. "How can you come down here, to your father's neighborhood, and act like this?" His brows were wild, laced with long, kinky gray hairs. Devil eyebrows.

I smoothed my skirt. "Thank you for your time," I said, and walked out.

~

When I got home, Michael and Malachi were out on the porch. They'd spent a lot of time together out there, sometimes talking or reminiscing, often laughing; listening to music; even just sitting side by side, reading. Or at least Malachi read, from a big stack of paperback novels he had picked up one afternoon in town—thrillers, mainly, which seemed to fit. He sometimes read aloud to Michael, who had trouble focusing on the small print in books.

Shane, eager to show me that he wasn't a complete idiot so he could get his freedom back, settled a little, even though I could see his restlessness in every movement.

Pueblo bored him. He'd never lived anywhere but a massive city, and the pace drove him batty, but at Michael's suggestion, he turned his attention to his music, developing new pieces, getting things ready for audition purposes, sharpening his skills, so often through those long days, the house thrummed quietly with the low thud of electric bass. Sometimes, when we were lucky, his tenor sailed out around the music, clear and true as crystal. He had a voice for crooning Motown, and it cracked me up to hear him put it to work on angsty teenage authority songs—but then again, who knew? One of those things he'd work out in time.

That afternoon, I found the taste of Abe's apple pie clinging to the roof of my mouth insistently. Clouds were piling up to the west, covering the sun, and it seemed like a good day to bake. Putting Mellencamp on the stereo—hoping maybe that it would draw the somewhat slippery Malachi into my kitchen, where I could flirt with him—I made the crust, which is the true secret of the taste of Abe's pie, and rolled it out with my prized marble rolling pin on the wide counter.

I'd fetched Shane off the side porch, where he was listening to the other guys, and put him to work slicing apples as I crushed the secret ingredient of the crust—gingersnaps—into crumbs. He resisted leaving the company of the males, but it was a job he liked, peeling the skins off in smooth, long curls. "Mom," he said, after a while.

"Mmm."

"I been talking to Jimmy online, at the library."

"Have you?" Jimmy Angelo was one of the old gang—a decent, solid keyboardist who'd sometimes played with the band and now made a good living doing various shows and studio work. He'd married two years ago and moved to Jersey, so I hadn't seen him much in quite a while. "How's he doing?"

"Good. Working a lot. Teresa just got promoted and said maybe she'll think about a baby in a couple more years."

I grinned, brushing flour from my hands. "That's what he gets for marrying so much younger than himself."

Shane didn't look at me. "I was wondering if maybe, if I keep it together and show you that I'm not gonna do anything stupid, if maybe"—he dropped the peeling into a paper bag, then finished so fast I could hardly make out his words—"you might think aboutlettingme go to livewithhim for my last year of school."

"Want to say that again?"

He took a breath, and I hated that he was scared to ask me, because that meant it was something he really wanted, and how could I let him go like that? A year early? Before I *had* to?

"Jimmy offered me a bedroom—they have an extra, you know—if I wanted to come back and get serious about the music. He thinks I'm ready."

"I'm sorry, Shane. I don't think so."

"I *knew* it!" He slammed the knife down on the table. "You're so overprotective it's strangling me! I'm seventeen, Mom, not twelve. It's not like I don't know how to take care of myself, and you know I'm not about to stay in any hole-in-the-wall town like this forever!"

"You don't have to shout, Shane." A familiar tension tightened my shoulders—Misunderstood Teen Versus Controlling, Short-Sighted Adult. "We can talk."

"That's what you always say, but it's you who talks and me who listens."

"I'll listen."

"No, you won't. I can tell by the way you've got your mouth that you're only gonna listen until I get done so you can say what you want to say." He stood up, his eyes narrowing. "Let me save you the trouble, okay? You're gonna say I'm too young, that I've just done something stupid and you can't trust me, that you'll worry about me." He leaned on the counter, all six-foot-two, broad-shouldered man-child. I could see unshaved whiskers on his chin. "Did I miss anything?"

God, I knew that tone of voice. I'd used it so often, never understanding how much it would hurt. "Nope."

"But the real reason you won't let me go," he said quietly, the bow pulled straight back from the shoulder, one eye closed to aim, arrow set to fly, "is that you don't want to be alone."

Bull's-eye. I rolled the heavy pin over the dough and said nothing.

"Oh, forget it," he said, and flung himself away from the breakfast bar. "You won't listen to me. Cut your own apples."

He stomped out the back door, and through the window above Saint Anthony's head, I saw him stalking away toward the orchard under those heavy gray clouds. Wind tossed his long, glossy hair around.

"Thanks a lot," I said to Anthony, and because I couldn't do anything about the kid, I pulled a Sylvia trick: I turned his face to the wall. "Sit there and watch and don't do a single thing to help, why don't you?"

The CD clicked off, leaving the room quiet. From the porch, I heard Michael's and Malachi's voices, woven together in a slow, easy kind of conversation that carried quite clearly on the rain-scented breeze lifting the curtain. I settled on the stool Shane had vacated and started peeling the rest of the apples, listening to the brothers shamelessly as thunder rolled closer. It wasn't a particularly interesting conversation—a discussion of current events, a slight tug-of-war over an issue in the news, then an easy move to a new topic. It was enough to reveal that Malachi, the big adventurer, was quite a bit more liberal politically than Michael. It was one of those odd little things that never failed to surprise me—my gay best friend, the ex-musician, who'd traveled the world and seen all kinds of people, was a fiscal conservative, mainly because he didn't believe the government had enough intelligence to take care of anything, and it was all best left in the private sector. Malachi, the one I would have laid money would be conservative, wasn't. At all.

I let an apple peel, unbroken from top to bottom, fall into the bag. On the television, a bright-red banner warned of severe thunderstorms in Pueblo West. In surprise, I looked out the window and saw the trees starting to toss in the wind coming hard down the highway, and far to the west, a line of heavy gray rain falling from clouds laced with lightning. Narrowing my eyes, I wondered if I had enough time to get the apples into their broth before the storm arrived, and decided to try. Another thing that sets Abe's pie apart is that he cooks the apples first. Trust me, it's one of the best pies you have ever tasted in your life. Ever.

The warnings on the television escalated—*reports of damaging hail; tornado sighted in Pueblo West*—and my mood rose with each warning whine. It was the first big storm since we'd arrived in Pueblo. After a few minutes, I decided not to take a chance—I remembered clearly a stove that had been hit when I was a child, because my mother had left a burner on low under the supper that was cooking when the lightning moved in—and shut everything down. Humming, I moved through the house, turning off switches and radios and unplugging clocks, then found a sweater and danced out to the porch.

The men were sitting in my aunt's rattan chairs. Michael and Malachi had been raised in the south and knew that kind of sky, but Shane, who'd at least had enough sense to get out of the orchard, had no idea. Thunder had been rumbling closer and closer, but just as I came out, a brilliant, jagged slash of lightning cut the black clouds, and practically before the light was gone, a sharp report of thunder came, almost painfully loud. I jumped reflexively, then laughed.

"God, Jewel, you look like it's Christmas morning!" Michael said with a chuckle.

"I love this!" The wind blew closer, biting and cold, bringing down the temperature ten degrees with a single heavy gust. It smelled of sulfur and earth and that piercingly rich note that is rain, and every hair on my body stood up in anticipation as I lifted my face to it, feeling the moisture my dry skin sucked in like the dry earth would take it.

A hush fell, birds and grass and river all waiting. Then a soft whoosh of sound, the rain moving toward us. The treetops at the far end of the property started tossing, gray and green and frenzied beneath the onslaught, and then it was on us, like a wave, a great roar of noise and water. Lightning danced, lashing out like a whip, the sound of it hitting trees deafening, crackling. "Once," I yelled over the noise, "I saw lightning hit a tree right over there. It exploded!"

Shane stood up and came to stand beside me, his brow furrowed. "Isn't it dangerous to be outside?"

"Not really." I had to shout it, and he waved a hand, leaning over the railing to look at the ground. There was little hail and not a lot of it, which allowed me to enjoy the rest of the spectacle without guilt. An insurance man had told me once, wearily filling out a claim for my aunt Sylvia's roof—her second in ten years—that hail damage in this stretch of land was the highest in the entire country. Big hail killed the crops, but these teeny little spitballs wouldn't do any harm.

But, oh, how it rained! Pounding, pouring, drenching rain, gallons and gallons pouring relentlessly out of that heavy black sky for twenty minutes. It didn't slow, either. It just stopped when it stopped, like someone turned off the faucet.

"Wanna see something cool?" I said.

Malachi grinned at me. "How cool?"

"Really, really cool. All of you, pile in the car. I'll get my keys and be right back."

I drove to the river first, and although it was churning a little more than usual, the waves of water had not really swelled it yet. Taking a series of back roads, avoiding the low-lying spots that would be filled with flash flood waters, I drove to a bluff on the east side of town and parked the car. "Can't drive any farther," I said. "We have to get out here and walk down."

Shane scowled. "It's muddy!"

"A little mud never hurt anybody." I got out and let them follow if they would or not. Skidding a little on the sloppy hill, I ducked under some drippy trees, and there it was. The guys were right behind me, and I laughed, pointing. "There!"

"What?" Michael said, and Shane said, "A river is what's cool?"

But Malachi said, "A confluence!" and made a happy little noise, running ahead of me. He smacked the back of Shane's head playfully as he went by. "It is cool, boy, don't you know nothin'?" He grabbed my hand and pulled me along. "Two rivers, coming together." He whistled. "That's still the Arkansas, I reckon, right?" I nodded and he said, "What's the other one?"

"My favorite in all the world," I said. "The Fountain. She's so deceptive and sleepy most of the time you can wade across and never get your ankles wet." Not now, though. "Up north, they call her a creek, and though they call her a river down here—"

"Rightfully so."

"—she is even too wild for that. The French called her 'the River that Boils.'"

His fingers squeezed around mine, and I wondered why that didn't feel scary, only right. His big, calloused hand wrapping around mine like it belonged there. He bent his head to peer at me hard. "You a river geek, too?"

"Too? Are you?"

He laughed. "Darlin', I've been crazy about rivers since I was a teeny little boy. Ask my brother."

"This one must seem pretty silly to be a favorite, then," I said, a bit defensive and ready to present my case for why my wild woman river was as good as any other.

But he shook his head, his eyes on the boiling, rushing confluence. "I understand it. This is a river La Llorona walks."

I looked at him, startled. "Yeah."

He let me go and raced down the hill like a ten-year-old, that long-limbed body oddly graceful for all his size. Shane rushed by me, pulled along as if he were attached by some invisible string. They ran all the way to the banks, and Malachi bent down and tossed something in, and Shane followed suit.

I looked over my shoulder and saw Michael ten feet or so up the hill, alone with the dark sky as backdrop, and he looked as powerfully Otherworld as I'd ever seen him, as if he commanded the magic that brought the clouds to this weight and darkness, as if all the power were concentrated in his slim body. His blond hair lifted in the wind, the only movement about him, and his mouth was very sober. I wanted to know what he saw with those pale eyes, what thoughts wove through him.

Below, Malachi whooped over something or another, and a soft, indulgent smile crossed Michael's mouth. He seemed to suddenly sense me standing there, and looked over. "Go on," he said with a tilt of his head. "Go play."

I'd really intended to stay there with him, but that strange invisible wall was up, and he wanted to be alone. I grinned and turned to tumble down the hill. "Wait up!"

~

I finally made it upstairs at ten. My limbs all felt as if they weighed five thousand pounds. Every apple, every discussion, every phone call and upset and minute of the day seemed to be etched on my spine—and I had to be up again at five.

Malachi was the only one who went upstairs ahead of me, and by the silence that greeted me when I hit the landing, he was out cold. His door was open, and when I turned on the bathroom light, I could see the barest outline of his body, face down as I had predicted, on the old double bed. As tired as I was, there was a lure to thinking about going in there and lying down next to his long, strong body. Not real thought, you understand, just that vague, tired, if-I-could-win-the-lottery kind of thing. In an ideal world, I'd be taking my shower and going into that room to lie down next to his body. Not for sex. I was way too tired for that. For—

I closed the bathroom door quietly, then turned on the water and let steam fill the room, tying my hair into a knot and shedding my clothes. My breasts fell down against my chest, and I didn't want to even think about what a rear view of my bottom would look like.

Which made me think of Malachi's behind under those covers. I took a breath. He wasn't what I wanted—not even close. What I *really* wanted was someone calm and easy, a steady man like Michael, to be there, warm and sleepy in my bed when I went to it, with no pressure attached. That was definitely not Malachi's style. Hot sex, definitely. Wild flattery. He'd probably even be okay with my body—*if* he'd ever seen a forty-year-old body, which I doubted seriously.

But calm and warm and easy? Not a chance.

Steam curled downward from the ceiling, and I stripped off my panties, thinking again of that rear view in a regretful way—but sick thoughts make sick bodies, and I remembered an exercise a midwife friend of mine had taught me.

I closed my eyes. Breathed deeply. Made myself think consciously of my fingertips and palms, and thank them directly for all the things they had touched and felt and found pleasure in. I thanked them for skill and speed and sensuality. Raised them to my gravity-ravaged breasts. For a minute, I had to pause, wishing in spite of myself for the perky breasts of youth. Took a breath, focused on thanks. They were still soft, still silky, probably still a joy in the hands of a man who genuinely liked women. These breasts had given me delirious pleasure and great pride and sustenance to my son. I thanked them.

The whole body. Belly, thighs, buttocks, feet. Ovaries, heart, kidneys, lungs. And last, but not least, vulva and vagina, the dark secret between my thighs that had been so very dangerous we couldn't even call it by its right name when I was a child. Only "privates."

Crisp hair against my palm, and the folds of flesh. I thought of Billy and his unerring ability to coax an outrageous response, and of Shane, emerging with such gusto even then, his outraged cry bawling into the delivery room before they had a chance to spat him on the bottom.

In that same spirit of thankful reverence, I showered, and afterward anointed all the thanked parts with sweet-smelling oils, rubbing them especially along the backs of my cracked heels and my dried-out elbows and my neck, which my mother had always told me would be the first to wrinkle. In this, as in many things, she proved to be correct. Rubbing moisturizer under my eyes with the third finger of my left hand, the very weakest finger and therefore the least likely to damage the delicate flesh, I wished that I'd listened to my mother more often.

My mother. How she embarrassed me when I was a young teen! Her piety, her plainness, her very Italian Italianness, in spite of the small rebellion of naming her daughters in such thoroughly modern ways. In my later teens, I worried about her, worried that my father didn't really see her or love her enough. In church, at the grocery store, at PTA meetings (all of which they accomplished together), women fawned over my father. The divorcées and widows worried me especially. They seemed so much more polished than my housewife of a mother. They wore eyeliner and face powder and perfume. They painted their nails and wore tight, short skirts. They especially displayed their bosoms. Discreetly at church. Less discreetly everywhere else.

In comparison, my mother looked . . . plain. Her long, thick black hair was an asset, but she didn't do anything with it, just wore it very long and straight, usually braided in a single long tail that fell to her hips. Her bosom was hidden beneath demure blouses. Her nails were unpainted, and she wore the same coral lipstick every day of her life. Didn't she see those women throwing themselves at my father? Didn't she think it was time to lose that extra twenty pounds?

It took me years to understand that my father was never—never—interested in another woman but his wife. He adored her. He planted kisses on her neck when she cooked and he didn't think we were looking. He patted her bottom when she was out in the garden. When he came home from work, she took him a beer in the bathroom, and they talked while he took his bath. Every night. Always.

So different from my life with Billy. Brushing the tangles from my wet hair, I wondered if my sisters had found that with their husbands. Jordan's Henry seemed capable, and he was certainly devoted. Jasmine's Brian was a high-powered car salesman and didn't strike me as demonstrative in the slightest, but who knew what went on behind closed doors? She seemed happy with the arrangement. They enjoyed doing things together, movies and a dinner out, sometimes the symphony or a play. Jane's Steve was mostly a mystery—I'd met him only twice, but there was passion in his big dark eyes and an almost painful devotion to my sister. Yes, of the four of us, I thought Jane would come closest to replicating the sound marriage of my parents.

And I'd gone the farthest afield.

Braiding my hair, finished with the many lotions and unguents and moisturizers necessary to preserve whatever youth might be left to me, I put on my pajamas and gathered my clothes from the floor.

But there, hanging forgotten on one of the three hooks on the back of the door, was Malachi's shirt. I had noticed it earlier, but my nose had been full of apples and pie dough and now it wasn't, and I could smell him in the fabric, a scent just a little deeper, a little richer than sun-dried laundry. The fabric touched my nose and forehead, and I let go, imagined breathing in these notes from his skin. His chest. That wide, supple expanse. I remembered how his back had felt when we were on the motorcycle, taut and strong, and knew his chest would be the same.

For five seconds, in that steamy, quiet bathroom, I let myself admit how much I wanted him. All day long I'd been noticing his mouth, a mouth that laughed easily and had big white teeth in it; his hands, enormous and full of dexterity; his thighs, so sturdy and powerful. His size appealed to me; it made me smaller in contrast, gave me that sense of delicacy that's almost impossible for a woman in my size category, and I know you're not supposed to say that you think about the size of a man's penis, but I'm sorry—we do. Not that it makes that much of a difference when a man knows what he's doing, but all things being equal . . . well, enough said.

A noise on the other side of the door jolted me out of the embarrassing swoon over his stupid shirt, and I yanked open the door, feeling the slap of my braid against my arm. It wasn't Malachi waiting in the hall, thank the saints, but in a way it was even worse. Shane. Blinking at me. "God, you were in there for ten thousand years."

"It's all yours." I clutched my dirty clothes to my chest and went to my room, carefully not turning my head toward the sex god's door, just in case my kid was watching. Sex and kids just don't go together, and it gets even stranger when you have a boy you know is thinking about it every three seconds all day long, every day. He would be so humiliated to know what was on his mother's mind.

After dumping the clothes on the floor, I crawled into bed and pulled the pillow over my head. Happily, sleep is never hard, and I forgot about everything as it washed over me, tugged me down into the deep ocean of it, where I was still anything I wanted to be and had nothing to regret.

MICHAEL

In his bed, alone in the night, Michael practiced yoga breathing against his pain and reached out for a picture to go with it, something calming and peaceful.

The afternoon came back to him, all of them down at the river. Under that slate gray sky at the confluence, Michael had stood straight against the plucking pain in his chest. Nothing physical. Physical discomfort had become his constant companion, and he was used to it. This was stranger, harder.

Three heads, all so dark. So dear. How was it that he'd never understood it was the small things that made life so sweet? Jewel's curls bouncing as she ran, the long mussed mass of it making him think of a mermaid's hair. Shane's thick, glossy black, so much like Billy's, who was—as he would tell you if you gave him so much as two seconds—one full quarter Oglala Sioux and on the tribal rolls at Pine Ridge, you could go and check. Not that Billy himself had ever been there, but it gave him a good tale to share.

And Malachi. Thick hair, unruly as hell when they were kids, so thick a brush wouldn't go through it and they had to buy him long-toothed combs. He'd scream for an hour while their mother patiently combed it out after a bath, letting it dry by itself into waves cut with a million colors. Michael had once tried to count the colors in his brother's hair—strands of gold and fiery red, darkest black and palest blond, as if every ancestor from every county in Ireland had contributed its legacy on one head.

It was hair just like their father's.

A half-buried rock stuck out of the hillside nearby, and Michael sat down, nodding at a pair of boys in oversize, very clean professional baseball shirts who made their way by. He saw tattoos on their hands, tattoos that contrasted strongly with the way they pushed and laughed at each other once they were past him. It was a tough hood, but even here, boys could play when nobody important was looking. They steered clear of the trio close to the banks, and Michael watched them for a while, letting that strange pain ease a little before he looked back to his beloved three.

It was love that made it hard, the whole dying thing. Thinking of not seeing Jewel anymore, or Shane, who was like his own kid. Or Malachi, who still hadn't forgiven their father, who still had that tight hard knot in him from so long ago. Maybe it wouldn't ever go away. Maybe that violent day was just gouged too deeply in the man's soul to erase. Michael couldn't imagine it; he'd only seen the bloody scene a few days later, after the cops and forensics people and everybody else got through with it. Malachi had heard the shots and raced out of his bedroom, a truck in his hand, and saw it all.

Poor kid.

Below, Jewel tossed her head at something Malachi said, and Michael watched as Malachi leaned in close to show her something he'd picked up. A shine bounced around both of them, shimmering and clear in the dark day. Clear enough that Shane stopped what he was doing for a minute to look at them. They didn't notice.

It was so plain now. Michael wished he'd seen it before. He hoped he had enough time to see it through. Wasn't an easy task, considering Malachi had the unfortunate tendency of running hard at the slightest sign of settling in. And Jewel had that little image problem.

But he thought he could go easier, knowing they had each other in place. A whole lot easier.

JORDAN'S HEALING OIL

Gather lavender and yarrow flowers just after dawn, before the heat of the day dries up the oil. Within an hour, pack a quart mason jar with an equal mix of lavender leaves and flowers, yarrow blossoms, and shredded white willow bark. Add 1 ounce powdered comfrey root. Fill the jar almost to the top with a high-quality, cold-pressed olive oil, leaving room for about an ounce of gum benzoin or rubbing alcohol at the top (keeps it from spoiling). Cover and let stand for two weeks to a month, shaking it once per day. Strain the oil through cheesecloth and pour into pretty bottles with corks. Excellent for eczema, dry heels, aching joints, general pain. Smells great!

Chapter Eight

Michael was sick all night. I heard him about two, pacing and giving the soft grunts that meant he was trying not to groan. Scrambling into a pair of sweats, I padded into his room to see if there was anything I could do to help. He looked up at me, surprised and relieved and wishing he didn't need me, an expression that always broke my heart.

"Come lie down," I said, patting the bed. "Let me rub your back for a little while."

"I'm all right," he said. Light from the windows caught the edges of his pale hair, the bridge of his nose. "Go on back to bed, Jewel. You have to get up in a few hours."

"Michael."

A startle of pain went through him, and one arm went reflexively around his thin middle. "Go, Jewel."

Gently I put my hand on his arm and tugged. "Come on."

He gave in. Sometimes it took longer, and I was relieved when he let go of the rigidness in his body, that rigidness that he tried to use to keep himself aloof, in charge, and gave himself up to me. In the dark, in the middle of the night, was almost the only time he ever could.

He stretched out on his stomach on the hospital bed my sister Jordan had scrounged up for him, and I felt the pocket of dead air around it, stale and empty of oxygen, filled only with the exhalations of a man in pain. I opened the window and tied up the curtain to let in some fresh air.

"Trying to kill me?" he said in his gravelly voice.

I smiled at the reference to night humors, the admonition of my grandmother to keep the windows closed at night no matter what. "Gotta leave a window open for the other fairies to come find you," I said, pouring oil in my hands. It was something Jordan made out of the herbs in her garden, a concoction that smelled like midsummer. She told me what was in it—lavender, for one thing, maybe something like horehound; she has a huge herb garden that she actually uses. I let the oil warm in my palm for a little while, then put it on his long, white back and started rubbing it in, gently, slowly, trying to ease away the tightness of pain in him. "Did you take any pain pills?" I asked.

"Nah. Makes me too dopey. I want to go fishing with Malachi in the morning."

"How about just some ibuprofen?"

He groaned softly when I hit a pocket of tenseness over his shoulders, and gave himself up to the process of letting me ease it away. "You don't have to pretend to be okay with him, Michael. He knows you're sick."

No answer, but under my fingers a bunching of the muscles told me he didn't like that, and I made a mental note to bring Malachi into the caretaking process the next time Michael had a really bad day.

Or was that fair? Maybe Michael had a right to choose what to show and not show; maybe he liked being the big brother who was strong. Maybe Malachi, like so many people—I almost said so many men, but there are lots of women, too—would be alarmed and dismayed, even disgusted, by illness.

On the other hand, maybe Malachi deserved the chance to do something for his big brother. As I rubbed oil from his shoulders to the small of his back, it gave me as much as it gave Michael—something concrete I could remember later, something to do in place of getting rid of the virus eating him alive.

"You know what I was thinking about?" Michael said quietly.

"Tell me."

"When you were so scared to go to cooking school."

With a rueful smile, I shook my head. "I would never have been able to actually walk through those doors without you." I'd been petrified, scared to the point of lint mouth.

"What scared you so much, Jewel? I mean, you grew up in a restaurant. What'd you think about when you couldn't go?"

I started on his right arm and took a breath, trying to remember. "I don't know, really. They all seemed so sure of themselves, so convinced of their absolute right to do whatever they wanted to do."

"That's how you were when I met you." He turned his head to look at me. "What changed, Jewel?"

"I don't know. A lot of things." Things I was looking for here in Pueblo, maybe.

"Billy?"

He liked to talk in the middle of the night, and it was a small enough thing I could give him, even if he was turning it on me tonight. "Well, that was one thing, I guess. Everything that happened with him."

"The girls didn't mean anything, Jewel. You know that."

The girls. The curse of the musician's wife. Billy had been better than most at resisting their overtures, but he'd had a few weak moments. "I know that," I said, dismissing them—then not quite able. "You didn't take lovers, though, did you? You were always faithful."

"Lotta good it did me." He put his chin on his fist and looked toward the window, and I knew he was thinking about Andre. "Wasn't quite the same situation, though. Boys don't come around like girls do."

"It's not the girls, anyway," I said. They really hadn't meant anything. "Just . . . his whole decline. Your brother was talking about Billy the other day, when he met him. He said he'd seen a bad end on Billy even then." I pushed the heel of my palm into the base of his spine. "Did you see that?"

"Yeah, probably." He sighed. "I know you loved him, Jewel, but he had missing pieces nobody could put right."

"I sure tried."

"Yeah. Probably bought him some time, too."

We went quiet. My mind was full of memories, and I could feel them echoing and repeating in Michael's head—Billy, so bad and beautiful and utterly doomed with his hair and tattoos and heartbroken guitar. "It wasn't me, or you," I said. "It was music that bought him time. If the music hadn't failed, he might have been an old man eventually."

"The music didn't fail him," Michael rasped. "He failed the music. He wanted it to be his slave, instead of the other way around."

It was true, though I'd never thought about it like that, and I felt a quickening of hope that maybe Shane wasn't doomed to repeat his father's life, even if he chose music. "Do you miss it, Michael?"

"God, yes."

"Will you sing for me?"

"Always." He took my hand and pulled me around to sit beside him. In the dark, he began to sing an old hymn, "Shall We Gather at the River?"

> Yes, we'll gather at the river,
> The beautiful, the beautiful river;
> Gather with the saints at the river
> That flows by the throne of God . . .

His voice, low and raspy and rich, poured over my skin and into my heart, as it had always done, and when he tugged my fingers, I joined in quietly, trying not to hear my voice or interfere with his. A breeze lifted the curtain and showed us a glimpse of the stars. Michael sang the whole song, only drifting a little by the end. His body was easing, and when he finished, I simply sat there holding his hand, listening to him breathe.

After a time, it seemed he'd fallen asleep, and I got up, about to creep out, when he said, "Jewel?"

"Yeah?" I whispered.

"Will you stay for a while?"

I didn't even answer, just went around to the side of the bed that he cleared for me and climbed up beside him. Like we were an old married couple, I pressed my body against his back and looped my arm around his waist, my cheek against the herbal scent of his shoulder blade. He captured my hand with his and pressed it against his chest, and just like that, he eased. Fell asleep. I could hear him breathing, wheezy but steady. It eased me, too, feeling his warmth, the steadiness of him, even the sharpness of his spine. It raised Billy's ire sometimes, to find us this way—I often thought it was as much out of jealousy over Michael as for me, to tell you the truth.

I don't remember anymore how we fell into the habit. Proximity, maybe. Loneliness. No, wasn't really fair. We clicked, Michael and I, that first day, so long ago, as if I'd found the brother I'd always wanted. No. Not even brother goes deep enough to describe it—finding Michael was like finding some missing piece of my own soul. It was never the slightest bit sexual.

In the dark of Michael's room, on his narrow bed, I pressed my thighs against the back of his, content to be in this minute, in this day, with him, and fell asleep.

∼

Blackbirds awakened me before first light. Their song wove its way into my dreams and whistled around inside them until I woke up, still curled close to Michael. He felt cool and utterly relaxed next to me, but the blackbirds made me melancholy. That song by the Beatles has to be one of the most piercing in all of music, and I found myself humming it under my breath as I got up and tiptoed out to the hall.

Just as I got there, Malachi came out of the bathroom, and I will say that for three seconds, I forgot I was wearing only a long T-shirt and my sweats, because all *he* was wearing was a pair of boxer shorts. White boxers, no frills, the most boring possible underwear a man could put on. Except that you can kind of see through them a little, and there was also a lot of dark, flat stomach and that chest I'd been fantasizing about last night. He was chewing on a toothbrush, his hair tousled still from bed, and I'd startled him.

Embarrassed him. He touched his belly with the flat of his palm, looked at me, at my breasts, back down to his body. "Uh, sorry," he said, voice gravelly and low as the rumble of a train so early in the morning. "I'll just run and get my . . . clothes. Jeans. Uh. Something."

His chagrin made me realize I was not exactly dressed for company, either. I nodded, not quite able to speak, and needing that bathroom pretty darn quick.

We both moved at the same instant. I thought he was going to turn toward his room, and ducked to my left to get around him, but he had stepped backward to grab something off a hook in the bathroom, and I misjudged the duck, so when he swung back around, we tangled. His elbow caught my shoulder, and his foot snared my toes. When I—flustered—tried to get out of the way, dodging under him, he was trying to move out of my way, and shifted the jeans in his hands to the other side. Something on them caught hard in a loop of my braid, and yanked so hard it brought tears to my eyes.

"Wait!" I grabbed my hair to keep it attached to my head and swung around to see what caught it.

Which put me right up under his arm, next to that flesh that really did smell like his shirt, only deeper yet. He grabbed my arm, and I was thankful that at least there was a thin layer of cotton between the possibility of bare flesh contact, though it didn't help when I found myself face-to-face with a pelt of dark chest hair.

"It's too early to play Twister," I said. "Can you get me unhooked and let me brush my teeth?" I could only imagine how my breath smelled and covered my mouth with my hand.

"It's the button, see?"

I looked at the button on the fly and nodded, waiting for him to free it, keeping one hand anchored around my waist, the other over my mouth. Maybe I was trying not to breathe in any more of that smell.

But he didn't do anything. Just stood there, holding on to my braid, wearing those sinfully thin boxers that tempted me to look (I didn't). I finally scowled up at him.

He'd been waiting, the end of the braid in his fingers, and he tickled my nose with it, winking when I gave him a reluctant smile. He let me go.

I stood at the sink to brush my teeth and saw how I looked. That's part of the trouble with me and men. It always shows in my face, that heat. Pupils dilated, cheekbones bright red, nipples standing at full alert. Oh, no, he hadn't bothered me at all.

"Shit." I said the word forcefully, bending down to scrub the night off my face. Scrubbed vigorously, telling myself all the reasons it would be a big fat stupid idea to have sex with my best friend's brother. A kid in the house had to be top of the list. A not-stupid kid to boot, one who'd notice immediately, and that would send the wrong message.

Madonna said, *What message would that be?* She was filing her nails in my imagination, bright-red nails. *That people have sex?*

She had a point. As did June, who said, *Stability is what that child needs. He's been through too many upheavals the past few years.*

It won't kill him if his mother has sex, said Madonna.

June spoke directly to me, that gentle reproach in her tone. *Jewel, you don't have to give yourself away like that all the time. Haven't you learned your lesson yet?*

The aim was so true, I knew that it was my mother's voice speaking. My father's. Right there in one delectable package of temptation was every reason my life was where it was.

Stung, I waited safely inside that crummy little bathroom until I heard Malachi go down the stairs, whistling some happy thing, before I dashed out and down the hall to my own room and closed the door. It was very dark still, and I had to turn on the light to find anything to wear. Jeans, the old ones, a pair of 501s that didn't do a damned thing for my big butt. I tossed them on the bed. Opened a drawer, wishing it was winter so I could layer on the sweaters, but I'd be cooking and it was going to be hot enough, so I settled for an oversize T-shirt that would hide every inch of my torso.

On went the bra, the T-shirt, down came the hair, which I brushed hard to get the waves out, then rebraided, just to be safe. No makeup. Flip-flops on my feet. I wished, momentarily, for a pair of glasses to hide behind, but I had had laser correction done a couple of years ago—neither glasses nor the contacts I mainly wore took all that kindly to the powders and grease that go along with cooking.

Armored, I turned off the light, peeked in on Michael, then poked my head around Shane's door.

His bed was empty.

Empty. He'd sneaked out again.

Forgetting everything else, I dashed downstairs, still hoping to be proved wrong. Sometimes he fell asleep there watching television, but not this time.

The digital clock in the corner said 4:11. Earlier than I thought, which was why the kid was busted. With firm purpose, I went to the kitchen to find Malachi making coffee, still whistling under his breath. "Are you desperate for that caffeine?" I asked.

"Not at all. I was making it for the house."

"Turn off the light, then, and leave it. Shane snuck out, and I want to catch him coming back in."

He winced and put the lid back on the coffee. "I'm finished with this part." He punched the button. "Be ready in just a few minutes."

"Whatever." I left him, going out through the side door to the porch, where I could see the road but Shane wouldn't see me. Out there, it was obvious how he'd left—scrambling from his room to the roof of the porch and a quick swing to the rail and out. I blew out a breath and prepared myself to wait. The blackbirds were still twittering in their melancholy way. I couldn't help but think of all the things that could happen to him, my foolish boy, in the middle of the night with a wild friend and a car and no doubt any number of legal and illegal substances.

It was impossible to sit still. I jumped up to pace along the railing, thinking a little anxiously of the pies waiting to go in the oven, of the possibility of landing the catering job for the Dante Alighieri society. I stared down the road and willed headlights to appear.

And because you never really got over a Catholic childhood, I prayed. To Saint Joseph, keeper of children, and the Blessed Mother, of course, and Saint Jude, and the Big Guy himself, just in case he might still listen to me once in a while. Prayed that they'd keep him safe, put angel wings all around him, protecting him even if they got into a wreck.

Malachi materialized out of the darkness, and I jumped.

"Easy, babe," he said, and gave me a cup of coffee.

I let go of a breath. "Thanks." Leaning on the porch post, I sipped it and returned to my silent prayers.

"Did you ever sneak out when you were his age?" Malachi asked.

"Yes. Why do you think it makes me so crazy? If I didn't know what he was doing, I wouldn't be so damned scared."

"He's not stupid, you know."

"You don't have to be stupid to get yourself killed—just reckless." And I should know.

"Not everybody is Billy, headed for a bad end."

I tsked. "What makes you think you know anything?"

He lifted his chin, meeting my eyes with an unapologetic steadiness that annoyed me even more. "Everything you think shows on your face. I bet you play lousy poker."

"It's not about Billy."

"Yeah, it is. You think cuz they look alike, that he's got a wild streak, that he's gonna end up in a coffin too soon, like his daddy did."

I tapped my foot against the porch boards, ignoring him.

He didn't take the hint. "Billy didn't have a goddamn thing all his life, Jewel. I mean, less than nothing, nobody to tell him he was good or right or kind. It's a miracle he managed to grow up at all, much less turn himself into somebody with something to offer."

"I know all this. What's your point?"

A shrug of that massive shoulder. "Shane's got you. Always has. He's got Michael. He had Billy for a while, and I do know that Billy loved that boy like he hung the stars."

From behind the dark walls where I kept Billy carefully mummified came a fist, landing a solid right hook to my heart. "He did." Since my heart had taken the blow anyway, I said, "He read to him every night, you know that? Read and sang, started teaching him to play guitar before he could even tie his shoes."

"There's nothing wrong with Shane except being seventeen and ready to fly the coop. He'll be all right."

"That's so easy to say when he's not your kid. There are a million things he doesn't know, doesn't get, and five hundred thousand of them could get him killed."

"Nah. He'll slam into a wall now and again—figuratively, you know, not literally. Get his heart broken, tangle with the wrong guy, make the wrong call, and generally fuck up. But that's just part of living, babe. I did it, you did it. We all do."

"Stop calling me babe and sugar," I snapped.

His chuckle, low and rich, countered the blackbirds' melancholy whistling. "All right, darlin'."

"You're incorrigible," I said, the anger deflating. I smiled at him reluctantly and sipped the coffee. To the east, the first hint of gray clung to the edges of the trees. "I just want things to be easier for him than they were for me. I'd like to spare him at least a few of my mistakes."

"Do you really? Which ones?" He leaned forward, bracing his forearms on his knees, the mug held loosely between his palms as he looked up at me.

"Don't give me that. The old 'the path we take leads to who we are.' I don't buy it, and neither do you, or you would have forgiven your father."

The first hardness I'd seen on his face filled it up then. Shuttered, battened down, closed up. "That's not my mistake. It's my father's, and I have a right to make judgments about what's okay and not okay."

"But we're supposed to forgive *ourselves* of everything, no matter how bad?"

"You've gotta live with what other people think, good or bad. But yeah, you have to get over anything you've done, as long as you've repented."

"But repentance means regret, Malachi. If you accept, that's not repentance."

He pursed his lips thoughtfully. "All right, you may have a point there."

My head abruptly started to hurt. "You know what? I really can't have some philosophical discussion at four thirty in the morning."

He lifted his chin in the direction of the driveway. "It's over anyway. There's your boy. I'll leave you to it."

I turned, forgetting Malachi in my relief. Relief that lasted exactly one half second, because it was a police car pulling up beside the bank of dark-green lilac bushes. I put the coffee down on the rail and walked around the porch to the front steps, where I stood, arms crossed, mouth hard, waiting.

A tall policeman, graying and weary by the set in his shoulders, nodded at me as he stepped out of the car, then reached to open the door to the back seat. Shane got out, stiff and thick limbed as Gumby, and I knew immediately that he wasn't just a little tipsy, the way he had been when I'd picked him up at jail, but something much worse.

The officer helped him, bracing Shane's elbow as he stumbled. I noticed my fingernails digging into the underside of my left arm and forced myself to let go, waiting for my son to lift that heavy head with its splendid fall of black hair so I could see his face. I wanted to see what drug got him, what chemical burned in his eyes.

In the split second before he did finally straighten, I saw Billy all too clearly, Billy as he'd been in those long days before he finally managed to OD on crack. Even then, I'd been amazed that the demon eating him alive had only made his beauty sharper, more brilliant—turned the cheekbones to high, sweeping shelves over which the blue eyes burned with the fever of addiction. He'd been like a candle that suddenly caught fire before it burned itself out.

Oh, God, please not Shane.

But if my stomach had been roiling with the possibility of drugs, it doubled over itself when Shane finally raised his head. I didn't see it all at once—it was hours before I truly clocked all the damage—but in that first instant, I saw the worst two marks: a lower lip so swollen he wouldn't speak well for days, and an eye as red as the dawn leaking upward in the east.

"A fight or an accident?" I asked, tumbling down the steps. My voice was oddly thin.

"Are you his mother?"

I nodded. Shane looked at me sullenly, or rather not-looked at me sullenly, his shoulder up defensively. My fingers itched to brush a heavy hank of hair away from that awful bruise, but I stuck them in my pocket.

"It was more of an ambush," the officer said. "He and his buddy were jumped." He scowled. "Everybody was ticketed for curfew violations, and that turned up his arrest the other week, but your boy here probably saved a little asshole's life by putting pressure on a knife wound."

Knives. A buzzing roared over my ears and departed. "Gangs?"

"Wannabes, anyway." The officer let go of Shane, and the boy staggered a little. "He refused treatment, so I brought him home, but I'd recommend a trip to the emergency room, ma'am." His eyes, the color of sherry in the dim light, were piercing. "And a good counseling program."

"Thank you." I reached for Shane, but he jerked away, nearly knocking himself down. I gave him that mother look—the fierce one—but it didn't work, since he still wouldn't meet my eyes. "You're right. Thank you," I said again.

He tipped his hat and drove off, leaving me and a swaying seventeen-year-old who was trying not to cry in the brightening dawn. "Pretty bad, was it?" I asked finally.

The tears fell then. Big and silent, rolling over his cheeks in mute distress. "Kid was only fourteen, maybe." The words came out broken, between what would be sobs in a girl. "Gashed . . . like a . . . fish."

"How did it happen?"

"I don't want to talk about it, okay?" He wiped a wrist over his cheek. "Not right now."

"All right." I wavered, over my head as always in emergencies. I don't know why that happens—the women in my family are usually good in a crisis. I never have been. My brain freezes. When Shane was six, he was playing Superman and jumped off the couch with a blanket around his shoulders and landed on his right wrist, breaking it neatly into a perfect Z. I'd been so zombied by the sight of it that I hadn't been able to move for a full five seconds, and then I'd promptly thrown up.

I was close to that now. "Uh, get in the car. I'll go get my keys."

"I'm okay."

"No. Sorry, you aren't. That lip needs a couple of stitches, or it'll be scarred the rest of your life."

He raised tender fingers to it. "Scarred?"

Ah, vanity, thy name is adolescence. "Yeah." I didn't wait for him to follow orders, just whirled around and started up the steps. I heard the door of the station wagon open and close as I flung the screen out of my way.

Inside in the dim foyer, smelling coffee and maybe bacon, I remembered the pies. The friggin' pies. I had to finish them this morn-ing and deliver or risk losing clients. Michael ordinarily pinch-hit for me in a situation like this—either he'd cook or drive Shane to the ER—but he'd had a very bad night, and nothing on earth would make me wake him.

For an instant, a feeling like despair crawled through me. It was too much—Michael and Shane and the big move and all the money strug-gles lately and my father being such a jerk. My own sexual frustration added to the mix did not help. I wanted to slide down the wall, curl up like a puppy, and wail.

But then it occurred to me that I had an entire family at my finger-tips now. Jordan, Jane, Jasmine. One of them would help. I picked up the phone, and stopped to consider who would mind least.

Malachi materialized in the doorway, wiping his hands on a dish towel. "Need something?"

He was awake and strong and healthy. Shane adored him. "Yeah, as a matter of fact, I do." I met his eyes dead on. "How are you in the emergency room? Shane got beat up pretty bad."

That slow, wicked grin. "I been there, once or twice, maybe."

"I'm *so* not surprised." I took a breath, feeling a little tension ease. "I'd take him, but I have to get those pies done."

"No problem."

My purse hung on the coat closet door, and I dug out my keys, wishing briefly and hopelessly for an insurance card. We'd had one for four entire years when Michael's restaurant was in full swing, and it had been a great source of peace of mind. I opened my wallet and found it contained all of thirty-six dollars, which I removed and put in his hand. "They'll have to bill me for the rest. You know the address?"

"Yeah." He touched my shoulder. "Don't fret too much, Mama. I got him covered."

"Thanks."

He started outside, then tossed the keys up in the air and turned around. "If I take the car, how are you going to deliver the pies?"

"Hmm. Good question." I glanced at the clock. "It's only five fif-teen. I don't have to start delivering until eight or nine. Surely you'll be back by then."

The dark, beautifully shaped eyebrows lifted skeptically. "Maybe emergency rooms are different around here, but it might be better safe than sorry."

The decision seemed way beyond me. Was it bad to send a banged-up kid on the back of a motorcycle to the ER with a guy he barely knew? All in pursuit of the all-mighty dollar? A good mother wouldn't work at a moment like this—she'd just do whatever she had to do. Make apologies.

But what about my work? I thought of the struggle—not just the need to feed myself, but the real need I felt to establish myself here with something I loved—and I wanted to cry again.

"Babe," Malachi said quietly, putting his hand on my arm. "The bike is perfectly safe. It'll take us maybe ten minutes to get there, and he'll be doped up by the time he gets out. It's not that big a deal."

I looked up into his face, seeing the kindness, the same goodness there that had drawn me so strongly to Michael. The Shaunnessey brothers might have their flaws, but there was a genuineness about them both that was rare these days. "Thanks. I'll save you a pie."

He put my keys in my hand. "That'd be great."

FROM THE FALCONI'S MENU:

Nana Lucy's Pork Chops in Red Sauce—A Falconi original. Two generous, thick chops slow-simmered in a richly spiced tomato and garlic sauce, served with our special-recipe stuffed shells. Mama mia! You'll write home about this one!

Chapter Nine

The pies were baked and loaded in the car by seven thirty, giving me plenty of time to swing by the hospital on my way in. There were six or seven others in the waiting room, some with very worried faces. The clerk behind the window was harried and curt when I asked about Shane. He wasn't in the ER at that moment, she said, but had been taken for x-rays to be sure there was no skull fracture.

"Skull fracture?"

She looked at me. "From the kicks." There was hostility in her tone, and I didn't understand it. "His hand, too, took a bruising."

Ah. The kids from the fight had probably all been brought here. Shane probably looked like the bad guy, since he'd been the white one in a neighborhood that pretty much wasn't. "What happened to the boy with the stab wound?" I asked, remembering.

"I'm not free to dispense that information."

With one last glance toward the doors into the treatment area, doors that were obviously not going to buzz to let me in, I said, "Thanks," and left.

For once the station wagon didn't scream on my rounds. Not once. It was as if the wagon knew I just couldn't stand that particular aggravation this morning, and the screaming might cost the car its life. It behaved admirably well at every stop, and everyone was pleased with the pie choice this time, except the harridan at a diner who had been after me for weeks to do some chocolate cream. I didn't like chocolate cream pie, for one thing, and while it was possible to transport Millionaire, which could be partially frozen, it was quite another game to try it with a delicate cream pie. I'd tried to placate her but had a sense that I was going to lose the account.

So be it. I stood behind my product, but life is too short to try to please the eternally displeased.

I left Falconi's for last. Since I'd started out early, I got there a little past nine, well before the waitstaff and bartenders arrived. Even better, my father's car was not in its usual place, and I remembered it was Friday, the day he went to the farmers' markets, driving in a 150-mile circle through the Arkansas Valley to the east. It wasn't strictly necessary, but he liked it, going out to haggle over flats of tomatoes, and onions fresh from the ground, and fresh basil tied in enormous hanks.

His absence meant I was free to go cry on the shoulders of whatever women happened to be in the kitchen today. I didn't know how badly I wanted it until it was in reach. There was no one in the dining room, only the sound of metal clanging and water running and voices coming out of the kitchen in the back.

I put the pies down on the bar, realizing this was the first time since I'd been home that I'd been here early enough to have the dining room to myself. When I was a kid, it had been the ultimate thrill to be in the place before or after hours—slipping out of the kitchen in the mornings to go color at one of the booths by myself, imagining it was mine, that the stools and the tables and the cocktail glasses all belonged to me, listening to the rise and fall of dish noises and voices from the kitchen and cars on the street outside. I reveled in the smell of garlic and bleach, the sticky, soapy smell of the bar.

I fell in love with the restaurant business at age three and have never gotten over it, that was the truth.

Remembering that little girl I'd been, I lifted the gate to the bar and went behind the counter to walk along the rubber matting that's supposed to save glasses and bartenders' feet. Touched the soda gun with its little buttons for cola and 7UP and soda water and tonic. Ran my hand over the bottles in front of the old, carved mirror behind the bar, put my finger in the bullet holes, *one-two-three*, that are gouged deep in the wood, the legacy of the darker side of the Sicilian world. Nobody ever talks about it—in fact, it's in very bad taste to do so—but I've seen pictures and newspaper clippings from those old days. I've heard the old men, when they were too far gone on homemade wine to care, tell stories about the Black Hand.

On the bar, the salt and pepper shakers were sitting on a tray, waiting to be wiped down and filled by the first waitress to come in. Idly, I looked in the cupboard beneath the far end of the bar and found the big containers of salt and pepper. Something else that's fun about restaurants—industrial sizes of ordinary items. Pickles and peppers in five-gallon plastic tubs, tomato paste in quarts, coffee by the case. Maybe these days everyone has seen them, thanks to Sam's Club and such places, but there was a time that knowing about them seemed like knowing a secret.

As I started filling the little crystal and silver shakers—sneezing as always when I got to the pepper—I listened to the voices spilling out of the kitchen. There was Nana Lucy, and then my mother, and my auntie Carol, their voices rising and falling in that singsong accent that's so peculiar to the area. I closed my eyes, just for a minute, to listen. The rise of inflection at the end of a sentence, making everything a question, the up-and-down, up-and-down cadence of it. You almost hear it in Brooklyn, but this is softer, not so guttural, both more Italian and more Spanish, spotted through with weird grammar borrowed from both languages and imposed on English.

I lost it, that accent. Not by accident. And I realized, standing there in the quiet, intimately familiar room that had belonged to my family for three generations, that Shane would never have it. Why did that feel so sad?

Someone in the kitchen laughed, a hoot of pure, females-only freedom, and it snared me. Putting down the pepper, I made my way to the doorway of the kitchen and stood there for a long minute, waiting for one of them to notice me. They were caught in their little world of spoons and big metal bowls. My aunt Carol, skinny and tiny in her plain white blouse, tended to the dishwasher, spraying stainless-steel bowls with water before fitting them into pale-green racks. Nana Lucy, her silvering hair caught in a net covered with tiny glinting beads in many colors, was perched on a stool by the butcher block counter scrubbed every night under her hawkish eye with bleach and three rinses of fresh water. Her gnarled hands were still as nimble as ever—I watched an onion disappear under the chop-chop-chop of her knife. My mother, feeding cheese to a grater mounted sturdily to the counter, had her hair bound under a bright-red scarf. She hated hairnets and would not wear one on a bet, so she'd purchased dozens and dozens of beautiful scarves in which she bound up her hair every day, like a Sikh. This one was silk, with a Celtic pattern on it. She was in the middle of a story.

"So Reenie goes up to her, right in front of the whole place, and says, that man is more trouble than he's worth. You could have him. And she dumps the pot in her lap, all over that dress." My mother's voice was already breaking at the end of the sentence, and she bent over, giggling helplessly. "And . . . then . . . no, wait, wait!" She held up a hand when Lucy would have interrupted. "She opened the salt and poured it on her hair!"

Carol, reddened hands on her waist, asked, "What did he do?"

"Oh, that's the best part: he jumped up from the table and ran after her, 'I'm sorry, I'm sorry.'"

Nana Lucy shook her head. "She deserved it." She caught sight of me. "Jewel! Is it that late already?"

"No, no. I'm early." I entered the enclave, put my hands on the smooth butcher block. "Who are you talking about?"

My mother's eyes crinkled prettily at the corner. "One of the waitresses—you know Reenie?—caught her husband out with his girl-friend last night. Your papa and I were there and knew the minute he walked in with her that there was gonna be trouble."

"He don't want to go nowhere," Nana said. "He loves those boys."

Carol made a sound, a softer, more sibilant "pish" that expressed derision as clearly as anything I'd ever heard. "Thieving woman," she said with a shake of her head. "Did she really think she'd take him?"

Mama and Nana nodded their satisfaction. It occurred to me that this was an almost Old World approach to the problems of infidelity. Startling, almost shocking, but also familiar.

"Need some help?" I asked.

"Sure. Chop the parsley if you want." My mother inclined her head toward a waiting bowl filled with ricotta. Stuffed shells were the special Friday nights. She looked at me. "You okay?"

I didn't answer. Didn't really need to. From a drawer, I took a paper chef's hat and stepped out into the hall to tuck my hair under it, then took a clean white apron from the stack by the door and tied it on. Ties to the back, loop back around to the front. Washing my hands, I said, "Can Shane come work here maybe?"

"What happened, baby?"

The parsley was waiting in a colander, and I took it out and found a knife. Putting the straight—never the curly—leaves flat on the wood, I said, "The cops brought him home this morning. He snuck out last night and tangled with a gang on the east side."

Identical shakes of the head, hands getting busier. I started chopping. "He has a split lip and a black eye and I don't know what else."

"Be good to keep him busy," Nana said, eyes on the onion she peeled. "Can he work?"

I turned the parsley, trimmed the stems, tossed out some squishy pieces. "He's good. He worked with me and Michael in New York all the time."

"He'd have to start with dishes." My mother stuck her hand into the pile of cheese, lifting it and loosening it before she cut another big hunk from the waiting wheel. "Nights, like everybody else."

"That would be good."

"How you gonna get him from here to there all the time?"

"I'll drive him. I don't mind." I positioned the deep-green herb under my knife and chopped as speedily as my grandmother, hoping she noticed. "He has his driver's license, but I don't trust him to come right home."

"Good idea." Nana Lucy shook her head. "Oh, Rose, remember your brother? Every week, it seemed like."

"I remember," Mama said.

"Which one?" I asked, thinking it was probably Silvio, who'd been dangerous and beautiful my whole life.

"Carlo," they said together. "He was a fighter, a lover," my grandmother added. "In trouble at school, with the priests, with the neighbors. Everywhere."

"Carlo?" I echoed, thinking of my plump, sober uncle in his neat blue suit. He'd sold cars for a long time, buying his wife a nice house in the tony suburb of El Camino. "He turned out okay, I guess."

Nana nodded. "They do, in the end. At least most of the time."

My mother looked at me. "Even you came home."

Even me. I lowered my eyes but could see only a blur of messy wet greens, and couldn't start chopping until my vision cleared. My mother put down her knife and came around the counter and put her arms around me. Her hands were cold, and I didn't care—I fell on her, putting my face against her neck, and I let go of the tears. "It was so terrible to see him like that! I brought him home because I didn't want that to happen, so maybe he could be safe, and it's not working and I don't know what to do, and I love him and he's good, but"—I took a breath—"his dad was a loser and Michael is dying and I'm an okay mom, but I can't be a dad. He needs a dad."

My mother stroked my hair and held me and let me cry. "He'll come to work here, Jewel. It'll be okay."

And I wondered, clinging to her in the restaurant kitchen where everything good and solid about me was born, how I could ever have left. How I'd ever believed Billy was worth it, that there could be anything better for me out there in the world than this right here. For a long, bitter moment, I regretted every choice I'd made when I was seventeen and filled with lust. I wanted my accent back, a good solid husband who'd have a potbelly by now, a handful of children who'd all been confirmed. It made me dizzy, I wanted it so much.

After a minute, my mom let me go, and I finished chopping the parsley, then went out and got the pies. Nana moaned, "Oh, the gingersnap crust!" She patted her bosom happily. I cut a generous slice for her, then hung up my apron and kissed them both. Michael was probably moving around by now, and maybe Shane would be home.

"Maybe he can start this weekend," my mother said. "How bad is he hurt?"

"I'll know more later. I'll call you."

~

The house was quiet when I walked in. Malachi's bike was parked in front of the porch, so they'd returned from the ER, but a quick tour showed both Michael and Malachi gone. Typical of men to leave a wounded kid alone. No mother on the planet would do that.

But, in good conscience, neither would Michael, so Shane probably looked worse than he was.

Michael's door at the top of the stairs was open, the bed neatly made. Someone had taken a shower recently; judging by the towels in a pile behind the bathtub, it was Shane. I peeked into his room and saw him deeply, soundly asleep. Snoring loudly. I breathed in the smell of the room, hoping for a ghostly hint of the boy he'd been, but there was only scrubbed male and an undernote of dirty socks. His shoulder, spotted with a little acne, stuck out of the covers; his big hand hung off the bed. Nope, the boy was gone—except in my memory. Quietly I closed the door.

A note in the kitchen, written in Malachi's sprawling hand, said they'd "Gone fishing. Be back later. Shane's fine. Three stitches, a bunch of bruises, no broken anything. He's had some good drugs, so he'll sleep long. Love, M."

The "love" made me smile. It wasn't a surprise, somehow.

Through the window, I saw that heat was rising across the fields, not yet shimmering, but starting to suck the gloss from the leaves on the trees. Probably hit a hundred today. I stepped out onto the back porch and wandered into the herb garden, surprised to have this unexpected time to do nothing at all.

Berlin trotted out behind me, and I bent over the cilantro, pinching some between my hands. The soapy scent eased the tight muscles in the back of my neck, and I drifted along the rows, thinking of a good hot salsa for this afternoon's dinner. Michael loved it, and fresh tomatoes were good for him.

At the end of the herb garden opened the big square of vegetables I'd planted. It was something I'd missed a lot during our years on the road, and when we'd settled in New York, I slept on a futon in the living room in a one-bedroom apartment in order to have access to a modest little balcony—actually not much more than an iron grate wide enough for one person—just so I could grow some fresh tomatoes and herbs.

This was so much better. The zucchini was doing its zucchini thing—sprawling wildly over everything. The day's squash blossoms were starting to close, but in the shadows beneath some of the bigger leaves, they still stretched open in glorious invitation. I knelt and fingered one of them, thinking in a vague way of a squash blossom and sun-dried tomato dish I'd created for Michael's restaurant. It had been one of the most popular things on the appetizer menu, and I thought about sharing it with my mother and grandmother, but knew they'd never add it to the Falconi's menu. No way. Too New World.

In between the squash and the straight rows of various kinds of tomatoes and peppers were nasturtiums and marigolds to keep away bugs, then another row of squash and pumpkins. The lettuce and broccoli had long since bolted, and I made a mental note to replant next week for a fall harvest of salads.

The hard, late July sun beat down on the part in my hair and on my arms, and I sleepily thought of the broad-brimmed straw hats that hung on hooks in the back room. I should have put one on to protect myself from wrinkles—you just have no idea how much damage this climate does to a woman's face—but it was too much trouble to go fetch one. I almost heard Sylvia tsk aloud.

Sylvia. I remembered summer mornings we'd spent on this very plot of land, companionably pulling weeds or harvesting herbs. I shadowed her constantly, coming out to the farm to spend the night whenever I could finagle it, which most summers was quite a bit. I loved getting away from the chaos of my house, my mother was more than happy to have one less kid to deal with, and Sylvia loved having a little helper who would do anything she asked without question. Even then, she'd been very old.

It was magic, being with Aunt Sylvia. She laced everything she did with stories of Sicily or herbal lore or tales of the saints—I had never met another person with her prodigious knowledge of the saints—and it seemed to me that she knew everything there was to know about everything. In the evenings, I sat on the porch and drew pictures of the cottonwoods with pastel crayons, and she praised every single one like it was a Monet.

Standing there with the smell of bruised marigolds wafting up from beneath Berlin's careless paws, I could almost see that girl I'd been. The ghost of her playing in the orchard, her hair falling upside down to brush the ground as she hung by her knees from a peach tree. Her shirt fell toward her neck, and she caught it, careful not to let her chest show.

She'd maybe been a little too thoughtful, that child, too questioning at times, but very happy. Eager to take her place in the world where she'd been born, delighted by the little things that made a woman's life, the simple calm chores of cooking and making beds, the more lush delights of gossip and canning, the delirious excitement of getting everything ready for a feast day—Christmas was good, but Saint Joseph's Day was even better.

Berlin snapped at a fly and vigorously scratched the spot where she'd been bitten. I kicked off my shoe and rubbed my toes along her side, wondering where that young girl had gone. How was it possible that she had turned into *me*?

My mother says I went boy crazy. But it wasn't that, exactly. I won't deny that hormones hit me hard, that I went to bed one night a little girl who liked pastel crayons and woke up the next morning completely and sizzlingly aware of every male on the planet. It seemed I couldn't *not* see them, that I hadn't noticed before how interesting they were, how decorative, how fascinating. How *different*.

But with that awareness came something more compelling. I saw men's lives.

The men in my world went places, and not just the market or church or a sister's house. They went out to drink with one another, sometimes for hours and hours, and they did not make explanations about the time when they came home. They went to the dog races with one another, and to garages to speak the mysterious language of engines. Men wrecked cars and had fistfights and were forgiven. They went to work and bowling. Men laughed loudly whenever they felt like it, not like the women who only really laughed with one another. And if somebody went "bad" for a while, carousing or drinking too much or having an affair, it was always a man who did it. Never a girl. Never, ever a woman.

Until me.

Even in my current melancholy mood, I had to smile. Somewhere between twelve and fifteen, I made up my mind that *this* girl was not going to be bound by those laws. No way.

I took up smoking. I learned to drink by stealing bottles of homemade muscatel from my uncle's basement—and trust me, that's the way to learn your limits real quick. I got on the Pill and learned to strut. I found out that a woman has an entirely different kind of power than men do.

In my auntie's backyard, I wandered over to the tomatoes. I'd picked over the Romas yesterday, but there was a bright, enormous Early Girl ready, and I plucked it, taking time to admire the plump, hot, red weight of it in my palm, thinking it really must have been a tomato Eve offered Adam in the Garden. So much more dangerous than apples.

Eve knew the power of temptation, knew that the right smile or a slant of the eyes or a certain loose-limbed gesture could command entire armies. Once I discovered that power, there had been nothing my parents could do, no matter how they punished or pleaded or dragged me to the priests. Their rules, their world had no meaning anymore. I got good grades and didn't screw up at school. I did my best to protect them from the reality of who I was becoming, but there was that little problem of the two degrees of separation in Pueblo—nothing ever stayed secret for long. I told myself I had to endure it only until I graduated from high school, and then I'd be gone. No way this little Podunk town was going to keep me.

So by the time I met Billy at the state fair the summer I was seventeen, my choices had already been made. I was just waiting for my ticket out.

Abruptly, I put an arm across my middle. Billy, Billy, Billy. The thought of him had been dogging me for days. The thought of all he'd been, all he'd destroyed—and how little I'd been able to do for him in the end. And in the attempt, I'd lost everything else, my father highest on the list.

"Jewel?" The word, coming into the deep stillness, made me jerk around hard enough that I almost dropped the tomato.

Malachi had come down the steps and well into the garden. "Hi," I said, and rubbed the tomato with the hem of my shirt. "Catch anything?"

"Not a nibble." He swished through the rows to me, his big feet in their work boots surprisingly graceful. Neither his silly fishing hat or vest dulled his sex god aura one tiny bit, and when he paused to toe a weed to death, he was about twenty times more alluring. Men who don't know a weed from a squash lose twenty points automatically in my book. "You all right?" he asked.

"Fine." I didn't look at him, concentrating instead on the tomato, pressing the firm, soft flesh with my thumb. "How's Michael?"

"Really tired." He sighed, squinted toward the horizon. "Maybe . . . uh, I don't know."

"What is it?"

He blinked at the horizon, hard. "Walking made him too tired to talk. Is that normal?"

I looked at the tomato, bit into it, took a long second to revel in the hot juice, mingled with seeds, in my mouth. "Mmm. Want one?"

"No thanks."

"Some days," I said, "he doesn't get up at all. Some days he'll walk all over and come home and cook for hours and be none the worse for the wear. It's all normal."

A mute guy-nod. He dropped into the easy squat of a man comfortable in the outdoors and tugged off his hat. The hard sunlight arced red and gold through his hair.

I put my hand on his shoulder in silent comfort and ate the tomato, giving him time. In the distance, the heat haze had formed, a shimmering, silvery plane over the sun-bleached grasses. It looked magical, like it could carry the weight of a couple of humans. I thought about wading into it, imagined it pooling around our ankles like water.

"How bad is it, Jewel? I mean, like how much time?" He lifted his head, put his hand around my wrist. "No bullshit."

I liked the feel of that hard, calloused palm, liked the size of it and the strength. "That's not really a question anyone can answer. People stay a long time right at this stage—months, years, even."

"But?"

"But anything could take him, at any minute." I shrugged. "A cold. A cut." I thought, but didn't say, *pneumonia, anemia, carcinomas, a bad hangnail.* So many things. The funny thing about AIDS was the way it made you appreciate the ordinary miracle of the body's usual line of defense.

I took a breath, couldn't quite meet that penetrating stare while I told the truth. "He started on antivirals pretty early, and they helped, but because he was on them for so long, the side effects started hitting him pretty hard. He's chosen to give up the drugs because they made him a lot sicker than the disease." I looked at the ground, noticing an ant laboring along with a crumb. "He's taking an aerosol antibiotic once a week, and drinking a tea that seems to help, and taking vitamins. That's it."

His thumb moved on my wrist, back and forth.

"So, really—" I began.

"I get it," he said gruffly. His mouth worked. "Gather ye rosebuds while ye may, right?"

A quick, sharp sting of tears made me blink. "Yeah."

He nodded, then took my hand and carried it to his mouth for a kiss of gratitude. I knew that was all it was—had been the recipient of just such a gesture from Michael a hundred times. It occurred to me that one parent or the other had been physically very affectionate—but I noticed the purse and clasp of his mouth, wanted to linger there with my palm against his lips, wanted to spread my fingers and touch the day-old whiskers on his jaw.

"Thank you," he said, then let me go. For a few minutes, he plucked weeds, then stood up. "I'm going to the market. You need anything?"

"Yes, please. Let me get a list." I paused, looking up at him. "I'm very glad you came, Malachi."

"Me too." He looked down at me, his eyes deep and unreadable, then touched my face. "I'm glad you've been there for him."

"Oh, no," I said. "It's always been Michael who was there for me."

I thought, just for a second, that he might bend down the rest of the way and kiss me. I had enough time to think what that might be like, how rich it would be to stand in the hot sun and kiss Malachi Shaunnessey ever so gently, how his hair would feel, brushing on my face, and what it would be like to feel his hands on me.

It was long, as such moments are sometimes, much longer in terms of everything that goes through your head. As if some ringmaster had suddenly pulled back the heavy curtains, I saw him very much more clearly. The alligator-wrestling angle was a front, a way to keep a very gentle heart safe from harm.

If he'd really been the kind of guy he pretended to be, he'd have heard of his brother's impending death and run off to the wildest outposts of civilization to drink himself senseless on the local brew and weep into wooden cups about his brother who was dying, far away.

Instead, here he was, doing what was important: being here. Spending time. Facing it.

It scared me to see that. Scared me a lot more than his big beautiful body or his delectable mouth or even his reliability around the house. At the exact instant he would have bent, I skittered away. "Let me get that list for you."

~

Shane stirred about three, groggy from painkillers and sleeping in a hot stuffy room. "I'm starving," he said, rubbing his tummy.

"Good. I've got a big dinner planned, but I could scramble you some eggs to tide you over." He settled heavily on the stool by the window and propped his elbows on the table. "That sound okay?"

"Yeah. Coffee, too?" he said hopefully.

"Sure." I pushed a pile of diced onion out of the way and wiped my hands on the towel tucked into the strings of my apron, all the while trying to assess his condition without staring. The eye was bad—as purple as pansies across the lid, which was less alarming than the red point of impact on his cheekbone. "How are you feeling?"

A shrug. His big fingers touched his stitched, swollen lip. "Okay."

I hummed along with the Boss as I got a fresh pot of coffee going, then filled a plastic bag with ice and gave it wordlessly to my man-child. He'd talk in his own time, and questions or nudgings from me would only make him retreat. I kept it matter of fact. "Head hurt?"

"A little." His eyes lowered, but he put the ice against his temple, wincing a little. "Not as bad as it did this morning."

"And no concussion or skull fracture?"

"No."

"Good." I took three eggs from the flat on the bottom shelf of the fridge and a bunch of chives from the crisper. No ham, but a few slices of bacon were left from yesterday's breakfast, and I took them out, too. Humming along with "Used Cars" to show I was perfectly content, I broke the eggs into a bowl.

"Why aren't you mad at me?" he asked finally.

"I am. But I think you got more punishment than you really deserved already. No point to me adding anything to it." Crumbling bacon into the bowl, I said, "You want to tell me how it happened? I don't see you as the type to rile up a gang."

"It wasn't like that." His thick hair fell forward, hiding his face for a minute. "We were just down there—where we were that one day it flooded at the two rivers?"

"The confluence?"

"Yeah. We went there. Just were sitting there on the hood when this kid comes running through the field, yelling and screaming about some girl, and before we knew it there were all these other guys coming after him." He scowled. "It gets kind of fuzzy right there, but the kid fell down, slammed right into my legs, and I bent down to help him, and—" He stopped. Peered at the counter, scratching with his thumbnail at an old scorch mark, went on. "He was covered with blood, and it got on my hands real bad until I could figure out where it was coming from, and then I could see it was bad. Really bad, so I put him down and put my hands on it, and then all these guys were yelling at us, telling us to give him up."

Carefully I didn't look at him and heated the cast-iron skillet. The butter sizzled into it, spitting and popping, and I poured in the eggs with their teeny tinge of green and chunks of bacon.

"I didn't really know what to do, Mom. I don't know how I could have let him go. He woulda died, I mean I know it, and even then, I was so scared when they were kicking me and hitting me that I was afraid it would be me who died if I didn't let him go, and I couldn't think what to do."

I closed my eyes against the vision of the cop coming to tell me my son was dead, beaten to death, instead of what I'd got. "You weren't fighting?"

"I swear I wasn't. I just held on to that kid, keeping my hand on that cut. He was young. Like maybe thirteen. Skinny and crying and choking."

"So when did the cops come?"

"Somebody must have called before, because they were all over the place really fast. Like three minutes after these guys showed up."

The eggs were finished, and I put them on a plate for him, found a napkin and a fork and put them beside the plate. I touched his arm. "I'm proud of you, Shane. You were really brave."

"No," he said, head bent. "I was scared."

"But you did the right thing anyway, and you saved somebody's life. That's a big deal, kiddo." I moved away to cover my emotion, picking up the skillet to take it to the sink. "A really big deal."

"Mom?"

I turned and saw what he needed. It was there in his big blue eyes, in the almost quiver of his lip, in the trembling of his hand that couldn't hold his fork. I went to him and put my arms around his shoulders and let him put his big head on my shoulder. That was all. He couldn't let himself sob—maybe he could do that later in the privacy of his room—but there were some tears. Mainly, it was the hard, deep hug of a boy who needed an anchor, and that was easy to give. So easy. I smelled his hair and rubbed my hand on his long, young spine, and eventually he took a deep breath. "Thanks," he said, and let me go.

ABE'S ASS-KICKIN' APPLE PIE

(written in pencil on a much-stained sheet of paper with MARION COR-RECTIONAL INSTITUTE across the top)

8 cups apples
¼ cup butter
½ cup brown sugar
¼ cup granulated sugar
2½ tbsp flour
1½ tsp cinnamon
pinch salt
1 tbsp lemon juice
1 tsp vanilla

Cut apples into thin slices. Cook in large pan with ½ cup water. While cooking, add butter. Mix sugars, flour, cinnamon, and salt in bowl. After apples are tender, add sugar mix, lemon juice, and vanilla to apples. Allow mix to simmer 10–12 minutes. Remove from stove and allow apples to cool. Once cool, place in pie crust. Be sure to slit holes in top crust. Sprinkle top with sugar if desired or mix 1 egg with 2 tablespoons water and brush over top crust. Also can add raisins to apple mix or mayhap nuts. Cook in oven 425 degrees for approx. fifty minutes.

For gingersnap crust:
2–3 cups crushed gingersnaps
¼ cup melted butter
½ cup sugar
1 tsp cinnamon
juice and grated zest of ½ lemon

Toss crumbs with melted butter. Combine sugar, cinnamon, lemon juice, and rind to form paste. Line bottom of dish with one-third of stuff. Add apples and cover with remaining crumbs (can put layer in middle if desired).

Chapter Ten

We ate late, just after sundown. The day had been miserably hot—I'd been right about the temperature, which had topped out at 102—and the weary swamp coolers, thumping all day in relentless, fatigued rhythm, upstairs and down, barely stirred the air. I made iced coffee and was glad for the cold, chunky salsa, the prosciutto ham and provolone cheese and sourdough bread. I'd brought a jar of cracked olives—my grandmother's specialty—home from the restaurant, and we ate the finger food while watching the moon rise. No one talked much. Michael was obviously not well, though he did his best to hide it. I saw the strain around his mouth, drawing up the flesh around his eyes, and I nudged him along when he appeared to be ready to stop eating. Over and over, just one more bite. An olive. A sliver of ham. Butter on the bread.

When we were close to finished, I jumped up. "Malachi, I forgot! I saved you a pie. Want some? Apple with some vanilla ice cream, maybe?"

"Sounds great."

"Michael?"

He wanted to please me, and it was his favorite. "A little. Not too much ice cream."

"Shane?"

Dully, he raised his head, and I saw that his left eyelid, which had dropped a little when he was tired since babyhood, was at half-mast. "Nah, thanks. I'm going to bed."

He helped me gather the plates and carry them to the kitchen, then went upstairs. A few minutes later, I heard the low strum of his bass coming through the floor and knew he'd be okay. The guitar was his way of unwinding, exploring his emotions. He used it like I used cooking.

I'd saved the most beautiful of the pies for Malachi, and admired it again as I cut pieces for all of us. I'd heard from my sister that my father had eaten nearly a whole one by himself the first time he sampled it, and the thought of thin, elegant Romeo eating so much at once gave me a smile as I carried the warmed slices out to the porch.

"What's that about?" Michael asked.

"My dad. He loves this pie. I was just wondering if he ate a whole one this time, too."

The smell of cinnamon and the undernote of gingersnaps filled my nose, and I took a bite, closing my eyes to fully appreciate the full depth of the flavors, mingling, swirling, dancing—

"What *is* this?" Malachi cried.

I started to say, "It's—"

He jumped up and spat over the rail. Stunned, I wondered if he was allergic to one of the ingredients, and felt immediately guilty.

But anger, like vibrato, moved in his low, dark voice. "Michael."

Mildly, he looked up. "It's just a pie. Sit down and eat. Or don't." He lifted a forkful to his mouth.

"It's Dad's pie."

"Yeah. I've been cooking it for years."

Malachi picked up the plate and, using the fork with a gesture that was plainly, deeply contemptuous, sent the pie sailing over the rail. Berlin, always ready, jumped up and trotted out into the yard to see what had been discarded.

Shocked by both his rudeness and the surprising evidence of very deep anger in what seemed to be such a mellow personality, I only stared at him. His body was rigid with fury, his shoulders straight and hard, his body poised for a fight. "Michael!" he said again.

Laconically, Michael said, "Jewel, I must apologize for my brother's rudeness. He's not usually such a redneck jerk, but every now and again, it does come through." He gave his brother a hard look, the one that would have had Shane hanging his head in a half second. It took about three seconds to work on Malachi. Then his body sagged, and he put his hands on his hips. Red flushed his cheekbones.

"My brother is right," he said after a minute. He looked at Michael with shame. "You were generous and kind, and I just acted the fool. I'm sorry."

"It's all right," I said. "Come sit down. You can have ice cream by itself if you want."

"I don't know," Michael drawled. "Anybody who acts like that oughta have to give up dessert for a day."

Malachi didn't grin. Didn't even smile. His jaw worked, showing a long cord in his neck. "Don't, Michael."

"Gotta get over it someday."

"No," Malachi said precisely. "I don't." With a shake of his head, he lifted a hand, started to say something, then just waved it all away. Without another word, he stalked off, those hard-heeled boots making a deep thump on the wooden floor of the porch. He disappeared, and a minute later we heard the bike start up and roar away.

"Uh, you wanna tell me what just happened?" I asked.

"Let him tell you when he gets back." He pushed the plate back, most of the pie still in a lump of ice cream. There was a fragility about his shoulders as he did it, a release of whatever he'd been hanging on to in Malachi's presence. "I think I need you to help me upstairs."

"Oh, God, Michael!" I jumped up and rounded the table, seeing now the melting in him as he let go, a crumpling like the Wicked Witch of the West. "You can't keep hiding how sick you are from him." Scolding to hide my fear, I bent and let him loop his long, stick-thin arm around my neck. "If you don't let him know—"

It took a lot for him to stand up, a fierce kind of concentration that's hard to describe unless you've seen it. Just so much effort to stand straight. A host of possibilities rushed through my imagination—explanations that didn't all lead to a crisis. "I'm going to call Jordan," I said.

"No." The word was breathless, but fierce. "Maybe tomorrow."

Tomorrow. That was his way of dealing with all of this. Tomorrow he'd be better. Tomorrow he'd take action. Without a word, I helped him inside, and we took the stairs one agonizing step at a time, pausing often to let him catch his breath. Sweat poured from him, and there was the sour, hot smell of illness in it.

You might think it was wrong of me, not to call my sister or take him to the hospital no matter what he thought, but I'd promised him early on that I'd never force him to do anything against his wishes. He made me swear on my mother, which is not something I'd ever do, but a blood oath was not a possibility, considering.

I got him to bed and took off his shoes. He was so weary he collapsed against the pillows like a puppet, angles of elbows and shoulders falling akimbo. I turned on the lamp and brushed a lock of hair from his face, seeing the blue veins below his skin. His breath was raspy but steady, and I took the big metal washbasin from the stand, filled it with warm water that smelled of lavender, and carried it back into the room. Through the walls pulsed the low sound of Shane's guitar, a heartbeat kind of sound, threaded through with Shane's lovely tenor as he worked out a song.

Michael smiled. "He's damned good."

"Yeah." I undressed him matter-of-factly, then washed him the way Jordan had showed me—it had been very awkward at first, bathing him like a child on those increasingly less rare times he found it beyond him—but it pleased me now to be able to do it. He hated the faintly metallic scent of illness on his body so much. "You want something else to put on?" I asked, giving him the painkiller I knew he'd need.

"Just the bedspread." His voice was thin, and as I bent close to cover him, he picked up my hand and kissed it almost exactly as Malachi had this morning. "Night."

"Who kissed your hand that way, Michael? Your mom or your dad?"

He opened his eyes, the blue a deep ocean shade that revealed nothing. "Ask Malachi."

I turned off the lamp and headed back downstairs to clean the kitchen. At the foot of the steps, I heard the bike, the sound of it mellow against the crickets whirring now as if in benediction. I went outside to gather the rest of the dishes. Big fat candles burned against the night, and I bent to blow them out.

"Oh, darlin'!" Malachi said from the other side of the rail. "Don't you know you never blow out a candle? You'll blow away all your good luck."

"Ah! Well, that explains a lot." I picked up the plates, scraping and stacking them. "I am sorry about the pie, Malachi. I didn't know it would upset you."

"It's not your fault." He leaned his arms over the rail, his mouth sad. He stared at the plates with a faraway expression. "Can you leave all that? Come for a ride?"

"Why don't you help me carry it in, and then we'll go? Otherwise we'll have five million ants in the morning."

"I can do that." We piled them in the sink and turned off the light. I didn't even need a little jean jacket, the night was so warm.

"Any place you like particularly?" he asked. "Somewhere there might be water to overlook?"

"I can think of a few."

He handed me a helmet and paused, frowning. "Why the change of heart?"

"What do you mean?"

"I thought I'd have to coax you to get you to take a ride. You're always so . . . wary."

"Am I?"

His eyes narrowed faintly, and I saw him look at my mouth, then back up to my eyes. The thrum of sexual energy crept into the moment, and we stood there thinking of kisses, wondering about what this little ride might mean. He nodded. "You are."

I tugged on the helmet. "Sometimes I just get tired of thinking."

He made a soft, slightly bitter noise. "Amen, sister. Let's ride."

And we did. Rode into the night with a soft, warm wind spinning around our limbs. I twisted my hair into a long cord and tucked it into the front of my shirt, anchored by my bra, and leaned into him without apology, putting my arms around his hard, long waist, my torso against his back, my thighs tight against the outside of his. I closed my eyes and let go, let go of me, of Shane and Michael and the past, and lived just in the moment. This moment, with a big healthy man on a motorcycle, a man I liked even if he was a sex god, a man—it surprised me a little—with whom I felt comfortable just being myself. It was kind of a rarity these days.

I directed him to a bluff to the west of town that looked out over the reservoir. Houses had cluttered the mesa considerably since I'd last been out here, and we had to drive a lot farther than I anticipated to get away from them, but finally he parked, and we got off the bike to settle on a cluster of boulders overlooking a steep drop to the water below.

"This is great," Malachi said, shoving his fingers through his hair.

I nodded, admiring the shimmer of lights, white and red and green, that marked the city. "I used to come out here when I first started driving."

"Alone?"

"Sometimes." I grinned. "Sometimes not."

"Good girl."

"Now that's where you're wrong, Mr. Shaunnessey. Not a good-girl bone in this entire body."

He chuckled. "That's what I like about you, Jewel."

I tucked my feet closer to my body and wrapped my arms around my knees. "Yeah, men always like that slut thing."

"That's not what I meant." He inclined his head. "I meant that you think you're this bad girl, and you're not. Not at all."

"Obviously you haven't seen enough of my résumé."

"I know what I see." He touched me then, just a single finger running down the outside of my arm, and it did what he intended for it to—gave me a rippling little shudder down my spine. "You're the one they turn to."

I looked at him, narrowing my eyes. "What does that mean?"

He put his hand on my knee, safe but ready, and I didn't do anything to dislodge it. "You take care of them, all of them. Even your dad, you know, you give him all this space, and I don't know that he really deserves it. But you do it with everybody."

I shrugged a little, daring to put my fingers on his wrist, looking at that strong, square joint to avoid his eyes. "That's just what families do. Big families."

"Who takes care of you?"

"I do!" I looked up to show I meant it and I liked it that way.

"Do you ever let anybody else do it?"

For a minute, I considered the question, rubbing my thumb across the silky hair on his upper arm. "Yeah, I do. My mom, my sisters. Even you—you're very reliable in a weird kind of way."

A flash of teeth. "That I am, ma'am." He turned my hand over, put our palms together. "That's not the same, though. You take little bits and pieces of help because you have so much going on all the time that you can't turn down a little help now and again, but mainly you do it yourself."

"What's wrong with that?" I asked with some irritation. "You can count on yourself."

"Everybody needs somebody, Jewel. Michael's as independent as you are, and where would he be without you?"

I made a noise of exasperation. "Where are we going with this, Malachi? I thought we came out here just to enjoy the peace and quiet." I shifted away, not harshly, just enough to give him the message. "Let's not do the analyze-Jewel thing tonight, okay? I've had enough of it the past three months to last me the rest of my life."

"Fair enough." He dropped his hand, gracefully accepting my limits. Idly, he picked up a stone and tossed it over the edge of the bluff.

Quiet enveloped us. Not a tense silence or one filled with things we wanted to say and couldn't. I admired the lights and the water and the sky, thinking no thoughts. "Tell me about your job," I invited after a while. "You're a tour guide or something?"

"Adventure tours."

I smiled, thinking of the image I'd carried of him for so long— drinking alligator blood and running with the bulls. "Very Hemingway."

He chuckled, such a low, rich, deep sound on the night, like black mink. "Maybe. But it's a good old time."

I thought of bugs and snakes and bad weather. "The Amazon doesn't sound like that much fun to me."

"It is, though. You like rivers, honey; that's some amazing river. She's powerful and mysterious and full of surprises." His voice, always heavily tinged with his southern childhood, slowed as if he had sunk into the current of a lazy river. "Sometimes, in the morning, I'd be the first one up, and it was like being the original man, squatting there at the bank, hearing all those strange birds and seeing them flash through the trees—" He made a clicking sound.

"I don't like bugs."

"Well, then, I'd take you on another sort of adventure." He narrowed his eyes and studied me, pursing his lips. "The Alps. You're a sturdy girl. You'd handle that pretty well."

"Sturdy. Oh, thank you so much."

He winked and lightly pinched the underside of my arm. "I like it. Healthy. You'd hike all day and be ready to party at nightfall."

I gave him a reluctant smile, liking that vision of myself quite a bit, and he knew it. "Italian Alps, though. My ancestors would insist."

"No problem. I love Italy."

"Have you been all over the world?"

He shifted, propping his knee up. "Not everywhere. It's a pretty big world, after all. Haven't made it to China or India yet. Keep meaning to get to Egypt to see the Nile—I mean, if you like rivers, that'd be one to see."

"Oh, yeah. And the pyramids. I'd love to see how the pyramids align with the stars. I'm a sucker for ancient Egypt."

"Good reason for me to think of an Egyptian adventure then. You can be the first one to sign on."

"It's a deal." I grinned at him. "First I want to hike the Alps, though."

"Got it."

"Did you really run with the bulls in Spain?"

An abashed little smile, oddly appealing. "How'd you hear about that?"

"Michael bragged about it to anyone who would listen for three seconds."

"Yeah?" A soft chuckle. "Cool. I did, actually." He cleared his throat ruefully. "Once was enough."

"Scare you?"

"Yep."

I thought about the film clips I'd seen, the bulls and the boys and men, the noise of it. Then I thought again of the Alps, cool and high and somehow serene. Malachi drifted off in his own thoughts.

After a long time, he said, "I really am sorry I was such an ass about the pie, Jewel. Took me by surprise, that's all, and I just—" He shrugged, then looked at me. "Reacted."

"You don't have to keep apologizing. I have a few father issues going myself."

"You know about my dad?" He brushed invisible sand off the boulder. "What he did?"

"Some of it. Probably most of it. Killed your mother's lover when she was in bed with him, right? And you were there when it happened." A little kid.

A nod. "Michael wants me to just put it down, you know? But he wasn't there." A pause. "He wasn't there."

"Did you know he's out of prison?"

He shook his head. "Michael knows better than to say anything to me about him. Most of the time." With a hint of that earlier violence, he threw another stone. "Makes no difference to me anyway."

"I can see that."

"What? You think it should?"

I smiled. "Not at all. That's your choice."

"I can't forgive him." A bitterness around his mouth again, but something else, too, that wrapped tight little threads around my heart. "I don't think about it every day anymore, but if I let down my guard, that nightmare is in my head—bam. Just like that. Still, after all these years."

"It might be kind of an obvious question, but have you ever had any counseling? Not every kid in the world witnesses a murder, after all."

He snorted. "No way." He gave an involuntary little shudder. "Can't see putting all my little pains and secrets out on some table for somebody to pick through."

"I'm here. You could tell me."

"I could." He turned his head, looking at me in the dark, and I waited. His eyes glittered a little. "I'd rather kiss you."

I shook my head, smiling. "I'm too old for you."

"Old?" He said the word in a satisfyingly astonished way. "Is that what you've been thinking?"

Trouble. "What do you mean, what I've been thinking?"

He slid that tongue out and touched his bottom lip. I rolled my eyes, but it was only to cover the fact that it really did hit me hard. I wanted that tongue in a big way. He shifted toward me, leaning his arm into mine, undeterred. "I don't usually have quite so much trouble figuring out a woman's defense when it's quite clear that she wants my body. You had to have some reason."

"Want your body? Whatever gave you that idea?"

"Oh, every little thing."

I raised my eyebrows in skeptical fashion, trying desperately to hang on to my dignity, though we both knew that it was hopeless already.

"Come here, sugar," he said, and before I could really do anything to stop it, he'd plucked me up like I weighed no more than a gumdrop and put me in his lap. "Quit lying."

He put his hands on my face and tilted my head and kissed me. I smelled cinnamon on his upper lip, and tasted vanilla on the lower, and there wasn't really anything I wanted to do to stop it. It was a long, slow kiss—just lips and little whispers of tongue behind it, long and slow and gentle, not the onslaught I'd thought he'd be capable of.

Tasting that sweetness, feeling his giant hands on my face, it occurred to me that he could be dangerous. In the flavors of that kiss were hints of lust, generous helpings of sex god, but the main note was need, that bewildered loneliness of a man in search of harbor.

I'd tasted that need on the mouths of men a dozen times. And I knew that I'd give him more than he asked for. But the danger I felt in his arms came from what he did to me. On one level, my blood pressure was building, and I could feel that heat rising in my limbs, and I liked the feel of his body and the fit of his mouth, but all the while that was going on, there was something else. The more he kissed me, the more peaceful I felt. Everything about my life that worried me or hurt me or scared me just slid away as I touched him. Peace came into my shoulders, spread through my chest. He felt like the smell of supper and the sound of Mass, like walking into my own bedroom and closing the door.

But that part didn't matter. For now, for this minute under a dark and peaceful sky, he was feeling the same ease I was, and we could share it for as long as we needed to. I opened my mouth to let the boy who'd been betrayed by his father come in and taste refuge. I put my arms around his neck. Slowly, he crept into the safety, his hands slipping down my neck, over my shoulders, his touch like rain.

His fingers slid under the straps of my tank top, and I shifted to make it easy for him to push them off my shoulders, a shiver of anticipation moving in me. It was so easy to pull my arms free of the fabric, easier still to help him by managing the clasp of my bra for him. So easy to cry out softly when his big hands reached up to cup my breasts, lift them with an accompanying sound of pleasure.

I had to stop kissing him for one minute. It felt so good, I wanted to feel only that—Malachi's work-hardened big hands moving on my bare breasts. I closed my eyes. "Oh, I've been wanting that."

"Yeah," he whispered, and pressed his face down into the excessive flesh. I could feel the trembling in both of us. I unbuttoned his shirt and pushed it off his shoulders so that we could rub together, flesh to flesh, as we kissed some more. Rubbing, sinuous motions of hips, of tongues, of hands.

"You feel so good," he said roughly, his mouth against my shoulder, my neck. He put his hands around my bottom and pulled me closer to his erection, and I wiggled closer still, laughing softly against his mouth as we settled into a satisfying bump and grind, slow and easy and sexy.

It went on for a long time, kissing in the soft night, our shirtless torsos brushed by wind and night and hands, our mouths dipping and swaying and tangling. Giving and receiving the relief of no thought. It wasn't even urgent to take off the rest of our clothes, somehow.

But there did come a point when it was time to quit. I lifted my head. "That's probably enough."

He had astonishing lashes, I noticed, long and thick and heavy. They cast a shadow over his irises, making it hard to read the expression there. I noticed his mouth instead, shiny with all the kissing. My chin felt faintly abraded from the growth of unshaved beard. He swallowed, his palms moving on my ribs. "Yeah. Probably time."

"Feel better?"

"Much. You?"

I lifted one shoulder like it was nothing. "Maybe."

It made him grin, eased the possibility of awkwardness between us now that we had to slide our bodies apart and put everything back together. I realized he would now see my belly, and the idea made me linger a little.

Maybe that was why I lifted my hands to his face, clasping his cheeks in my palms the way he'd done me. I thought of a dozen things I could say, but I kissed him instead. Softly. My lips to his, gentle as a promise.

And who knows why these things happen. But after all those other kisses, this one changed everything. A pierced sound whispered between his lips, and I caught it in my throat as I traced the shape of his big, hard-angled face. Touched his cheekbones and his jaw, even the corner of his eyes where the lashes tickled my ring finger. And because I was looking at him, I saw the ripple of pain he tried to hide, that man thing that was so poignant, that need and wish and sorrow and longing—all of it inexpressible—and my heart was snared. They don't know, these guys, how to go anywhere but into a woman's arms when they hurt, and they think they like breasts and bellies and sex so much because they have no idea how to get what they need any other way.

And it's so easy to give them that union. Open your arms, kiss their lips, and invite them in. And when they're lying there, spent, head against your neck or breasts, they can breathe for a few minutes. That's why they fall asleep so fast after sex. They're so exhausted by the time they get there that there's no other option.

But Malachi had a whole lot more going on—or maybe it was scary for him, too. He put his hands on my arms, almost urgently. "Let's stop now, Jewel," he said gruffly. "We've stopped thinking long enough."

I smiled. "Okay." With an ease I might not have felt a few minutes before, I slid off his lap and sighed. "If you say so." In the quiet loneliness of night and prairie, I turned my back and reached for the moon, letting starlight and the mother light fall on my naked breasts.

Malachi tossed my shirt at me. It landed across my shoulders, and I laughed as I pulled it down virtuously over my chest before I turned. "Close your eyes."

He inclined his head, tugging his shirt on his arms. "Won't matter. It's branded, right here." He tapped his temple.

"Okay," I said with a shrug, and put on my own shirt. Braless. I have to admit I knew he'd like the feeling of that against his back on the way home, and as if he knew that, he grinned.

"Aren't you forgetting something?"

"Nope."

He retrieved the lost bra from the ground. "I'll just hang on to this then, if you don't mind."

"Feel free."

In unspoken agreement, we turned toward the bike and put on our helmets. He tucked my bra into his shirt with a wink, then sobered. Putting his palm to my cheek, he said, very seriously, "Thank you, Jewel."

I lifted up on my toes to press one last kiss to his gorgeous mouth. "Trust me, the pleasure was all mine."

FROM A HOMILY BY POPE SAINT GREGORY THE GREAT:

Devotional Readings: Mary Magdalene

We should reflect on Mary's attitude and the great love she felt for Christ; for though the disciples had left the tomb, she remained. She was still seeking the one she had not found, and while she sought, she wept; burning with the fire of love, she longed for him who she thought had been taken away. And so it happened that the woman who stayed behind to seek Christ was the only one to see him. For perseverance is essential to any good deed, as the voice of truth tells us: "Whoever perseveres to the end will be saved."

Chapter Eleven

The sisters were all summoned to be fitted for bridesmaid dresses. I drove to Jordan's on a Saturday morning a week after that wild night with Malachi, glad of the respite from what had been an absolutely grueling seven days.

The way Jordan's house sat on the hill, it caught all the best morning sunlight. Cottonwood leaves glittered, moving on some unseen breeze, and the freshly mudded adobe glowed a rosy gold. I parked, seeing Jordan and Henry walking up from the river, a basket in Jordan's hand. Their heads were close, both of them with long curls, slim shoulders, she just a little shorter than he and much rounder. It was the sweet peace of a couple in harmony, headed for the house they'd filled with their love, and I envied them fiercely for a minute. A long, solid relationship like that was rare. They had been married nearly eighteen years, and it appeared they would not have children—not for lack of trying—and yet they still walked like that in the morning, heads bent together in quiet accord.

I'd never known that with Billy, not really. We'd shared a powerful connection, but it had never been particularly peaceful. Not this kind of shimmering, soft quiet. Billy hadn't had a quiet spot in his entire being.

Jordan saw the car and waved. I got out, waving back.

"Morning!" Henry called, tossing long curls out of his face. "Have breakfast with us?" He held up a handful of what looked like river grasses, and I wasn't sure, even looking at his face, if he was kidding.

"Wild rice?" I guessed.

Henry grinned, winking at Jordan. "No, mon, a peace offering for the gods, you know."

I laughed, glancing at my watch. "We don't have time. Mama will have a fit if we're late."

Jordan kissed him easily and ambled over. "You ready for this?"

I rolled my eyes. "Ugh. Have you heard anything?"

"Jane has good taste," she said hopefully. "Maybe it won't be too awful."

I lifted an eyebrow. "Have you ever seen a *good* bridesmaid's dress?"

"Um. No." We both climbed in the car. "So," she said. "I hear Shane's doing good at the restaurant. Charming everybody, working his way right up to prep cook in a single week."

"He loves it. If I'd realized, I would have done this ages ago." I backed out and headed to town. "He's even asked if he could borrow the car to take a girl to the movies next weekend. He's got Sunday night off."

"Ooh, what girl? Somebody from the restaurant?"

"A busgirl. I haven't met her—her name is Alicia."

Jordan gave an earthy roll of laughter. "Oh, are you in trouble."

"Why?"

"Oh, God, Jewel, she's like a tiny Aphrodite—stacked and perfect and full of fire. And she knows exactly what she wants."

"Sounds like Shane's type, all right."

"And how's every other thing?" She lifted a brow, and although I wasn't absolutely sure she meant Malachi, that was who was in my mind. Heat touched my ears.

I hadn't seen much of him since that night on the bluff. There didn't seem to be a rush to get to the next step, although we both knew it was coming. And I held the anticipation of it close, a secret to take out and examine late at night when I knew he was asleep in the room down the hall.

But life, this week, had intervened. I landed the Dante Alighieri catering gig and spent whatever extra time I had meeting with the organizers of a fundraising event. Shane started work at the restaurant and had to be ferried back and forth. And Michael . . . well, Michael wasn't thriving. He'd had one little crisis after another, and it looked like he was stable again, but it had been exhausting. I'd peeked in on him this morning, and his color had been a little hectic, his skin dry, but when I frowned over him, he insisted he was fine.

Relatively speaking, anyway.

"Jewel?" Jordan asked.

"Everything is fine." I pulled up in front of the bridal shop and parked, counting the cars of everyone else. My mother's Chrysler, Jane's neat Toyota, Jasmine's SUV, several others that looked like young women's cars that I assumed belonged to the four of Jane's friends who would complete the wedding party. "Ready, Freddie?" I said with a sigh.

"As I'll ever be. How fat do you think we'll look?"

"I will look very fat. You will be fine."

"God, please not pastels."

A gaggle of voices met us as we went in—I could hear Nana Lucy's above everyone else's, scolding the dressmaker for something. My mother was trying, as usual, to be peacemaker. Jane and Jasmine stood to one side, biting their lips. I looked at Jordan. "This looks promising."

"Oh, very."

It wasn't until I rounded the last stand of evening gowns that I saw my father sitting with my uncle Carlo in a pair of easy chairs. My heart slammed hard into my ribs, and I was already turning around unconsciously, unaware of it until Jordan grabbed my sleeve. "You're gonna have to learn to deal with him sooner or later. The family isn't *that* big."

Don't ask me why a pair of middle-aged men would find this entire process so interesting, but it was often the case in my family that a couple of guys came along to anything big like this. Maybe they wanted their opinions heard, they wanted the women to look good, but not too good. I never asked, but I probably should have been prepared for the possibility.

It wasn't like he paid any attention to me anyway. My grandmother got her way about whatever had incensed her—she usually did. I gathered it had something to do with hemming. Not the length, but the method of stitches in the bridal gown, which Jane was wearing right then.

She spied me, and a happy bright smile spread over her face, that youthful glow that made me feel decrepit. "Jewel!" She spread her arms. "What do you think?"

"You are so gorgeous," I said sincerely. It was a confection of a dress—billions of yards of soft lace and seed pearls, a nipped waist and deep bodice that displayed her dewy, youthful bosom perfectly, finished off with a long, long train that would delight the youngest cousins who would get to carry it up the aisle. "It's fit for a queen. Turn around." I sighed happily. "Oh, you're going to be the most beautiful bride that ever was."

"Thank you!" She hugged me happily.

Then the matron of the shop brought out the bridesmaids' dresses. I managed to keep my face straight, but Jordan was straight-up horrified. They were not only pastel, but pastel *satin* in baby bootie colors—all those nauseatingly adorable shades. The style was simple enough, but simple in that way that would make my arms look fat, emphasize the belly that had grown way too old for these kinds of dresses.

"Jane!" Jordan protested. "I'm going to look like a cow in that!"

"Oh, no! No, you won't!" She was busy passing out candy colors to various people. Her little skinny friends, not a single one bigger than a size eight, were cooing happily. Sure, sure. They had a chance to show off collarbones and delicate wrists. My collarbone had disappeared years before, and I didn't hold out any hope that it would appear between now and the wedding.

Still, it was Jane's day, and I gave Jordan a hard look, accepting my pastel-purple dress with a bright smile. Lavender was an awful shade for my skin. The only one worse was yellow, which was what Jordan pulled. She gave me a sickly smile. Our coloring was almost identical.

We were directed to various dressing rooms, and Jordan nabbed one with a full door. Inside, she bent over, crushing the satin against her body. "Oh, God, Jewel!" she squeaked, her eyebrows to the middle of her forehead, her eyes dancing with something close to hysterical laughter.

I could feel it coming and put my hand to my mouth. "Don't." I deliberately turned away to put the dress on.

"What size did she get me?" Jordan muttered. I glanced over my shoulder to see her flipping the tag. She made a noise. "Twelve. A size twelve with this chest. Right."

"Just put it on. That's what we're here for, to get the sizing right."

"The wedding is in two weeks. How can they fix this much?" Swishes and grunts as she struggled into it. With a sinking heart, I pulled mine up, seeing the bulges below the waist, the not-straight line of waist to hip to thigh, trying not to see the way my skin turned a particularly exciting shade of sulfur against the purple.

"Ugh," Jordan said. With a sigh, she said, "Zip me up, will you?"

She pushed her hair out of the way, and I tugged up the zipper, only having to force it for a little way right through the waist. "Oh, it's going to be fine, Jordan. They'll just have to let it out a little right here." I pulled her hair up into a loose mass. "Your back and shoulders will look great."

She stared balefully into the mirror. "Yeah, Jewel. Just keep talking."

"Girls!" my grandmother said, rapping sharply at the door. "Hurry up. We ain't got all day."

I turned to let Jordan zip me. And this zipper took a little more forcing. I could hear it groaning from my waist all the way up to the top, no matter how I sucked in my stomach. In the ever-so-flattering, fluorescent-lit mirror, I watched the satin stretch like an overextended balloon over my flesh. Jordan snorted when I turned around.

"Oh, thanks!" I said, but she looked at me, and I looked at her. She pressed her lips together, sucking them in until there was no lip skin visible. Her nostrils quivered. I tried to resist, but the edge of a snicker slipped out before I could catch it.

Her figure was quite perfectly voluptuous in normal clothes, but the yellow satin made her look like an aging barroom whore. I could barely breathe, and when I did, about half of my breasts fell out of the top of the dress, where they'd been squeezed up. I felt my lip shivering and pointed my finger at her sternly. "Don't do it, Jordan. I mean it. I can't breathe, much less laugh."

"You look"—she covered her mouth and opened her eyes wide, blinking rapidly—"like Miss Piggy!"

My own nostrils flared, and I felt the tickle at the back of my throat, that tickle that meant she was about to send me over the edge. Determined to resist, I stuck my piggy nose up in the air and regally headed for the door, satin swishing around my legs. Behind me, the danger quaked in Jordan, and I knew one of us had to keep it together. I didn't dare look at her as we two cows—pigs?—trundled out, trussed hard into our satin.

The others looked fine, of course, just as bridesmaids should—thus the *maids* part of the word—even Jasmine with her skinny little butt, but there was no mistaking the horror on the younger girls' faces when they saw us. Nor the shock of my mother and grandmother when they saw my tattoo, bold as sex itself, a scarlet rose across my right breast.

Jordan, half in humiliation, half in the helpless hilarity that had infected her the minute we stepped into that dressing room with pastel satin, said in a choked voice, "Miss Piggy with a tattoo!"

As long as I didn't look at her, I'd be okay. I swallowed several times, struggling to keep my mouth in a straight line, but it wiggled in spite of me. The tickle in the back of my throat danced upward into my sinuses, forward to my lips. Little tears blurred my vision.

But Jordan was already gone. "Well, gee, Piggy," she said in a Kermit-like voice, laughter welling up like water starting to trickle from a split pipe. "It's you . . . it's you . . . it's *you*!"

The pipe burst. She bent over, roaring, shaking, and squealing, and I was lost. I put a hand on my chest to keep my boobs from falling out completely and let 'er rip. We've always done this to each other, fallen at stressful or bewildered or ordinary moments into our own little World o' Hilarity, and once we get going, there's no stopping it. People stand to one side, giving us polite half smiles as we feed each other a word, a gesture, a glance to fuel the giggles.

And I could see them all, the entire circle of women and girls looking on like we'd gone over the edge as we hooted and strangled and clung to each other. I'd just about get it together, then I'd see the edge of her belly pushing at the skirt, or she'd do another Kermit imitation, and we'd be off again. I could feel the irritation of my mother tugging at us, feel Jane's complete bewilderment, and caught Jasmine rolling her eyes, but none of them could halt us until it was finished, and that was that.

We both knew it was inappropriate in this circumstance, and we were trying to get it together when the side seam in my dress gave way with a very loud sound, and the pair of us collapsed completely, falling to the floor in absolutely lost, hysterical giggling, our eyes running with tears, cheeks aching. "I'm sorry, Jane," I choked out. "It was too tight."

"Migg Pissy," Jordan said, strangled, and at that, Jane started to laugh, too.

"Get up!" The voice was a roar. "Right now! You are making fools of yourselves and everyone here."

My father, of course. And although it had been a long time, a very, very long time, since any of us had heard that particular tone, it worked as well as it ever had. Like a bucket of cold water, it splashed down over the heat of our giggles and chastened us.

I realized I still had my hand over my chest, that the split seam had left a good six inches of my side exposed, and my rose tattoo was as shocking a thing as any woman had ever done in this family. When I looked up, it seemed they were all staring right at me, disgust on their faces.

My father was looking down at us with fury and a hard mouth. Some demon—or maybe a goddess—pulled out a whip and cracked it. I lowered my hands, tossed back my hair, and met his eyes. "You like the tattoo, Papa?"

And for one long minute, his black eyes burned into mine. He saw me, really looked at me, eye to eye, for the first time in twenty years. It was electric, that second, and long, and I dared to let hope swell in my heart for the space of it. Anger I could manage. Anger could be changed. Distrust, even disgust, or whatever emotion he chose to focus on me would be okay. I'd take it.

But then he cursed, low in Italian, too profane even to write down, and turned his face away, making a sign against the evil eye.

I jumped to my feet, that demon running amok now for sure. "You can't ignore me forever, Papa! I live here. I'm part of this family!" Tears, and not giggle tears, welled up in my eyes as he kept walking. And in a fit of temper I reached down and grabbed a loose shoe, hauling back my arm to throw it at his smoothly combed head.

Jordan grabbed my wrist in time, and I only threw a curse after him, as profane as the one he'd spit on the ground. I spit, too, and my hair stuck to my cheeks, to those humiliating tears.

He walked out. I didn't watch his entire progress. I turned my back so that I wouldn't, but I heard the door swing shut behind him, ringing the little bell hanging from the ceiling, and it was the only sound in the entire shop.

A dozen women stood still as ice, not a whisper of satin or a heavy breath, just frozen, dead silence, but beneath it I felt their emotional hands reaching for me, covering the tear in my dress, patting my hair into place. The younger ones sent their spirits to fret over me, their physical eyes big and round and hoping never to be me, vowing right then to be good mothers and wives so they'd never have to be shunned like that in public.

I tossed my head, feeling my earrings swing cold against my neck. "To hell with him," I said. "Sorry, Nana. And sorry to you, Jane. I didn't mean to cause a scene on your big day."

It broke the silence, and they all started talking, whispering like birds, chirping to one another and to me and to the world, spirits lifted by the drama or maybe just their beauty. Only my mother, mouth hard and flat, said nothing. Her large dark eyes burned into mine, censorious and pitying at once. She shook her head.

I lifted my chin and met that pitying gaze with all the force in my body. Quietly, June Cleaver said in my head, *You're gonna want your mother one of these days.*

Madonna argued, *Well, maybe she needs to get a clue about how to love her daughter.*

She does, June said. *That's why she's disappointed.*

To hell with her then, too, Madonna said. And I tossed my head and turned away at the dressmaker's urging, feeling sick to my stomach and brutalized, but determined not to show it for a second.

"Jewel."

Malachi's voice, coming from behind me, so dark and thick and heavy, was utterly out of place. Great. I took a breath, feeling too much chest falling over the top of the stupid dress, the air on my side. Thought about the whole scene just past that he'd surely witnessed.

And my father had seen him, too.

Squaring my shoulders, I turned. And stilled. He looked liked a giant from outer space in that little shop, his angles and darkness and maleness exaggerated by the loops of pale-green lace hung on the wall behind him. His black boots had left dusty marks across the thick white carpet; his hands—usually so competent—hung loosely at his sides.

His face, I finally noticed, was ashen. "What?" I cried, forgetting the dress and fight and everything else. "Michael?"

"I had to take him to the hospital. He's there now."

"Oh, no, Malachi! The hospital? Why?"

"He couldn't breathe—couldn't talk. I called the ambulance." He shifted, kicking one foot out in an attempt to keep the emotions from turning to something horrifying like tears. "He has pneumonia."

I closed my eyes, reaching for the calm and good grace necessary right now. "Did he have to have the respirator?"

"Yeah."

I glanced at Jordan sympathetically gripping her skirts. She knew what I knew, that Michael had strict do-not-resuscitate orders, which meant he didn't want the breathing help. He had probably been extremely confused by the time they got him there and been unable to express his true wishes, and Malachi, wanting to do the right thing, had done exactly the wrong one.

But there was no need to go into that right this minute. "I'll get changed," I said, and bustled with as much dignity as possible toward the dressing room, stopping to kiss Jane. "Sorry, babe. Maybe you oughta drop me from the bridesmaid list."

"Not a chance." She looked at the woman orchestrating everything. "Can you get the new dresses here FedEx by Monday?"

The woman scowled. "Impossible."

My grandmother drew herself up—all four feet eleven inches of her, her black eyes turning venomous—and the woman added hastily, "Tuesday. I'll get on the phone right now. You'll have to give me some secondary color choices, though."

"That's fine." Jane grasped my elbows and kissed my cheek.

My mother, relieved to have some practical problem to solve, said, "Make them both fourteens, and I'll do any alterations. They have too much bosom for these dresses."

Her practicality was somehow reassuring. "Thanks, Mama."

She patted my arm, inclined her head toward the door. "Go. We'll take care of it."

"Shane—"

"We'll take care of him."

So I scrambled into my jeans and normal shirt, tossed Jordan the keys to the station wagon, and hurried out to join Malachi, who was pacing in the parking lot like a restless wolf, back and forth. When he saw me, he stopped, right where he was in a pillar of sunlight breaking between two buildings, and I saw him struggling for control. Without a word, I went to him and put my arms around him, knowing he'd collapse around me for a minute, and he did. I felt the subterranean trembling in his limbs, his terror, his howling grief and worry, and I just held him tight.

After a minute, he took a breath and released me. "Thanks."

I nodded, rubbing his upper arm a minute. He took the helmets from their hooks under the seat and gave me one. It was only as I climbed on the back of the bike behind him that I saw my father sternly staring off to the west, ignoring me.

Perfect.

I ignored him, too, and we pulled out to go to Michael.

FROM THE MUSIC BOX MENU:

In the Mood Temptation Torte—A concoction only Andre and Michael could have dreamed up together: rich, dark chocolate cake layered with thick cream and ripe cherries, drizzled with a sinfully delicious chocolate syrup. If this won't seal the seduction, honey, nothin' can.

Chapter Twelve

It wasn't until we were in the hushed corridor of the ICU waiting room that all of it hit me. The scene with my father—how could I have been so stupid?—the ride on the bike with Malachi's tight, tense body in front of me, feeling like it wasn't flesh at all but shaped out of metal or rock, ungiving and absolutely rigid.

And Michael. Of course. But it was harder to let that in, the reality of the fact that he was back in the hospital, the place he most adamantly did not want to be, and worse, hooked to a respirator to help him breathe. I'd learned, though, how that knowledge would come. It would slide in sideways, like fog creeping under a door. By morning, I'd know it. Feel it. The awful reality that he was back in the hospital, edging closer to that—

I sucked in a breath.

For now, I could concentrate on Malachi. In the somehow cold light of the clean, quiet room, he was motion and movement, caged restlessness. He didn't have to say it, standing up for the fourth time to pace forward to the windows that overlooked the hallway beyond, but he did. "I hate hospitals."

I only nodded, thinking with a little tear across my heart of Michael, tethered to machines he hated, machines that would save his life one more time.

One more time.

I said, "Did you see Shane at the house?"

Malachi paced two steps. Shoved a hand in his back pocket. Peered at an exit sign. "He called. Said he'll be late."

"Malachi, come sit down."

He flipped a glance over his shoulder. Flight yearning showed along his jaw, and I could see the green light of the Amazon flickering beneath the surface of his dark eyes, the glaciers of the Alps, the yellow waters of the Nile. Anywhere, anywhere, but this small, airless, and sterile room.

"Please," I said, and held out my hand. "I want to talk to you for a minute."

He moved like a Transformer in a cartoon Shane used to watch, each step thick and heavy in his boots, his knees bending like they were badly oiled. He ignored my hand and sprawled into a chair, leaving one empty between us, then dropped his head into his hands. "What?"

Even there, with so much else that needed my attention, I noticed things about him. The vein up his arm drew my palm. I fit my heart line to the river below his flesh.

"Your brother has a DNR order, Malachi. Do you know what that is?"

A scowl. "I watch television."

I waited, my hand right where it needed to be. Finally he said, "Do not resuscitate." His neck softened first, bent and let his big head drop. His hair swayed down over his face. "He is going to be so pissed off at me."

I laughed at the tone—the misery of a kid who has a big punishment waiting. "Yep."

It startled him. "Why are you laughing?"

"Well, it isn't funny, but the tone of your voice—"

"I don't have anybody else, Jewel," he said gruffly. "Nobody. It's always been just me and him."

Not quite true. I said nothing but held the name of his father in my mind—Abe, Abe, Abe. He must not have heard me, though, because he just stared at the steel toes of his boots with misery.

"If he could," I said, "Michael would stay, just for you."

"How can you be so calm about it?" he asked fiercely. "Just let him go?"

"What else is there to do?"

"Fight."

"It's not my fight. Yours, either."

"Then I'll make him fight."

"He's done fighting, Malachi. He's tired."

"He's only forty-five years old!"

I thought of the sun lines around Michael's eyes, the fan of them radiating out into that magnificence of cheekbones, the bones that had made him so photogenic. I thought of the deep, clear blue of his irises when he had asked me to promise I would not make him suffer as Andre had.

Malachi stared at me with narrowed eyes, the adventurer's battle arm ready to chop down trees and wade through snake-infested waters, but absolutely helpless against the minute invaders that would take his brother. I gave him Michael's words to me. "They've been really great years."

Malachi, the alligator-wrestling tough guy and ladies' man, bent his head and wept.

I moved over to the next chair so I could reach him and put my arms around his massive shoulders and let him cry into my neck. "I don't want him to go," he said.

"Me, either, hon." I took a long breath, pushed the reality away. "Me, either."

~

They let us in to see him for five minutes at a time, one person, once every hour. I lied and told the hospital personnel that he was my brother so that all the others in my family who would eventually show up could take their turn with him. It was the least I could do to make up for my scene at the bridal shop—let everyone who loved Michael sit with him a few minutes each day. I gave up my time for them. Nana Lucy would need to pray. My mother would need to pet his brow and talk to him sensibly. Jordan would need to check his meds and make sure they had everything right. She would cry when she saw the respirator, as I had.

When my five minutes came, late in the day, I paused outside the door and took a long, centering breath, trying to shape myself into a canvas upon which Michael could paint anything he needed. I opened the heavy door and went into the dim, windowless room. The only sound was the whoosh of the respirator. A light blinked on the IV machine.

His body was so thin now that he looked like a skeleton beneath the covers, his collarbone peeking out of the top of the blue-printed cotton gown. For Andre, we'd made some in brilliant peacock shades because he'd been so offended by the sheer ugliness of hospital attire. The memory made me smile as I walked quietly to the side of the bed, loath to disturb him if he was honestly sleeping.

But he raised his fingers in a feeble wave as I came up, and his eyes were open. "Hi," I said, smiling. I brushed his hair off his brow and rested my palm on his forehead. "Sorry, buddy."

A shake of his head—*don't go there.* His lids closed and I felt the ease that my hand lent him. I started to sing quietly, a lullaby in Italian, and brushed his hair back gently, over and over, the same gesture I used to use to lull Shane to sleep.

It's so hard to know, these days, how to deal with someone who is dying. It used to be normal—even I remember the elderly aunts and grandfathers who were cared for in the houses in my neighborhood, the odd younger person nursed through the end stages of cancer or some other shocking thing that drained them of life too early. It wasn't exactly common, but it wasn't uncommon, either. In those days, before everyone was whisked off to the hospital for the end, the women in my world took care of the dying as a matter of course. I rode with them as they took meals to shut-ins, as they scrubbed kitchen floors or vacuumed carpets for the ill one. I heard my grandmother reading to my grandfather every day, heard her whistling even when I spied her wiping away a tear when she bathed him.

So easy. Michael's hands were cold and dry, and I took a bottle of lotion from the table and warmed the lotion in my palms, then rubbed it on his knuckles and wrists, smoothing lotion all the way up to his elbows. When the nurse signaled that my time was over, I kissed his fingers. "Love you," I said with a smile. "I'll break you outta here just as soon as possible."

He couldn't smile around the tube in his throat, but he blinked, once, slowly. *Yeah.*

~

Malachi found me in the kitchen at nine. The sun had set. Shane was at the restaurant and would spend the night with Jane at her new house. Shane and Jane. The names ran through my head in a litany, rhyming absurdly.

"Jewel," Malachi said.

I glanced up from the masa in my bowl. "Hi. How you doing?"

He ambled in, a little frown of puzzlement between his brows. "Who's coming over?"

I looked up. Twenty-seven peach pies cooled in the racks by the wall—ready for delivery Monday morning. A lasagna with spinach and pasta reclined on the counter next to chocolate chip cookies stacked in golden mountains. On the stove bubbled the meat and chili mixture that would go inside the tamales—I'd had to make a special trip for the corn husks—and the candle I bought in that aisle was burning in the window, a rose-scented Virgen de Guadalupe.

"I can't help it," I said. Wiping my hands on my very grimy apron, I reached for a glass of water and took a long drink. "Help yourself. I didn't really make dinner."

He frowned a little, then shook his head and reached for the burner knobs on the stove. "Why don't you go take a shower and we'll go out?"

"Out?"

A restless shrug. "Yeah." His eyes, clear and dark and unapologetic, met mine. "I think I'd like to get drunk. You need it even more than I do."

"Hmm." I weighed the danger of being alone and drinking with Malachi against the idea of trying to go to sleep naturally whenever I finally exhausted myself here. A cord of tension throbbed in my neck, and I blinked. "I don't know."

He took the spoon out of my hand. Put it gently in the sink, turned off another burner. "You're wiped out, babe."

"Yeah." I let my hands fall to my sides. "All right. Let me put the food away and catch a quick shower."

"I'll take care of the food." He untied the knot of my apron at my belly button, and somehow I didn't mind the forwardness. For once, maybe it would be okay to let someone else take care of things. "Anything particular I need to know?"

"Stuff that spoils goes in the fridge." I pulled the apron off over my head. "There's Tupperware above the sink for the rest of it."

"All right." He moved with the solid sureness of a man unafraid of anything—even a woman's kitchen—and opened the cupboard, cocking his head over his shoulder. "I can handle it, Jewel, I swear."

It didn't take long, since I decided not to wash my hair. A quick shower to wash away the flour and food, the grime of a long, bad day. I tossed through my drawers for something wicked, setting my jaw as I thought of my father this morning and my mother's scolding eyes, and to spite them, I chose a black leotard with a deliciously low-cut neckline. To hide the extra flesh around my middle, I put on a vest that didn't interfere with the view of my tattoo. The hair came down, long tangles of curls. In the low light, I could be mistaken for five years younger—which was enough for me just then. The final touch was a wicked little necklace Michael had given me for Christmas one year, a delicate string of dark metal and red beads that brought just the right attention to my cleavage.

That's my girl, Madonna said.

June had nothing to offer. It was probably too slutty for her to bear.

When I came back down, Malachi was standing on the porch. He didn't say anything about my appearance, which did slightly hurt my feelings, just handed me the helmet, and we rode out. I directed him to a cozy bar not far away, one that was agreeably dark and had an excellent jukebox for the stray couple who wanted to dance. Some nights there were a lot. Some not so many.

We settled in a booth near the single pool table and the small dance floor close to it, and ordered from the weary young woman. "Tequila, gold," Malachi said. "Straight up, with a beer chaser."

I raised my eyebrows. "Serious about this, aren't you?" To the waitress I said, "Tomato beer for me."

"Bottle or draw? We got Miller Lite and Bud on tap."

"Draw. Bud, I guess." Live dangerously—a few extra calories wouldn't kill me this once.

"I'm sorely disappointed, Ms. Sabatino," Malachi drawled. "Not even one shot?"

"Trust me, me and tequila don't mix."

The waitress looked at me. "Make it two shots," Malachi said before I could shake my head.

I asked her to change a five-dollar bill to quarters for me, and while we were waiting for our drinks, I went to the jukebox and started punching in numbers, guessing Malachi the southern boy would like Thorogood and Lynyrd Skynyrd, of which there was a plentiful selection. He joined me, nodded at the selections, and added some Springsteen. And then some Bonnie Raitt, who sliced and diced my heart every time with that earthy voice of hers. "You don't strike me as the sort to enjoy Bonnie Raitt," I said with a little smile to cover my dismay. I didn't want him to like her. It gave him another layer, and he already had more than I wished to acknowledge. So much easier if he was just unapologetically a bad boy doomed to a life wrestling alligators.

"I'm full of surprises, sugar." He winked, naturally, and showed that long line of smile.

I shook my head with amusement and peered down at the song list. Five more. I flipped the page and made a soft sound of surprise. "They have 'Longing for You'!" I punched the numbers in delight. It had been Michael's best work—both in lyrics and voice—and had been the only truly successful song he and Billy ever recorded.

"Man," Malachi said, "I haven't heard that in so long." He chose a couple more songs, then took my hand to lead me back to the table. I saw women noticing him, shooting me small, quickly hidden glances of envy, and grinned. "What?" he asked.

"It really is pleasant to appear in public with a sex god."

He laughed. The first time all day. "We do have our uses." We reached the table, and he held on to me for a minute, putting our bodies close as he looked down at me. "I guess you'd know a little about that."

"About sex gods?"

"About being one."

I pulled away lightly. "That would be goddess, wouldn't it?"

Another small laugh, one that felt like a victory, as he slid in across from me. He blinked and pushed hair off his face. "I remember when I thought Michael was going to be really, really famous," he said.

"Me too." I thought of those old days, the promise that gilded every moment, the slightly drunken sense of possibility that somehow just never materialized. They'd had decent sales on the first album, and the second had produced "Longing for You," the song that made Michael's voice famous, but the third bombed.

"You were there, Jewel. What do you think happened?"

"Oh, I know exactly what happened—Michael fell in love with Andre, and love was more important to him than fame."

Malachi's face went very sober. "Did he make the right choice, Jewel?" The words rasped out, raw and rumbling.

The waitress brought our drinks, and he paid for them, and I thought back. "Did you ever meet Andre?" I asked. There was a little tightness in my throat, and I took a sip of tomato beer to cool it.

"What the hell is that?"

I grinned, familiar now with the horror the concoction roused in the uninitiated. "Beer and tomato juice. It's a fixture here—I was amazed when I left town and bartenders had no idea what I meant when I ordered a red beer."

He made a face, and I pushed the glass across the table. "C'mon, alligator man, try the local cuisine."

Suspiciously, he lifted it and took a ginger sip. His mouth turned down at the corners, and he took another. "Not bad." Another. "In fact, it's excellent."

I motioned to the waitress to bring a glass of tomato juice for us to share. She nodded, and Malachi gave me back my glass. "So," I asked, "did you ever meet Andre?"

"Once, a long time ago. I'm ashamed to say I wasn't always real comfortable with it, you know, the gay thing." He shifted, turned his shot glass in a perfect circle on the table. "I don't know why I thought it mattered. And it wasn't like he was ever"—a distant little frown—"anything *but* gay. He loved Andre, I know."

"Yeah." I thought about it. "When I think of what might have been if Michael had stayed in the music business, I remember a trip we all made to Ireland when Shane was about ten. Billy was . . . on his way down, and we didn't see him too often, but the money was good in the restaurant, and I was doing well with a catering firm. Andre booked the trip for all of us, as a surprise for Michael's birthday, because he always wanted to go to Ireland so bad, you know?"

Malachi nodded.

"Andre did everything, and he found ways to make it particularly good for each one of us. We stayed in these wonderful little bed-and-breakfasts all over, which was for himself, because he was just besotted with the service industry on all levels. Blarney Castle for Shane, who was madly in love with the idea of kissing the stone. An evening at a music festival for Michael." I felt the sudden pierce of tears in my throat and had to stop.

"What was yours?"

"A goddess site." Considering all that had happened today, the memory was somehow a cheering one. It was hard to imagine a goddess of any ilk caving in to family pressure to behave herself. I looked at Malachi earnestly. "What I remember, though, is the way they looked at each other when Michael saw the shores of Ireland the first time. We flew into London, then took a ferry across the channel, so Michael could arrive as his ancestors left. He just stood at the rails and stared at that green, green coast, and Andre was beside him, and—" I had to blink hard, pause for a minute. I could see them so clearly in memory, Andre as dapper and dashing as Armand Assante, dark and swarthy and clean, Michael taller and leaner and stronger, so blond. Both of them healthy then.

Malachi touched my hand.

I brushed away an escaped tear. "Anyway, he was just a very special person. He and Michael were as in love as any couple I've ever known. They made each other happy. I don't think music would have given Michael what Andre gave."

He looked at me. AIDS hung between us, loud and unspoken. I shook my head. "It could have been either one of them, Malachi. It's not like Michael was celibate before they met. And it doesn't do any good to blame. It's an awful disease, and no one should have to go that way."

He bowed his head, ashamed. "Yeah. I just hate it. You want to blame something, anything. Make it right."

"I know."

"Whew." He inhaled, exhaled hard, blowing it all out. "What a day, huh?"

It rippled through me, the thorns of Michael and my father sticking in my heart. "Yeah." I scowled at him. "We don't have to talk about it, do we?"

A glitter in those bright eyes. "Not much of it. But I'm dying to know what your father said to you in Italian."

"You were there for the whole thing?"

"Even more than that." With a quick, focused gesture, he slung back the shot and slammed the glass back down. "I saw you and Jordan come out of the dressing room."

"Oh, brother." I winced, then grabbed my shot and drank it. Coughing a little, I sipped some cooling beer, then said, "So you got the entire show of my humiliation."

"I'd say yeah. My favorite part was the tattoo." He chuckled. "You'd have thought you'd come out of there without your clothes on."

I laughed, touching the scarlet rose. "Like it?"

"It does draw the eye." He sipped some beer. "Wasn't quite as popular with the family, was it?"

"I'm the family slut. They'd be disappointed if I didn't uphold my role."

"Now." He leaned forward. Hair fell down and touched his cheekbone. "Why do you keep doing that?"

"What do you mean?"

"Playing like you're so bad for them, when you know you aren't."

A wash of heat touched my face, and I looked away. "You just get stuck, you know? The good sister, the bad sister, the smart sister, the pretty one." A shrug. "You and Michael only had to divide things in half. We had to go a little farther to define ourselves."

"Just doesn't seem like you're enjoying yourself much. Why keep it up?"

I drew a line in the condensation on the outside of my glass. "I *don't* want it anymore," I said quietly. "I'm tired of it. I want my father to see me as I am, as a normal woman. I want my mother to stop looking at me like I'm going to screw up every second. I want my grandmother to stop telling me I'm too old to leave my hair down." My heart started to pound. "I want them all just to see that I made some mistakes, but

I wouldn't trade it. How could I? If I hadn't walked the road I did, I'd be someone else entirely."

There was something very gentle in his smile just then, a smile that softened those Hershey's chocolate eyes and made him look—oh, I don't know—normal. "Exactly."

"Maybe I don't even believe all that."

"Why not?"

"What are you, my psychotherapist? It's not exactly like you've dealt with your issues any better."

"We're not talking about me right now."

"And I don't want to talk about me."

"So just tell me what your father said in Italian."

A slow, agonizing twist of the knife. "It's a really nasty version of *whore*." Quickly I lifted my bottle and took a long drink. "Bad to the Bone" came on the jukebox, and I said, "You want to dance?"

"Not right this minute."

It annoyed me. "Well, then we get to turn the table, Mr. Psychoanalyst. You get to talk about why you won't forgive your father after twenty-five years. He made a mistake. One mistake, and he lost everything over it."

"He killed somebody, Jewel. That's a lot worse than one thing."

"He killed your mother's lover in a jealous rage." Inclining my head, I added, "And I believe it was because he caught her in bed with the man. Not exactly an uncommon story, you know?"

"He did it with his ten-year-old son in the house, sleeping in the other room!"

"And your mother brought her lover home to that same sleeping ten-year-old."

"Not the same."

"I think it is." The waitress stopped at our table, and Malachi motioned for two more shots. I said, "Your parents were so caught up in the drama between the two of them that they let their children down. Over and over."

"Does Michael actually talk about this shit?"

"Malachi, we've hardly spent a day apart since the night I met him. I was bound to hear the story sooner or later."

He bowed his head. Turned the beer bottle in circles, one exact rotation at a time.

"What do you remember?" I asked. Then, because the shutters went up, added, "About your parents, I mean."

He took a breath, wiped his face, looked over my shoulder at the past. "Fights. They fought so much. And then everything would be cool for a long time, usually after we moved to a new place. Then they'd start in on each other again."

"Was it your mother who was a toucher?"

"A toucher?"

"Yeah, you know, both you and Michael have that habit of touching people. I figured your mother was demonstrative like that."

A strange expression touched his mouth, made his eyes distant for a moment. "Maybe it was Michael, then. My mother wasn't like that, really."

"This gesture," I said, and picked up his hand and kissed the back of it.

A soft smile broke over his mouth. "Now *that* was my mama. She also used to sing all the time."

"That's where Michael got it."

"I think so."

As if it had been conjured by our discussion, "Longing for You" poured into the room. Michael's voice, low and slow and rich, flowed into the room. I saw heads lift and faces smile as they remembered the song, or maybe just something they'd been doing when they heard it. It was a love song with heart, one of yearning and hope and with a deeply erotic undertone of need. A pair of lovers moved out onto the dance floor to do an easy bump and grind to it, gazing into each other's eyes. "I think he'd just met Andre when he wrote this."

Malachi's eyes twinkled. "Think they'd mind if they knew?"

"Some of them." I smiled.

He stood up. "I'll dance to this one."

I hesitated for a minute, not sure I could really manage this particular song and Malachi's long, taut body all at once. He tipped his head, a dare, and held out that big hand. I stood up and let him draw me onto the little area cleared in front of the jukebox.

So big. It was a rare pleasure to stand chest to chest with a man, hip to hip, and still have him be taller, tall enough I had to tip my chin up to look at him when he pulled our bodies close, his thigh boldly sliding between mine, his hand on the small of my back, his eyes glittering with sex and the need to forget the rest of the world.

"Take me away, darlin'," he said.

I closed my eyes and let it go—let it all go—thought only about his hands and his hips moving so close, and the promise of his mouth. He smelled like Safeguard and shaving cream and Tide, and beneath my hands, the muscles of his back moved in sleek shifts.

After a long time, I looked up to find him looking down at me. There was no shift in his expression, no smile this time or light word, just his big dark eyes steadily looking down at me. And for some reason it was okay to look back, to just let him see inside as we swayed. I had enough sense to think, *Uh-oh,* but not enough to do anything about it.

Right there in front of the whole bar, he bent and kissed me. "Wish I'd met you about fifteen years ago," he said.

I heard the part he didn't say, *Before it was too late.* I only smiled and took his hand, and we walked back to the table.

FROM THE *PUEBLO CHIEFTAN* WEDNESDAY FOOD SECTION:

Our Favorite Entries in the Annual Chili and Frijole Festival

#7 Crudo Chili—The only true cure for a hangover. Fresh Pueblo, jalapeño, and serrano chilies stewed with pork, onions, and tomatoes. Hot enough to blister the roof of your mouth, but it works. Not that we know from personal experience or anything.

Chapter Thirteen

The night was soft when we tumbled out of the bar. "I don't think either of us is in a state to drive," I said.

"Nope," he agreed cheerfully. "What do you suggest, darlin'?"

Overhead the stars stretched—endlessly both tempting and unattainable. I tilted my head back to admire them and nearly overbalanced. There'd been a *lot* of tequila. "I dunno. A cab?" But this made me laugh. At two a.m., no cabs would really be available.

"Too far to walk."

"Yep." I peered up at the sky. "Is that Jupiter, d'you think?"

"Which one?"

I pointed, but my finger wouldn't stay. I dropped my hand. "The bright big one."

"Mmm." He tucked his hands in his pockets, three sheets to the wind if balance was any indication. "Maybe."

Three guys came out, and I recognized one of them. "George! Is that you?"

He brightened, which was good for my ego. "Jewel? I saw you dancing."

"And you didn't come over to say hello?"

He put a hand on his chest. "And get my heart broken?"

I laughed and moved closer. "Are you anywhere close to sober, George? And driving?"

"A little." He looked at Malachi. "You need a ride, maybe?"

"We both do." I tossed my head and pulled away the long strands of curls that fell in my eyes, knowing even as I did it that he wasn't looking at my hair at all, but the shift of breasts that came with that gesture. "Not far—'member my aunt Sylvia's place?"

"Oh, sure, sure." His hand moved on my back, a hand that said he wished he didn't have to bring Malachi, too. "I'll drive you."

His buddy rode in the front, and they got into a mysterious discussion of engines. Malachi took up 67 percent of the available back seat with his thighs and shoulders and arms, and it was only that much because he was trying to give me enough room. Streetlights flashed through the window, showing me glimpses of his big hand resting on his thigh. Flash-flash-flash. Each flash gave me something new—the taut, iron-hard appearance of that thigh. The curl of his long thumb. The half-moon shape of his nails. Really good hands, good wrists. Not too much hair on the forearm.

Giddy with dancing and liquor, I wasn't careful about keeping to my space. There was just too much to like about sprawling. I leaned my head back, not daring to close my eyes, and rested my hands on my belly. Our thighs touched. My elbow bumped his, and he moved, trying to give me room, then let it settle back and slide close.

And then I did close my eyes, risking the swirl of too much drink in order to immerse in the steam coming out of our pores. Mine. His. Desire was thick and sweet between us, basting my flesh and sinking into my muscles and swelling up basic molecules. I loved the smell of him—that scent of sun and wind, mixed with a little hot man and smoke from the bar and a hint of caramel.

He moved his arm again, a slow drag against my breast, and his hand fell on my thigh, rubbed down to my knee. I turned my head, smiling a little, and he was looking down at me with an odd expression, not what I expected. "What?" I asked with a smile.

He flickered a glance toward the front seat and back to me, shaking his head.

It might have been all of six or seven minutes before we got there. A long time to feel your blood boiling for a particular man who really does have exactly what you want. It was way past the point of simple want, at least on my part. Every cell in my body hummed with it. Lust, I thought with a hint of laughter and turned my face into my hair. Just call it lust and be done.

George leaned around. "Take care, Jewel."

I waited for Malachi to unfold his long self. Put my hand on George's arm. "Thank you."

"Anytime for you, babe."

I kissed him, once on the lips, surprising him and myself, then scrambled out of the car behind Malachi, who was standing there under that wild canopy of stars, waiting for me.

But was he *waiting* waiting, or was all the sex in my head? Because he only took my hand as we walked up the steps. No wild hot kiss, which I'd been half-expecting.

And, okay, there was a time to be the maiden, a time to be the pursued and the hunted. There was also a time to call a bluff. At the top of the stairs, I tugged him to a halt, then jumped up another step and turned to face him. I put my arms around his immense shoulders and bent in and kissed him.

He kissed me back, but with restraint. I frowned, straightening. "Did I miss something?"

His hands rested easily against the flare of my hips. "I want it to be better than this."

"Better?"

"Yeah." His eyelids went heavy, smoky, and I saw the rumbling heat there. He lifted a hand and put it around my breast. "I want to remember how it tastes. How it feels. What you look like. I don't want it all lost in some tequila haze."

His hand nearly covered me, and I ached to feel it there, exactly where I'd wanted it, but I didn't like the depth of what was coming out of his mouth, and it made me reckless. I covered his hand with my own. "It's not such a big thing. Just a little friendly lust."

He didn't say anything, just hooked a hand around the back of my neck and pulled me down to his mouth for a kiss so deep, so rich, so full of promise I found myself dizzy. "Really?" he said quietly. "You really think I'll be just one of your guys?"

"It's not that."

"What then?" His mouth closed on my neck, hot and wet, and his tongue made these amazing little patterns over my skin. Somehow, then, we were sitting on that top stair, me in his lap. I think he picked me up and just sat down, but it was while he was doing that thing with his tongue, and I didn't really notice we'd shifted until he stopped. "Why don't you tell me, Jewel?"

"Tell you?"

His hand moved. "Tell me why it won't be such a big thing."

"No," I said softly. "That's not where we were." I struggled a little against him, wanting to get my hands on that shirt. If I could put my hands on his skin, I thought it might be possible to convince him it would be okay if we went upstairs. But he held me with no effort, my left arm pinned against his oaken side, my right arm caught at the elbow in his massive, easy grip. It didn't hurt. My head was cradled against his biceps, my bottom neatly in the dip between his legs. Against the side of my left thigh, I could feel his erection, fierce and steady, and with a little sigh, I wiggled against it. "You don't want to be just one of the guys."

"Right." His hand tightened on my elbow, holding me still.

I relaxed my body, looking up at him, feeling the slight brush of the wind move my hair against his leg. "I just *want* you, Malachi," I said quietly. "I don't want to wait."

He slid his fingers along the edge of my leotard. I wished, suddenly, for something easier to take off. Hadn't thought of that. Looking down at me steadily, he moved his fingers over my skin, teasing. "Is that right?"

"Yeah."

"I think I can give you a little something, sugar. A taste to tide you over, hmm?"

"Not fair!"

"No?" He said it kindly, but with distraction, because by then he was working that leotard off my shoulder, catching my bra strap with it, and I felt suddenly dizzy and closed my eyes. In a swift, electric movement, he freed one breast, and I went soft at the feeling of air on my naked skin, the sound of his voice, that erotic bass. "Ohh, that's pretty," he said, but didn't touch. Not for a minute. His fingers hovered just above it, as wind chilled the spot and I started to quake a little. All at once, he bent his head and took me in his mouth while his other hand slid between my thighs, hard. Hand, mouth, and me like a kerosene-soaked rag—I'm embarrassed to admit it took about three seconds. Malachi moved his mouth from my breast to my lips when I fell over that edge, kissing me to keep the little mewling noises down, and maybe to absorb my protests. "Will that hold you till morning?" he asked, eyes glinting.

I broke away from him, humiliated. Or tried to break away. He didn't let go, and until he decided to do it, there wasn't much I would have to say about it, though I tried. "Let me go!"

Instead he pulled me into him, kissing my ear and my cheek, laughing as I fought him, and it was frustrating to realize that he was still hard as rock beneath my thigh. "Jewel, listen," he said, laughing and ducking as I got one hand free and smacked the back of his head. "Listen!" He caught my wrist and gave me a look, raised eyebrows that meant business.

I stopped. "What?"

"Tried to get out of this gracefully, but you're gonna make me say it all out, aren't you?"

"Say what?"

He shifted up into me, pressing himself close to my body. "I want you—God knows I do—but we had way too much tequila back there, and it's just not gonna be all that good tonight." The gravelly voice was low, echoing through his chest into my body. "Get it? I want it to be better than that, Jewel. It's worth waiting for."

"Oh," I said. "Oh." And nodded. "Sorry."

He laughed, putting his face on my neck. "Nothing to apologize for."

"Tomorrow, then?"

"Oh, yeah."

"Promise?"

"Cross my heart and hope to die," he said, pulling my shirt up. "Stick a needle in my eye."

"All right." Now how to depart gracefully? Get up, go in the house, and fall into my bed.

Luckily, we were both drunk. Together we stood and shifted and brushed ourselves off, then went upstairs and made out at his door for a long time before I ambled into my room, stripped off my clothes, and fell into bed naked for the first time in years. It felt good, at least as long as I could stay awake to enjoy it. My last thought was that I should have taken some aspirin and had some water. The hangover would be a doozy.

~

I read once that John Steinbeck liked his liquor, but he hated to admit to hangovers. There was a story—I had no idea if it was true—that one morning after he and a group of friends partied hard, a friend asked him how he felt. "Oh, I'm fine," Steinbeck replied. "Of course I do have a headache that starts at the base of my spine."

Exactly.

The first hour or so, I had to be careful not to jar my delicate head in the slightest. The second hour, after three cups of strong coffee, three Advil, and some scrambled eggs, the physical misery had eased enough that humiliation could take first place. I couldn't sit still to read the paper, because the damned evening kept rising up in front of my eyes, taunting me with my hands on Malachi, then his hands on me . . . oh.

So I tackled the kitchen, which was stuffed with food from my cooking spree the night before. Malachi was still asleep, so I put my music on the headphones. Upbeat stuff. Silly songs, like "Please Mr. Postman," and music by the Temptations. Good rhythmic beat for the work. By the time I finished scrubbing the cupboards with a mix of Murphy Oil Soap and water, I'd worked up a light sweat and felt about a thousand times better. The oak cabinets gleamed that soft, warm yellow, and I stood back to admire them in the fine, soft light of morning, singing along with the Marvelettes.

His hands were around my waist before I even caught a glimpse of him, and I startled so hard I dropped the broom, hastily tearing off the headphones as he swung me around.

Malachi, of course, the one I'd been dreading and anticipating in almost equal measures all morning. He seemed to have no such ambivalence and pulled me over his big thigh, his hands sliding up my back. "Morning," he said, and his eyes were a deep, smoky color, thick with anticipation.

For one second, I wanted to give myself up to it. To him. To the lure of those hands and that mouth—oh, I knew what they could do—and that wicked grin.

But my own actions of the night before, my needy wish, rose up to humiliate me, just as I'd been afraid they would. I ducked away from him a little.

"Oh, no, you don't," he said, "don't you dare."

"What?" But I couldn't look him in the eye. It was hard enough just to stand there, smelling soap and feeling the humid dampness of his skin beneath his clothes. A freshly showered man is surely one of God's greatest pleasures.

"Steal away." He captured my head in his giant hands and kissed me. A sweet kiss, and one I could resist.

"It's a bad idea, Malachi," I said, slipping away from him like I knew what I was doing. Blindly, I went to the sink and started running water. "I was drunk last night, or it wouldn't have gone that far."

"Liar." He came up behind me and put his hands around my waist very lightly, the heat of his palms crumpling my shirt against my skin. I could feel his body all down my back. Then he bent and put his mouth on my shoulder, on the skin just beside the fabric. An open-mouthed kiss, full of wiggling tongue I wanted elsewhere.

"All I've been thinking about since I opened my eyes is getting you naked," he said. That soft baritone rumbled. He moved his mouth a little higher, on the side of my neck, and kissed me again, his hands staying perfectly still, which I was not entirely certain I wanted. "I've been thinking about sliding my tongue all over this hot body of yours, sugar. *All* over it." His teeth captured my ear. "And I've been thinking about yours on me."

Me too.

There was really no alternative. Sex now or sex later, it was going to happen. As I turned, he picked me up and put me on the counter, and I instinctively wrapped my legs around him, working my own buttons as he worked his. "This is inappropriate," I whispered, shedding my shirt, then the bra.

"Life is inappropriate," he said, but then he was kissing me and moving those fantastic hands. I worked his belt, then the buttons of his jeans, wanting him all the way naked, and he was glad to help, shifting his body backward to let me push the jeans off his hips—oh, and I did love the feel of that high, hard, naked rear end against my hands. It was sleek and powerful with the movements of his body, and when he kicked off his jeans, I raised my head.

"Oh," I said softly, admiring him. "You are so much more gorgeous than I thought."

He gave me a sleepy-cat blink. "It's all yours."

But first he bent that big lion head of his and breathed over my breasts. Didn't touch. Just admired for one long minute, then sighed and bent close and put his mouth on me. And I couldn't remember why or what or anything. I just put my hands in his hair and let him work his magic, let the heat and sizzle of it rise through me, burn my skin, the back of my neck, my lower spine.

Then I was kissing him again, and touching him, stroking that lovely work of art that I'd known would be just as aggressive as it turned out to be.

Shane's voice broke through the glaze like a baseball through a window. "Hello!"

For the space of an agonizing half second, Malachi and I stared at each other. Then, in a move I would be forever grateful for, he pulled me off the counter, pointed toward the pantry, gathered our clothes, and dashed in behind me, closing the door just as Shane reached the kitchen, calling out again, "Hello?"

It was a small pantry, especially when I was sharing it with Malachi. He turned toward me in the dark, his shoulders shaking with laughter, and I punched him a little, feeling around for the clothes he'd brought in with us. But instead of letting me have them, he raised his arm and put the bundle on the topmost shelf.

"Oh, this is too good," he murmured close against my ear, and I heard the glee, the anticipation of it, just before he dropped down to his knees. I started to push away, but he captured my wrists in one giant hand and pulled them behind my back, pressing me into the wall behind.

And started licking. Open-mouthed, across my belly, my ribs, my breasts, up my throat. When I struggled, he tightened his grip, and I felt the curve of his smile. Behind the door, Shane flipped on the television, and I barely repressed a groan.

It was so wicked and terrifying, so decadent and delicious, that I couldn't have stopped him on a bet. The chances of Shane opening that pantry door were slim to none, since he'd never done it as long as we'd been there, so the only challenge was being quiet.

Not such a simple thing, because Malachi got serious. Long and slow, up and down. His free hand played bass to the lead of his mouth, arousing every cell from my forehead to my toes until I was literally shaking all over.

Only then did he stand and kiss me, pressing that naked body into my half-clothed one, kissing and kissing and kissing, rubbing himself across me in the most erotic way. "I need my hands," I whispered urgently, trying to pull them free. My breasts and his chest slid sweatily together and apart. He pressed his hips tight for a minute, tightening his grip on my wrists, and it was one of those little things, those tiny, tiny gestures that distinguish a good lover from a truly splendid one. A new rush of erotic anticipation danced through my body. I struggled against him, wanting to touch him.

"Not yet." He bent close enough to kiss me and worked his hand into my jeans, worked his way between my legs, and found the heart of the matter, and I was so weak, so aroused that it was last night all over again, only more intense, so intense that it brought back my hangover headache.

In the dark, thick and close, he took my hand and put it on him, kissing me with nearly violent thrusts as I relaxed and gave back what he'd given me. It was tight and hot in there, and our chests got slick with sweat, prickling and slippery. Part of me was aware of Shane, just on the other side of that door, hearing his little noises as he poured a glass of milk, rattled around in the cupboards, and finally—thank God—tromped up the stairs over our heads.

Malachi moved immediately at the first step on that stair. He shoved off my jeans, lifted me up in his powerful arms, and slid home. Hard. I wrapped myself around him, holding on around his shoulders, legs tight around his waist, knowing I'd have a bruise on my back from where I banged the wall at that first, dazzling thrust.

Oh, nothing, nothing, nothing in the world comes anywhere close to that moment, that instant of joining. After so long, so very, very long, all I wanted was to stay right there, in that single, hilt-deep thrust, holding on to a big, sexy, sweating man who was kissing me like he'd die if he didn't keep it up. My hair fell around us, brushing his arms, mine, our shoulders, whispering down my back. His hands and arms were amazingly powerful, and we held there, suspended for an exquisite, brilliant stretch of time.

Nothing, nothing, nothing in the world comes close to that moment. Except the moments afterward. We moved, constrained by the environment but lent great athleticism by desire, in a vivid, intense, amazing kind of sex. And when he made it to the finish line, it was violent and intense, and he nearly bit my lip in his satisfaction, his fingers almost painful on my buttocks, and he held there so hard and sharp and deep that I could finally make it *with* him, instead of selfishly taking my own pleasure.

It could have been weird, after, but it wasn't. I slumped against his shoulder, letting my heart slow down, hearing his pound against my ribs, and closed my eyes. "I knew it would be that great."

He moved his scratchy chin against my forehead. "Me too." I felt him swallow, and his arms were starting to tremble. I eased my feet down, took my weight. Smiled in the dark, knowing he couldn't see it, but he'd hear it.

"Maybe you can make it to my bed one of these times."

He made a soft sound of regret. "I want it to be now." He touched my back, my arm. "I want more."

"Tonight."

"It's a deal." He leaned there against me for another long minute. "I guess you want me to get your clothes?"

"That would be good."

"No, it's very bad." But he did it anyway, reaching up to pull the tangled jumble off the shelf. I felt around for my bra, then my shirt. My jeans were tangled on the floor with my underwear, and it wasn't the easiest thing in the world to get them back on. I started chuckling when I had to use his arm to brace myself. "It was a lot easier to get everything off."

"Motivation is everything."

When we'd put ourselves more or less back together, Malachi eased open the door to make sure the kitchen was empty, and we slipped out. His hair was wild, and I giggled and smoothed it. He swung me around and pushed me against the fridge and kissed me again, a fierceness to it that didn't surprise me in the slightest. "All I'm gonna be thinking about all day is tonight."

"Ditto." At a movement from upstairs, we pulled apart. "I'm going to go freshen up."

He let me go. At the door, I paused and looked back at him, and saw the strangest expression on his face. Not the wicked gleaming I would have expected, or the flushed pleasure of a man who'd just had really great wild sex in a closet.

No, when I glanced back, he was standing by the window with his hands on his hips, his face in profile to me. And I would have sworn that what he most wanted to do was weep. Pierced, I rushed up the stairs, not wanting to know if it was joy or sorrow that put that emotion there—in the end, it didn't really matter. The result would be the same. I'd found my man, and he'd found his woman, but life would never let him take that gift.

At the top of the stairs, I ran into Shane coming out of his room. A guilty flush burned from my breasts to my eyebrows, and I hoped he didn't notice. "Where were you?" he demanded. "I called and called."

"Um. I was outside."

"I thought we could make Michael breakfast," he said, "take it to him at the hospital."

"All right. Let me grab a shower."

His eyes narrowed suddenly, and he shook his head in disgust. "Never mind," he said, then went to his room and slammed the door.

I looked down. My shirt was inside out.

MICHAEL

They tried to make it festive, a celebration, an occasion of joy—Nana Lucy and Jewel's mother and the sisters who blurred when he tried to rasp out their names in thanks. Nana held his hand tight and chanted the rosary, the cadence of her voice weaving into the rhythm of the breathing machine, which blurred into memory.

Andre was with him only when he slid farthest away, an angelic figure with his eyes alight in humor. Andre the angel, he said in his mind, and it made the angel laugh. Michael wasn't sure sometimes if it was Andre, actually, or if it was the form the angel had taken to comfort him, but he figured it didn't matter all that much. The purpose was comfort, and comfort he did.

In between the short visits, he lay alone and trussed, tied to the earthly realm by needles and tubes, and the truth was, now he had no choice but to get through the pneumonia this time. He'd promised Andre he would not die in a hospital, the most solemn vow he'd made in all his life. He intended to keep it.

To keep his despair at bay, he thought of the timing. There was the wedding. And the state fair. That was important, part of the circle.

When Jewel came, her hair down and free, her hands full of food, she put her head down on his chest. "I'm sorry, love."

He touched that wild hair, the hair that had snared Billy so long ago and would snare Malachi now, feeling a great rush of love. He couldn't speak, so he squeezed her arm.

The smell of her filled his head, the scent of cloves and shampoo, a scent he'd always thought of as red, as vivid and warm, like Jewel. Everything in him just eased as he breathed it in, and he closed his eyes.

FROM THE COLORADO STATE FAIR CONTEST BOOKLET

"QUEEN OF THE KITCHEN":

To be eligible, an exhibitor must be a Colorado resident. Competitors must enter at least twelve of the competitive Pantry Department categories shown below and place in ten. Exhibitors are automatically entered in this special contest when entries are made in the following categories: Canned Fruit, Canned Vegetables, Jellies, Preserves and Marmalades, Butters and Jams, Pickles, Yeast Breads, Microwave Cookery, Nutritious Snacks, Quick Breads, Round the World Baked Goods, Pies, Cakes and Sponge Cakes, Cookies, Dried Foods, Candy, Baked Goods with Honey.

The Queen of the Kitchen Award will be determined on the basis of total ribbon points won, with points to be counted as follows: first . . . three points, second . . . two points, third . . . one point.

Chapter Fourteen

Late that afternoon, I drove Shane to Falconi's for the dinner shift. He didn't speak to me the whole way, and my attempts at conversation died in a syllable.

Instead of going home afterward, I went out to Jordan's place. The low buttery light of early evening gilded the world as I got out of the car, splashing across the trunks of trees, making the tall stands of dry grass look soft. From the old juniper by the house came the sound of wrens and sparrows at supper, the chittering, squealing excitement seeming out of proportion until I climbed onto the porch and saw Jordan's cat, an aging gray tabby, sprawled beneath the tree. He raised his head at my approach, squeaking in his ruined little voice, and I paused to scratch his big head. He purred a smile.

From within came the sound of a dog whining, and Jordan popped her head out. "Jewel! Hi!" She pushed open the screen door to let her monster dog out to greet me—an enormous mutt with the lean shape of a Great Dane and the sweet face and fur of a golden retriever. He leaped out to greet me, lifting on his hind legs to gently put his forepaws on my shoulders and give me a kiss if I were willing. Charmed as always, I offered my chin, and he let me hug his neck. "Ah, you're a good dog, Wolfenstein."

Jordan had a handful of red grapes and offered me one. "What's up? How's Michael?"

"Okay." I felt vaguely ashamed that I had dragged my distress and upheaval into this peaceful place, but we all did it. All ran to Jordan with cuts and bruises and weary hearts, and she—like Sylvia before her, I suddenly realized—always had some plaster to put over it, a tea or a song or a medicine.

"But?"

I stuck my hands in my back pockets. "I kinda want to talk. You have time?"

"Ooh," she said with a wicked lift of her eyebrows, "I hope it's about Malachi."

I lifted a shoulder. "Sort of."

"Come on in. I'm trying to get my herbs ready for the fair."

I laughed. "Not really? For a bracelet?" If you entered goods into the pantry contests, you could buy a bracelet to get into the fair every day, much cheaper than paying admission.

"Yep. They don't do bracelets anymore, though—it's a little card now."

"What could be that interesting that you'd need a pass for the whole time?"

"Tradition," she said with a grin, and I followed her to the kitchen. "It's what we do, you know?"

I settled at the heavy table and watched as she trimmed and tied hanks of rosemary. "Does everyone still enter something to get the passes?"

She nodded. "Every year. Jane did really well last year—especially in the canning. She took three blue ribbons and two reds." Twisting heavy white thread tightly and neatly around the stems, she brushed out some imperfections from the branches, and the scent filled the room. "Mark my words, she'll be Queen of the Kitchen one day."

I rolled my eyes. "When I was away, I had a whole spiel on the state fair and Queen of the Kitchen. It's so unbelievably corny."

She looked at me steadily, a little smile on her lips. "Is it?"

"Queen of the Kitchen?" I said. "A state fair, for God's sake? How provincial is that?"

"Probably a lot." Still that smile lingered, secretive and somehow knowing. "You've just forgotten, Jewel. Remember how excited we were the year Auntie won Queen?"

And suddenly, I did. It had been Sylvia. She had spent weeks and weeks getting ready. To take Queen of the Kitchen, the cook had to win the most blue ribbons in the entire scope of the Pantry division of the state fair contests—and that meant a huge number of entries. Pickles and canning, jellies and jams and preserves, quick breads and yeast breads, cookies, pies, and cakes.

"I think I was ten or eleven," I said, and brushed a lock of hair off my forehead, remembering the constant heat in that kitchen, the rounds of dark-brown breads, the shine of jars wiped down with vinegar water, the careful wrapping and transportation of the goods for the judging. And then we'd sat on bleachers in the Creative Arts building, hot and sleepy, watching the judges take a teeny nibble of this, another of that. They pinched the breads and rolled the dough into little balls, scowled and conferred, tapped and broke. "Okay," I admitted, "that was pretty cool."

"I was ten, so you had to be eleven. I wanted to be the judges so bad, so I could eat all that stuff!"

She'd been plump in those days and far too fond of sweets. "That's only because Mama deprived you."

"No, it's because I was greedy!" She laughed. "I still am—I just keep temptation out of the house. I don't know how you do it, cooking all those pies." She looked up. "You should enter, Jewel!"

"It's too late, isn't it?"

"No!" She opened a drawer and pulled out a little book, flipping open the pages of contest regulations. "You can't do your pies because you do that professionally, but maybe something else? Tomorrow is the deadline for entering, and you have to pay for the pass when you pay for the entries."

"I can't see how I'd want to go to the fair ten days in a row."

"Seventeen. They extended it."

"Oh, even better!" I shook my head. "How many funnel cakes can you eat, after all?"

"It's something to do. People-watching and all the music and the booths—we go every day usually. And even if you didn't use it, Shane would love it."

"True." I chuckled and picked up a lavender wand to smell. "Wonder if he'll run off with some wild chick?"

Jordan looked at me in horror. "Oh, I forgot, Jewel. I forgot that's how you guys all met. I'm sorry."

"Nothing to be sorry for." But the lingering shame of that rebellious act made me remember why I'd come over in the first place. "I seem to have a talent for screwing up."

"No, you don't, Jewel. It's just that everyone always wanted you to be somebody else. I hate it that you're sinking back into that apologetic mode. You had so much fire while you were gone—and your bravery made me brave."

"It did?"

"Of course it did. Do you think I could have let myself fall in love with Henry if I hadn't had you ahead of me? Do you think Mama and Pop would have accepted him if they hadn't seen how much worse it could get?"

"I never thought of that." Henry was of mixed race, the son of a West Indian mother and a Hispanic father who'd met his wife on a Caribbean cruise he'd won from a radio station. "So I've been bad to pave the way for you." I grinned. "At least somebody got something out of it."

"You got a lot, Jewel. Don't give me that." She began lacing together a new collection of herbs, matching the stems by length. "Shane. Michael. Even Billy, before he lost it so bad."

I brushed lavender over my nose. "Yeah."

"What's eating you?"

"Shane is not speaking to me."

"Mmm. How unusual in a seventeen-year-old. Why?"

Now that I had come right to it, I didn't know if I could tell her. Or if I should. Or if she'd be shocked. I picked up three pieces of yarn and started braiding them.

"Ooh," she said in a throaty voice. "This is about Malachi, isn't it?"

I lowered my eyes. Nodded.

"Jewel, the minute I laid eyes on him, I knew you'd sleep with him." She laughed. "He's *so* your type."

Stung, I protested, "I don't go around sleeping with every guy I meet, Jordan!"

"That's not what I meant, and you know it."

"No, I don't know. What did you mean, then?"

With that particularly exasperated huff of a sister, she said, "You like sex, Jewel. You always have—and what's wrong with that?"

"Oh, I don't know!" I stood up and paced three steps to the wall, turned around. "Ask my dad. Ask my grandmother, who told me I'm too old to wear my hair down anymore." Flinging up one arm, then bringing it back down, I said, "Ask my son, who didn't speak to me the entire day because he came home and wanted to make breakfast for Michael, and he couldn't find me because I was in the pantry with Malachi, and then didn't even have the sense to get my shirt back on right side out."

Her shoulders were shaking with laughter before I made it to the end of the story. "Oh, that's priceless! In Sylvia's pantry? With the Jolly Green Giant?"

"Yes." I started to smile.

"Oh, I never thought of that. Can me and Henry borrow it sometime?"

"For the full, erotic effect, you really should be hiding from a kid who almost surprised you." I strove for a light tone, but it came out edged with misery.

"Jewel, kids don't like to think of their parents having sex. It's a fact of life. It's also a fact that parents do."

"I'm sure he's getting an earful at the restaurant."

"Probably," she agreed, "but that's not your problem. You can't live your life trying to please other people. Sooner or later, you have to accept who you are, warts and all."

"I have more warts than most people."

"No, you don't."

I sank back down in the chair. She just didn't know. Because she loved me, because she was a champion born, she championed me. "Thank you."

Quiet fell between us, and I heard the wind starting to blow. "You know, Jordan," I said, "I really like him. Malachi."

"What's wrong with that?"

I shook my head.

"He's kind of a lost soul, isn't he?"

"Yeah. My other specialty."

She smiled fondly. "You always have collected the lost ones. What was that kid's name who lived by the school?"

I hadn't thought of him in thirty years, but his name popped into my head instantly. "Francisco Vigil." A sturdy, dark-brown boy whose parents spoke no English. They lived in a tumbledown, two-bedroom house, all nine of them. Francisco was in my class, and because I was a good reader and he wasn't, the teacher put me to work helping him sometimes. Casting myself as a saintly girl upon whom the Madonna would smile benevolently for my Good Works, I threw myself into teaching him better skills.

But he tugged at my heartstrings. His hair was badly cut, and he had exactly one pair of pants and two shirts. By Friday, they were always grimy, but he wet-combed his hair every morning, and his hands and face were clean every day. It really hurt me that my lunch box was crammed full of good things to eat and he always unwrapped a single peanut butter and jelly sandwich on white bread. Not even

Wonder—just the plain loaves that sold three for a dollar at the local convenience store. I started saving my oranges for him and splitting my cookies. I asked my mother about putting the family on the church poor list.

I laughed a little, remembering. "Poor thing. I can't imagine what he thought of me."

"Jewel, he was crazy about you! And we were all kind of jealous in the end, because he was kind of dangerous, and you seemed brave."

"He was hardly dangerous." I thought of his big dark eyes, so steady and clear, his earnestness as he labored over his reader. "He did learn to read, though. I guess that's good." At the end of the year, he moved away, and no one ever saw him again. The city condemned the house—actually three houses in a row, owned by a rat of a slumlord—the following spring and tore them down.

"Malachi isn't lost like that, though," she said. "He's running hard."

"He'd run now, if it weren't for Michael."

"What makes you say that?"

I hadn't even known I believed it until I said it aloud. "It's hard to stay aloof from community here, you know what I mean? He's getting sucked in, and he's afraid of it."

"Is that it?" she asked quietly.

I thought of his low, deep sigh when I fell on his shoulder. Thought of my instinctive need to put my arms around him when he'd come to the bridal shop, and the deep trembling need in him when I had. I thought of the ease with which we'd kissed and played the night out by the reservoir. Thought of the long, long time we'd spent looking into each other's eyes while we danced.

But those things were too deep and personal to share. "I don't know," I said. "But if he lasts one day here beyond Michael's funeral, it will be a long stay indeed."

"Poor thing. I'd hate to have to run like that my whole life."

"Not everybody wants roots like ours, Jordan." I chuckled. "I'm not even sure I want them most of the time."

"They may not want them," she said, "but everyone needs them."
A wink. "And there is something between nothing and way too much."

I laughed. "True."

~

When Henry came home, obviously tired from a long day in the sun, I made myself drive back to the house. All the way there, I tried to figure out what I'd do about Malachi, how I should act, what we needed to say to each other, or whether we needed to say anything. We were alone in the house again tonight, at least until Shane got home, and that seemed to put a lot of pressure on the idea that we should have sex again.

But I wasn't sure I wanted to. All day, the feeling of him around me, in me, kissing me; the look of his smile and the throaty baritone at the bar last night—it seemed too much, too dangerous. Right this minute, I could walk away and feel only a little pinch. If I let myself get more involved with him, started liking another little thing and another and another, there'd be too much to miss when he hit the road.

As it turned out, though, he wasn't at the farm when I got there, and that was worse. The animals came running to meet me after I unlocked the front door—Berlin tapping down the stairs to get her head rubbed, the cats twirling around my ankles in a much more self-serving way. They wanted the empty food dish filled. Like, yesterday.

Dark had fallen, making the lamplit rooms inside too lonely, too quiet, and I made some tea to carry out to the porch, a nice cup of Sleepytime to head off the lingering hangover headache that had dogged me distantly all day. I settled on the front steps, where I had a view of the road and the top of the trees tossing in a light wind.

And for the first time I realized that this was what my life was going to be in a year or so. No Michael. Shane would head off to his life. Malachi would be in Egypt or Barcelona or some other exotic place. My sisters would all be married, busy with their own families. My parents—well, who knew what would happen there?

I would be forty-one and forty-two and forty-three, alone, knocking around Sylvia's big house with too many cats and a dog.

The recognition settled like a lead weight in my chest, too depressing to even cry about. I saw the years stretching ahead of me like a dusty road leading out to the prairie. Dun colored, bone dry, all life sucked out of it by gusts of hard, dry wind.

It was terrifying. What would I do? How would I find companionship? I thought of some of the women I'd known, divorcées or widows who dolled themselves up to go to the clubs on the weekends or hung out at museums and coffee shops and Barnes & Nobles, their smiles too bright, their makeup too polished, and I felt sick.

I was no longer young. I wasn't old, but the blush was off the rose, as Nana Lucy would say. I'd taken a big chance on a dream that now seemed foolish and shallow, and now, instead of a nice, comforting, stable life, with a husband to lie down next to at night and a network of comforting women friends, I had nothing.

It made me think of Sundays. As a little girl, I had loved them—waited all week to put on my good dresses and patent leather shoes. I loved the bustle of our big breakfast and the rush to get to Mass on time—remember, my mother had three little girls to brush and comb—and the rituals at church. I loved the smell of incense and the way the light broke through the big stained-glass window. I loved afternoons filled with the smell of roasting meat, and the steamy darkness of winter suppers.

When I hit the wild days, Sundays bored me stiff. I got a job and worked them, just so I wouldn't have to sit around the house and listen to football and yawn while everybody flipped through the thick newspapers. When I was a teen, Sundays embodied the stasis and provincialism of my world, of the tightly knit community and the city itself.

And I gleefully escaped them. Sundays with Billy were filled with sex or lazy drives on his motorcycle, or spent sleeping in recovery from a concert the night before.

When Shane was born, Michael abruptly started cooking breakfast on Sunday mornings. Big southern breakfasts, with fried potatoes and bacon and grits and homemade biscuits. Billy took to them like a starved child, and it became our ritual, Michael cooking every Sunday morning no matter where we were or what we were doing. When he met Andre, they both came over, and even when Billy started falling to drugs so badly, he often showed up on Sunday mornings.

With a wretched twist of shame, I realized I should have known that Shane would show up this morning—Sunday—to cook breakfast. It seemed a terrible breach that I'd forgotten.

Sitting there in the dark, with crickets whirring and Sylvia's solid home behind me, what I wanted more than anything was to go back in time and rewrite my life so that my Sundays would now be what I was sure they were in my sisters' houses. With a deep sense of lost chances, I realized I should have given them to Shane all along.

I heard the motorcycle before I saw the headlight cutting through the night. For a minute, I thought about jumping up and running inside, so it wouldn't look like I'd been waiting for him, but the idea presented so many complications that in the end, I didn't move a single muscle.

Or maybe it was just that he was so welcome on this lonely night, looking so competent and strong as he parked and climbed off the bike. I could see weariness in his step as he walked toward me, and his very presence meant we'd now have to deal with all that . . . stuff, but it didn't matter. My heart lifted, just seeing him, just having someone else here with me so I didn't have to face the night all alone.

But even that thought had a layer of lies in it. It wasn't just somebody; it was Malachi. The difference mattered.

"Hey," he said, collapsing one step below me. "You're looking about like I feel."

"Which is?"

"Worn out." He looped his hand around my ankle. "You okay?"

"Not really. I'm fairly wretchedly depressed. How about you?"

His smile was shadowed. "The same."

"I know a cure," I heard myself say, in spite of my resolve. "Doesn't last that long, but it works pretty well while it's in place."

"I'd love it, sugar, but it's causing you too much trouble." His fingers moved on my ankle bone. "Shane'll be home soon, right?"

"Yeah."

"Well, I guessed that maybe he was none too happy when he didn't have a single word to say to me the whole day until we ended up in the men's room at the same time and he gave me a gentlemanly little warning."

"What? Did he really?"

"Yes, ma'am."

I couldn't help a little chuckle. "What did he say?"

Malachi didn't laugh with me. "He said you'd been through enough, and he didn't want to see you get hurt, so I oughta just leave you alone."

A mix of humiliation and motherly satisfaction went through me. "Ah, he's seventeen. Sex is all wrapped up in romance and black-and-white values." I shook my head with what I thought was just the right touch of irony. "He still thinks it's a man who takes and a woman who gets used."

"Are you using me, Jewel?"

I met his eyes. "Maybe a little. We're using each other to get through a hard time. Is that so bad?"

He moved, with that same feline grace that always took me by surprise, and caught my head in his big hand and kissed me. It was a savage kiss on one level, thick with the unresolved need we both felt to be properly naked and in a comfortable place to see what the whole thing would be like, and it gave me a rush to be wanted like that, to want it so much in return.

But as if he knew that was where my head was, it turned into something else. He tilted his head ever so slightly, and his lips were softer, more tender, his tongue dancing with mine in a waltz, not a tango. I felt his breath on my cheek, felt myself falling into that sweetness. I put my hand in his hair and stroked the silky length of it, breathing in his taste, his smell, his warm body.

And it was corny, but it made me dizzy again. Lighter than usual, airier, more at peace. Before that really registered, he gently lifted his head. "We've both been around the block a few times, Jewel," he said, his voice rumbling nearly below register. "We both know the difference in a kiss like that, and maybe it's just gonna be smarter for both of us to leave this right here." He swallowed, his thumb moving on my jaw. "I'll never stay. I don't know how."

I brushed my fingers over his cheekbone, his jaw. "I know."

He bent close again, pressed his mouth to mine, then let me go.

I took a breath, pulling away, somehow feeling a lot more at ease. "Well, glad we got that out on the table. Are you hungry? I have enough food for an army in there."

"Now, that does sound good."

"C'mon. I'll fix you right up, soldier." I stood up, and he followed me. At the door, he took my arm and pushed my hair away and kissed the back of my neck. "Thank you, Jewel."

I didn't say anything, just opened the door and went inside.

~

Tuesday, I was summoned to Nana Lucy's house for a fitting. The dresses had arrived as promised. Jordan was working a twelve-hour shift, so I had to go alone. Believe me, I did not want to, not after the little scene on Saturday. We'd all seen one another at the hospital, but they never lectured in front of other people.

Nana Lucy still lived in one of the old neighborhoods, called Goat Hill because a long time ago people grazed goats there. It stood over the highway, reached by climbing narrow, hidden roads. Nana moved there as a newlywed and had lived there for more than sixty years. She raised her children there, had planted the gardens for sixty seasons.

Her house was an old bungalow, stuccoed in a tasteful pale tan with dark-brown shutters, and had that fussy neatness that lets you know an old person lives within. Her grass was never more than one inch high, and a boy came in once a week to keep the flower beds free of weeds. The hoses were rolled up and her car was never parked anywhere but on the pristine driveway beneath the squeaky-clean carport. She swept her sidewalk every single morning.

It was my mother who opened the door, with bobby pins in her mouth and one hand holding up her hair in the back. She waved at me, then started sticking pins in her hair, prying them open with her teeth. Little pieces stuck up all over, and I said, "Hang on, Mama. Let me help you. Where's the brush?"

Inside, the house was as neat as outside. Plastic runners covered the carpet down the halls, and plastic covered the lampshades—a habit I'd always found peculiar, but had probably once had a genuine purpose. In the days before the steel depression of the early eighties, the mill pumped out loads of sulfur and coal dust that settled on everything. People had called the city Pew-town for years because of it.

"Over there," my mother snapped, pointing at a natural bristle brush as she tugged out the pins. "I don't know why I can't get it up right this morning."

"Where's Nana?" I fetched the brush and pointed at a chair at the dining room table.

My mother sat, her fingers worrying themselves in her lap. "She's in the garden. Don't ask me why she had to go pick zucchinis right now, when there are a million things to do, but that's what she's doing."

As she talked, I took out the pins and unbraided my mother's hair. "Oh, Mama," I sighed as it fell free, even thicker and blacker than I remembered, each strand as shiny and healthy as a child's. "You have such wonderful hair. You should wear it down sometimes."

"At my age? Don't be silly." But her hands settled as I started brushing it, and she straightened in a kind of acknowledgment.

When I was a little girl, I loved playing with my mother's hair. We fought for the privilege of brushing it out at night, to the point that we had to take a day of the week. "Tuesday always was my day to brush your hair out," I said.

"Amazing you still remember that."

I put the brush down and started weaving the hair into a braid. "I remember everything about my childhood. You wouldn't believe how much."

"Do you, Jewel? Isn't that funny?"

"Not really." I thought, but didn't say, that it was because I'd left.

"Remember those little dolls your dad used to make out of hollyhocks?" She put her hands flat on her thighs. "You wanted me to make you a skirt just like the round petal of a hollyhock."

I remembered. I also remembered that she'd done it—sewing wrinkled red handkerchief linen to a wide, lime-green waistband. "I wore that thing to death."

"Yes, you did."

I rolled the braid into a bun that distributed the weight over as much of her scalp as possible. "I don't know how you wear it like this, Mama. Doesn't it give you headaches?"

"I'm used to it."

"The headaches or the hair?"

"Both." She handed me the last pin and stood up when I fastened it. "Let's get this done so I can get to work."

"You're not still trying to do both work and the wedding this week, are you?"

"I couldn't take two weeks," she said with a scowl. "I'm taking next week off to make sure all the little stuff is finished right." She bustled over to a box on the table and pointed to my shirt. "Get undressed."

"Right here in the living room?"

"Who's gonna see?" She looked pointedly at the heavy blinds protecting the furniture from the hard, southwest sunlight. "Just do it, Jewel. I'm in a hurry."

Stung, I pulled the shirt over my head, oddly shy to have my mother see my body after so many years. At least I'd worn modest undergarments today, a bra that hid the tattoo, for one thing.

She brushed away the tissue paper lining inside the box, and I sucked in my breath in happy surprise. "Is that one mine?"

She made that peculiarly dismissive noise. "I told Jane you two couldn't wear those soft colors, but she wouldn't listen until she saw how they washed you out. She also didn't listen when I told her to get fourteens." She shook out the indigo dress. Still satin, but a rich, rich color that I would not mind wearing at all. "Jane, she's like you, Jewel."

"She is?"

"Take off the jeans, too." She held the dress close to her, as if I'd soil it with chocolate-smeared fingers. Shyly, reluctantly, I did as she asked, wishing she'd at least let me shimmy out of them beneath the skirt. Too conscious of my round belly and big thighs, I waited for her to put it over my head.

It fell down around my body in a swish of luxurious heaviness, and she zipped the back easily—until she got to the bust. "Damn," she said, as foul a swear word as she ever uttered. "You're even bustier than my sister."

I frowned. "Hmm. I have an idea." Reaching behind me, I unfastened my bra and pulled it off through the sleeves, then bent over from the waist and squished everything upward and center. Still bent over, I said, "Try zipping it now."

With a little cry of satisfaction, she did it. "Now let me look at you."

I straightened and the fabric held everything in place for the moment. "What do you think? Too much? I can get a corset or something like that to keep everything in place for the wedding. If necessary, I can change right afterward."

She was silent, and I looked up. Her head was cocked, a sad smile on her face. "You are still so beautiful, Jewel." She tugged a hank of my hair over my shoulder. "Even when you were a baby, people used to stop me in the street so they could look at you. Not around here, of course, but everywhere else."

Not around here because the community would have been respectful of her worry over the "evil eye" being cast on a baby. "Thank you," I said quietly.

"I have always worried more about you than all three of the other girls put together. And you can still surprise me." She smiled and turned me around to face the long mirror in the corner. "Look at yourself."

In that instant, looking at myself in the long oval mirror, I knew my mother loved me. The color was exactly perfect, bringing out a topaz light in my eyes, pointing out the strands of red and gold in my hair, turning my skin a burnished pale honey. And the style that had seemed so tacky in the dressing room bridal shop now looked like a Victorian ball gown, especially when she reached out and pulled the sleeves down to reveal my shoulders. "The other girls were shy to try this, but that's how they're supposed to be worn. A woman's shoulders are made to be displayed."

I touched the tattoo. "I can cover it with makeup for the day."

"Good idea."

"What are you going to wear, Mama?"

She gave me a distracted smile. "Oh, probably that lace dress Sylvia gave me for Christmas a few years ago. It's a nice color."

"The peach dress?"

"Mmm," she said around a mouthful of straight pins she used to nip in the waist of the dress.

"Mama, no. That dress is a lot more than a few years old. You've had it since I was in high school."

She took the pins out, frowning at the fit. "Well, but I haven't worn it more than five or six times."

"No, you need a new dress."

"Costs too much. You know how much it costs for a wedding these days?"

I turned and took her hands in mine. "Please, Mama? Let us buy you one, all of us girls. We could make a day of it—drive up to Nordstrom's and find something really beautiful."

She was shaking her head before I finished. "No time for that. Got so much cooking to do, and these dresses to fix, and a million other things."

"I can help with the cooking."

"Oh, you have too much on your plate as it is."

"No pun intended," I murmured.

"What?"

"Nothing." I was calculating how to get her a great dress, one that would reveal her in all her beauty for once in her life. "Really, Ma, I'll do some cooking. What's left?"

She let go one of those sighs and shook her head. I'd ask my grandmother. And talk to my sisters about the dress idea. Maybe getting to Denver to go to Nordstrom was too much—there was a shower this week, and a lot more prep to do for the wedding—but maybe Dillard's.

She unzipped me. "Do you think Dad's ever going to forgive me?" I asked as she carefully lowered the fabric from my body. I stepped out equally carefully, and then dived for my jeans.

"He will." She patted my arm. "You'll see."

"When?"

Carefully she settled the dress over a ladderback chair. "Might go easier if you leave that man alone."

"By 'that man' I guess you mean Malachi?" I sighed, pricked with anger even though I knew it was true. Malachi summed up in one luscious package all that my father thought was wrong with my morals.

She didn't answer. And Nana Lucy came in carrying what looked like a hundred green penises, forty of which she shoved into a bag for me to take home. "I can't use this many zucchini, Nana! I have a whole patch of my own."

She might have been deaf. "Freeze them."

There was no point in arguing. I tried to forget the bag on the table when I left a few minutes later, but she sent my mother out with them. "Nice try," Mama said.

Maybe I could make some fried zucchini for dinner. I wondered if Malachi liked it.

FROM THE MUSIC BOX MENU:

Zappa Zucchini—The delectable Jewel Sabatino made this one up (see her squash blossom appetizer above). Thinly sliced, lemon-marinated zucchini grilled golden with cherry tomatoes and freshly ground black pepper.

Chapter Fifteen

During my exile, August was the month that came to mind when I thought of Pueblo. Winters here are mild and unremarkable. The spring is lovely—wet and cool in the evenings, clear and golden in the mornings. It's a city filled with crab apple trees that bloom all at once and yards full of tulips, then irises, then the first early-summer roses and lilacs.

By July, the sun is starting to suck the green from the landscape and all but the most exuberant of flowers—God bless marigolds and petunias!—have hidden themselves until September.

And then comes August. In August, the blaze of the relentless sun irons the color from everything, and you move in a sort of blinking daze. Sprinklers run all day and night, and you can smell the green and silver sprays of water pouring life into lawns and trees. The sound of them clicking or swishing, together with the thumping of swamp coolers and the whir of overhead ceiling fans, accompanies every movement.

In August, hundreds of thousands of elm trees—too fragile for the heavy snows or the high winds, but so fertile they grow everywhere anyway—offer nearly bare branches to the blisteringly clear blue of the sky, their leaves devoured all summer by mustard bugs, who then slime everything beneath with their offal.

But this August brought something new. Woven through the new but familiar pattern of days, like some nubby, hand-spun wool through plain muslin, was Malachi. Even as the days blurred together beneath the force of sun and Michael's decline and the increasingly hectic preparations for the wedding, I knew his stamp would linger in my memory—the scent of his skin seeping over the dry ragweed smell of the fields; the glitter of his dark eyes alight in the soft gray evenings; the low, rich sound of his laughter laced through the birdlike chatter of females in such an uproar.

In August, Malachi became my rock. He was there, reliable and consistent, capable and kind and wise, through everything.

On August first, the temperature was 101. On the second, it was 102, where it stayed, relentlessly, day in and day out, for six days, when it jumped to 103 before settling back to 101 for a week. Unusual to hit so high, so long, but it did.

Jasmine and Shane took it personally, grumbling from one task to the next in wilted hair. Michael was protected from it in the hospital, but Malachi and I moved his bed downstairs to the parlor for his return, where he'd have the benefit of the breeze that blew in from the porch. If the heat was bad enough, he could sleep in the hammock slung between two hooks outside. I was also thinking of those narrow, steep stairs and how exhausted he'd been climbing them. This would make it easier.

Naturally, since there was more to do than could be done anyway, I started landing an average of one or two new accounts every week and realized I'd need to find a professional kitchen before much longer. In New York, I'd rented a restaurant kitchen in the wee hours of the morning, when it would have ordinarily been empty. It wouldn't be hard, especially with my family connections, to make a similar arrangement here.

Malachi made himself indispensable—pitching in with uncanny accuracy wherever he was most needed. He often ferried Shane back and forth to work, fed the animals, swept floors. My family grew used to asking him to take care of things for them—one day it was driving my grandmother around to three doctor appointments in her staid gray Buick. Another, he made phone calls for Jane, who was so overwrought at all that was left to be done that she broke down and had hysterics.

Another, he ran my pies to every account in town and came home with a wad of tips he gave to me with a wicked twinkle in his eye.

The best times were when we sat with Michael, who grew stronger every day, and I learned their history, both together and apart. When I learned how deeply they'd both been wounded, and how strong they each had become at the site of the scar.

On Thursday evening, I dropped Shane off at the restaurant. Malachi rode along so we could stop in for dinner at the hospital. Michael had been taken off the respirator and moved to a regular room, but they weren't about to release him for another four or five days, and he was quickly becoming the most irritated—or irritating?—patient on the ward. I'd stopped earlier in the day at Pepe's, a gourmet Italian/Mexican deli out in Blende, to bring him olives and goat cheese and sun-dried tomatoes. I'd cooked one of his favorite dishes, lemon-grilled zucchini, and Malachi smuggled in a good red wine in the waistband of his jeans. The nurses looked the other way when we spread the feast out, and Michael turned the television to ESPN because Malachi could not get enough of sports all day long every day.

"Man, I can't wait for football season," Malachi said with that yearning in his voice.

"Tell me about it," Michael breathed, and cut me an amused glance. "Almost time, Jewel. Aren't you thrilled?"

"Oh, definitely. Can hardly wait." I rolled my eyes.

"You don't like football?" Malachi said with an edge of exaggerated surprise.

"I'd rather walk barefooted through goatheads." I lifted a forkful of cheese and roasted peppers, eyeing his shoulders. "I guess you were every coach's dream, though, huh?"

Michael, ever the older brother, snickered. "Not exactly."

"Hell, how could I follow Michael? They all thought I'd be some big superstar like my brother the quarterback, and all I had was size."

I grinned. "You didn't teach him the Game of Games, Michael? Some older brother you were." Michael had been all-state quarterback his senior year in high school and could have gone to college on a football scholarship, but chose instead to hit the music road with Billy.

"Hey, I tried," he said. "Boy had the coordination of a Great Dane puppy."

I laughed, and so did Malachi. He lowered his head, a little abashed. "It's true. I tripped on mosquitoes in those days. Broke the coach's heart, it did, especially after my sophomore year."

"Lord, that was a summer!" Michael said, shaking his head. "You know how it was when Shane turned fifteen? Ate you out of house and home?"

"Like he doesn't now?" But I remembered the difference. Entire boxes of cereal, whole gallons of milk, giant pizzas with all the trimmings, double orders at Burger King—with shakes instead of soda, by his own choice—all in a single day.

"Oh, no. You have no idea. When he was fifteen, that May," Michael said, animation lending his razor-thin face an illusion of health, "Malachi was, what? Five eight? Five nine?"

Malachi nodded, doing a fair job of devouring a loaf of french bread by himself now.

"In October, he was six three and still growing. He ate from morning till night every single day and was still skinny as a rail."

I kept myself from eyeing his gorgeous thighs, which were not at all skinny now. A restless little wish for his body roamed across my mouth and breasts, and I pushed it away. "That's quite a growth spurt."

He glanced at me, as if he'd felt the pulse that suddenly started thudding in my belly, and his eyes grew liquid, wicked, amused. He winked lightly, dispelling the tension. I shook my head at his wordless bawdiness, and he laughed.

When I looked back at Michael, there was a very small smile around his mouth. "Anyway," he said. "The boy had the size, and the coaches were slobbering, but he couldn't hold a football to save his ever-lovin' life."

Malachi held his hands in front of him, examining them. "Shame, ain't it?"

I thought of what else he could do with those hands. "Everybody's got a different talent." I licked my lower lip.

"True enough, sugar. True enough."

"Wait a minute," I said, narrowing my eyes at Michael. "I'm confused. I thought you left home when he was younger than that."

Michael nodded. "Mama got herself a real good job in Biloxi, got herself a good church congregation, and she settled for the first time. They didn't move anymore, so I stopped in as much as I could." He frowned, staring into the past. "I knew you then—that was after the second album."

I peered at a forkful of peppers, thinking again how much younger Malachi was. "That was the summer Billy and I went to Sicily." I wrinkled my nose, thinking I'd been trying to get pregnant in Lucca Sicula when Malachi was having his growth spurt. "You're a child, son, a child."

His eyes crinkled at the corners, deep fans of sun lines born on his wild adventures. "Nah, you're just old."

"Ah, too true."

"It's just right, biologically speaking," Michael said. "Women need a man a little younger."

"Michael!" I protested, embarrassed in spite of myself.

He looked at me innocently. "What? You think he never heard of sex? He ain't that young."

Too much. I narrowed my eyes at him—he was always matchmaking me with someone. My love life after Billy had been his personal quest.

"Malachi," Michael said, "would you run and fetch me some soda water out of the machine at the end of the hall?"

Clueless as all men, he jumped up. "Sure, bro. Be right back."

As soon as he was gone, I stood up so I could get close and talk quietly. "What are you doing?"

He took my hand, hard. "Don't talk. Just listen for once, will you?"

I nodded but didn't smile.

"I see you lookin' at him, sugar, in a way you haven't looked at anybody in a long time. Maybe ever. And I see him looking back the same way. You'd be good for each other."

I glanced over my shoulder. "It's sweet of you, but no." I squeezed his fingers gently. "Remember Johnny." Johnny had been a decent enough sort, a Queens native with an accent just Italian enough to make me homesick. He'd been attractive, never married, with a house of his own in Jersey. I'd liked him well enough, but he'd fallen head over heels in love in six weeks flat, and it took me a year to get rid of him.

He waved his hand. "Johnny was Andre's idea. I never did much care for him."

"And Thomas?" A svelte and charming sociopath who captivated me for weeks, then stole $3,000 from the register one night when nobody was looking.

Michael winced. "Not my best call." When I would have come up with another disaster of a name, he said, "What about David?"

I had to concede that hadn't been bad. We'd dated for a long time, at least by my post-Billy standards, which was about eight months. I hadn't been ready for a commitment, and he was ready to settle down and have children, so we parted friends. "He was okay."

"And who introduced you to Billy, hmm?"

I laughed. "Now which side of the line should I put that on?"

His clear blue eyes sobered. "The good side, Jewel. You had fifteen good years."

I'd been kind of hoping for fifty. "At which point he self-destructed like a bomb from *Mission: Impossible*."

"You gotta make peace, honey. Sooner or later, you've gotta just claim your life."

An unexpected pinch of tears made me blink. "No, I don't." I heard Malachi's step behind me. "And stop matchmaking," I whispered.

~

221

Although he gave a good show for a solid forty-five minutes, maybe an hour on a good day, Michael tired very quickly, and after supper we left him with a big pile of magazines and novels and the channel changer. I kissed his head on the way out, feeling the thinness of flesh over bone on his brow, the furnace of illness in his pores. "Sweet dreams," I said.

Outside, the sun had set, and the world had cooled a solid fifteen degrees. Without the iron of that sun beating you to death, eighty degrees at 20 percent humidity is pretty damned pleasant, and I wasn't in a hurry to get home. "Shane doesn't get off for a couple of hours. You want to go find a beer somewhere?"

"Love it."

We went to a hole-in-the-wall tavern downtown that had been there as long as I could remember, a comfortable neighborhood bar with tall booths and a dart game going on in back. He ordered tomato beers, and we carried them outside to the patio. A folk guitarist wearing a long flowered skirt and a macramé top sang a wistful ballad. Her fine blonde hair lifted on the wind, and although she was not particularly pretty, she had that rosebud dewiness you start to notice the minute you've lost it. When she saw Malachi wander out, she missed a chord, and he gave her an easy grin. She smiled back, instantly smitten, and sang the next song toward him.

A gold ring looped through her belly button.

I focused on the tub of geraniums to my left, suddenly very aware of the round of Malachi's biceps pushing against the plain white cotton of his shirt, of the shape of his wrist and hand on the table, the sense of his thigh not that far away from mine. Beneath the sound of guitar and girl-voice was the omnipresent summer music of crickets and cicadas.

"God," Malachi said suddenly, nudging me with his elbow. "This guy looks just like Billy! Look!"

Coming through the back gate was a young man, maybe twenty-five, with the long, ropy build that seemed to lend itself so well to guitar players. He was dressed in black, head to toe, black leather pants that caught the light in strategic spots, black bandanna tied pirate fashion around his head. The dark hair fell nearly to his waist in rippling waves. It was a style—bad-boy rock and roller—but there was a greater similarity, too. A darkness clinging to his mouth, a loping way of moving.

It was enough to make a stab of something go through my heart. "Amazing," I said quietly, shaking my head.

The man paused broodingly to one side, scanning the grounds from beneath hooded lids, a study in ennui. His wrists and hands sported tattoos and rings. "Billy used to get a tattoo whenever he felt really bad about himself," I said before I knew I would. "He always said it was a celebration, but it wasn't."

Malachi looked at me with the graveness that could sometimes give his normally playful expression so much more depth. "You still miss him," he said in some surprise.

I lifted a shoulder, still snared by the look of the young man. The resemblance was eerie, and I felt echoey emotions bouncing around the air, shimmery memories of Billy twenty years ago, when he was still so full of himself and his dreams, always vulnerable to the darkness, but genuinely brilliant. "I know a lot of people think I just ran off with him to get away, or because he was a musician on the rise," I said, "but I loved him. I really did."

"We all did, Jewel." He looked toward the youth, back to me. "I thought he hung the friggin' moon."

"Yeah. Exactly," I said, shifting so that the guy would be out of my line of vision. "I keep thinking about the state fair. Michael has it in his head that he really needs to go, and I keep thinking there's no way I can do it." I swallowed, glaring into my red beer. "Not because of Michael or any regrets, which is what he's thinking, but I don't want to go and think about how much hope Billy had that night I met them."

He touched my hand, waiting. I looked back at the Billy clone and let the sword of loss he roused come through. "We *connected*, all three of us, that night. I was as devoted as I knew how to be, as supportive and strong, encouraging." I frowned. "I didn't freak when he started getting lost, either. I mean, I saw what was happening, that he was just kind of sliding down this . . . this slope, and he kept slipping out of my grasp."

"Suicide is always rough on the people it leaves behind."

"It wasn't suicide!"

"Well, not in the sense that he took a gun and shot himself, but what do you think he was doing, Jewel? The way he saw it, he was a failure."

"But he wasn't. He was a good musician—he could have had studio work for the rest of his life. Even when he was really getting bad at the end, when I had to make him leave—Shane was only about eight or nine, and I didn't want him hurt, you know?"

He nodded.

"Even then, they were still calling to have him come work. It was worth it to them." I peered into the past. "And before he let it all get to him, he was good to us. He was a good father, a good husband, not that we were exactly married."

Malachi took my hand. "Throw it in the river, babe."

"I have no idea what that means."

He made a gesture with his hand, tossing an invisible something into the air. "Take all the parts you can't do anything about and throw 'em in the river. Keep the things you can use, the good days, and let the rest go."

He made it sound so easy. "I don't know how."

"Yes, you do." For the first time, I realized he was very close, his long-lashed eyes starry and liquid in the low light. I don't know which of us moved first, but somehow, we were kissing. Gently. The best kind of kiss in the world, or one of them, the soft give-and-take kind, the comforting kind with just a hint of more lurking.

It was so exactly what I needed in that particular moment that I shifted a little to let him in, inviting the sweep of tongue, bracing myself with one hand on his thigh. For a minute he hesitated, and I opened my eyes to see him looking at me, very close, and then his lids swept down, and he came inside, almost against his will, and I followed him back.

Kissing. Most men just don't get it. They get past it as quickly as they can, diving onward to earthier things. The man who knows how to kiss and likes it, who isn't afraid of it, is a gem indeed, and Malachi liked it. He was good at it. There was as much an art to it as there was to a handshake, and it had as much to say about a person.

Malachi's lips were relaxed but not squishy. He didn't crush my mouth or grind my teeth or shove his tongue halfway down my throat. He . . . played. Danced.

He pulled away first. "I really like kissing you," he said a little roughly.

"I bet you ruined your chances with the girl, though."

"The girl?"

I straightened, trying to blow it off. "Yeah, the girl with the belly ring."

He snorted. "*Way* too young, sugar." He picked up his glass, drained it, looked around for a server. "I think Billy Boy is her guy, anyway."

"Ah, of course." For a minute I felt sorry for her. But that was foolish—the kid only looked like Billy. That didn't mean he had to end up like him.

"I do like the belly ring," he said, and leaned closer to me. "But not as much as your tattoo." He made a show of pretending to look down my shirt.

I tossed my head. "Too bad. So sad. You let a seventeen-year-old talk you out of it, so why would I bother with you?"

He laughed, and leaned in closer, his breath on my neck. "What makes you think I'm not going to do anything?"

I looked at him. "Whatever you say." He was lying, and I knew it, and he knew that I knew it. He wanted to be in my bed almost as much as he didn't. I scared him—and since my ambivalence was hardly resolved, I figured that was a good thing. "You know what you're missing."

"Yeah," he said with a sigh. "Yes, I surely do." He stood up. "I'm going to get another beer. You want one?"

"No, thanks. I have to drive."

~

Friday morning, Shane arose with the sun and me and rushed through breakfast so that I could drop him off at the restaurant before I made my rounds with the pies. He was going to stay with my mother tonight and tomorrow to help cook, and it made me feel oddly uncomfortable that he was spending so much time with my parents. Shane had surprised me with the wish to stay and help tonight with the millions of pizzelles that would be made for the wedding. "You don't mind, do you, Mom?" he asked. "Me helping Nana cook?"

I looked to the left, waiting for a break in traffic, so he wouldn't see my face. "No, why do you ask?"

"I dunno. You just seem kinda funny about it."

Pulling into traffic gave me a minute to come up with a response. "Does my dad talk to you?"

"Sure. He has all along, when you weren't around."

"That's good," I said. And it was. I was just . . . jealous, maybe. Jealous that my son could go to the house I grew up in and hadn't set foot inside of in twenty years. That he could work in the restaurant, drinking Cokes in an apron after the dinner rush. "You like him?"

"Mom."

I peered out the windshield at the red stoplight, willing it to turn green now. "Yeah?"

"If you miss him so much, why don't you just talk to him?"

"It's not that easy." I thought of the day in front of Jane's house when I'd tried, when I'd held out my branch of peace and he'd ignored it completely. "He's stubborn."

"He misses you, too."

"Maybe. That doesn't mean he can forgive me."

"I don't understand that," he said.

"I know." I cleared my throat. "Don't spend too much time worrying about it, all right? We'll work it out someday."

At the restaurant, I spied only my father's car in the lot and gave Shane the pies to take inside. "Mom. Won't you try?"

"Not today."

He shrugged, annoyed with me, and I even understood why. But there wasn't a chance in hell I'd open myself up to an all-out rejection from my father in front of the boy who had begun to love him.

After I delivered the pies to the various spots on Friday's list, I met my sister Jane down on Union Avenue. We had a dual purpose— instruction in sexy underwear for Jane, and a dress for our mother.

I arrived first and parked across the street from the enormous red sandstone Union Depot, a landmark in more ways than one. Like so many such places in cities across the country, it had been built on a grand and glorious scale, with elaborate wood trim and stained glass. It had been an enormously busy hub before air travel, particularly during World War II, when troops were moving in and out constantly.

But the station's greatest claim to fame was from the Great Flood of '21, when the Arkansas River nearly took out the city of Pueblo. During the height of the cataclysm, water had risen to the clock on the tower, and as I always did, I lifted my eyes to the imaginary mark so far above my head that I had to squint against the brilliant blue sky to see it. I never had been able to truly get my mind around that much water, and I couldn't now. They said it washed all the way across what was now the highway and up Goat Hill. Afterward they harnessed the river with huge levees behind the station.

Along the street, merchants were opening their shops, putting out chairs and tables on the sidewalk in front of the cafés, rolling out the bright canvas awnings, taking down the protective gauze from the windows full of boutique goods. Standing there, touching history, touching time and geography, a little piece of myself settled back into my heart with a sigh.

I didn't see Jane, and she startled me a little when she touched my arm. "Good morning!"

"Hi!"

She inclined her head. "What's that smile for?"

"I was just thinking how amazing it is that the city has turned itself around so much." I looked at her. "You probably don't really remember how bad it was."

"Not really." She wrinkled her nose apologetically.

We started walking, and I pointed out an old, faded sign with broken lights that would have once flashed an arrow to the sleazy bar below. "When I left, this whole area was pretty slimy. Rough bars and dirty junk shops, that's it. Half the rest of the buildings were closed. There were fires down here all the time." We passed an empty building that waited for someone to restore it, the windows protected by plywood. "Everything looked like this." I looked up at the obvious renovation taking place on the upper stories—more pricey lofts for young professionals. "Only not so clean."

"Pueblo never seems to change that much to me."

"Well, some things always stay the same," I said slowly, remembering. "But it was bad here when I left. So many people lost their jobs with the mill, and they ended up losing their houses and their cars and everything. And they didn't have any money to spend on going out to the bars or the restaurants or the stores, so everybody else started losing money, too. It was depressing. Now—"

She laughed. "Now it's growing."

"It didn't die after all, I guess."

"How could a city die?"

"A lot of people thought it would." We got to the end of the block, and I stopped in front of a naughty, upscale underwear shop. "Are you ready?"

Her eyes widened as she looked up at the sign. "Yikes!"

"C'mon, kiddo. Nobody bites in here."

It was fun. A lot more fun than I had expected to pick out sexy nightclothes for my perfect little sister. She would look so good in all of it that it was really just a matter of helping her to figure out what kind of sexy she liked and felt comfortable with. Some women like feathers and froufrou, some like slinky and elegant, some like trashy, some like virginal. Jane was not in the latter category, or we wouldn't have been there at all, but that was all we really knew. For the first ten minutes, she kept referring her questions to me, as if I had some magic font of knowledge, and I finally pulled about seven different kinds of things off the rack, in all different colors and styles, and said, "Try them on. See how they feel. See what makes you feel fabulous."

Giving me a doubtful look, she clasped them all to her chest and marched off.

While she was in the dressing room—for a really long time, I noticed with a grin—I flipped through the lingerie. Most of it was designed for women either a lot younger or a lot thinner than me, but there were some nice, heavy satin gowns in garnet and emerald that I liked, and a very wicked red corset that I judged would take off the top of Malachi's head. He was a man who would definitely like trashy. For a long moment, I imagined myself in it, a saloon madam, maybe, and thought of how his face would look if I put it on and showed up in his bedroom. Bet he wouldn't be worried about a seventeen-year-old's opinion *then*.

A black leather miniskirt leaped into my hands, and I paired it mentally with the red corset. Bad. Very bad indeed. Especially—I looked at the wall where the stockings were lined up—with black fishnets and high black heels. Wicked, wicked, wicked.

I put it back—the money alone was impossible—and shook my head. It said something about my personality that I was less worried about what my kid might think than Malachi was. Something not very good about my personality.

Suddenly I was ashamed to be in here with all the erotica on the wall, with thong bikinis, ashamed for letting myself imagine seducing a man when my son was in such a troubled place, when my best friend was dying, when my father still wasn't speaking to me for the same kind of crimes.

It all mocked me with its shallowness. The games and toys seemed tawdry, the tattoos tacky.

"Jewel?" Jane stuck her head out of the dressing room door. "Will you come here a minute?"

Wiping the sudden depression off my face, I moved forward. "Sure, sweetie. What is it?"

"I'd like your opinion," she said, and her cheeks were flushed. "I mean, it's kind of racy, you might not want to see all that, and I'm sorry for asking if it makes you uncomfortable, so you can say no if you want, but I'm—"

I put my fingers to my lips, smiling to put her at ease. "Your body won't embarrass me."

A sigh heaved out of her. "Good. I just can't decide between two of them." She waved me in, holding her blouse against her chest modestly. The dressing rooms were plenty big enough for both of us, and I closed the door firmly behind me. When she just stood there, blushing, her blouse clasped to her, I said, "Close your eyes."

She did.

"I guess the one you're wearing is the first one?"

She nodded. Around her crisp white blouse I saw the edges of black and a long, A-line skirt. A silken weight of lace roses, very elegant. I somehow wasn't surprised she'd liked this one. Gently I reached out for the blouse, and she let me have it. "Keep your eyes closed if you want," I said. "Sometimes that's easier."

It was beautiful, of course, its sexiness in what it hid as much as what it revealed. It only hinted at the naked body beneath it. Her creamy shoulders glowed against the black lace. "It's gorgeous," I said. "Very 1930s. It will be perfect in your house."

"Will it make him wild, do you think?" She opened earnest eyes now, taking a deep breath that illuminated her graceful sweep of collarbone.

"Absolutely."

"Okay. That's the first one." She eyed the other, tossed over the built-in bench.

I turned around. "Tell me when you're ready."

The quick agile movements of shedding one, then donning the other. "I have to keep my eyes closed this time," she squeaked. "You can turn around now."

Laughing softly at her appealing modesty, I turned and whistled low. "You want them both, babe," I said. It was black, too. And a lot more revealing, but in the best possible way. "This is an entirely different mood. Maybe this would be good for one night a little later in the honeymoon."

"He kind of likes fishnets," Jane said, putting her hands over her face. "I think he'll really like this one, and I'm the one who really likes the other one."

"Then you definitely need them both. One to perk you up when you're sensing he's in the mood and you aren't—"

"Oh, I can't imagine not being in the mood."

I chuckled, turning to face the door. "I'm not looking anymore," I said. "So get them both just for fun."

"I think I will." There was no sound. I suspected she was admiring herself in the wicked body stocking she had enough sense to realize would please the bad-boy side of her ever-so-respectable husband. For some reason, it put a lump in my throat.

"Oh," she said quietly, "I really can't wait. My skin feels like it's on fire. All I think about"—her voice was muffled as she pulled something over her head—"every single minute, and I'm not kidding, is our wedding night. I don't know how I'll stand to wait the whole entire day."

It made the knot in my throat worse. "I love it that you haven't slept together."

"Yeah, I'm glad in a way. It'll be"—her voice got breathless—"fun to discover it all with him."

The knot moved through my throat to the backs of my eyes, and I blinked hard, wishing with everything in me for the discovery of sex with a man I'd be with for the rest of my life. "It will be more than you even imagine right now," I said, and hoped my voice sounded steadier to her than it did to me. "The best."

She squeezed me from behind, giggling and happy. "Thank you, Jewel. You are so awesome to do this with me."

"My pleasure," I said. "Now, let's go find something for Mama and get some lunch. I haven't eaten since five this morning."

~

We didn't have a lot of luck at the first two shops we tried—most of the fashions were too young or extreme, nothing my mother would wear on a bet. We had not been entirely certain about size, since Mama wouldn't discuss her weight and cut the tags out of her dresses so no one would ever know, but on that, Jasmine had come through. She hadn't been able to come shopping with us today, but she had slipped into Mama's room one day and measured one of her dresses with a tape measure at bust, waist, and hip, and we figured she was a size eight. Ten at the most. Impossible that my little mother and trim father had had such Amazon daughters. Except of course that it wasn't.

In the third shop, we found it. A classic mother-of-the-bride dress in soft champagne silk, a scoop-neck, sleeveless sheath with a waist-length jacket made of matching lace. "Ooh," Jane breathed as I pulled it off the rack. "This is it."

"I wish we could talk her into wearing her hair down or something."

"No, not down," Jane said, shaking her head. "But loosely gathered on her head, don't you think? Her hair is her secret thing, you know, like for Pop alone. I think that's kinda neat."

Ah. Of course. "I guess it is."

~

When I left Jane, I ambled back to my car, sluggish with the heat of the sun and the long, long day of shopping. I was sleepy and peaceful and content. She made me feel ancient, but in a good way, not like a crone but a priestess, and when the lingerie shop came into view, maybe that was why I slowed. Testing myself.

And suddenly it occurred to me that I knew exactly what to get her for her wedding gift. Let everyone else give her Crock-Pots. From her bold, wild sister would be at least one thing that was unbelievably racy.

The clerk smiled, remembering me from earlier. "Forget something?"

"A surprise for her." Jane had said that her fiancé liked fishnets, and with a happy, close smile, I marched over to the racks and found the red corset—medium—and the leather skirt. Jane was younger than I, but she was as voluptuous as the rest of us, so I tried it on, finding it pretty tight. Just right for her. On the way past the wall of stockings, I chose a pair of fishnets, with a garter belt, naturally.

"Oh, very sexy," the clerk said.

"Yeah." It cost a pretty penny, pennies I couldn't really afford after the dress-buying spree, but life came around only once.

"Do you want me to wrap it?"

I shook my head. "I'll take it like that." I wanted to stop by and show Michael. Just for fun.

MALACHI'S FRIED FISH AND POTATOES

Ain't nothin' fancy about this meal. Cube a few potatoes, no need to skin 'em, and toss them in whatever oil you have handy, though olive oil is real good if you're not camping. Bacon grease is also terrific, but a little more trouble if you're cooking over an open fire. Watch out they don't burn.

While you're cooking the potatoes, take your basic white fish, any style, and clean and debone. Slice the fish into manageable pieces and roll them in a mix of cornmeal, flour, salt, and pepper. Fry in a hot skillet till done, and serve with beer.

Chapter Sixteen

The day had turned deep gold by the time I got back out to the farm, and I found myself thinking about Malachi. Without Shane, we'd be knocking around the house alone, and I felt a little apprehensive as I pulled up by the lilac bushes. There were no pies, no wedding goodies to cook, and even if there had been, I was really too tired even to think about standing up in a kitchen all evening.

Heavy clouds were gathering to the west, but the sun was just ahead of them, and it fell in dusty reddish gold bars through the elms lacing their arms overhead. It was the stillest time of day, and as I closed the car door, I heard the faint strains of music coming from the house. No other sound whatsoever. No engines, not cars or tractors or planes. Too early for crickets, and the cicadas must have been taking a break.

The music seemed to be coming from the back, and I walked around the outside of the porch, looking for Malachi. He didn't hear me come up, and I caught him in a rare moment of revealment—his legs propped on the railing in their boots and jeans, his shirt open in deference to the heat. His hair, really getting too long now as the weeks passed, was a little tousled, as if he'd had his hands in it, and on his slanted and carved face was a distant expression.

I stopped, pierced a little by how much I liked looking at him, how dear his face had become over the short time he'd been here. It occurred to me that I'd become very dependent on him these past few weeks, dependent on his reliability, his easygoing humor, which was so welcome in a family of such intense personalities, his way of simply taking care of things that otherwise went undone.

It scared me, suddenly. I had not allowed myself to depend on anyone in a very long time. I took care of things myself. I liked it that way—if you didn't put too much trust into somebody, you couldn't get hurt, right?

For a minute, I felt a panicky sensation in the back of my throat, as if I couldn't quite breathe. Then I realized that there had just been so much going on that I'd taken the easy help he offered. I didn't expect him to stay. Didn't expect a declaration of love or a proposal of marriage. My independence was safe.

Still, I felt bereft, wondering if I'd ever see him again after Michael died.

Feeling as if I were invading his privacy with my silent observation, I moved into his line of vision. "Hey, soldier," I said, carrying my packages up the stairs to dump them on the table. "How you doing?"

He picked up a long-neck bottle of Bud and examined the last two inches of beer left in it. "Guess I'll be better when I get me another beer. You want one?"

"Sure. I'll get it." I took the strap of my purse from my shoulder and started to turn.

"Nope. For once, you sit." He pushed on my shoulder lightly. "I'll get it. You want anything else?"

It wasn't until I was sitting that I realized just how very tired I was. Gathering the heavy, hot mass of my hair from my shoulders, I said, "Water?"

"No problem."

I twisted my hair into a rope and tied it into a knot at my neck. Not exactly an elegant style, but it worked. A light breeze swept over my nape and spine. So much better.

Malachi was back in a second, carrying a very big glass of ice water and two beers. "I made dinner, too. Nothing like your cooking, a-course, but I hustle up a mean fish."

"You cooked?"

He sat down, put his beer on the table, and bent over to unlace his boots. "Got lucky this morning and bagged a couple of nice bass out at the reservoir."

"That's great." I drank the water first, big long thirsty gulps of it, drinking until my stomach felt a little too tight.

One boot came off, and he stripped off his sock, stuck it inside, and started on the other. "You were out cold."

"I was a little slow this morning." I finally noticed the music. Bonnie Raitt's "Angel from Montgomery." "Mmm, I love this song."

"Love the whole CD," he said, and pulled off the other sock and boot.

His feet were long and sturdy, with graceful high arches and knotty looking toes. "What size shoe do you wear?"

"Fourteen." Inclining his head, he slanted a grin at me. "Sometimes fifteen."

"Shane wears a thirteen. It must be hell for you to find shoes."

A half shrug. "I'm used to looking hard for everything I wear."

Eyeing his long back, it occurred to me that I still sometimes forgot how enormous he was. He just didn't have the usual big man mis-shapenness or clumsiness. Everything was in perfect proportion, just larger than average. "It really is kind of amazing that you didn't end up in sports of some kind."

"Ain't it a bitch?" He laughed a little, showing me that crooked eyetooth that was so oddly appealing. "Just was no damned good at any of it."

"Well, except wrestling rivers and fish."

He shot me a grin, making the sun lines crinkle. "I guess that counts."

"I'd say it did." Easing into my chair a little more deeply, I took a sip of beer. A tiny little sip. This tired, with so much on my mind, I didn't want to lose my head. "I went by to see Michael on the way home. They're going to let him go, maybe Monday."

"I spent the afternoon with him. Took the fish by to show him." The smile wavered, and he swallowed hard. "I'm about to carry him out of there myself."

I touched his arm.

"You hungry?"

"I could eat." I started to get up.

"Let me do it, Jewel. You're always waiting on everybody." Far away, thunder rumbled low and long against the mountains. He glanced toward the west. "It's nothing fancy, just some fish and potatoes."

"I can help."

"Just sit." He dug in his pocket and threw me a lighter. "Take care of the candles."

I moved the bags off the table, making a mental note to take them inside before it started to rain, and lit the pillars and tapers and the nearly spent stubs of some votives in their varied containers. A soft wind, pushed ahead by the rain coming toward us, made the flames flicker. Darkness was falling in earnest now, and the candles, narrowing our world, made me feel cozy.

Malachi brought out two plates piled high with fried fish and potatoes, the silverware rolled in napkins in his other hand. "Want something else to drink?"

"I'm fine, thank you." I inhaled the scent. "Smells wonderful."

"This is about the extent of my cooking," he said, "but I think I make it pretty good."

And it was excellent, as the simplest foods often are, seasoned with salt and pepper, fried crispy with the insides still tender. We didn't talk much at first.

"Guess I should have thought about some wine," he said.

"No, I think beer is just right with this. Hearty." To illustrate, I took a big swig. "It's really good, Malachi."

"Thanks." I sensed a little shyness about him tonight. A wish to please, maybe. "How'd it go today with Jane? You guys went shopping for wedding stuff or something?"

As if it was a movie, Bonnie Raitt started singing "Love Me Like a Man." "Something like that," I said. "She wanted honeymoon items, actually." Carefully I wiped my greasy fingers on a napkin, once, then again. "I picked up a present for her. You want to see?"

"Sure." It was the reply of a man being casually polite. I took out the red corset, putting it up against my body, then laid the leather skirt across my lap. I wiggled my eyebrows. "Smashing, huh?"

His expression didn't change. "Nice," he said, and popped a potato in his mouth. Leaning back, he lifted a shoulder. "It always seemed to me that bare skin was enough."

"Really." I hoped it didn't sound as irked as I felt.

"What could be better than naked?" His position showed me a long strip of chest and belly between the flaps of his shirt. Deeply tanned flesh, supple and hard as—I couldn't think of anything except *man*. I wanted, with sudden ferocity, to see him naked again. And not for five seconds in a kitchen before we got caught, but where I could admire all that length and suppleness at leisure.

It still miffed me a little that he was unmoved by my ploy, and folding the pieces, I shrugged. "Naked is good, I guess."

He chuckled softly. "Naked is the whole point, isn't it?"

I couldn't look at him. Shoved the pieces back in the bag and took a long drink of beer to cool my overheated throat. Chest. Groin. It didn't reach that far, and I wiped a little sweat from below my ear with my wrist. "Eventually," I answered finally.

He kicked his feet out in front of him, looking at me steadily.

"What?" I snapped.

"You want to get naked with me, sugar?"

I snorted. "Not with a man who calls women *babe* and *sugar* all the time."

"All right, then." He took a leisurely swallow of beer. "Jewel, you want to get naked with me? Because I'd sure like to get naked with you, and maybe we don't have many chances."

I smiled slowly. "The answer, Malachi," I said, standing up and picking up my bags to keep them safe from the rain that was coming, "is yes." I walked to the door. "Last one naked is a rotten egg."

He jumped up, and we raced inside, banging the screen door behind us. I dropped my bags on the dining room table and saw that he'd already lost his shirt. "Not fair!" I cried. "You started out way ahead."

"I'll let you catch up." He dropped the shirt over the back of a chair, rubbing his belly in that way men always do, easy with the feel of themselves. "Better yet, I'll just get naked and watch you get yourself naked."

"Upstairs," I said, reaching for the waistband of my jeans. I shimmied out of them. "And you have to go up first because there's no way I'm walking in front like this."

"You go up the front stairs. I'll go up the back."

Quizzically, I smiled. "Why?"

"Naked when you reach the top of the stairs."

A shiver touched my neck. We parted.

I climbed the stairs, pulling my T-shirt over my head at the landing, then my bra off on the next step, feeling deliciously wicked at being naked in some part of the house that wasn't a bedroom or bathroom. I reached the top of the stairs with my panties still covering me, and couldn't quite get the nerve to take them off.

Malachi had fetched a candle from the kitchen and carried it in his big right hand. The light flickered over him, hiding and revealing the buttery look of his flesh—the astonishingly gorgeous length of him, long torso and longer legs. His shoulders looked sleek and round, and I stopped in almost overwhelming desire for a minute, my clothes forgotten in my hand.

"Naked," he said.

I peeled off my panties, and he moved toward me. "Now, what costume could be better than this?"

"Easy for you to say," I whispered, unable to get more volume than that as his arm looped around my back, his palm spreading over my bottom. "You're perfect. The rest of us have things we'd just as soon hide."

He kissed me. Bent that giant lion head and captured my mouth, using his arm to pull me against him, a sensation that gave me a jolt so violent in combination with his mouth that my knees nearly buckled. I had the sense of the candle aloft to one side, casting yellow light over my eyelids, lids I closed against the onslaught.

He lifted his head, his eyes sober and sparkling at once, and took my hand. "Bed," he said, and led me to my room. He put the candle on the dresser, and we fell on the unmade bed together, limbs and lips and hands tangling in that acute, needful way people who've been resisting will do when they finally give in. "You don't know," he said in his raspiest voice, gathering my breasts into his hands, "how often I lay down there in that room and thought of this."

My heart pounded, sending extra blood around wherever it was needed. "Yeah?" I asked breathlessly. "And what'd you think about doing?"

He reached behind him and tossed the cover over me. "I would think of you naked under a sheet," he said in a low voice, smoothing that sheet over my breasts, almost to my neck. "Sleeping on your back." I closed my eyes, a pulse fluttering in my throat. "And I'd think about coming in here, and slowly pulling down the sheet"—it slid downward, an inch at a time—"until I could see your breasts, imagining how beautiful they would be." He used his hands, his mouth. "How responsive."

"And then what?" I breathed, my hands moving on his thigh, tight and tense from his position.

"And then you'd wake up, and I'd kiss you." He did.

"Didn't I do anything back?" I pushed at him a little, touched the weight of his sex teasingly.

"Maybe."

"In my imagination," I said, sitting up, "it was a little different."

"It was?"

I pushed him down on his back. "You were sleeping, and I crept into your room, and woke you up with my mouth." I illustrated, slowly and erotically, and like all men at such moments, he only made an incoherent sound, low and deep. He put his hands in my hair and pulled it around us, smoothed it over his belly, and I used the hair, too, laughing low in my throat at the strangled sound, which also gave a little more excitement.

"God, Jewel," he groaned, and pulled me up to him, to his mouth, and I couldn't be aloof or pretend to be wicked or playful or anything else. I kissed him with my heart on my lips, and I tasted his, and we made our way to joining with the ragged sound of hungry breath, crying out together when it was accomplished.

And in that single second, we both paused. Malachi lifted his head, and I opened my eyes, and we hung there, eyes open, lips softly greeting, once, twice, three times. I felt my trembling and his, all through us, and then we tumbled into the deep, taking refuge from each other in each other.

When it was right, it was *so* right.

Everything disappeared but Malachi and the force of us joining. There was only now, this very minute, burning white and blue, with Malachi moving with me, in me, over me, through me.

Only him. Hiding and revealing himself, ducking away and dipping back for a kiss, driven to join, to take refuge, to relieve his pain, his loneliness here with me, and I opened all the way, taking the chance again, because it was impossible not to give that one thing that it was possible to give. Shelter. Peace for five minutes. A heart beating warm in the darkness. To take the gift of his sensitive hands, his giving mouth, the unbelievable, unmatchable pleasure of being with a man I really wanted.

Malachi and me. Me and him. Rain falling outside, patting against the windows, our hands sliding, lips falling on chins and necks and chests. Thunder and the hard, rocking, fierce motion. The smell of him and me, and the rain, rain wafting in light sprays over my face as I held him, his enormous body spent, his nose against my neck, his mouth in breathless, butterfly kisses over my throat.

When it's right, it is *so* right.

~

We lay there, spoon fashion, ghostly light coming through the curtains like a blessing. His arm lay heavy across my side, his hand clasped in mine. My rear end rested against his hairy thigh, and against the hollow of my back, I could feel the damp softness of exhausted penis. In appreciation, I pulled his hand to my mouth, kissed his fingers. "Oh, that was good," I said on a sigh.

He kissed the place at the base of my neck that gives me shivers every time, kissed it with that slow laziness of a satisfied man. He moved his bristly chin against the spot. "Told you," he rumbled.

I laughed and shifted a little, rubbing my foot on his shin. "So you did."

The long fingers slid from my grasp and moved to cover my breast, an easy clasp. "God, that's nice," he said, and his lips touched my back again. "So soft. Nothing in the world has that exact kind of weight. When I was about thirteen or fourteen, I wanted to have breasts of my own so I could just feel them all day long."

Laughing, I turned over and faced him. Light caught on a swoop of hair, and I lifted a hand to touch it. "Boys are so vulnerable to breasts. When Shane was that age, he kept downloading pictures of these women with triple-Z breasts. Stripper variety. The most amazing breasts I've ever seen."

"What did you do?"

The light edged his nose, too, and tipped the very edge of his lashes, hiding his eyes. I moved my leg over the outside of his to feel the slide of his skin and that crisp hair against my inner thigh. "We talked about it."

"Yeah?" He moved his palm along my ribs, up and then down again. His toes touched my ankle. "What did you tell him?"

"That I understood why he wanted to look at those pictures, but that real sex was a lot better." With one finger, I touched the edge of his jaw, wanting with a fierceness that surprised me to kiss him again. So I did. Slowly. "That no picture in the world can come close to the real thing."

"Good answer." He kissed me back. "And what did you think about sex when you were thirteen?"

"I didn't."

"Liar."

"What does that mean?"

He laughed. "You've been thinking about it since you knew it was in the world."

"I don't know why you'd say that, Mr. Shaunnessey."

"You love it, Jewel. Everything about it."

"I do." I closed my eyes to breathe him into me, the prickle of sweaty skin, the solidity of his body next to mine, the smell of him, the sound of his breath. "Yes," I said, moving my hand and feeling the slight tensile shift in his organ against my palm, my fingers. "I really do."

"So what did you think about when you were thirteen or fourteen? When boys are looking for breasts in size Z, are girls thinking about dicks the size of pogo sticks?"

"No," I said. "I did want to see a penis, you understand, but my fantasies were about pressing my breasts against a boy's naked chest. I thought I could be happy with that."

"Like this?" He moved close. Crisp hair pinged over my skin.

I hadn't thought of hair at thirteen. I just didn't know how good it would feel. "Sort of."

He bent and opened his mouth over one nipple. "Or was it more like that?" He suckled and let go, and in spite of everything we'd done already, a blip of arousal slammed between my thighs, and I laughed.

"It would never have occurred to me to think of that much."

He lay back. "So who taught you to think of it?"

Dangerous territory, that. "Let's not spoil this."

"Will it spoil it?"

"Probably."

"Why? Was he better than me in bed?"

I thought of the back seat of his Fairlane, and the hurried moments in an empty apartment borrowed from a friend. "No."

"Then tell me."

"You first," I countered. "First lover."

"Nope. I asked first."

I sighed, turning over on to my back. "Jesus Medina." Not *Gee*-zus. Hay-soos. At the sound of his name, a face long forgotten pressed into my mind. I'd loved his name so much. "He was the most dangerous boy in school—even had a tattoo around his arm. I was sure I could save him."

"Save him from what?"

"I don't know. Himself, probably. We worked together at a restaurant in town." The moment rushed back. The table by the window, where it was so hot, the sun shining hard through the windows to light on his hair that was so long and straight, so black it didn't reflect any color but white. He had lifted long, almond eyes, faintly hostile. Eyes that turned soft when they lit on me.

Jesus. A whirl of images came back. Those big white teeth that showed when he let go of his defenses and really laughed. The wide mouth and good lips, and a kiss that could melt diamonds.

I would have done anything for him. It made me quiet, remembering.

Malachi's hand moved a little, prompting. "And what happened? Why did you pick him?"

As if there had been a choice involved. "I didn't, really," I said, and knew it was a lie even before he snorted. "Okay, I did. I knew from the first that he was the kind of boy who knew what to do, you know?"

"Yep."

"I was still a nice Catholic girl at the time—thought I'd been pretty good at following the rules. But he just had this aura that made me think about it all the time, what real sex would be like." I stopped for a minute, then went on. "It was his bare feet, actually. I was sitting with him at a party, and his feet were bare, and they were so beautiful that I just wanted to touch him so badly . . ." I shook my head. "How weird is that?"

He only looked at me softly, his hand moving on my body.

"Now you," I said, feeling revealed.

"Kimmy Johnson. She was twenty-three, and I was sixteen."

"Now why doesn't that surprise me?"

"I have a history of older women."

"Thanks very much for reminding me."

He chuckled, rubbing his chin on the top of my head. "Thought I'd died and gone to heaven, yes, I did. We had one seriously hot summer."

I tried to figure the age difference—by then I'd met Billy and Michael. We were probably already in New York. It made me feel old, and I pulled the sheet over me.

He pushed it off, leaning close with that bad-boy grin. "Five years is a lot when you're sixteen. Not so much in your thirties."

"Forties. I'm forty."

"Oh, well, then forget it. You really are old."

His grin was wicked, wild, so free. I looked up at him, shifting my head on the pillow so that I could really see him, and I had one of those aware moments, a space of a few seconds that I could really be alive in, seeing his aggressive nose and the fall of his dark hair across his neck. I touched the length of his throat, realizing that this whole thing hadn't been for him at all. I'd done it for me, and not because I was desperate for sex, but because I'd wanted to lie here like this with him, feeling whole.

Feeling whole. How could that be?

"The difference is," I said, making my voice light, "is that you could have women who are twenty."

"Nah. Twenty-year-olds are too idealistic."

"What's wrong with that?"

He shook his head. "They always think sex is love."

I made an outraged noise. "That is so sexist, Mr. Shaunnessey!"

"It's also true. How old were you when you fell in love with Billy?"

"Seventeen. Much younger."

"Mmm. And would you fall now?"

I lifted up on one elbow, narrowing my eyes. "I don't know. He was pretty lost."

"Would you have sex with him?"

I thought of Billy's long black hair, the depth of his eyes, the way he could get that expression on his face that turned my body to instant mush. With a wry grin, I said, "Probably."

"There you go."

"Have you ever fallen in love, Malachi?"

He pulled back and looked at me for a long minute, and I could see the worry in him that I'd asked such a question. "No." And the way he said it, I could tell he meant it.

"How did you avoid it?"

A shrug. "I just have."

"Never a twinge? Never even a bad crush?"

"If it gets there," he said, "I leave."

"Run."

"Same difference."

I smiled, suddenly very sure, and bent to kiss him. "What are you going to do this time?" I whispered, and rubbed the length of his belly with an open palm. I didn't close my eyes, and let him see the amusement his little paper walls gave me.

He didn't bother to protest, but pushed me back on the pillows, an edge of aggression to his movements that amused me even more, and I chuckled.

"I'll figure it out," he growled, and kissed me.

NANA LUCY'S NOVENA

Novena to Saint Therese of the Little Flower (Patron Saint of AIDS patients)

Saint Therese, the Little Flower, please pick me a rose from the heavenly garden and send it to me with a message of love. Ask God to grant me the favor I thee implore and tell Him I will love Him each day more and more.

The above prayer, plus five Our Fathers, five Hail Marys, and five Glory Bes, must be said on five successive days, before 11 a.m. On the fifth day, the fifth set of prayers having been completed, offer one more set—five Our Fathers, five Hail Marys, and five Glory Bes.

Chapter Seventeen

Michael came home on Monday morning. From his bed by the dining room windows, he could talk to someone on the porch or see into the kitchen. It was the heart of the house.

He was weak but in good spirits that day and the next. Our whole goal—and by ours, I mean Michael's, mine, my family's—was to see him strong enough by Saturday to go to at least part of the wedding and reception. Shane had already volunteered to be the one to bring him home when he got tired, bring him home and stay with him. He did add that he hoped it would be all right if Alicia, the girl from Falconi's, could come with him. Michael and I exchanged a look over that, and Shane had the good manners to blush.

Michael rubbed his shoulder. "I'd love to meet her, kiddo. If she won't be . . . bothered."

"Oh, no. I can't see why she would. It's not like you're contagious or anything."

"Does she know what his illness is, Shane?" I asked.

He bristled, his accent equal parts, suddenly, of New York and Pueblo. "What, d'you think I lie about it?" His brows pulled down, heavy and dark. "You think I'm ashamed or something?"

"Nobody thinks that," Michael said mildly, rubbing Shane's back. "But it's a small place. Maybe not everyone is hip as you."

Shane looked up, his eyes wide with shimmering tears. "I'd rather I never had the chance to be hip to this," he said.

"Me too," Michael said simply. He looked out the window, as if spying someone walking beyond the porch, and a gentle smile touched his lips. "But that's the gamble, ain't it? Roll the dice and see what you get."

"It's not fair," Shane said.

"Why not?"

I went into the kitchen to finish rolling out pie dough, far enough away to let them talk, but not so far I couldn't shamelessly eavesdrop. Shane had been circling this for days, and I was relieved that he'd finally been able to bring it out in the open.

"It's just not," he said now. "There's a million people out there who are just a waste of friggin' oxygen. Why can't they be the ones to die of some killer disease? Why does it have to be you? Why'd it have to be Andre?"

Michael was silent for a long minute, but you learned when you talked with him to expect that, and Shane waited along with me. Finally, Michael's low, gravelly voice drawled, "You figure disease should be a punishment, then? Cancer for murderers, AIDS for rapists, like that?"

Miserably Shane said, "Well, no."

"I know you don't think like that, boy. Judgment's a bad road to walk, cuz sooner or later, you'll be the one on trial for one thing or another."

"I know."

"Come on and sit down."

From my spot by the kitchen window, I heard the scrape of a wooden chair against the wooden floor, and out of the corner of my eye I also caught sight of Malachi's foot sticking out into my view. He sat close to the kitchen door on the wraparound porch. Michael wouldn't be able to see him, but I suspected he knew his brother was there anyway.

Michael went on. "Lotta folks would say I was paying for my sins with this disease, and you're gonna hear 'em say it if you haven't already, so you may as well be ready. Don't get mad, don't think there's anything to it. They're just trying to find a way to make themselves safe in a dangerous world." A pause, and I imagined Michael's bony hand on Shane somewhere. "What you know, and what I know, is that there's nothing safe at all about life, and you might as well go on and live it, instead of hiding in some corner."

"But I'm going to *miss* you," Shane said in a small voice.

"I know, son. But we've had good times, haven't we?"

"Yeah. But I had good times with my dad, too, and I still miss him. It doesn't help all that much to just remember."

"Yeah, I know."

I stopped pretending to roll out the dough, my eyes filling with tears. With a deep breath, I stood up and went quietly out on the porch, where Malachi was sitting on the floor, his feet out in front of him, his face sober. I sat down next to him and took his hand.

Inside, Michael said, "You believe in angels?"

"No," Shane said with disgust. "I don't believe in any of that crap. God and angels and voodoo. It's all bullshit."

In spite of myself, I was shocked. It wasn't like I was a good religious girl anymore, but the idea of anyone not believing in some kind of religion made me really sad. It was my own fault, though. Had I ever taken him to church regularly? No. Another mark against my mothering.

Michael said, "When I was a little boy, my mama used to take us to Sunday school when she could. Wasn't like she could settle in to one church or anything, because we moved so much, but when things were all right between her and my daddy, we'd all find some little-bitty church in town and go."

I looked at Malachi, my eyebrows raised in a question. In all my years with Michael, I'd never heard this story. Malachi gave me a rueful smile and nodded.

"D'you hate it?" Shane asked.

"No, I liked it. Made me feel good to think there was angels lookin' out for me."

"Whatever."

"I figure," Michael drawled, "that I can put in a special request, be your guardian angel till you don't need me anymore. So then all you have to do is just holler, and you'll know I'm there."

Shane let go of a soft, heartbroken sob. "That's just bullshit, man."

"Well, I don't happen to think so, but you're welcome to your own ideas. Just remember I said it, all right?"

Next to me, Malachi's shoulders were shaking, and I looked at him, alarmed and afraid he was weeping, but it was laughter making him shake. It took everything he had not to fall over. Perplexed, I gave him a questioning look, and he shook his head.

"I'll remember," Shane said.

Malachi lost the fight. He let loose a wild whoop of laughter and fell over on the porch floor. "The archangel!" he cried.

"Don't you forget it, either," Michael called.

~

In spite of that depressing little talk, Michael improved dramatically every day. It had been like this with Andre, too. Up and down, sometimes really up and really down, though when he started to decline, he'd been a lot sicker a lot faster.

Michael made me think of a candle, a white taper, slim and straight, the flame burning clean and dripless even to the very end. I tried not to think about how close he had to be getting to the bottom, but I understood what his T cell count meant. His burning improvement was an illusion. Or maybe, like a dog or a cat that simply goes to the end, happily ignorant of the progression of its disease, he was living every day. Not such a bad thing.

On Friday, Malachi carried him to the river at dawn so they could fish. I stood in my bedroom window watching them, my fingers pressed to my mouth. Malachi carried his brother as if he were a child, and Michael, once so big and strong, let him do it. I was glad of that—that Michael was letting go of the aloof independence that had always marked him, letting the rest of us do things for him. He accepted our offerings in the spirit they were intended, a way to make his way, and our own, a little easier.

In the soft light of dawn, their dark and light heads together were beautiful, and I could imagine them as children, when it would have been Michael piggybacking Malachi. Brothers. Not that different from sisters, I guessed.

And I was suddenly and fiercely glad that I'd written to Malachi over and over and over to get him to come here. It had made Michael so happy to spend time with his brother, and from what I now understood of Malachi, he would never have forgiven himself if Michael had died without this chance.

Shane appeared at my door. "Whatcha doing?" he asked, and fell on my bed with a tangle of cats, putting his face against one, his hand on another, letting the third crawl up on his bare belly.

A wave of deep fondness rolled over me—he'd always been the *sweetest* child, with a depth of goodness and kindness that colored everything he did. He always watched out for the little kids in a group, keeping them safe as if he were the only one around to do it, and he stuck up for the weak and small, collected strays with an unerring eye. In New York, I would often have a litter of lost boys in my living room, begging for broiled cinnamon toast and popcorn and cups of tea I fixed for them while I listened to their stories. Not their real stories, of course, because boys just didn't do that. No, they just talked; talked and talked and talked, their eyes bright under badly cut or purple hair. At such times, Shane was loud and gave them a hard time and laughed, more or less ignoring me, but I knew why he brought them to me. It pained him that they didn't have this little oasis of quiet and mother in their lives, and he wanted to share it.

This morning his eyes were swollen with heavy sleep, and his lip showed a shadow of dark bristles, and yet I saw the little boy and the bigger one beneath the man-child one when one of the cats reached out a paw and touched his mouth, then bent her head to his forehead and purred.

I wanted to curl up with them, boy and cats, but settled for dropping to my knees beside the bed and reaching out to rub Giovanni's silky back. "You're up early."

He yawned. "Couldn't sleep anymore." He kissed the paw on his mouth. "I was dreaming about a song and wanted to get up and write it down before I forgot it."

"Did you remember it?"

"Scribbled it on the back of a pizza box in my room." His indigo eyes, made deeper by the sleep in them, rose to mine. "Do you think I might really be able to do something with my music, Mom? No crap. The real thing."

"Yes," I said firmly and without hesitation. "It won't be easy. No artist has an easy life, but you know that."

"Yeah." He narrowed his eyes, looked away. "But is it worth it?"

"I don't know. That's something you'll have to find out for yourself."

He took a breath. "I'm afraid of being lonely."

I touched his head, the long length of glossy hair. "You'll always have me, kid, no matter what." But more soberly I added, "Loneliness is part of the game, though, I'm afraid. No one thinks the way you do, except other musicians, so you have to find and keep those connections." I thought about the healthy musicians I had known, and despite the press stories, there are a lot of healthy ones out there who live good, solid, honest lives.

"It's not easy," I said again, "but what would the rest of us do without music? We rely on all of you to accept that not-easy life so that we can get through ours. The upside is, you will know more perfect love in a day from it than most of us see in a lifetime. That's your reward."

He listened intently and silently, very seriously absorbing my words. "How do I . . . how do I stay together through it, Mom? That's the part that scares me." A pause. "Dad. Some of his friends. They just self-destructed."

Hard question. "I don't know, exactly, Shane. I wish I had some magic formula for you, because God knows that's the last thing I want for you." I drew a lock of his hair through my fingers. "There are some obvious things—stay away from the drugs and booze. When you find people you can really trust, do whatever you can to preserve the relationships. Don't make enemies if you can help it."

He nodded, liking the sensibility of those suggestions.

It wasn't enough, though, and I frowned, trying to focus what I knew had short-circuited Billy. "One of the things that makes you a musician is that you feel things more than other people do, and that can be really hard when the feelings are painful ones."

"Like Kurt Cobain."

"God forbid! What you have to do, I think, is learn to accept all your feelings. They're your material, and all of them are good and real, and if you feel them honestly, you'll be able to use them."

"Wow, that's just like my dream." He sat up on one elbow, tossing his hair out of his face, and I had to let him go. "I was watching this woman dance, you know, like in a sari, and she had all these veils, all different colors, and all of them were feelings. Like sadness was this pale, kind of silvery gray, and I could hear the sound of it." His face took on a glow, and he gestured with one big hand. "Love was pink and red, mixed up together. She was dancing with one, and then another one, and she'd put each one around her and let it cover her all up, then let it go and pick up the next one." He stopped and gave me a pleased little frown. "It was a cool dream."

"Really cool," I agreed. I never dream like that. Not even in color. "I wish sometimes that I had some artistry in me, so I could have dreams like that."

"Mom, you are an artist! Food. You're so good!"

I smiled. "Thanks. But it's not the same thing."

"Sure it is." Something crossed his mind, and he scowled.

"What is it?"

"Nothing." He shook his head. "You never see yourself like everybody else does, Mom." To my amazement, his eyes filled with tears, and I knew it was the sorrow coming out, the sorrow over Michael, over the big changes Shane was facing in his life, the fact that our chances to sit like this, talking quietly in the softness of a summer dawn, were narrowing. "You're cool, Mom. And beautiful. And I like it that you didn't cave in to what everybody else wanted for you. I wouldn't even be here if you had."

And my own eyes grew wet. "Thank you. That's one of the nicest things anyone has ever said to me."

We didn't hug. Not right then, even if I would have liked it. It would have been too icky. "Are you hungry?"

"Starving."

I stood. "Let's go get something to eat, then. Maybe later you can play some of what you wrote this morning."

"It's not ready yet. I will when it is." He sat up, his hands in his lap. "Mom?"

Twisting my hair into a knot, I turned with raised eyebrows.

"I was a jerk about—well, that one morning." He bowed his head, lifted a shoulder. "If you like the guy, you should do what you want."

"Mmm." He meant well, so all I said was, "Thanks."

"But I hope you'll be careful," he added. "I mean, I just don't think the guy's gonna stick around, after . . ."

"No, I'm sure he won't."

He let go of a held breath. "Green eggs and ham?"

I wrinkled my nose. "How about some blueberry muffins?"

Looping an arm around my neck, he said, "You make the muffins. I'll handle the eggs. Michael likes them. He'll need to eat when he gets back."

~

There were a million things left to do, and I had no time for anything except panicked, last-minute wedding business the rest of the day. I ran

256

from shop to house to church to hall in the heat, heat that finally broke at five, when a swift downpour cooled the air off for the rehearsal dinner. I'd been worried about the wedding preparations all week, knowing I'd have to deal with the presence of my father, but the mercurial fluid of family provided a buffer for us, and it never even became a problem. I relaxed and laughed with my sisters about a million things. Jane was jittery but almost ablaze with happiness.

Saturday morning dawned clear and dry. By prior arrangement, Jordan was going to pick me up, and we'd get ready at the church with our sisters, in order to leave the car for Michael and Shane. Malachi would ride his motorcycle in. I showered and washed my hair, combing out the long, tangled curls as I sat with Michael, who ate an entire plate of scrambled eggs and had a kind of cheery good humor that boded well for this day. When Jordan honked, fifteen minutes late, I grabbed my bag of makeup and kissed him on the forehead. "See you later."

He grabbed my hand. "Be yourself, Jewel. Promise me."

"Who else could I be?"

"You know what I mean. The real you. Don't let them take all that away."

"I promise, Michael. Cross my heart and hope to die."

"Stick a needle in your eye?"

Jordan honked again, urgently. "Yes. I have to go. See you at the church."

Be myself. As we drove into town, commenting on the predictions for heat, then torrential rains that were the day's forecast, I mulled that over. I pretended I knew what it meant, but did I? There were so many ghosts of me in a family gathering like this that I had a hard time picking which one was the real Jewel. I'd run into all of them over the past few months. There was the little girl who loved Mass and hung upside down in the orchard at her aunt's house. The socially responsible preadolescent who earnestly participated in food drives and reading programs. The wild child who became the restless one who turned into the woman who could throw a backpack over her shoulder and climb on the back of a motorcycle and leave home without a backward glance. The mother, the wild woman, the little girl, the business owner, the friend, the lover, the sister, the daughter.

It made my head hurt. We all had these splits in our personalities, I knew that—no one is all one thing or all something else—but there was a bigger schism in me than in most of the women in my world, and I didn't know where the bridges lay between the parts of myself. The daughter and the lover did not seem to coexist all that peacefully, for example. If I denied one, the other had to go, and I wasn't willing to do either.

The wedding was to be held at one of the best churches in town. It was my favorite place as a child, but in my years away, they'd pulled down the old brick building, leaving only the gymnasium, and built a grand and beautiful new building, which I naturally hated. The Shrine of Saint Therese. When I was a girl, the priest was a small Irish man with a wonderful, lilting brogue who was much beloved by the parishioners, and he was still around, though the duties had been overtaken by a younger priest.

This morning, I discovered that the church was beautiful after all, a slate-colored arch against the brilliance of the sky. Jordan and I followed the sound of women's voices down a hallway to a room bursting with the notes of a dozen perfumes and powders and cosmetics and high, lilting chatter, the dazzlement of stockings and ribbons and girls in pristine bras and women powdering their bosoms against the heat.

I stopped just inside the door and closed my eyes, breathing it in. It smelled like Sunday mornings. Someone had brought doughnuts, and their fresh sugary smell mixed with a hint of coffee and baby powder. I thought of patent leather shoes and ribbons for my hair, and I laughed in purest joy when my grandmother said, "Jewel Sabatino, stop mooning around and get over here and get dressed."

I put down my bag of cosmetics and looked for Jane, peeking around her young attendants, who looked like calla lilies in their satins. Jane sat on a chair near the table with the doughnuts, dressed in a long slip, stockings, and shoes. Her hair was swept into a french knot through which had been strung tiny pearls, work I recognized as my mother's. She was eating a glazed doughnut with a serene kind of radiance that was totally at odds with the uproar around her. "Hey, kid," I said. "Aren't you supposed to be freaking out by now?"

She grinned at me. "I think they have that covered."

I laughed. "Should we give Mama her dress now?"

"Get dressed first, so Nana doesn't have a coronary. Then we'll do it."

"I have a surprise for you." I gave her a box that contained the corset, black leather mini, garter belt, and fishnet stockings. "Don't open it until the fourth day of your honeymoon."

"Fourth, huh?" She raised wicked eyebrows. "I can't wait."

"Jewel!" Nana Lucy bellowed.

"Okay, okay!" I shimmied out of my jeans and T-shirt, revealing the scarlet corset and black panties beneath. I'd made a special trip to get a second corset. Jane cracked up, and my grandmother huffed, and Jordan gave a little squeal. "I *want* that!"

My mother, pins in her mouth, looked at me. For a minute I couldn't tell if she was annoyed, and a pinch caught me. It was meant as a little joke, not any kind of defiance. Then she shook her head, but she was smiling. "Daredevil."

I grinned and clasped my hands on the lower swell of my breasts. "Good support, eh?"

Nana put the dress over my head while another girl helped Jordan with hers, and we turned toward the long mirrors to look at ourselves. My mother had changed the colors for both of us, that beautiful blue for me, a deep rich gold for Jordan, and we smiled at each other in the mirror. "You're so beautiful," I said.

"So are you."

For the first time, I saw why people often thought we were twins. Standing there in blue and gold, our shoulders glowing against the satin, long curls and plenty of cleavage and identical smiles. "Wow," I said. "When did you start looking so much like me?"

"No, you look like me, lucky thing."

The brazen rose tattoo on my breast caught my eye, and I brushed my fingers over it, turning to dig in my bag for the cover. Carefully, so as not to mar the edge of the dress, I bent into the mirror and started dabbing it on.

Jane, watching calmly from her corner until that minute, stood up. "Jewel, what are you doing?"

"Covering it up."

"No! I love that tattoo." Drawing herself up to her full height, she swiveled her blonde head around to my mother and grandmother and Jasmine, who had opened her mouth but then closed it. "I'm the bride, and I get to say. Leave it."

"But Daddy—" I said.

"Is fussy and old-fashioned and really needs to get over himself."

I heard Michael say in my head, *Be yourself.* With a tissue, I wiped away the cover. "You're the boss, babe."

FROM THE *PUEBLO CHIEFTAN*, AUGUST 29:

Sabatino-Candelario

Steven Candelario, son of Rick and Shirley Candelario, Pueblo, and Jane Sabatino, daughter of Romeo and Rose Sabatino, also of Pueblo, were married recently in a Mass at the Shrine of Saint Therese in Pueblo.

Maid of honor: Jennifer Corsi; bridesmaids: Jasmine Abruzzo, Jo Gutierrez, Sally Pacheco, Jordan Olivas, Jewel Sabatino, Elizabeth Hair, and Sharyn Cerniglia.

Best man: Mario Quintana; groomsmen: Brandon Mascarenas, Peter Stroo, Adam Pino, Robert Santos, John Romero, Alex Candelario, and Elias Candelario.

The newlyweds will reside in Pueblo.

Chapter Eighteen

There is nothing in the world like a big Italian Catholic wedding. Unless maybe it's a big Spanish Catholic wedding. That brilliant August day, we got both at once.

The church was packed, every pew brimming with well-dressed well-wishers. As we attendants marched up the aisle, I reveled in the beauty of them all, the children in their first patent leather shoes and precious toddler-size suits and ties; the grandmas in their pearls and pumps and matching handbags and hats; the young girls self-consciously beautiful in dressy dresses they didn't get to wear very often; the boys tugging at their ties when the girls looked their way.

We took our places and turned to wait for the bridal entrance. It made me nervous, knowing my father would escort Jane up the aisle, and to calm myself, I looked into the crowd. In the second pew were Shane, Michael, and Malachi.

Malachi. I'd never seen him dressed up, and the sight was not calming. He'd had a haircut and a shave, and looked as smooth and clean as a spread in *GQ*. The suit was sand-colored linen, with a silk shirt and a red tie beneath it. With a start, I realized it had belonged to Andre, though it had never looked quite like this on him. Spying me, Malachi looked me over very slowly, head to toe, lingering at the expanse of tattooed cleavage as he licked his bottom lip.

With a dignified lift of my chin, I looked at my son, who sat on the other side of Michael, and grinned. Shane had slicked back his long dark hair and put on a black suit with a charcoal shirt and tie. He looked like nothing more than a modern-day version of a gangster, and when he pulled out a mock gun and shot me, I realized he'd done it on purpose.

Between them sat Michael, so thin that his suit hung on his bony shoulders, a fact I was sure pained him. And yet he managed to look dapper in spite of it, a red handkerchief sticking out of his pocket, a red carnation in his lapel. A bowler hat rested in his lap. He gave me a thumbs-up and touched his chest to indicate the tattoo.

Impossible he would not always be here in my life. For a long time, I held his gaze, hoping he knew how much I loved him.

Then the music swelled, and Jane came in on my father's arm, and my eyes blurred dangerously. He had a proud look on his face, the father who'd managed to raise a virgin bride in the modern world. A beautiful, dutiful, wonderful girl who would go to her wedding bed unsullied. A woman who was feverish with joy in this moment, a woman who would say her vows and mean them, who would take her place in the world he understood in ways he understood.

They marched up the aisle triumphantly, dotted with colored light falling through stained glass, and for me the world narrowed in a strange, powerful way. Narrowed to the smell of incense and candles, to this bride and her groom, who shattered us all. Brides are radiant, joyful, beautiful. This groom was all of that and more. His face held hectic color, and none of us missed the way he had to keep wiping his eyes as she advanced or when she took his arm with pride and excitement. We endured the Mass, all of us, and then the vows were said, and when Jane, in a clear, fluting voice said, "I do," her poor groom had tears of joy on his cheeks, and he wasn't ashamed of them. When it was his turn, he said, "Yes!" so loudly that a pleased roll of laughter went through the room.

There wasn't a dry eye in the house. Especially mine. I tried for a while to discreetly wipe away the emotional tears with a tissue, but the thing got so soaked and everybody else was so obviously moved, too, that I gave up and let them drip.

And I had to admit, one of the things I wanted, standing there, was to be married like this, in a church with a Mass by a priest. The real thing. I wanted to take my place in this community, *my* community.

But did I even fit anymore? Had I ever?

I just didn't know. I didn't know where I fit or where I belonged or what the future would hold, and that was the terrifying part. Not knowing. Maybe that was the good side of tradition. My sisters and mother and grandmother all knew where they fit, what function they performed. Even Jordan, who had adopted a slightly unusual lifestyle with her mixed marriage and counterculture ways—she was Sylvia, and all the healers before her. Jasmine was the pampered beauty who raised the social standard. Jane was the salt of the earth, and somehow I knew she'd be the mother of many sons. My mother was the wizard, running everything, and would take her place in the matriarch position when my grandmother vacated it.

I'd never be matriarch, queen of the clan. I'd never be salt of the earth or the healing woman or the social standard. I'd always be the bad girl, the woman the others pointed to as an example of what not to do—because it was a sure way to end up alone. Take a chance on a wild man, and he'll leave you behind. Take a chance on the big world, and what did it get you? Right back where you started, only your father will never speak to you again, so you'll have lost, no matter how much you were trying to win.

Standing there branded with my rose tattoo, I lifted my chin and focused on my beautiful sister, on her beautiful, wonderful day. It wasn't as hard as you might think to smile and be glad for her.

~

From the wedding, we all drove to an old warehouse–turned–banquet hall in Blende. My mother had wanted the Colorado Building at the fairgrounds, but since the state fair was starting the following week, there was no possibility of that. And it wasn't, I thought, ducking out of the blistering noontime sun, that there was much difference between them. This was a long rectangular building, with a stage at one end and the kitchens at the other. My sisters and I had been in here for hours the night before, hanging the decorations—reliable crepe paper and silver cardboard wedding bells and even some thin, gauzy fabric over the windows. A band in crisp summer uniforms was assembling on the raised dais that served as a stage, and the cake—a masterpiece of intricate layers—was situated beneath a pagoda of the same thin netting.

Within a half hour, the buffet was opened, and a long snaking line formed around the edges of the room. It moved slowly and left no one unsatisfied. Our whole family had been cooking for a week, but so had Steve's, and it was as if all of Pueblo culture had come together right there at my sister's wedding—tamales in their husks piled next to enormous trays of lasagna and a steaming Crock-Pot of green chili stew, with piles of thick, homemade tortillas next to a huge tray of antipasti, my grandmother's special cracked olives at the center.

So much food. It perfumed the air. I filled a plate for Michael with a little of everything, hoping to tempt him into eating something, and carried it with my own brimming plate back to the table where he was holding court.

I don't know how many times I'd seen him do this. He just settled somewhere, and people gathered around. Once, I thought it was his great beauty that drew them—a beauty both earthy and ethereal, so striking you couldn't help staring a little when he first came into a room. But I'd learned it wasn't his beauty. Even now, when his illness had left him scarecrow thin, and he sat in a wheelchair, people still gathered around the flame of Michael, as if he truly were the king of fairies, the benevolent granter of all wishes.

I halted a few feet away, admiring him amid his admirers. Some of them, especially those about my age, knew he'd enjoyed a few minutes of fame and wanted to breathe it in, but even they were drawn in by that indefinable something. I watched a little girl give him a Tootsie Roll Pop, and her little brother, no more than four, showed off his truck. A cluster of guys my age or so approached and offered their adulation.

He caught my eye and winked. I put his plate down for him. "Your highness."

He chuckled, sounding like himself, and I forced myself to simply sit down and enjoy the moment without judging his condition every five seconds. "D'you see your child?" he asked, immediately picking up his fork. He lifted his chin toward the platform at the back.

"What is he doing?"

"Looks to me like he's gonna play."

And that was exactly how it looked. Shane was bustling around with the other members of the band, connecting equipment, testing mikes and sound levels, moving with such sure expertise that I was a little taken aback. "Did he tell you anything?"

"Not a thing." Michael shook his head, a smile on his mouth. "Maybe it's just seeing him on a stage, but he really looks like Billy to me today."

Malachi, who had two brimming plates filled with everything from chicken wings to tamales to three kinds of salad—potato, bean, and green—said, "Who does?"

I gestured toward the stage and grinned again at how wonderfully clean and dangerous Shane looked. The girls had to be swooning. "Who gave him the Al Capone idea?"

The brothers shrugged and said together, "Not me."

"It looks good on him."

A woman in a navy linen dress and spectator pumps, her hair cut into a glossy black fall, came up to the table. "Jewel?" Her perfectly made-up face said she expected me to remember her. She touched her chest. "You don't remember me, do you?"

But her voice brought her into focus. "Oh my God!" I laughed and stood up to give her an impetuous hug. "Callie Perez, right?" I stepped back to admire her. "You grew up great."

"It's Martinez now," she said, but with that breathless laugh that showed she was pleased. "I was such a dweeb in high school, it wouldn't have been too hard to improve."

"No, you weren't," I protested, and looked at Michael. "You two would have loved each other. She's read everything in the universe."

He gave a polite nod, having learned that not everyone wanted to shake hands with a person who obviously had AIDS, but Callie immediately stuck out her hand. "You're Michael Shaunnessey. I'm awed."

He winked. "Don't be, darlin'."

"Oh, but it's fun." Her smile was white and genuine. She turned to Malachi. "Hi, I'm Callie."

"Nice to meet you," he said with every ounce of his southern charm on stun. She blinked a little, and I gave him a look. He wiggled his eyebrows over her head, unabashed.

Callie turned her attention to me. "I won't keep you," she said. "But I promised myself I would come tell you something."

Intrigued, I prompted, "What?"

She glanced toward the guys, hesitating, and with that particular kind of female body language that was so unmistakable, stepped back a few feet. I followed, as I was meant to do. "I can remember that day in front of the school like it was yesterday," she said. "October. The light coming through the leaves, and Billy Jake standing there by his motorcycle, his hair lifting on the wind . . ." She grinned, shaking her head fondly. "My heart was in my throat, watching you walk toward him. We just froze, all of us, that whole lawn full of kids, watching you take something so boldly that none of us would dare."

Unexpected emotion welled in my throat, and I swallowed.

"It was like a movie, Jewel. And you weren't just my hero that day. You gave a lot of us courage."

I hugged her, as much to hide my sudden tears as to thank her. "You will never know how much I needed to hear that today."

"Oh, I think I do." We separated, only a little awkward, and she stepped back, as if I were the ex–rock star, not Michael. She gave a little shrug. "I just wanted to tell you."

"Thank you."

When I sat back down, I couldn't help glancing over to where my father sat at the head table with Jane and Steven. My father was laughing at a joke someone made, and his whole face lit up, making his eyes crinkle, showing off his fine, straight teeth. He leaned over to return the joke in some way, stabbing his finger in the air to emphasize the point, and both of them cracked up even more.

He was getting old. There were wings of white across the sides of his head and sprinkles of it through the rest. His hands, ever capable, were looking a little gnarled at some of the joints.

Malachi reached under the table for my hand. "Does having Daddy in the room mean you're not going to dance with me today?"

"No way."

"No way, you won't dance with me?" His eyes glittered. "Or no way, Daddy'll stop you?"

I looked at his mouth. "No way he's going to stop me."

"Good girl." He pretended to take something out of his pocket, mimed licking a pencil. "I'll save you a reel, then, before my dance card gets full."

I remembered his expert dancing at the club that night. "You're going to be busier than you know, sweetie."

∼

By midafternoon, the band and the cash bar had considerably loosened the crowd. A predictable wave of thunderheads rolled in, darkening the room but in no way dampening the spirits of the revelers. Including my own. Michael showed no signs yet of being overly tired, and finally glared at me when I asked him for the tenth time, "Are you okay?"

"Babe," he said, drawing me down beside him, his hand feeling strong around my wrist. He kissed my cheek and said, "Don't take this wrong, but there aren't that many weddings in my future, and I'm enjoying myself. Don't hurry me off to my bed."

I smiled. "All right. Sorry." What was the absolute worst that could happen, after all? It surprised me that I could think in such a joking way about it, but there was something peaceful about that, too.

I danced all day, with cousins I hadn't seen in twenty years and had forgotten. With uncles who smelled of Old Spice and Brut, with Spanish grandpas who'd learned the two-step in New Mexico at age four and had indulged at least once a week ever since. We did the chicken dance, laughing happily. We ate. The wine flowed, the cake was cut, toasts were made.

But the delirium of the day for me came from Shane, standing up there so handsome and suave, singing as beautifully as Michael, who'd taught him, and playing even better than his father, who had also taught him.

Michael just kept shaking his head as Shane did one more thing and one more, singing in Spanish he'd learned in only a few weeks, crooning out love songs in very bad Italian. He told me later that he'd been spending every night after work with the band, who'd lost a singer three weeks before the wedding and had never had a good bass player. My father had arranged it.

Of course. Because my father would have realized—or someone would have heard it and realized and told him—that the voice, trained by Michael, was the voice of *my* father, a voice so clean and deep and true that people often turned around when he spoke in a crowd, and stopped dead when he sang in church.

And I could tell my father knew it by the way he watched my son with his dark eyes filled with pride. At least, I thought, peering over the shoulder of my rotund cousin Leo, I'd given something back to my dad for all the trouble I'd caused. I wondered, suddenly, if he realized that Shane was a Sabatino, not a Jake. A boy to carry on the name.

"You must be so proud of him," Leo said.

"More than a little," I admitted.

"All's well that ends well, eh?"

I smiled up at him. "Sure."

No one, of course, commented on the fact that the sisters all sat at the head table with Jane, except me. Wars in such a huge family are a delicate thing, and to keep the peace, an unspoken set of rules were followed. If my father danced, I stayed off the floor, for the most part. And when it became clear that I was a popular partner, he started declining dances. When he got in line for food, I waited until I was far behind him, and we never went to the bar or the cake table at the same time.

Even so, the timing gets off a little once in a while. Overheated and flushed in my satin gown, I went to the bathroom to wash my face, noticing as I peered in the mirror that my eyes had that telltale shine of slight tipsiness. "Time to slow down," I said aloud to my reflection.

"It was time for me an hour ago," another woman said, a young Hispanic professional sort with long dark eyes. "Not so many weddings a year you can't indulge them, though, eh?"

I was grinning when I came out and ducked behind a guy in shirt-sleeves—which put me face-to-face with my father on his way to the men's room.

We both halted, stunned to silence, our eyes catching and holding for a space that felt much longer than it was. For one lightning stretch of an instant, I thought I saw a softening, thought he might be about to open his mouth and speak to me.

Instead of waiting, then being disappointed, I ducked my head and dashed around him, nearly tripping on my skirt in my haste.

Close call.

A little while later, when the band was on a break, I saw him capture Shane and lead him over to a table in the corner. I leaned close to Malachi. "Now, there's the table you want to sit at," I said as an old man lifted a bottle to my father. There were introductions being made, the lift of the chin in acknowledgment. My father drank, passed the bottle to Shane, who carefully didn't look my way as he lifted it and drank.

Michael raised an eyebrow at my soft sound of protest. He shook his head, and I knew he was right—that bottle was acceptance—but it was still hard to see my kid drinking right in front of me.

"What are they passing around?" Malachi asked.

"Homemade wine. Muscatel. The man in the blue shirt makes it every year. He's famous for it."

"Go snare us a bottle. I like to sample the local cuisine."

I made a dismissive sound. "Not for women."

He chuckled. "Really?"

"Pretty much."

"Amazing." He gazed over the party with a measuring expression. "I've never been to anything like this in my life."

"You're kidding!"

A one-sided shrug. "How many of these people are you related to?"

I took a breath, narrowed my eyes. There were about three hundred people in the room. "Probably at least half of them. Maybe a hundred, hundred and fifty? The rest are on Steve's side."

"That's amazing."

"Find it a little overwhelming, do you?"

"It would be hard to live around so many people who knew you, I think."

"It is, sometimes. But sometimes, it's really good, too."

"I guess you'd always know somebody had your back. Or you'd have a place to land."

I thought of the web, the net—sticky safety. "Something like that."

He looked at me. "As long as you follow the rules, right?"

I nodded a little sadly, thinking of my recognition during the wedding that I would be the one they'd point to as an example of what not to do. "They'll still make a place for you," I said. And because he looked so good, because I had nothing to lose, I leaned over and kissed him.

His grin was a thousand watts. "Is that your place?"

"You betcha."

"Think they noticed?"

"I don't care today."

His gaze was steady. "Yes, you do."

I looked involuntarily at my father and Shane, settling in for the telling of tall tales at the old men's table. The bottle made another round, and I grinned. "He thought he got a headache from tequila."

While the band was on break, a selection of prerecorded tunes was playing, and I stood up abruptly. "Dance with me, will you?"

For a moment, he hesitated, his expression impossible to read. "Maybe that's not what you really want."

"If you don't stand up and dance with me, you'll make me look really bad."

He unfolded, bigger than a grizzly, and let me lead him onto the floor with a sprinkling of other couples. When the band was on, it was hard to talk, but this was more intimate and not quite as energetic.

I held him loosely so that I could look up at him. "When you leave, they'll forgive me," I said with a smile. "The grandmas will start looking for a divorced man, or a widower, maybe somebody with kids. The aunties will ask their friends at work, and talk about me. I'll be hitched in a year."

"And I'll just be a fading memory."

"No, you're going to send me postcards from exotic places, so I have some link to the wild world outside."

He sobered. "I can do that." He rubbed my spine with the tips of his fingers. "Maybe before you get all the way settled in, you could meet me in the Alps."

"Maybe." But we both knew I never would. For a long minute, we let that knowledge rise up between us, both comforting and sad. I smiled to lighten it. "I can promise I'll think about you sometimes on summer nights when it rains."

"That would be good."

Because he would leave, I could say things more freely than I would have ordinarily. "You know, if you and Michael and your parents had lived here, things would have been very different for you."

He gave a derisive little snort. "Yeah, Michael would have fit right in."

"He'd have been fine. Everyone would have known he was gay and hoped they were wrong and said prayers and lit candles for him, but they would have watched out for him. If he'd grown up in my neighborhood, he would have had to fight, but I know he did some of that anyway."

Malachi nodded.

"The big difference would have been with your parents," I said.

The careful distance. "Why?"

We turned, and Malachi edged his body closer. "The relationship was volatile and passionate," I said. "But they did love each other."

"I guess."

"Everyone would have known it. When they got into their fights and one or the other showed up at their local bar, there would have been somebody on alert. Nobody would have gone home with your mother. And if there was a stranger around, he'd have been politely escorted away."

Malachi rolled his eyes.

"Or they'd have picked a fight with him," I said with a grin.

"That I can believe."

"And when your dad started getting too drunk and talking trash? Somebody would have just either drank him under the table or stuck with him till morning."

"I don't buy it, Jewel. No community does that, not consistently." But even as he spoke, a flicker crossed his eyes.

"What did you remember?"

He scowled at me. "Why do you do that all the time?" It came out *all a-time*.

"Do what?"

"Come up with something like you can read my mind."

I grinned up at him. "Because I can."

"Yeah?" He lifted his chin, a challenge. Given to another man, it would have been a squaring off, but what it revealed to me was the underside of his jaw, a place I knew from experience smelled of a special soap he always used, a plain brownish bar laced with herbs. "What am I thinking right now, then?"

I inclined my head. He wanted me to think he was looking down my dress, but he couldn't hold it long enough. He stumbled a little, kicking my toe. "Sorry," he growled.

What was he thinking right now? He was surprisingly easy to read for a man who'd spent his whole life covering his emotions. "You're wishing that you *had* been raised in a place like this, that you had a nana and a few million cousins to catch you when you fell and a dad you could pretend to ignore." I half smiled at the darkening of his irises. "Oh, I forgot. You do have the dad part."

The cheekbones went dark, intensifying the angle. It occurred to me vaguely that he must have some Native American blood somewhere, and it surprised me that I'd never noticed it before. It was plain in Michael's face, too, if you ignored his coloring. The slash of cheekbone, the downturn of the mouth.

"Tell you what, sugar. I'll write my daddy a letter and tell him all is forgiven if you can get yours to dance with you."

"Hit a nerve, huh?"

"I dare you," he said.

I only smiled, feeling heat rise between us with his anger. It lashed out, whipping across my torso, down the front of my thighs. On my back, his fingers curled.

"Double dare you."

"And I decline," I said easily. "You'll do what you need to do. Just like I will."

The song ended. We stopped, but neither of us let go right away. "You really piss me off sometimes, Jewel, you know that?"

I laughed. "And why is that, Malachi?"

"You just think you know everything."

"You mean I don't?"

"No." His jaw set for a moment and his mouth was tight. "What I was going to say is, why don't you come with me? You don't belong here any more than I do."

Come with me. It pierced me in a dozen places, a hundred ways. Run away again, this time with a man who had made it an art form. "Climb the Alps?" I said. "See the pyramids?"

His fingers laced through mine. "Yeah. It would be so good, Jewel."

A laugh went up from the head table, and I looked over my shoulder. An ordinary group, really, who would lead ordinary lives. The butcher, the baker, the candlestick maker. Jordan saw me looking and winked.

"Why don't you stay, Malachi?" I looked at him steadily. "I'll go to the Alps with you, to the pyramids, but I need to be here with my family now. I missed them too much to ever really leave them again."

He looked around, panic on his face. "I can't." He let my hand go and spun away on his heel, going outside, where the wind was beginning to whip up. If his brother hadn't been on his deathbed, I knew he would have climbed on his motorcycle and been gone.

It made me smile. I floated back to Michael and kissed his head. "I could have used him a lot sooner," I said.

He reached up and put a hand on my wrist. "I never saw before how much alike you are."

"I don't really see that."

"I know." He turned my hand over, his palm as dry as an elm leaf. "When does the fair start?"

"Friday."

"We're going that day, right?"

"Sure, if you want to."

"I do." His thumb moved on my hand, and I could feel him slipping away into that distant place. "How does it work out, in terms of the way it was when we met?" He dragged himself back into the moment. "Was it the first night of the fair then?"

I smiled, brushed a lock of hair from his shoulder. "It was indeed, sir. Twenty-three years ago. Amazing, isn't it?"

"I'm real glad you went that night."

And suddenly everything in my world shifted, like somebody pulled a string in my imagination and all the pieces fit together. I looked down into the aquamarine color of his eyes, and knew that *this* man had been the reason I'd gone to the fair, and run away. It was Michael who'd freed me, not Billy.

I loved him so much. "You are so amazingly beautiful," I said, and kissed his lips lightly.

An outcry at the front of the room went up, and I saw the band members reassembling. "Time for the money dance," I said, eyeing Shane as he picked up his bass. He laughed at something one of the other guys said, showing his big white teeth. The tight gangster queue was coming undone, leaving a few strands to fall across his handsome face. So bad, so beautiful, so talented, my Shane. I would miss him when he headed out into the world, but somehow I felt he was going to be just fine.

"What's the money dance?" Michael asked.

"Watch." The dapper Romeo, a half foot shorter than his daughter, was leading Jane out to the floor as a lively dance tune struck up. Other couples followed. My father pinned a bill on her dress. "Sometimes," I said, "they steal the bride and ransom her. The point is to get money for the newlyweds." Jane was handed off to another relative, a big stocky construction worker who danced like a tree, then was spun around and was given to a boy about ten, who gazed up at her adoringly and pinned his money to her waist, his cheeks as red as tomatoes.

I rested my chin lightly on the top of Michael's head. "Next life, would you be straight so we can get married?"

"That'd be all right, I guess. What if we're both girls, though. Or guys?"

"Just don't go anywhere when you get to the other side. Wait for me, and we'll figure it out."

He leaned backward, turning his head into my chest. Light struck his irises, turning them a crystal color. "Will do."

I leaned into his shoulder. "I'm going to be so lonely without you."

"Nah, you'll have what you need, sugar. You always do."

"Sugar?" I laughed and settled next to him. "You've been hanging around your brother too much."

He watched the dance without speaking. Then, "Life's just too damned sweet, you know it?"

"Yes, it is." I took his hand loosely in my own. "What's been the best part, Michael? Music?"

He shook his head, a smile on his mouth. "Thanks for bringing me here, Jewel."

"Oh, sure. Everybody oughta go to an Italian wedding at least once."

"Not here, today," he said. "Here, to this town, these people."

"Michael—"

"Listen, okay, for just a few minutes." He tightened his fingers around mine. "There's some things I've been wanting to say to you, and they're important."

"I don't want to talk about this right now."

"This is a good time. We're happy today."

"But . . ." I didn't want to talk, because it made it too soon. I could feel it creeping up on us, on him, that scythe, but talking about details made the blade shimmer in the sun. I took a breath. "You're right. This is good. And you know you can count on me."

He gave me information on his papers, on documents he thought I would need. He'd written everything out and put it in a drawer in his room, and a friend back in New York had the key to a safety-deposit box that was to be opened when I called. It held his will and sundries.

"There's one more thing, Jewel, and this is the hard one."

"Shoot."

"Get my father here for the funeral. And don't let Malachi leave until he gets here."

I smiled, thinking of our dance. "Now *that* will give me some pleasure."

"Thank you." He let go of a breath, and holding hands, we watched Jane collect a fat wad of bills while her new groom discreetly got ready to go. Jane's face was flushed and shiny, and I wondered if her heart was pounding. "Oh, they are going to have such a good time tonight," I said.

He nodded, smiling fondly. "I'd sure like to dance."

"Let's do it, then!" I stood up and pushed a tangle of chairs out of the way, clearing a spot for us no more than three feet square. But we wouldn't need any more than that. "Right here. We'll just have our own little shuffle on our own little square of floor." I stuck out my hand, and he took it, standing slowly. I bowed. "Sire."

A million times I have danced with Michael, in dozens of clubs over the years. He waltzed and tangoed like a master, but just now we slid into a shuffling two-step that didn't go anywhere but in a circle. His body felt as insubstantial as the wind, so thin and light it was as if the fey folk were calling him to the other side a molecule at a time.

But it was still Michael, his voice humming through his chest in that familiar way, his neck and the curve of his shoulder smelling faintly of Aramis, his fine hair brushing my cheek. His broad, long-fingered hands held me as we swayed, and I closed my eyes, letting all my love pour through me, brilliant as the light of a million candles. I breathed him in, close to my heart.

"The best part, Jewel," Michael said, low against my ear, "was you."

And I knew, right then, but I didn't let on. I just lifted my head and smiled at him. "I love you," I said.

He tucked me close, and we shuffled in a weak circle. "You can't help it."

MICHAEL

He awakened just before dawn, the house silent around him. He turned his head and saw a particular blue in the sky beyond the windows. For one long moment, he relished it, that bright intense color, and the scudding of clouds beginning to obscure it. It would rain.

He had seen the sky gather rain clouds this way thousands of times in his life, in hundreds of locations. He never got over the beauty of it. Of thunderheads moving with authoritative darkness over the blue, blue sky. He had ridden in planes above those banks of clouds, and never failed to feel a little prick of sadness that he was above, not within, not below—feeling clouds, feeling rain, admiring lightning.

The house around him was very still. Everyone still slept. Only he was awake to appreciate the power and beauty of the approaching storm, to smell the rain on the breeze coming through the small opening of his window.

It had been a while since he'd been able to really walk without anybody helping, but this morning, he slid his legs to the side of his bed and put his feet on the floor. He felt acutely the brush of light cotton against his knees and across his chest. He felt the floor press up against the soles of his feet. He took a breath and loved the feeling of air in his lungs.

Peering through the window, he admired the wide grassy fields, and the muddy, deceptive flow of the Arkansas beyond, rushing to fill farmers' fields with irrigation water. He thought of the places he and Jewel had seen on their way west from New York, thought of cottonwood trees, and the fishermen up early on the banks. He thought of the union of this river with the great Mississippi, and it pleased him.

His strength was small, but there was enough of it if he moved slowly. On a notepad he scrawled a few words so they'd know he was at peace, then he walked on his own power through the door and out into the world. The wind brushed over his face, cool and soft as a lover's breath. It rustled leaves in the trees overhead, and he stopped, sweating, to admire the sound.

Peacefully, slowly, he walked to the river, stopping whenever he needed to, in no hurry. He admired spiderwebs hung between branches, and the flight of a magpie overhead. He took time to notice the darkening of the sky and the first ripples of lightning. Morning thunderstorms were rare, but he welcomed it.

At the riverbank, he had to rest a very long time. His body, thinner than it had been when he was twelve, shivered and quaked at the effort he expended. It was a long time—long enough that clouds covered all the blue in the sky—before he had the strength to move again. He had hoped to go naked, as he had come, but in the end, he had no more strength. He swallowed the pills he'd brought with him and waited, sitting on the bank for a long, long time, until the first raindrops began to fall.

It was a good day to die.

He had loved living. Loved every small thing about it. And he would dignify that by choosing this day to leave it, a day when the river ran swiftly, when rain pattered among the cottonwoods, a day when the people he most loved in the world slept entwined in each other's arms.

Some might call it a sin, but he knew it wasn't. It was dignified. It was tribute to all he loved, all he had experienced, all he'd been lucky enough to know. As he lay back to let the rain cover him, he thanked the beings that had allowed him to be here, and closed his eyes, and let them carry him away, his soul sliding into the swift current, into the river of time.

PRAYER TO SAINT JOSEPH FOR A HAPPY DEATH

O Blessed Joseph, you gave your last breath in the loving embrace of Jesus and Mary. When the seal of death shall close my life, come with Jesus and Mary to aid me. Obtain for me this solace for that hour—to die with their holy arms around me. Jesus, Mary, and Joseph, I commend my soul, living and dying, into your sacred arms. Amen.

Chapter Nineteen

It was lightning that awakened me, not a loud crack, just a low, faraway rumble, like drums. I lay in the warmth of the bed, listening with my eyes closed to the rain coming down against the windows, blowing a fresh clean scent through the world, a promise that the day would not be hot. The breeze was even cold, and I could take some pleasure in the anticipation of fall, when I'd dig out the heavy quilts and we'd have to turn on the heat.

Next to me, Malachi slept like a dead man, the muscatel having done its work, and it made me smile fondly. Oh, they'd loved him, those old Italians, something I should have seen. If anybody loved a big alligator-wrestling, hard-drinking ladies' man, it was a macho old Italian. He was one of them in three minutes.

I left him sleeping and tiptoed downstairs in my robe, headed for the kitchen and coffee. The light was dim, and I didn't see what was wrong when I went through the dining room the first time. It was only as I was measuring grounds that I stopped and went back to the doorway to double-check.

Michael's bed was empty.

I stared at it for a long, long minute, thinking he'd gone to the restroom—though I knew very well he hadn't since I'd just been in the downstairs bathroom. My vision grew acute as I stared at that empty bed, and details imprinted themselves on my brain—the small geography of shadows left by the rumpled covers, a whole world of hills and valleys and canyons and plains in a white sheet that looked pale gray in the low light.

The imprint of his head was still on the pillow. I went there first, putting my face down in it gently so as not to mar the shape, just inhaling the scent of his hair, the lingering hint of illness that never seemed to entirely cover the robust patchouliness of Michael.

My hands were shaking as I straightened and picked up the note.

The best that you can hope for is to die in your sleep. Love you all. Bye (and thanks for all the fish).

A hundred times I'd tried to imagine what this would be like. How I'd manage it. How it would go.

Nothing could have prepared me for the real thing. My mind went blank, but my body simply gave way, as if I had no spine, no bones. I fell straight to the floor, the note in my hand, the rain beyond the window. I couldn't even cry.

No bones in my body and no activity in my brain. I stared at the narrow planks of the hardwood floor, noticing the grain of one board looked exactly like a weather photo of a hurricane, while the one next to it made me think of the shivery lines on a graph that measured heartbeats. I'd had one when Shane was born, and had watched it shivering up and down with his speedy heartbeat for hours and hours. Michael had been there.

Then.

And now he was outside in the rain, and he needed me not to fall apart. It was easier than I thought to get to my feet, though it did make me a little dizzy. I walked upstairs to my room. Malachi's foot stuck out from beneath the sheets, and I bent to put my hand around his arch. "Malachi," I said, surprised at the husky power of my voice. "Wake up. I need your help."

He was noiselessly, completely awake. I'd never seen anyone go from sleep to awake so fast. "What is it?"

"Michael's gone."

"Gone—" He sat up straight. "Oh." He swallowed, then tossed the covers back and put his feet on the floor. I handed him his jeans and then found my own. In silence, we put on socks and shoes. "He go to the river?" he asked, his voice a little rough but pretty steady.

I nodded.

It didn't occur to either of us to take an umbrella. We walked through long, yellow grass, rain wetting our heads, making my hair heavy against my back. Beneath an ancient cottonwood, Michael lay stretched out in the rain, his body so absurdly, painfully thin.

His body. It was so obviously just a body.

Malachi knelt and lifted him in his arms, so gently I nearly fainted with it, and carried him home. We laid him out on his bed, and I washed him, head to toe, brushed his hair, dried him carefully, and put him in his favorite shirt and jeans, even shoes and socks, before we called the coroner to report the death. Malachi made a pot of coffee and put a song on repeat on the stereo, "Long As I Can See the Light," an old CCR song that moved quietly through the house on mournful notes of saxophone. "Do you mind?" he asked me, bringing me a cup of coffee.

"No."

It wasn't until I woke Shane, and he pushed by me to go downstairs and somehow make sure I wasn't lying or mistaken, that the quiet stirred. Even then, Shane came into the dining room and turned on the light, and his honest child's heart simply burst. He put his head down on the bed next to Michael and wept silently, his shoulders shaking. I stood next to him, touching his back, wishing for that easy flow of tears, a way to block the thickness building between me and the world.

And when Malachi, big and solid and tough, sank down into a chair and put his head in his hands and wept, not in any kind of hysterical way, just deep, heartfelt, silent tears, I wanted to express it, too. Howl. Scream. Something.

Instead I went to the kitchen and picked up the phone, dialing Jordan first, who would help me get the word out. I didn't think I could stand to say it over and over again, and she would help me. As I was talking to her, I got out a heavy ceramic bowl and added flour, baking powder, salt. Muffins would be good on such a cold morning.

And the rain just fell and fell.

~

The thing about family is that they move in at such moments. By mid-morning, my house was filled with women cooking. By noon, there was a steady stream of cousins and siblings and children and aunts and uncles, coming by to pay their respects, every single one of them carrying a covered dish. Someone—maybe it was even Malachi—called the officials, and between my mother, Nana, and Jasmine, they settled on arrangements.

The only thing I remembered to do that day was take care of Michael's request. I carried the phone into my bedroom, into the silence that still smelled of Malachi, and dialed a number in Ohio. A man answered. An old man, one who'd smoked a lot of cigarettes back in the day when that was still allowed in prisons. It was a polite hello, drawled out softly in Malachi's very deep voice.

"Mr. Shaunnessey?" I asked.

"Yes, ma'am. What can I do for you?"

"Well, sir, I'm afraid I'm calling with bad news. My name is Jewel Sabatino, and I'm—"

"I know who you are. Michael's friend." His voice roughened. "Reckon, since you're the one took care of him all this time, you're calling to let me know he passed, huh?"

"Yes, sir. I'm sorry." I blinked. "He wanted you to be here for the funeral, and if it's all right with you, I'm going to arrange a flight for you tomorrow."

"He said that? He wanted me there?"

"Yes."

"It'd be my privilege, young lady," he said. "I'mna have to take you up on your offer of a flight, because I ain't got two nickels to rub together right now, but you just let me know when and where, and I'll be there."

He could be a pallbearer. I drifted a little, thinking. Him, Malachi, Shane . . . and who else? Maybe Henry would do it. I wouldn't have minded, but a casket is heavy, and I'm strong but not that strong.

I realized Mr. Shaunnessey was talking. "I'm sorry," I said. "I didn't catch that last part. I'm not . . . I just . . ." A well of emotion came out of nowhere suddenly, and I had to stop.

"Sugar, you have every right. Go on and cry if you need to. I'll listen."

And I almost did, right there, break down and sob, but there was something in me so afraid that I wouldn't stop if I started that I managed to get it back under control. "I'm okay. I should have the details for you in a couple of hours, and I'll call you then, all right?"

"That'll be fine." A pause. "Is my other boy there?"

"Yes."

"Good" was all he said.

~

The day blurred after that. I know I moved through it, applying myself to details like where and when and how. I made phone calls to all the people in New York and LA who would want to know, and listened to a lot of those people cry. Some of them made plans to come in for the funeral, musicians mostly, and some of the inner circle from the restaurant. Hotel rooms had to be found for them.

Shane and I planned the wake, to which everyone enthusiastically added. My uncle Zito, who ran a wholesale distribution business, contributed the wine and spirits. Three of my cousins pitched in for a couple of kegs. Jasmine, immaculate in her blue silk dress, spent the afternoon on her cell phone arranging for chairs and tables to be delivered, for ice and condiments, and a million other details that would have purely escaped me. Between all the food service people, we covered the feast pretty easily. We agreed, my sisters and mother and nana, to leave Jane alone to enjoy her honeymoon. If she called any of us, not a word was to be spoken, and I knew Michael would have wanted it that way. Jane, practical girl, would agree. The beginning in this case was more important than the end. She and I would find a way to create a memorial to Michael when she got back.

Malachi disappeared. Shane went looking for him late in the afternoon, but he'd gone somewhere on his bike, and nobody knew where. By that time I could tell my family was worrying about me, and someone took charge of getting me a Valium scrounged from someone's stash, and when that only intensified my confusion, they put me to bed. Jordan sat with me, watching the television, until I fell asleep.

Maybe it was just a defense, but I slept like it was me who died. Slept deep and hard, waking every so often through the night with a sense of confusion to see someone else beside the bed, sometimes my mother, sometimes a sister, sometimes Shane.

It was never Malachi, but I never surfaced long enough to figure that out, and to be honest, I wouldn't have cared anyway. I wanted Michael to comfort me over Michael's death, and it didn't matter that it didn't make sense.

Malachi showed up in the morning, haggard and in need of a shave. He didn't say a word to anyone's questions, just smiled wanly as he cut through clusters of my relatives to where I sat on a kitchen stool, peeling apples for Abe's pie. I hadn't told him yet that Abe was on his way. I didn't know if I would.

"I need to talk to you," he said, taking my hand.

"But I'm—"

"Excuse us," he said to the others, dragging me outside behind him into the steamy, overheated midday garden, then beyond.

"What are we doing, Malachi?" I asked impatiently, pulling back on my hand. "I have a million things to take care of."

He didn't answer, but tugged me through the garden, accidentally stomping the edge of a zucchini plant and noticing with a little "sorry." I leaped over it, caught up with him. "What's going on?"

He stopped, finally, in the shadows of the orchard. "I been working on these trees," he said vaguely. "Can you tell?"

Confused, still not really with the program, I scowled at him. "Couldn't this wait? I really am busy."

"I know." He didn't let go of my hand, though, as he pointed upward. "Got a couple of books out of the library and did some pruning. You're not strictly supposed to do it in the summer, but you had some rot and disease going here. The crop won't be great this year, but you could make real money outta this orchard in a couple years if you get it together."

Maybe, I thought, this was just his way of dealing with things. Everybody was different. "Thank you, Malachi. That was nice."

He bent then, and kissed me. Hard. Backed me into a tree and pressed our bodies together, a small sound of sorrow coming from his throat. For one minute, I let him absorb what he could, but it didn't touch me.

Dispassionately, I opened my eyes, looking at his sorrowful face and feeling his big body against mine without a single answering spark in any cell of my body. It was like he'd already left. When he sensed my disinterest, he raised his head, and I ducked away. "How long until you leave?"

"What?" He looked so confused that I almost felt sorry for him. Almost.

"I hope you'll stick around for the funeral. Even with you, I'm a pallbearer short."

"What are you talking about? You think I'd cut out before the funeral?"

I plucked a leaf from a branch. "How would I know?"

"Oh, shit. You're pissed that I took off last night, right? But it wasn't for a woman, Jewel. I just . . . needed to be out of there, away from all those people, so I could grieve in my own way."

"I was barely conscious, so no offense, but I didn't really notice."

He put his hands on his hips, brows pulling down. "Look, I'm tired and not really thinkin' that clearly. If there's something I'm not picking up on, you're gonna have to just say it straight out."

I wanted to hit him. The burst of anger was so hot and clear and direct that I had to take a step back. "There's nothing to say." I backed up another step. "I have to get back. There's a lot to do."

The frown deepened. "Are you all right, babe?"

"I'm fine, *babe*." I shook my head and headed toward the house, not looking to see if he followed. After the shadows of the orchard, the sun hit me hard on the top of the head, heavy as a dropped iron, and I had to stop, blinking hard against encroaching prickles of black, focusing on the white-painted clapboards of the kitchen. Through the window, I could see Shane holding a colander, an apron tied around him.

A little shattered voice cried, *Michael, what will I do?* But I shushed it and kept putting one foot down in front of the other until I had the screen door to hold on to and the cool of the deep shade running in a three-inch strip around the house.

I was swaying pretty hard, and even if I was furious with Malachi, I was grateful when he caught me with one big arm around my waist. He was strong and sturdy, something to hold on to in the spinning of a world that didn't have any markers. "I got you, honey, just lean on me and we'll get you a drink of water."

"I'm all right," I said.

"I know you are," he said, as if he were speaking to a cranky four-year-old. "Glass of water won't hurt nothing, though, will it?" He steered me through the tangle of people in the kitchen and dining room, their faces blurring absurdly, in and out of focus, and out to the side porch. "Head between your knees," he said, settling me in a chair, and someone must have helped him because there was a glass of water in my hands, and he held it a little longer than I thought I needed him to. When I got it to my mouth, the water was so cold and silvery going down my throat that I thought it had been too long, that I hadn't been drinking enough water.

"Thank you." I looked up at him, and he was peering back at me with those way-too-vivid eyes that almost hurt me they were so beautiful. The rippling edge of a scream came up through the back of my brain, and I gritted my teeth against it.

Only a little longer. Just get through this part, and I could go completely crazy if I needed to. Get Michael buried, see Malachi off . . . and, well, I couldn't lose it entirely, because there was Shane to think of, but maybe Jasmine and Jordan could keep him for a few days so I'd have some time alone.

Malachi's big hands closed around mine. "Jewel, why don't you let a little of it out?"

I took a breath. "I'm okay." Then I thought of his father, coming in a few hours, and wondered how to tell him. If I should tell him. "I'm making your dad's pie. Just a warning."

"I smelled it."

I remembered his dare at the wedding. And I will never be able to say what made me do it—maybe I had to be just so far beyond caring that nothing mattered—but I said, "Will you get the phone?"

He went inside and came back with it. "A miracle no one is on it."

Before I could lose my nerve, I punched the buttons for Falconi's, and Lorenzo answered. "Hey, guy," I said, meeting Malachi's eyes. "It's Jewel. Is my father around?"

"Sure. Let me get him for you."

"Tell him it's me."

A noisy pause. "I will."

My heart wasn't beating any faster. My hands didn't sweat. A couple of tears leaked out of my eyes while I waited. I heard a clatter and then my father's voice. "Hello." Abrupt, but not brusque. Worried.

"Daddy, I have a favor to ask you," I said, and my voice, which had been very stable to that minute, turned croaky.

"Whatever you need," he said.

I couldn't speak for a moment, couldn't get enough air through my throat. "Um . . . I need one more pallbearer. Can you help me?"

"Yeah," he said. "Sure, of course."

"Thank you, Daddy."

"Whatever you need, baby," he said.

Oh, it was dangerous to talk to him. "I have to go," I said, trying to maintain some kind of control. "I'll see you tomorrow."

"You take care, Jewel. It's not so easy, saying goodbye to somebody you love a lot."

"I will, thank you."

I cut the connection, tossed back my hair from my hot eyes, and said, "Your father is going to be here at four o'clock."

He dropped his head in his hands. "Ah, hell."

"You want to pick him up?"

"I—uh—" He turned his lips down, blinking hard. "I don't think so."

Nodding, I said, "Shane can do it."

I went back inside, and my mother was waiting. She hugged me. "Good girl," she whispered, and I felt her tears on my neck. "Thank you."

I patted her arm. "Let's get back to work."

~

Shane found me a little before three. Somehow—I couldn't really remember getting there—I was sitting in a plastic lawn chair in the shade of a tree in the backyard, watching a crew of male relatives, all of them Falconis, getting things ready for the barbecue we'd have. Shane had the keys to the station wagon in his hand. "I need directions," he said.

He looked pale, and violet shadows stained the hollows below his eyes. "Sit down for a few minutes," I invited. "You don't have to go just yet."

Reluctantly he dropped down beside me, resistance in every line of his long body. "I'd really just like to get outta here, Mom. No offense." He winced a little, looking at a pair of six- or seven-year-old girls screeching out in the orchard. "But this is crazy. I don't know how you stand it."

There wasn't a smile anywhere in me, but I looked at the circle of cars lining the drive and lifted a shoulder. "It's always been like this. It was terrible when your dad died, trying to take care of everything. You need family for this."

He raised his eyes. "You talk different when you talk about family, you know that? I always noticed it, but now I know where it comes from."

"Yeah? How's it different?"

"You just start talking like them." One side of his mouth lifted, an Elvis expression I suspected he'd once practiced, but now was natural. "You sound like Pueblo then."

"Hmm. I thought I lost my accent."

"No way."

"My dad is going to be a pallbearer," I said suddenly.

"Cool."

"You don't sound surprised."

He shook his head. "Mom, he misses you bad. All he talks about when I'm there is you."

"He does?"

"Every day, Mom, he finds a way every day to ask me questions about you. 'Does your mom put cinnamon in this pie?'" He adopted my father's lilt exactly. "'Your mom teach you that song?' 'Your mom ever tell you about the time we went up to Denver to see the opera on her sixteenth birthday, just me and her?'"

A fierce pain went through me. The opera—that had been such a special evening. I dressed up, and so did he, and we had dinner, then went to see *La Bohème*, and as we drove home, a hundred miles in the dark of a summer night, we talked and talked and talked.

"Why didn't he talk to *me*?" I asked.

He shrugged. "Don't ask me. I'm still trying to figure out the family stuff here." He touched my hand. "He loves you, Mom."

"I know."

He left then, and I was too exhausted to do anything more than just sit there, the world blurring out again. I was still there when Shane returned, a tall thin man in the car with him.

I had always imagined Abe Shaunnessey to be an older version of Michael. The man who got out of the car, his hair badly cut, his clothes old but painfully clean, was instead the spitting image of Malachi. Same dark hair, same dark eyes, same hard-hewn swooping angles of jaw and cheekbone and nose. He looked to be about sixty, a hard-lived sixty, of course, but not yet worn out. He was thinner than he should have been, and down on his luck, but his grip was strong, his gaze direct when he grasped my hand. "Thank you for taking care of him all this time, Jewel. He loved you a lot."

Malachi came out the back door and just stood there, hands loose at his sides, his mouth drawn in a hard line. Abe turned around, his shoulders square, and said, "Hello, son."

Malachi closed his eyes, and it almost seemed he would faint there in the hot sun, but then he came down the steps. I watched it in slow motion, my perspective divided almost as if I were in two places at once—looking at them from above and from the side, so I could see the part in Malachi's hair where the sun burnished two hot reddish lines through it, and the gray in his father's, which was a slightly faded version of the same dark brown. I could also see Malachi's face and his father's shoulders, which looked suddenly vulnerable when Malachi's huge hands embraced them. Cicadas set up a racket in a nearby elm, and two of my cousins argued over where the barbecue pit should go, and a cat skittered through the grass at my feet.

Above and straight on, I saw their faces. Tears wetting Abe's craggy features. Something far deeper covering Malachi's. His eyes were closed, and his hands were in fists, and I don't think I've ever loved anyone in my life the way I loved Malachi Shaunnessey in that moment, seeing his heart break and his walls come down. It moved through me in waves of red and yellow light, strong as sound, washing away everything else, even grief.

And knowing not even this would keep him didn't change it, but it made me look at him, memorize the shape of his fingers, the tips white where he was holding his father's thin form; look at the angle of hip to leg, the uneven fall of his hair. It wasn't like looking at someone else, but at a part of my own body. It was the same way I felt about Michael, that he could never be gone because he was living inside of me, forever and ever, as long as I walked the earth, as long as there was breath in me. That was what love did, the sweetest part. I didn't have to make sense of it or justify it or even have it returned. Love just arrived and filled you up and that was enough.

Sitting there, in the sun, missing Michael, I realized it was something I was really good at. Maybe it was the best thing I did. Loving Michael and Malachi, loving my mother and father and sisters and cousins and uncles and aunts and all the ones in between. Loving my son so much it sometimes overwhelmed me.

And loving Billy. It had been the right thing to do. There, half-crazy with grief, filled in every cell with a kind of rocketing, blistering recognition of my own life, I could see that loving Billy had given him everything he could possibly accept—someone he could count on, no matter what, to love him. A child who would carry him all his life. Someone to turn to. Someone to worry about him.

But he'd given me so much more. He'd given me a chance to taste the world and live in it, a chance to love wildly. He'd given me a son who was the best thing I'd ever offer the world. He'd given me Michael, who would always be my truest and deepest friend. Even that day, I knew that.

Billy had even brought me, in a roundabout way, the love of my life, who'd walked in that first day smelling of clothes hanging on my aunt Sylvia's line, and stolen my heart.

I stood up and leaned in to kiss them both on the cheek. "Come in and have something to eat," I said, my hand lingering on Malachi's arm a little longer than on his father's. "There's plenty."

ZITO'S WHOLESALE LIQUORS INVOICE:
ITEM PRICE

3 kegs beer, 2 Budweiser, 1 Bud Lite donation
2 5-liter boxes CAS white zinfandel donation
2 5-liter boxes CAS table red donation
1 case 12-oz. plastic cups donation

Chapter Twenty

The day of the funeral comes back to me in bits and pieces. It was sunny and hot, the kind of still, close day when everything living scurries away to the shadows and waits for night. I remember it in the contrast of that blazing sun and the shadows it created—the shattering brilliance of the church windows, the sweat on the faces of the pallbearers, the depth and coolness of the grave.

Afterward, the wake at Sylvia's house—my house—the rectangles of the windows in the dining room bright in the dimness. The fabric of my uncle T.J.'s coat, nubby and brown as he stood talking with Shane, his arm around my son's shoulders. The smell of aftershave and lotions and basil and tomatoes and coffee. The press of kisses imprinted my face, dozens of kisses, pats on the cheek, squeezes of the arm, deep hugs. Never wordless. *We liked him, Jewel. He was good. You're good. We're proud of you.* And, *What a good boy you've raised, look at him taking care of things,* and *I hear he's a good cook,* and *Isn't he handsome* and *He sings like his grandfather* and *The girls must be beating a path to his door, I bet.*

So soon after a wedding, it was easy to pick out the differences in family gathered for this—there were even more people coming in and out than there would be for a wedding, coming to offer whatever they could, like the kegs and the wine and the music. Like my cousin Vince finding a hammer in the back room to fix the loose step on the porch so nobody would trip on it. Like Jasmine finding a notebook for people to sign so that I'd be able to write thank-you notes later, and my mother taking over the care and feeding of the New Yorkers and Californians come to pay Michael their respects. One of them was Jimmy Angelo, the one who had invited Shane to come live with him for Shane's last year of high school. Jimmy had gained weight since the last time I'd seen him, and his hair was thinning across the top, but his arms were sturdy and strong as he embraced me. "Let's find some time to talk, huh?" he said.

I nodded.

It was good to see them, even better when three or four of them brought out their instruments in the backyard and played a tribute to Michael—singing all of his songs, every single one he'd written.

Shane sang my favorite. Next to me, Abe sighed with a kind of pained sound. "He sure looks like you, don't he? But he sings like Michael. Boy had the best training in the world."

I poured some more beer into his plastic cup from a pitcher on the table. It was getting dark now, the crickets and cicadas coming out to lend their song to the dance. "Where did Michael get his voice, Abe? Was it from you?"

"Nah, I can't sing a lick. His mama always had aspirations that way, you know, but she didn't have no range, and once she stopped being the cutest young thing, she stopped landing gigs." He sipped his beer, his face shining like his wife had just stepped out into the next room. "Broke her heart clean in half, it did."

"She was always beautiful, from the pictures I've seen anyway."

"She sure was, Jewel." He drew in on his cigarette, and I noticed that his fingers were cracked along the tips, the telltale sign of a mechanic. He'd scrubbed them well, but nothing ever got rid of grease that went that deep. I wondered if he could fix the scream in my car.

"You know," he said quietly, "she's been gone nigh on fifteen years, and I didn't see her for three before that, and there's not a day that goes by that my heart doesn't ache a little with missing her."

I nodded, touching his hand. "I can see that."

"Folks are sure foolish." He shook his head. "Makes me happy to think of Michael and her on the other side, waiting for me when I go."

It startled me a little, and I blurted out without thinking, "You think she's waiting? Did she forgive you?"

His eyes stared into the distance. "Sure she did. She wasted away without me, darlin'. Only reason I didn't waste away without her"—his mouth twitched in emotion—"is cuz I was tryin' to get home to my boys."

And I realized it was probably true. "I'm so sorry."

He sighed. "My own fault."

"That doesn't make it any easier, though, does it?"

"No. I reckon it don't."

From the corner beneath the trees came an explosion of laughter. We both looked over. Malachi had been herded by a band of my male relatives into a knotty little group that was intent on fine drunkenness. A sacred duty when a man's lost his brother, and one they took seriously. They wouldn't let anybody get sloppy—though Malachi would be given that freedom if he showed an inclination—but they'd take the time to listen to him, tell stories of their own brothers, living and dead.

"He looks right at home," Abe said.

"He fits right in," I agreed. My son, who should have, started to sing with a pack of wild men in wild clothes and wild hair and wild hearts. He'd never stay, my boy. His heart had been burned early with the imprint of his father's music, and music would be his mistress. I guessed, sitting there in the darkness, that I'd raised him right after all. He'd had the perfect training for that world—how to survive and how to screw yourself up and how to make it work.

I'd miss him. So much.

Through the roar of the others, I heard Malachi's laughter weaving under all of it, thick and deep and rich. "He's got restless feet, though."

"Malachi?" Abe said nothing for a minute. "I don't think it comes natural to him, not like Michael and me. Malachi was always more like his mama, wanting to set down some roots, crying about the friends they'd made, the gardens they planted."

"And now he's the one who's leading adventure tours all over the world."

"Only cuz he's scared."

"Probably." Across the open lawn, Malachi raised his glass at me. I raised mine in return. *"Salud,"* I said aloud.

A figure emerged from the darkness, dapper and perfectly pressed even after so many hours of eating and drinking and talking following the funeral, except for a betraying lock of hair falling on his forehead in that rakish way. He carried a plate of food, which he put down in front of me. "Your mama sent this out," my father said. "Said you need to eat some more."

"I'm not very hungry," I said.

"I know." He sat down with us, pushed the plate and fork toward me a little. "But you don't want to get sick. I remember when my brother died, I had trouble remembering to eat."

I looked up at him, at those deep beautiful eyes that were finally focused on me, the rift just—gone—and I realized I'd always known it would go this way, that when I really needed him, my father would be there. And I knew, finally, what I'd been waiting for.

The dam I'd carefully constructed that morning of so much rain simply gave way. A trickle, at first, a sudden spring of tears that overflowed and fell on my cheeks, then more, and more, and more.

My father said, "Come here, baby," and I fell forward heavily, knowing he'd be there to catch me in the net, the web, of his arms. In the arms that had cradled me from babyhood, I wept, feeling those hands that had made me hollyhock dolls smooth my hair, that voice I had missed so much murmuring quietly, "It's okay, let it out. You just cry, Jewel. You just go ahead and cry."

~

Malachi found me about midnight. In the kitchen, all the food had been put away, and the dishes done, and nearly everyone had gone. A few of the younger cousins lingered, along with Jordan and Henry, out in the back where citronella torches tried to hold off the mosquitoes that bred by the river no matter how dry and hot it got over the rest of the city. I sat on the side porch by myself, looking at the sky and thinking about nothing, just listening to the homey sounds of a loose group of musicians at play. Sudden thrums of guitar or snatches of song, spontaneous riffs weaving together, laughter and commentary. It sounded, I thought distantly, like they were getting serious about something now—somebody repeating something over and over on a guitar while someone else wove some sax through it, and someone else belting out wordless voice notes. A properly melancholy minor key, the song of men expressing their sorrow—and celebration.

I heard Malachi's heavy step on the wooden boards, coming around from the front. I looked up. "Hi."

"Where've you been? I been looking all over for you," he said. Weariness weighted every syllable. "Even went down to the river to see if you might be there."

"I took a shower."

He took my hand in both of his. "Guess we got over our father issues, didn't we?"

"Guess so."

"Michael engineered it all."

It hadn't occurred to me, but of course he had. "Yeah."

"I'm leaving in the morning, Jewel."

I looked at him. Nodded. "I thought you might."

He lifted my hand and pressed his mouth to my palm. "Will you . . ." His mouth worked, the same gesture I'd seen his father make earlier. He cleared his throat, raised his head to look at me with those brilliant, sad, brokenhearted eyes. "Can we go upstairs?"

"I'm too tired for sex," I said. "Thanks, anyway."

"Not sex," he said, letting go of a sigh. "I just want to hold you."

"We can do that." I touched his face. "Don't go without telling Shane, all right? He's gonna miss you."

"We talked already."

"Good." I stood and tugged his hand. "Come on, big boy, let's go on up."

In the moonlit darkness of his room, we shed our clothes and lay down, finding each other across the bed. The windows were open to catch any spare breeze that might cool the thick air, but it was very hot, and our skin burned and sweated wherever we touched. It didn't matter. We curled up together. Swept by some impulse, I found myself humming the song that had been in my head all day, "Shall We Gather at the River?" Malachi hummed along, picking up the refrain when we got there, and I felt his heart breaking, felt his sorrow as he pressed his forehead to mine, whispering, "I love you, Jewel."

Tears fell on my neck, and they felt like an anointing, lighting a pure white light inside of me, a light that grew and grew, flickering at first, then steadied as my certainty solidified. "I love you," he repeated, the sound so quiet I barely caught it, and then again, he said it, raggedly, "I love you. I never knew what this was like."

I caught his big head and opened my eyes. "I know, Malachi." Then I kissed him and rested my head on his chest, listening to his heartbeat. "You don't have to leave, you know."

His hands tangled in my hair, and there was trembling in them. "Come with me, Jewel. Please." He smoothed my hair urgently from my forehead. "There's a whole world out there, a million places I want to show you."

"No." I put my hand on his face. "If you want to, you can stay here. And we'll visit any place you want."

"I can't," he whispered. "I can't."

∼

And he didn't. I wish I could tell you that I woke up in the morning and he'd had some epiphany that let him go out and buy me a big flashy ring I could use to make my sisters jealous, but he didn't.

He left me sleeping, something he'd probably had some practice at doing. The first I knew of his going was the sound of his motorcycle starting up in the gray light of dawn. I didn't throw on my clothes and go running out into the morning, but I didn't stay in bed listening to him drive away, either.

I got up and put on my robe and went to the window with a view to the east, a view of the road that leads to the rest of the world. It took him a few minutes to clear the local roads and hit the highway, but I saw him, a lone rider heading toward the dawn. I watched until he sailed over a hill and disappeared.

From the door, Shane said, "Are you okay, Mom?"

I turned, smiling even though I had to wipe my cheeks. "I'm fine." Tugging the tie of my robe, I added, "Go back to bed, sweetie. You were up late."

But instead he ambled over in his new man's body, on giant man feet, and bent down to hug me. "How about if I fix you some eggs or something?"

"You don't have to take care of me, Shane. I'm going to be okay."

"I know that. You've done all right so far." He rocked me back and forth a little, and it made me think of Michael with a burst of love and sorrow.

"Listen," I said, pulling back. I sat on the bed and patted a place beside me. "Jimmy and I talked last night."

He bowed his head, lacing his long-fingered hands together. "I changed my mind, Mom. I'll hang here until I finish school."

"No." I shook my head for emphasis. "I had already decided, watching you at the wedding, that there's no reason for you to stay here." I swallowed. "You're ready. It's time for you to go find your life."

"Mom!" He lifted his head and looked at me with his father's eyes. Or rather eyes the color of his father's. Shane's held a level of maturity that Billy had never reached. "No way! I can't leave you here, all alone like this!"

Which was exactly the reason I had to make him go. He would try to take care of me and fret about my well-being when he needed to be thinking of his own life. I also knew that he'd be grieving over Michael badly for months, and being busy with his own life and goals would be the best way to offset that. "I appreciate that, but I'm hardly alone. In case you haven't noticed, I have about ten thousand relatives in this town."

Betraying hope flared. "Jimmy's leaving tomorrow, though."

"Better get cracking, then, huh?"

~

There was an admirable-size crowd assembled at the airport in Colorado Springs for his send-off, even if it was the crack of dawn. My mother and father, Jordan and Jasmine and Jasmine's kids, even Nana Lucy, who didn't like being left out of anything.

Shane was a little embarrassed, wanting to be cool in front of Jimmy and the other guys, but he was also glad. Nana put a Saint Christopher medal around his neck and told him to keep it on. He promised he would. My mother gave him a basket of food from the restaurant, which would be very welcome on the long flight, and hugged him tightly, tears in her eyes. Jordan and Jasmine each gave him a little something—a gift-wrapped box from Jordan that I knew held condoms and that she told him to open on the plane, and a fat envelope with money from Jasmine. "Open a savings account," she said. "If you ever need *anything*, you call me, you hear?"

He bent down to hug her, his face showing his fondness. "I promise, Auntie."

Eight-year-old Danny cried on his shoulder, even though he wanted, really bad, to be a tough guy.

My father took my son aside, but not so far away I couldn't hear him. "You can be anythin' you want, Shane, but remember you're a Sabatino, and be an honor to my name."

Shane nodded soberly. "I would never do anything to hurt you, Papa."

"I know," my father said, and kissed him hard on the cheek, his hand tight around his head. He used it to pat his face after, a gesture that somehow pierced me. "Call me when you can, huh? Tell me how things are going."

Shane nodded, nearly in tears, then hugged him hard. "I'll miss you."

"You'll be fine," Romeo said, and went over to join the others, jingling his keys in his pocket to cover his strong emotion.

I just stood next to him, my kid, until they called the flight. I memorized the feeling of his tall, ropy body next to mine, inhaled the soap-and-man smell of him, remembering a thousand other notes he'd once carried—baby powder and Diaparene, sand and sun, Play-Doh and brownies and Kool-Aid. He didn't say anything. We'd talked so much the past twenty-four hours about what he could do and what he couldn't do and how to behave and everything else that there wasn't much else to say. I trusted Jimmy to look out for him, and trusted his wife to give Shane the mothering he might need. The Jersey neighborhood he'd be living in was pleasantly upscale, and my gut said he'd be okay, that this was the right thing to do.

When the flight was called, the other guys picked up their packs and shuffled off to the gate, a familiar game for most of them.

Then it was just me and Shane. He glanced over his shoulder. "I gotta go."

I'd told myself I wouldn't cry in front of him, and although I had to blink very hard to actually avoid spilling tears, I stuck to it. "I know." I gave him a brave smile. "Be careful. Be good. Don't hold back on your dream."

But he was the one who cried, and not even blinking could hold it back. I felt the hot tears splash on my neck as he hugged me hard. "I love you, Mom. I'll call you every Sunday, no matter what, no matter where I am."

"That's great."

The last call came, and he straightened. "It's time."

"Yeah. Bye, babe. See you soon."

And he turned, all six foot two of beautiful young hopeful male, his pack slung over his back with everything he needed in it, and I would have done every single minute of my whole life over again, every miserable moment, every sorrow, every joy, every everything to come back here and see him off to the life he was meant to live. I felt myself grow smaller and larger at once, aligned with everything in the world, all of history and all of the future. Everything that had happened had resulted in this moment, with Shane prepared, as nothing else could have prepared him, to live a long, healthy life making art for the rest of us.

"Hey, Shane," I said, remembering at the last minute.

He turned but kept walking backward.

"I'll put a candle in the window."

He grinned at the old code phrase between me and Billy, and lifted a hand and dipped out of sight.

To fly.

FROM A POSTCARD SHOWING SEVEN FALLS, COLORADO SPRINGS, COLORADO

8/18

Hey sugar—

Didn't get far my first night somehow. It's real pretty here. I dreamed about Michael last night, just sitting on the foot of my bed. Think about the Alps, huh? Or maybe the Nile.

Love, M

FROM A POSTCARD SHOWING NATIVE AMERICAN DANCERS, NORMAN, OKLAHOMA

8/20

Hey babe—

These guys made me think about Billy. Think he'd have done better if he'd taken up drums? Dreamed about Michael again. Just sitting there on my bed. Weird. Should be home in a couple days and will head out shortly thereafter. I'll send you a postcard from Africa, maybe.

Love, M

FROM A POSTCARD SHOWING MAGNOLIAS IN FULL BLOOM, BILOXI, MISSISSIPPI

9/10

Hey darlin'—

Still dreaming about Michael every night. EVERY night. Never says a word, just sits there at the foot of my bed, looking at me. I almost called today, but realized you'd probably be out delivering pies. Wanted to know if you're dreaming about him, too. Getting things together for a quick river raft trip in CA. You'd like it. Come if you want.

Love, M

FROM A POSTCARD SHOWING A WHITEWATER RAFT TRIP

Thinking you'd like this river. La Llorona doesn't walk here, though. Michael went away. Doesn't sit on my bed anymore. Don't know whether to be sad or glad.

Love, M

Chapter
Twenty-One

I went to the fair alone in the end. And didn't last an hour. It was too sad. Too many ghosts walking around there for me—ghosts of myself and Michael and Billy. Ghosts of time past. I ate a funnel cake and called it a night. By next year, I'll probably be more in the mood.

I did a lot of things alone over those last weeks of summer. Slept alone, ate alone, cooked alone. It was amazing how lonely that big old house was without any voices but my own in it. I spent a lot of time visiting with my sisters, and my mother started having me over for dinner a couple of times a week. I went. Love has no pride, as Bonnie Raitt says, and I needed them in a big way.

There was a blessed conspiracy afoot to keep me busy, everyone taking turns needing me for something or another—Jane and her house and shopping, then the baby shopping, because of course she came home pregnant; Jordan dragging me out to her house for breakfasts and a few therapeutic margarita nights; Nana and her trips to the doctors; my father and his wish for advice on the menu of Falconi's. Advice, by the way, that he actually listened to. Shane had told him a lot about the Music Box, Michael and Andre's restaurant, and he'd been impressed by some of the meal choices. Time, Romeo said, overriding even Nana, to bring Falconi's into the twenty-first century.

Shane called every Sunday afternoon, and a lot more besides. He was pretty lonely and lost the first couple of weeks, but once school started, he cheered up. Girls always make the world look better. Jimmy had hooked him up with two other young musicians, and they landed a gig in a nearby hamlet within a month. The club was small, but prestigious—agents and music-label folk were known to scope it out for new talent.

I spent whatever extra time I found on my hands working in the garden or walking by the river. It seemed maudlin at first, but somehow the sound of the water, the flow of those ions in the air, maybe, comforted me. I felt close to Michael there, and Malachi, and myself. Berlin and I walked a lot through those months, and I even lost a little weight.

Every night, I lit that red pillar candle.

~

The one thing no one did for me was introduce me to anyone. No aunties with some suitable older fellow who'd lost his wife. No dashing divorced guy with a couple of kids who needed a mother—which I wouldn't have minded, by the way. No coworkers who might drink a bit much from Henry's construction sites, no doctors or technicians or cheery male nurses from Jordan, or mortgage loan officers from Jasmine. No teachers, no joggers, no cooks or bartenders. No one. From anyone.

I thought at first that they were being respectful, you know—so much had happened and they were giving me time to grieve. So, by the middle of October, I let it drop, here and there, that I wouldn't mind the idea of getting on with my life.

Still nothing.

Which left me lonely, sitting on my steps as I had that summer, looking down the years of my life that were going to be every bit as dry as I'd feared. I'd wither out here with the goatheads and the orchard, forgotten like an apple fallen overripe to the ground.

I was lonely. Lonelier than I'd ever been in my life. All the work, all the family, all the new acceptance I felt about myself and my choices didn't do a damned bit of good when the moon rose, heavy and yellow, over the river that October night. A harvest moon, as big around as the earth itself. It painted its cool light over my arms and face, cast a magical glow over the fields and trees, making me think of Michael. "You could come to my dreams," I said aloud. "I'm kind of jealous that you showed up to Malachi and not to me."

The light just glowed, endless and eternal, from the disk of the harvest moon. I went upstairs, alone, and got ready for bed. In the window of the bedroom, the red candle had nearly burned to the very end, and standing there in my sweats and T-shirt, my hair tied back in a sensible braid, I looked at it, so small against the hugeness of that moon, and thought how foolish I'd been to believe that Malachi would return. Everything had pointed against it. Every bit of logic, everything I knew about men, everything.

And yet, somehow, that last night, I'd discovered faith in him—my faith in that light that burned between us, that peaceful warmth that had felt so steady.

Even a woman who knows better can sometimes fall prey to foolish fantasies, and there was nothing wrong with that. But Malachi wasn't coming back, and it was time for me to make a new life on all levels. I bent over the flame, taking in a deep breath to blow it out. Headlights flashed against my eyes, and I stopped. Watching those lights on the road below.

A hard, sharp, painful hope twisted in my breast, and my heart started to pound. I waited, watching those lights come fast down the road, bumping in the potholes—a truck, I gauged. A million trucks came down that road every year.

I don't know how I knew. There was a part of me, the logical part, the grounded part, that was bracing for disappointment even as I turned and headed for the stairs, taking them two at a time. As I hit the ground floor, the lights swung into my driveway, flashing across the big panes in the front windows that I'd washed three days ago. I was thinking there was some leftover lasagna and some pumpkin pie in the cooler, and I could make some coffee, because he'd be hungry, even as I was thinking it might just be an emergency, that someone needed me for something.

I was waiting on the porch when he opened the truck door and stepped out, a puppy scrambling out behind him, a little German shepherd with clumsy paws and a black nose. It whimpered a little but raced toward me when I came down the steps and whistled softly, scrambling into my arms, a big ball of clumsy fur that offered a shield as I looked up at Malachi.

He lifted a shoulder. "He adopted me. I wasn't really thinking about getting a dog, but he wouldn't leave me alone."

The puppy licked my chin happily, and I smiled, bending my face into his still-soft fur. "How could you resist?"

"Obviously I couldn't."

I put the puppy down and went forward. "You look like hell," I said. And it was true. Hair mussed and too long, hollows under his eyes, a three-day growth of beard on his jaw. He closed his eyes for a minute, his hands loose at his sides, then opened them.

"Oh, my God," he said heavily, and embraced me.

Not a little, loose hug, either—both long arms all the way around me, pulling me into his body tight, his face against my hair. "Jewel," he said, a sigh of relief. His arms were squeezing the breath out of me, but I didn't mind it. I clung to him just as hard, breathing in that scent of line-dried clothes, that homey smell that was his and should have been a clue to me all this time.

He smelled like Sylvia's yard. The yard that was his, that was mine. I thought I could hear my auntie chuckling in great good humor.

"Oh, God, Jewel," he said again, "I missed you like a leg." He kissed me hard, and I tasted all those days he'd missed me, all the days I'd missed him, and then fought my way free of him, stepping back to get some sanity.

"Are you here to stay, Malachi? Or to try to convince me to wander the world?"

From a pocket on the front of his shirt, he took a folded piece of paper and handed it to me. I opened it, perplexed, and read, "Arkansas River Whitewater Rafting." It appeared to be something official, but I couldn't really tell what. "So?"

He held the top of the paper and pointed to the very bottom, where there were two signatures. Malachi's and one I didn't recognize. It was a deed of sale.

I swallowed. "You bought it?"

"Yeah." He cleared his throat. "I'm not asking you to just take me on faith, Jewel. I know my history won't make it easy to trust me, trust that I mean what I say. You don't have to live with me or anything—I got an apartment in town, and we can . . . court like normal people. Whatever you want to do, I'll do it." He swallowed, lifted a hand to my hair, dropped it. "I never loved a woman before. I didn't know how bad it would feel to be without you, and I'm willing to do whatever it is you need until you can see your way to letting me be your man."

"My man?"

And those dark eyes lifted to mine without a wince or a pain and said, "Your husband. If that's not too corny." He twisted a piece of my hair around his finger.

"That was the right answer," I said, and burst into tears, right there. And like any man, he was bewildered about what to do about that, so I picked up his big arms and put them around my shoulders and put my face against his chest and cried. "I was so afraid to believe in you. I gambled my whole heart that you would figure it out in time."

Now he started to get it, and rocked me back and forth. "I never felt like any place was home until now. I was afraid of how badly I wanted it." He kissed my head. "I love you."

Dizzy over faith rewarded, over the promise of the future, I pressed my face into his shirt. "I know," I said, and smiled when he laughed.

~

Wrapped in Malachi's long, warm body, I slept.

And dreamed that Michael came and sat on the bed next to me. He was himself again, his hair gleaming and long and almost gilded with light, his shoulders broad and full, his laughter bright and rich. "I was here all the time," he said, putting his hand on my leg. "But now I know you'll be okay, and I'm going on." In the distance, smiling gently, was Andre, or maybe not Andre but just another angel.

Michael kissed my forehead and started to go, but then he put his hand on my belly. "Name her Michaela, will you?"

I protested that I didn't want a baby, but Michael only laughed.

I woke up, and Malachi was waking up, too. "I dreamed about him again," he said, pulling me tighter, that giant hand going protectively over my belly, which wasn't young but probably wasn't so old it couldn't carry a baby for Malachi at least once. "He talked this time."

I put my hand over his. "I know."

It's all good, as they say.

Acknowledgments

Ram Samuel made me sign in blood that I'd credit him with the recipes he guards like secret gold. Thanks to him for letting me use Ram's Ass-Kicking Apple Pie and J.O.'s Barbecue Sauce recipes. Thanks to the many readers and writers who sent me their special favorites, especially Virginia Kantra for Grandpa's Pork Chops, and Kaite Mediatore for sharing her story of zeppoles. Vince and Sharyn Cerniglia shared not only great recipes but some wonderfully evocative stories. Thanks to Jim Pagano and the adventurous group from Denver, Colorado, for letting me tag along on the walking tour of the old neighborhood—it was one of my best days as a writer, ever. Thanks to my mother, Rosalie Hair, who fell in love with the artifacts and stories pouring into El Pueblo History Museum from the Pueblo Italian community and said, "I really think you need to see this stuff."

Others who contributed directly or indirectly: Sam and Kay Coris, who were in my thoughts a lot as I wrote; their daughter Jennifer, whose wedding inspired the one I wrote about here; Miriam Pickard, who was so generous and kind, and would have loved this book; Jack Passanante, who shared stories; Sally Pacheco and Adolph Chacon, who not only know a whole lot about that sticky web of family but are also examples of why I love Pueblo; Sue Longsdorff, for hundreds of miles of walking, talking, plot points, and support. And, finally, very special thanks to Connie.

About the Author

Photo © 2009 Blue Fox Photography

Barbara O'Neal is the *Washington Post, Wall Street Journal, USA Today,* and Amazon Charts bestselling author of more than a dozen novels of women's fiction, including the #1 Amazon Charts bestseller *When We Believed in Mermaids* as well as *The Starfish Sisters, This Place of Wonder, The Lost Girls of Devon, Write My Name Across the Sky,* and *The Art of Inheriting Secrets.* Her award-winning books have been published in over two dozen countries. She lives on the Oregon coast with her husband, a British endurance athlete who vows he'll never lose his accent. For more information, visit barbaraoneal.com.